Vampires Inc.

Book One

Rick Taubold
Chris R. Hosey

Double Dragon Publishing

Vampires Inc.

Double Dragon Press

Published by
Double Dragon Publishing, Inc.
PO Box 54016
1-5762 Highway 7 East
Markham, Ontario L3P 7Y4 Canada
http://www.double-dragon-ebooks.com
http://www.double-dragon-publishing.com

ISBN-10: 1-55404-691-2
ISBN-13: 978-1-55404-691-1

A DDP First Edition June 29, 2009
Book Layout and
Cover Art by Deron Douglas
http://www.derondouglas.com

DEDICATION

From Rick:

For my wife
&
In memory of my parents
Robert H. Taubold 4/20/1918 - 10/27/2005
Dolores V. Taubold 8/28/1920 - 9/10/2007

From Chris:

To the life and times of my father
Richard James Hosey Jr. 10/26/1944 - 5/8/2006

ACKNOWLEDGMENTS
by Rick

Chris Hosey has an amazing talent for creating wonderful characters. To maintain continuity and a consistent style, I have been in charge of the writing, but the original concept was Chris' and it's set in his hometown. His collaborative input and insights made the novel richer than any solo effort could have.

I thank my many friends in the Zoetrope writing community for their support, advice, and critiques that made this novel better.

Thanks to the talented Kelly Jaakkola for her honest critiques and for keeping me from getting sloppy.

My brother Lance, with his constant encouragement, support, and advice, has helped me navigate the world of publishing.

Shaun Radley inspired his namesake character of Drake Radley and advised me with Drake's rap talk.

Sean Dent and Mick Halpin assisted with the Ireland settings.

Jonathan Redhorse, a good friend and a remarkable writer, supplied information for the Denver settings.

Thanks to Kim McDougall for fine tuning the French phrases.

Will Etter graciously let me borrow his surname for the vampire character of Dietrich Etter.

Scott Gamboe, fellow author, good friend, and police officer provided some technical expertise.

Finally, many writer friends, too numerous to name, gave me encouragement and invaluable feedback. You know who you are. Thank you all.

CHAPTER ONE

Detroit, Michigan—Tuesday, October 14, 2003

Eli glanced at the wall clock in the rear of the lecture hall. He'd finished fifteen minutes early. "We're done for this evening. Next week there will be a short quiz at the start of the period on tonight's material. Any questions?" Several students groaned, but no hands went up. "Please read chapter thirteen for next time."

While he packed up his notes, one of the female students approached him. "Professor Howard, I just wanted to tell you how much I'm enjoying this class. Your perspective makes it sound like you were there and experienced it."

Every semester that he taught Black History 1865-to-present, he could count on at least one student making that remark. He always replied with, "I was born in 1838 in Jackson, Mississippi. I *was* there." The student's eyes would invariably widen and a smile usually—but not always—would follow from the assumption it was a joke.

"I appreciate the compliment, Miss Michaels." Eli shut his attaché case. Out of curiosity, he tapped into her thoughts.

She wasn't sure which surprised her more: the remark itself, or her history professor pulling a presumed joke out of thin air.

"And I will see you next week." He donned his leather coat and left, with her gaping after him.

Outside, the Wayne State University campus streets glistened from the brief thunderstorm of an hour before. The storm had left muggy air and deserted campus streets in its wake.

Ahead of him, a young woman exited a classroom building carrying a folded denim jacket on top of the books under her arm as she walked toward the parking lot. His light-sensitive eyes easily discerned her attractive facial features and flawless skin. He also spotted the two individuals lurking in the shadows nearby. He stopped next to a tree and set his attaché on the ground. The Blue Light Phone at the far end of the lot wasn't close enough for quick access by either of them.

Three cars remained in the parking lot. The woman pulled a set of keys from her jeans pocket and pointed her keyholder. The door locks on the red Saturn thunked. Maybe she'd reach her car in time and he wouldn't have to intervene.

The two men sprinted toward her. She jerked her head up at the wet squeak of sneakers on the asphalt and quickened her pace. The more muscular of the two, a clean-shaven White in his late twenties or early thirties, darted out of the shadows. The woman lunged for her car and slipped on some wet leaves. She caught her balance, but her books, jacket, and keys fell and scattered on the asphalt. The man pressed himself against her back, squeezing her between him and the car. She screamed.

Eli fought to control his emotions. He projected a thought at the man. No effect. The distance was too great even for him.

The man clamped his hand over her mouth. "Shut the fuck up, bitch!"

She struggled and attempted an aikido maneuver Eli recognized, but she wasn't experienced at it. The man turned her around and wrestled her to the ground, ripping her blouse in the process. She screamed again.

The man slapped her, then pinned her arms and straddled her. "Don't piss me off, bitch. Ain't no one around to hear you."

The second man, slender and a few years older, exited from the shadows. "Hurry up, Donny. I want some, too."

"Get your lazy ass over here and gag her!" He leered at the woman. "Quit fightin' and you might enjoy it."

Emotions too long suppressed rose inside Eli. Several long strides brought him behind the two men. Now he was close enough. His telepathic stun temporarily disabled the second man. Almost simultaneously, Eli dug his fingers into the back of the other man's neck and yanked him off the woman.

"What the fuck!"

He spun the man around and stared hard at him.

"Who the fuck are you?"

The man jerked back; Eli's strong fingers wrapped around his neck and found the pressure points. Deep inside him, a door unlocked. Behind it lay memories of a different world, a different time, and a different Eli Howard, one well acquainted with anger and violence. The worst of those memories pushed the door ajar.

The man choked; his face turned red. The smell of his fear mingled with the humid, fall-scented air. With his feet nearly dangling, the man's eyes began to close.

Eli abruptly dropped him. He stepped around the woman to where the second man was reviving and pulled him up by the jacket. Forming his left thumb and forefinger into a V, he pressed them under the man's throat, lifting him, while gagging him. He drove his free fist into the man's nose.

The man gurgled. "Fu—" escaped his lips a moment before the telepathic blast put him to sleep.

Eli stood there, facing away from the woman while he reined in his emotions. He couldn't change what she had seen, but in her hysterical state of mind she might believe some of it imagined or exaggerated. He turned to her.

"Are you all right?" he asked in a tone he forced to be calm and soothing.

She scrabbled away and pushed her back against the side of her car.

"I am not going to hurt you. I'm Professor Howard, and I teach night courses here." He proffered his hand.

With short, rapid breaths, she pressed her hands onto the pavement. An imposing, six-foot-three Black man—he hadn't gotten used to being "African-American"—dressed in black and with a shaved head would not instill confidence under the best of circumstances.

He stepped back and took out his cell phone. "I'll call the University Police."

She shivered against the car while he reported the incident. Distrust filled her eyes.

"They're on the way. I'll wait with you until they arrive."

"Th-thank you." Her sobs had lessened.

He proffered his hand again. Trembling, she reached to accept it. He effortlessly pulled her to her feet, then retrieved the items she'd dropped and handed her the jacket. "Put this on."

She turned away while she did, as if she'd just realized her state of undress.

He pointed at the two unconscious men. "They won't bother you further. If you wish to file a report, I'll be your witness."

She shook her head. On the streets of Detroit, unless the attempted rape could be proved, little or nothing would be done. On campus, she stood a better chance of justice. The University Police, while commissioned police officers, were a different breed. Still, she would have to file a report and relive the nightmare.

In the distance he heard running footsteps. Moments later, two male officers arrived. "What happened?" one asked.

"I'm Professor Howard," he said. "I was on my way home when I saw those two men," he pointed, "running at this woman." He had already fixed the rapists' faces in his mind. "I tripped one. He landed on his face; I think he broke his nose. The other one had grabbed her and torn her blouse. I pulled him off by the throat, overzealously perhaps."

The officer nodded and proceeded to cuff the two men.

"Are you all right, Miss?" the other one asked.

Her breathing had become less labored, but the tears were starting. "If h-he hadn't been here..."

"Do you need me for anything else?" Eli asked the officers.

"Not right now, sir. We'd like a statement, but you can do that tomorrow. Is there a number where we can contact you?"

After giving them his home and office numbers, he walked out of the parking lot and turned right onto Second Street. When the weather accommodated him, he preferred walking to driving. Reaching Woodward, he headed north. Years of practice with his telepathic powers had enabled him to make people not notice him on these streets. Tonight, he didn't care. Let them see him.

Crime had existed in Detroit for decades, but never this bad. For over eighty years, Detroit had been his home. He remembered when young women could walk these streets without being assaulted. Detroit used to be a proud and safe city, where white people weren't afraid to go Downtown.

Three blocks later, a hustling drug dealer shoved a small packet at him. "I'll make you a deal, special price tonight."

Eli stared at him. A simple telepathic command made the dealer drop the packet and run. If only it were that easy to rid Detroit of all the drug dealers. He picked up the heroin and put it in his pocket to dispose of later so some kid wouldn't get his hands on it.

A woman stepped into his path. "Fifty to make ya happy? Hundred for the night."

Young, still attractive. For how long? "No, thank you."

When she reached out to rub his groin, he stopped her. "It's half price. *Big,* han'some men don' come by here much."

He peered into her mind. She had a kid. Handing her a hundred-dollar bill, he said, "Buy something nice for your son."

Detroit was rich in Black history. Once comfortable with his vampire side, he'd come here to explore his racial heritage. He chose a random cross street and walked east. From one of the rundown houses raised voices pierced the night air: shouting; cursing; blaming.

At Oakland he turned north again and several blocks later entered the Boston-Edison district. He stopped in front of an old house, once a prominent dwelling in this neighborhood. Now it was forgettable. A cracked sidewalk led up to his porch and the dark living room beyond it. Adrian must be out clubbing instead of enjoying the new big-screen TV he'd convinced Eli to buy.

"You have to keep up with the latest technology," Adrian had said.

Just as well Adrian wasn't here. The twenty-two-year-old didn't always take things as seriously as he should and frequently resisted advice and guidance. On the other hand, the suggestion that Adrian take money from his trust account to purchase the TV had resulted in, "I thought the trust fund was for my retirement. You've got more money than you could ever spend anyway."

Smiling at that thought, Eli resumed walking. After tonight's events, several things inside him had to be reconciled.

***

Detroit—Wednesday, October 15, 2003

Eli came up beside Ling Lu on the Detroit RiverWalk, looking out across the black, nighttime water. With the moon and a few distant streetlights the only illumination, his night sight easily discerned the details of her Asian beauty and the warmth of her brown eyes. Her modern suit had classic Oriental red and black colors. She didn't wear this one often. In it her slender body appeared delicate. Ling was anything but.

He gave her a light kiss on the right cheek. "Thank you for meeting me here."

"Your call worried me." She turned her head at him. "You look like hell."

He shut his eyes. All last night, he'd walked, finally returning home to sit in his library, reading, meditating, finding ways to distract himself so he could relax and get some sleep.

"I'm tired of it," he said. His soft voice barely rose above the faint rippling of the water. "I'm tired of all the pain here." He rubbed his hands down the sides of his face and braced his palms against the metal railing.

"But it can't touch us," she said.

He didn't believe that. "In 1920 when I arrived, Detroit was so different. Today, kids can't play safely on the streets, they respect nothing, and everyone sells drugs."

From the corner of his eye, he saw her shake her head. "You're living in the past, Eli. These are human problems, not ours; they'll pass us by."

All vampires received that same indoctrination. He couldn't fault her for echoing it. "If humans die out, so do we," he said. "We're still mortal; we still depend on them."

"They've been around longer than we have, they outnumber us, and they haven't died out yet."

"It's not like our kind haven't tried more than once to encourage it," he said. "I know you care about them."

She studied him. "Since I'm twenty years older, take some advice from your elder and don't get involved."

He thought of her as a sister, never as an *older* sister. "My mother would probably have said the same thing. She died three years before I was changed, a blessing in a way. She wouldn't have understood what I became."

"You're already doing enough," she said. "You teach young people how to avoid the sins of their predecessors."

"That's too slow a process to affect the present." In some ways he was proud of the dual aspects of his life. As a teacher, he helped others understand man's conflict and struggles. Would the day ever come when he'd be teaching about vampires?

"Why do you want to help humans now?" she asked. "What has changed your attitude?"

He clenched his jaw as he stared out across the water. "Last night, on the campus, I nearly killed two humans who tried to rape a woman. I…lost control."

He heard her breathing speed up slightly. "I'm not surprised. You declared yourself a pacifist and have ignored what's going on among our kind for the past half-century. You've had no stress. Your hot-blooded emotions haven't been an issue."

She knew most of his past, but he knew little of hers before she came to the U.S. "I'm a pacifist for good reason." His hands gripped the railing.

"I don't doubt you believe that." She put her arm through his. "When we first met, sixty years ago, you still had a feisty spirit. Despite the best intentions, no man or vampire—not even Eli Howard, not even over the course of a century—can force himself to change so drastically." She had so much wisdom. Her voice became stronger. "One vampire against all the evil of humankind is too large a task for even the great Eli Howard. Even if you—we—can prevent a few crimes, even if we do make a small difference, humans will undo it soon enough."

"Does that mean you'll help?" he asked.

"I didn't say that. I do agree that crime here is a little out of control."

"A little?"

"What can only two vampires do to stop it?" She put her head against his shoulder.

"Between us, we've got over three hundred years of experience with humans," he said. "We can make the city better. Others of our kind will observe and follow our example to make their cities better. It's not like we have anything else to do."

"Do you honestly believe those interested in keeping crime and their drug trade alive will let you terminate their activities? Where whole governments have failed, you expect to succeed?"

"I thought you, out of all of us, would understand," he said.

"I do, Eli, but the odds are not in our favor. If one sleepless night has you this haggard, I don't want to see you when you fail in this endeavor."

"I'm that bad?"

"Tonight you are not a handsome man." She bent his head down toward the water. "The ripples are doing you a favor. Maybe talking to Dietrich and the Council could help. They're meeting here at the end of this month."

He already knew what the answer would be. Dietrich was his mentor, and the Council's adviser, but he wouldn't help in this. Beyond keeping the two species from fighting one another, Dietrich didn't care what humans did to or among themselves. As for the Council, they'd follow Dietrich.

Years ago, Dietrich and he had disagreed over how and how much vampires should be involved in human affairs. Dietrich sidestepped the issue by suggesting Eli get his Masters and teach. They had not corresponded since. He found it ironic that this semester he was also teaching a special topics course in peace and conflict studies.

"We both know they won't do anything," he said.

"And Ysabel?"

Ysabel De La Cruz, the head of the Council. She lived in Detroit. He couldn't remember when he'd last spoken with her. *Yes, she'd listen. Whether she could help…* "Maybe I'll call her," he said.

"Have you thought this through? How will you carry on this fight and still teach?"

"I only teach part-time."

A faint sigh escaped her lips. "What you propose is a full-time job. Have you talked to Adrian?"

"I'm not sure he should be involved."

"You've mentored him well," she said softly. "Give him the benefit of the doubt. This is more his generation than ours you're dealing with."

Ling put her arm around his waist while he gazed into the river. The peacefully rippling water offered no answers and no reconciliation with last night's events.

CHAPTER TWO

Detroit—Thursday, October 16, 2003

Glad to be home after a night of strenuous partying, Adrian Shadowhawk pulled his yellow Corvette into the garage, next to Eli's.

He got out of the car and stood outside in the clear, starry night wondering why Eli had called him. Eli almost never called him. As far as he knew he hadn't committed any major infractions of the Rules—no more than usual, anyway.

The small table lamp in the living room barely shone through the heavy, living room curtains. He went inside and was about to remove his jacket when he noticed a light coming from the library. *Might as well get this over with.*

Eli's swivel chair was turned away from him and facing the bookcases behind the desk. The light on his desk lamp was set on its dimmest setting.

"'Zup, Eli? I got your voicemail. You wanted to see me?"

Eli swung his chair around.

"Whoa. You overindulge in something? You look like shit."

"Still that bad?"

"And a quart low besides. I keep telling you fresh is better than that canned stuff."

"Why didn't you answer your phone?"

"I shut it off so I wouldn't have cell phone interruptus." Adrian rolled his eyes. "I'm a creature of the night, and someone was helping me appreciate what the night had to offer. You sure you're okay? Some problem I should know about?"

"It's nothing a few hours of sleep won't help." Eli gestured at the chair in front of the desk. "Have a seat."

Adrian slouched into it. Whatever Eli had going on, it didn't seem like anything *he'd* done. "What's on your mind?"

"I do hope that hair's an accident."

"I think it goes very well with my fine Lakota skin."

"You look like a blue porcupine."

"Just colored gel. Washes right out. They call it color without commitment, and it's perfect at the clubs. I bought neon orange and neon green, too."

"Lakota?"

"I *am* full Lakota, after all. I think I should get back to my roots. What do you think?"

"I think Adrian Shadowhawk has been gambling with humans again."

Here it comes. Pick-on-me time. "Just poker. Unmarked deck, straight dealing. Honest—"

"Honest? You didn't use your telepathic ability even once?"

"You know mine's piss poor. 'Sides, I promise I didn't use it...once. Do you think we ever could, like, communicate completely without talking? That'd be so cool. Maybe we could find a way to make mine stronger."

"What happened to your charitable, strip-poker games where you donate the lost clothing to the poor?"

"There's a clothing glut at the moment."

Eli's eyes narrowed. "Really."

"That's what I was told."

"So you invented feed-me poker."

This couldn't be about that, could it? "You lose, you feed me. I think it's highly creative." Adrian opened his mouth and rubbed his tongue over the tips of his normal, human incisors. It wasn't fair that vamps didn't have fangs. "When are my fangs gonna grow?"

Eli narrowed his eyes. "Aren't the blood lancets working out?"

"Waste of time unless you're into nouvelle cuisine mini-meals. And quit poking into my head!" He scooted up, reached into his jacket pocket, and put his latest acquisition on the desk: brass knuckles with needle fangs attached. "Bought this cool tool from an online site that sells it along with other nefarious pieces clearly not intended for benign purposes. The fangs are hollow. I can imagine some nasty uses. Hurts more and leaves two tiny marks for several days, but this way I'm not gonna suffer from malnutrition. I'm a vampire, and we're supposed to be badasses. No pain for them, no gain for me."

"That's not how I taught you to behave toward humans. I hope these humans willingly let you feed on them."

"They sure do! I found a sweet technique. I fang 'em in the neck and suck at the little bit of blood while I press on the neck pressure points you taught me about. I bring 'em to the edge of unconsciousness, then let 'em bounce back. They think I'm really draining their blood. 'Course I don't tell them I'm not. They say it's like a near-death experience. And it's drug free—I know how you hate drugs. They love it, and even pay me for the service. Win-win."

"That's a dangerous practice, Adrian."

He thought about that. "I use alcohol wipes on the fangs to sterilize them first, but maybe I should print up some consent forms to cover my ass."

"Those pressure points can kill."

"I'm real careful."

"And it's dangerous to expose us to humans."

"Right. Like humans don't already know we exist. Get this. Two nights ago they invited me to a sex orgy. That's why I wasn't home. Some of the guys had me feed on them while they were doing the women. It was my cycle-time, so when my high-powered vamp saliva got into their wounds... You should've heard 'em scream when they blew."

Adrian leaned back in the chair again. "At the after-party, one of the women wanted me for some one-on-one. Sucking on all that fresh human blood amped up with hormones made me *sooo* ready for it. She had me begging, Eli. Then two more wanted me." He sighed and rolled his shoulders. "I was pretty whipped when the night was over, but it was sooo sweet." Adrian put his hands behind his neck and stretched. "Last night wasn't bad, either."

"Adrian..." Eli's voice had that parental warning tone.

"Yeah, I used protection." He bobbed his head, reciting, "'Female vamps are sterile; males aren't.' I'm glad I had some magnums with me. All that extra human blood inside me made it—"

Eli leaned forward and folded his hands on the desk, staring. His pupils dilated. He was pissed. "Before I changed you, Adrian, I told you there were rules to follow. You agreed to them."

Adrian put his hands on his thighs. "Yeah, yeah. The Be-Nice-To-Humans Commandments: One, don't feed on humans without their permission; two, don't kill humans; three, don't change them. I didn't break any of those."

"The fourth one? Don't let them know what you are."

"So what? It's not like we're getting negative press."

Eli continued to stare at him. "The idea is *no* press."

"We're not evil; we don't hurt them."

"It's perception, Adrian."

"Fact is, I'm keeping 'em off the streets where the real bad shit is. I'm protecting them. What's wrong with that? What's the big fucking deal, anyway?"

Eli didn't move. His gaze drilled into Adrian. "The big...*deal*, as you so colorfully described it, is that larger issues are at stake here, ones that go far beyond your limited viewpoint."

Way to go, Adrian. He's royally pissed off now.

"Your careless actions could endanger all of us everywhere in the world. Vampires have existed for thousands of years, more or less in anonymity among humans. In 1905, a group of zealots decided to make themselves known. Their actions resulted in violent confrontations and thousands of deaths across Europe and Asia. Many of our kind were killed as well. It took us two years to end the conflict. I helped restore control, and I have no wish to see that happen again."

For a moment, Adrian didn't know what to say. He'd never heard of this. "Chill! I'm not gonna start a war or anything. Besides, *you* broke the *third* rule when you changed me."

"With your full and informed consent. You were dying before you deserved to."

Adrian took a deep breath to collect himself before he answered. "And I appreciated it. I'll try to be more careful."

Eli relaxed. "That's all I ask. I apologize for being a bit harsh, but these rules exist for a reason."

"I understand." He'd have to ask Eli more about this 1905 thing sometime. Not now, though. "Something else you wanted?"

Eli looked thoughtful.

"Oh, I get it. You're calling in the favor, aren't you?" Adrian leaned back, put his feet on the desk, and crossed his arms. "No prob. What does my old, wise mentor want from his devoted student?"

One of Eli's eyebrows rose slightly. Whatever was on Eli's mind had him depressed, and Adrian had never seen Eli depressed before. "Hey, I know. I'm having a vampire movie marathon this Saturday—here of course, 'cuz we've got the big TV. I didn't think you'd mind if I invited a couple of human friends over to watch *Blade* and *Blade-2*. You're welcome to join us, might cheer you up. You know, you sorta look like Blade. You got the sunglasses-and-leather-coat action going—well, not at the moment. If you let your hair grow, you could stunt-double for him."

Eli rose. "Let's go for a walk. I want to show you something."

Okay, what the hell was going on? What happened to the lecture for his bad behavior? He deserved a lecture for his bad behavior. He'd psyched himself up for it—except Eli wasn't delivering. He appreciated talking with Eli, even if they didn't have a lot in common, being from different generations and all. Sometimes he even learned useful shit.

They strolled around the neighborhood. Eli pointed out houses Adrian had seen before but ignored. "You're walking through history, Adrian. This is Boston-Edison. If you'd lived here in the early 1900s, you might have seen Henry Ford himself or other notable men of the auto industry, like Stanley Kresge."

"Who?"

"Kresge started a chain of dime stores that became Kmart Corp."

"I always wondered what the K stood for."

They passed a boarded-up house. "Long before you were born, this was a busy, middle-class neighborhood. My people—the Blacks—felt they deserved to live in such places and they fought for that right. Within a few decades, the Whites had vacated and the neighborhoods fell into decay and ruin amid recessions and riots.

"Detroit's population has an unusual history. In 1920 it was nine hundred ninety thousand with four percent Blacks. By 1950 it had doubled, but with sixteen percent Blacks. Today, the total population has fallen to less than in 1920—"

"And African-Americans make up over eighty percent," Adrian said. "See, I don't wallow ignorance."

Eli nodded. "Do you know why the Black population changed as rapidly as it did?"

"I suspect you're going to tell me."

"In 1913 Henry Ford placed an ad offering equal pay to all workers, regardless of race, and that attracted us here."

"You didn't need a job, did you?"

"I came here for different reasons," Eli said.

"I'm guessing you have a point to this history lesson?"

Eli faced him. "I want to do something about the problems plaguing Detroit."

Sure, Detroit had a few problems, maybe more than a few. "As in…?"

"Make the city safer, get rid of the street crimes, the drugs…the rapes."

"Hmmm. Sounds like a *lot* of work."

"Yes, it will be."

"And I suppose you expect me to help. If I wanna play, I gotta pay, right?" He patted his stomach. "A little extra exercise couldn't hurt. I'm starting to put on weight, too much couch potato. It's been a while since I did any street brawling, but it's not something you forget." He squeezed his upper arm muscles. "Have to get myself back in shape first."

He gave Adrian the strangest look. "On the streets is exactly where I *don't* want you."

"I'm confused. Where do you want me?"

"Behind the scenes, putting those computer skills you keep bragging about to practical use."

"My hacking, you mean? That's illegal."

The eyebrows rose again.

"I just do it to my friends, for fun, nothing bad… But you're talking about hacking the bad guys who're doing illegal stuff, right?"

Adrian rubbed his chin. Okay, he didn't need to get in shape, but he could use it as an excuse to hang out at a gym, do some workouts and impress the ladies there with his enhanced vampire strength and see where it led.

He squinted at Eli. "We'll need lots of help. Do you think the Vamp Council will relax their stodgy rules about changing humans? I know a couple of human hackers who'd be perfect. That way I could have some vamps my age to hang with."

"The Council won't help with or condone my plan," Eli said.

Now Eli had his attention. "You're talking vigilante-style clean up, aren't you? Sweet!"

CHAPTER THREE

Detroit—Saturday, October 11, 2003

"Cocktail parties *suck*!" Drake Radley flipped a finger at the full-length reflection staring back at him. He thrust his other middle finger up next to the first. "Times two."

He stormed out into the hall. Why didn't they make him stay in his room and study or something? Wasn't it a parental imperative to ride your kids' asses about studying? Oh no, not Ethan and Val-not-Valerie Radley. *They* had cocktail parties, and *they* expected their one and only offspring to attend them. In a fucking tux!

Okay, just because it was a Saturday night, and he was a smart kid who didn't need to study much, why couldn't he just stay in his room and listen to his music? Oh, right. They'd covered that topic at dinner—

"You're part of this family, heir to the business, and you need to learn how the real world operates."

And—of course—Valerie uttered her usual line, "Your father only wants what's best for you."

He gave her a curt, "Fine."

Ethan slammed the tabletop with his fist and Drake jumped in his chair. "Watch your tone, young man! If we'd sent you to that private school like I wanted, you'd have learned respect and wouldn't be listening to that filthy rap music."

Military school, he meant. "Yes, *Father*."

Ethan left the dining room and Valerie said, "He does love you, Drake. Give him a chance. Why don't you meet him halfway?"

Halfway? There's no halfway. It's Ethan's way or no way. The only reason Ethan didn't send him to that school was his mother refused to let it happen. She wanted her son here, no argument allowed.

"I'm trying to help you understand him, Drake."

"Don't bother," he'd said.

The typical Radley dinner conversation, whenever Ethan showed up. Which was thankfully almost never.

Drake lightly fingered the hard-gelled spikes of his sandy hair. Ethan hated his punk look, but the most he could do among his guests was give Drake a disapproving glare. *As if he could melt the spikes with his stare.* Sometimes he wondered how Ethan would react if he ever heard him use the f-word.

Drake walked to the top of the stairs and scanned the crowd of suits and cleavage-baring cocktail dresses. Not that he didn't appreciate cleavage, but most of it belonged to hags three times his age. The only non-hag looked more like jailbait. She was clinging to the arm of a guy who probably retired twenty years ago and hadn't put her in his will yet. How could this old fart score when he couldn't?

He let out a sharp breath between his clenched teeth. Better get his ass down there and mingle—or float, as Father Dearest would say. If he didn't show, he'd hear about it later.

Plodding down the uncarpeted stairs, Drake made as much noise as possible, but the din of the revelers drowned him out. He checked his gold pocket watch, the one Val's dad had given him for Christmas two years ago. His father expected him to wear his Rolex at The Parties. *Screw that.* Not that he didn't appreciate having a two-thousand-dollar Rolex, but it only reinforced the smart, rich-brat image that had haunted him all through school. Other kids had a circle of friends. He had a small semicircle, and that only because he bribed them with free meals or movies.

Standing at the bottom of the stairs, he checked out the guests. Forty-five minutes into The Party and already several were drunk and disorderly.

Drake floated himself to the bar for a Coke. In a cocktail glass. Filled with ice, it held like two ounces of beverage.

Why couldn't he have a whole can? Because it would be tacky for the son of Ethan and Val Radley to carry a can of Coke.

No beer for him, either, because he wasn't legal. What would Ethan's drunken clients think if he allowed his underage son to drink anything alcoholic?

His mother saw him from across the room, smiled, and waved him over. "Very nice, dear," she said.

"Thanks."

Compared to some of his friends, he'd lucked out in the mom category. For being forty-seven, Valerie still looked great. Her blue eyes sparkled. Unlike the facelift poseurs, her naturally wrinkle-free skin wasn't shriveled by hours in tanning booths. Her blonde hair, also natural, glowed as it brushed the shoulders of her black dress. She was smart, not blonde-like at all, and used to help him with his schoolwork, until she started going with Ethan on his weekend business trips.

"Go let your father see you," she said.

At the other end of the room, Ethan was with some guy, probably a customer. Drake wandered close enough to listen over the dull roar in their great room. The guy was talking really loud.

"Ethan, the problem is your prices aren't competitive," the guy said.

"My people have done the market research, Dick. I agree that some of our prices are higher for low-volume runs, but Radley Biotech uses state-of-the-art equipment. We can produce higher quality in the same or less time as our competitors. When you go with higher volumes, our cost is less per unit than theirs."

"When I don't need large volumes, I'll pay through the nose!"

"We're willing to work with our customers. I'd like you to talk with my research and sales people. As long as you maintain a certain level of business with us, we can arrange to meet your requirements at prices you'll find attractive."

The guy pushed his half-full drink glass at Ethan and nearly spilled it. "Your problem is you pay high taxes for doing business in a city that's one giant slum."

"My company is in the suburbs." Drake saw his father straining not to comment.

"Detroit has a high Black population? What's the percentage of Blacks on your payroll, Ethan?"

What the hell did that have to do with this conversation? His father's expression said he wondered the same thing. *What an asshole.*

"As you noted, Dick," Ethan said, calmly, "the Black population is high."

"My point exactly!"

His father noticed him standing there. "Ah, Drake, I'm pleased you joined us."

Like he had a choice.

"Dick, this is my son, Drake. Drake, this is Dick Holt from Cleveland, one of my prospective clients."

"Heir to the throne, eh, son?" Dick Holt extended his hand.

Drake forced a fake smile and reciprocated. Dick's hairy hand vise-gripped his and pumped it furiously. Drake winced. "Maybe you can convince your old man that if he wants my business bad enough, he's going to have to make some compromises."

God, what a prick! When Dick released his death grip, Drake muttered, "What goes with 'Dick', has four letters, and begins with 'H'?"

"Pardon?"

"*Dick,*" Drake said, louder. "Nice name. Your parents must've not liked *you* either."

Behind him, his mother said, "Drake!"

Ethan's face got real red. "I apologize for my son. Drake's in those troublesome teen years and sometimes he doesn't think before he speaks." Ethan turned to Drake. "I think you'd better go upstairs." Through clenched teeth he added, "I'll deal with you later."

S-wee-t!

The knock on his door came a few minutes past eleven. Drake, in cargo shorts and T-shirt had parked himself in front of his PC and was playing a video game. "Who is it?" he said loudly.

His father had already shoved the door hard enough to bounce it against the doorstop. He halted halfway to Drake's desk. Drake kept watching the screen.

"Look at me, young man! What you said tonight to Mr. Holt is unforgivable. He's a *customer.*" His mother entered the room and came up behind his father.

"*Prospective* customer," Drake said, "and he'll get over it. Besides, you aren't gonna get his business anyway."

"Regardless, what you said to him was rude," his mother said. "I taught you better than that."

He caught that she said "I" not "we." He paused the game and focused on her, still standing just behind Ethan. "But he *was* being a dickhead."

The corners of her mouth curved slightly upward.

His father scowled. "You not only showed a lack of respect for us," he said, "but you embarrassed me, my guest, and yourself."

His mother shook her head slowly. Just when he thought she was on his side, she'd taken Ethan's again.

"For your little antic, you lose your Jeep," Ethan said.

What! "But I need it to get to school!"

"That's true," his mother said.

"Let him take the bus like everyone else." Ethan glared at him. "This conversation is over." He marched out.

Saying nothing, Drake looked to his mother for sympathy.

"I'll drive you to school on Monday," she said.

"Whatever." He went back to his video game.

She lingered a moment before she left.

***

Detroit—Saturday, October 18, 2003

Drake fidgeted on the sofa in his living room and checked the pocket watch he'd been holding for the past fifteen minutes. Seven forty-three. He pushed a curtain aside and checked outside. Where were those two? They were supposed to be here by now. If they didn't show, it would be too late to find another ride. He'd been planning this all week. Well, he could call a taxi, except he wasn't exactly sure where he was going. Jason said he knew the perfect club, but you had to be eighteen to get in. He told them that wasn't a problem. Not for Ethan Radley's son. His pocket change had purchased him the fake ID. No way was his ass staying home tonight.

He'd been dressed and ready an hour ago: slightly sagged jeans—he wasn't into showing off his butt—oversized, white T-shirt, the silver wallet chain draped over his pocket.

A horn honked outside. He bolted off the couch. The horn honked again. He opened the front door and waved at Todd's piece-of-shit car. Todd revved the engine to show off his barely functioning muffler. Drake made sure he had his house keys and wallet before he locked the door behind him.

Jason yelled out the passenger's side window, with a cigarette dangling out of his mouth, "Dude, let's go!"

Drake sauntered toward the Franken-car.

"Hurry up! Get yo punk ass movin' so us white boys can par-tee."

Drake got in.

"Nice duds," Jason said.

"Perfect for where he's goin'," Todd said and gave Jason a high five. They both laughed.

Drake had hardly closed the door before Todd put the car into reverse, gunned the engine, sped backwards out of the driveway, and slammed on the brakes. Drake shot forward and almost banged into Jason's seat. Before he could recover, Todd yanked the gearshift into drive and hit the accelerator again. The car lurched, slamming Drake back against his seat.

"Don't forget to fasten your seatbelt," Todd said, before laughing.

"Asshole," Drake said.

"That a comment against my expeditious driving?"

Jason jerked his head at Todd. "Dude, where'd you learn that hundred-dollar word?"

"From some college girl I picked up in a bar a couple weeks ago. She was all hot and horny and dragged me back to her place. Who was I to refuse? She had her clothes off before we even got to the bedroom, then ripped mine off and practically raped me. Afterwards, she said women didn't appreciate expeditious lovemaking."

"That's 'cuz she didn't come."

"Hey, not my fault. My nine-incher makes most women come at the sight of it. I offered to eat her pussy, but she said that was disgusting. Go figure."

While they bragged about how often they got laid, Drake did his best to ignore them.

Todd lit a cigarette, too. By the time they reached I-94, a haze of smoke had filled the car. Drake tried to open his rear window, but the handle was broken. He coughed and reached across to open the other window. It didn't help much.

Twenty minutes later, they were Downtown near the river, heading north on Beaubien Street. Todd turned left onto East Congress and stopped halfway down the block. "Here you are, Rapper Boy."

Drake squinted out the window at the old building and the line of maybe twenty people waiting to get in. "This is the club?"

"This is *the* club," Todd said as he and Jason smacked fists.

"It's ghetto," Drake said.

"This is Ling's Place, where the bad boys play. You gettin' out or don't ya think you're bad enough?"

Drake opened his door. Todd stuck his hand back at Drake, wiggling his fingers. "Um, our agreement? Gas money plus tip, you said."

Drake leaned over and took out his wallet. "Twenty, right?"

"That's what we agreed, unless you want to contribute more."

Drake gave him a twenty, and Todd stuffed it into the pocket of his leather jacket. "Appreciate it, man."

"You're coming in too, right?" Drake asked.

"Sure. Just goin' to find us a prime parking spot."

Drake pointed at the lot on the other side of the street. "Over there."

Jason poked a finger at Drake. "How about *you* get your ass in line and save us a spot so's we can all get in faster? See ya in a few..." He coughed out a barely audible, "...hours."

"What?"

"Kiddin'." Jason punched Todd in the arm.

Drake got out on the passenger's side. As soon as he shut the door, Todd hit the gas and the car screeched away.

He stared after them. Not being able to drive his Jeep royally sucked. *Fuck it all!* He came here to have fun. *The rents are away, Drake's gonna play.* He stuck his hands in his pockets and walked toward the club.

The club was an old bank building, nothing special, not much different from the abandoned building next to it. The cornerstone said 1961. A guy and girl in heavy goth makeup, each with multiple earrings, exited and walked down the front stone steps. As he got in the line, two guys ahead of him turned around. They had shaved heads and wore black leathers and combat boots—and they were holding hands. One of them stared at him then slowly scanned down Drake's body, lingering on the vintage high tops, then raised his head again.

Drake gave him a brief nod and leaned sideways to check out the other people in line. Except for three punkers, the rest were goths, no one dressed like him. Todd and Jason had lied. Well, what'd he expect from a couple of fucking losers?

Four stone steps led up to the door. Two intimidating bouncers stood at the top checking people—dark slacks, white muscle tops with writing and some kind of logo. They were of African-American persuasion. He figured he'd better refer to them that way to avoid getting his ass in trouble. The first guy, definitely over six feet, did police-style body searches on the guys; for the girls he only checked their purses.

The second bouncer was huge. Guys like him posed on the covers of weight-lifting magazines. He checked IDs and collected money. A scantily dressed girl whispered in his ear and no money changed hands. The rumors about sex favors must be true, like in the old Dire Straits song, *Money for Nothin'*."

The three punkers didn't get in. At first he worried until they passed him on the sidewalk. Jason said this club was eighteen-and-over. Those three didn't even shave yet! He wasn't worried. Even though he'd just turned seventeen in August, he easily passed for eighteen or nineteen.

He shoved his fingers into his pockets, leaving his thumbs out to rub along the top seam of his jeans pockets. That was cool, right? He brushed the tip of his right sneaker over a crack in the sidewalk. The guys ahead of him, still holding hands, moved up. He checked his pocket watch. Where were Todd and Jason? It shouldn't take ten minutes to find a parking spot, should it? He glanced over his shoulder. The three people behind motioned him to move up.

Without paying attention, Drake took a couple of steps and ran into one of the gay guys. "Sorry."

"Hey, handsome," the guy said none too quietly.

His partner scrunched up his face at him and gave Drake a dismissive wave. "Eew."

"It's not you; it's the clothes," the first one said. "But I wouldn't mind seeing you out of them." He gave Drake a hopeful expression.

Drake nervously looked around then back at the guy. "Uh, sorry, I'm waiting on a couple of friends."

"A threesome? I'm jealous."

His partner slapped him, on the arm. "Tramp."

Five minutes later, he was up. The first bouncer looked him over. "ID?"

Wait a minute, wasn't the second one the ID checker? *Shit.* They weren't going to let him in. Drake handed him the fake ID. The bouncer examined it carefully. "New here?"

Drake nodded. The guy had some serious face craters.

"Figured."

What did he mean by that?

The bouncer gave him a thorough body search, practically feeling him up before he jerked a thumb at the second bouncer. "Go see Ty."

Drake moved over. His hand shook as he held out a twenty.

The bouncer took it. "You want change, or do I get a tip for lettin' your sorry ass inside?"

Drake shrugged, happy to get in; the bouncer waved him by.

He stepped inside. Strange music assaulted his ears. *Twenty bucks to listen to that shit?* The volume surprised him, though, not all that loud, not even earsplitting. At all the parties he'd been to, the DJs liked to crank it. He could talk over this without yelling, like a cocktail party for the kiddies.

Inside, the place was still a bank. Well, almost. The bar ran along the former tellers' stations, although the barriers between tellers and customers had been removed at all but the two far ends.

Next to the entrance, in the DJ booth, stood a half-naked woman seriously tattooed and pierced. Several overhead spotlights lit her and a sign that said, "DJ Femme Fatale." Very femme.

On each side of her, two equally half-naked goth women gyrated to the music. He wasn't into goth, but the sight of these three women sent a serious rush of blood into his groin. Very fatale. With his loose jeans and the dark, crowded room, he hoped no one would notice his bulge.

Overhead, dozens of small, colored spots hung from the ceiling. The clubbers danced in and out of the shafts of light. To his surprise the lights weren't the tacky blinking kind. Some of the clubbers wore glow necklaces or blinking trinkets. Most were goth-attired and some had fake fangs. Most appeared older than he was; none were dressed like him.

He passed under a UV spotlight. It made his already conspicuous white shirt glow bright blue.

The gothic undercurrent united the club's unexpected multicultural mix. He figured it would be mostly Blacks. Two Asian guys off to one side each popped something into their mouths. In a far dark corner, and barely visible, a couple was enthusiastically making out. The guy's mouth was on the girl's neck. Drake squinted for better focus. Did she have her hand down the front of the guy's pants? A handjob right here in front of everyone? He couldn't see where the guy's hands were.

The music segued to a techno piece. He *hated* techno. Did the DJ take requests—like *no* techno? He leaned into one of the spotlight beams and checked his watch again. Twenty-five minutes and still no Todd and Jason. He should have waited to pay them. They were probably off somewhere getting high first, which meant he'd have to ride home with them in that condition. *Fuck them.* Lots of fine babes in here. He'd find one not already hooked up and maybe he'd get lucky like that guy in the corner.

Slowly winding his way through the ravers toward the bar, someone groped him, but he didn't see who. It wasn't the gay, bald guys, at least. They weren't anywhere nearby.

"Coke," he said to the bartender and took out his wallet.

The bartender opened a bottle of beer and put it on the bar. Drake wanted to take it, but he pushed it back. "I didn't order this."

"Yeah, you did." The bartender ran a finger over the label. In big letters it said, "Ling's Brew." Drake squinted at the small writing. *Near Beer Cola.*

The bartender held up two fingers. Drake gave him two dollars and dropped a third into the tip glass. The bartender nodded and moved to his next customer.

Grabbing the bottle with his left hand, he took a cautious sip. It tasted like a cola, not as sweet as the brand-name stuff, and it had a peppery bite he liked. He drank some more as he peered past the back of the bar. Beyond the shelves holding the liquor bottles, the bar was open in back, unlike the ones he'd seen in movies. Off to the left, in a small room, a security guard sat in front of monitors. Straight behind the bar, stood the old bank vault with its door open. A light glowed inside, and he could see part of a desk. *An office inside the vault? Sweet.*

The music changed. To a rap piece. *Finally. Tupac. "How Do U Want It." Sweet.*

The song ended too soon for him, and his bottle was empty. He was about to raise his hand to catch the bartender's attention when someone bumped into him.

"Hey!" a voice said.

Drake turned around.

A big guy with long sideburns, a ponytail, and a dragon tattoo on his right forearm, loomed over Drake. He held out his empty drink glass and glanced down at his wet muscle shirt, now stained with whatever had been in his glass. "You spilled my drink, asshole."

"Sorry, but it wasn't my fault," Drake said. "You bumped into me."

The guy pushed his face closer to Drake's. "You callin' me a liar, little man?" Drake got a blast of his alcohol breath.

Behind the guy Drake noticed another guy hurrying to get away. "How about I buy you another drink?" Drake said.

"Not good enough, runt. How about we go outside?"

"Leave him alone, Bart," a new voice said. "He didn't run into you. Someone else did."

Drake looked at the newcomer with spiked green hair, black leather jeans and jacket, and combat boots.

"This is none of your fucking business," Bart said.

"Back off before I make it *Tyson's* business."

"Who the hell is Tyson?"

"He's the mountain-of-muscle bouncer out front."

The kid must mean the bouncer collecting the money.

Bart bared his teeth and brought his fist under green hair's chin. The kid didn't flinch. He sure had balls because this Bart guy was a couple of inches taller and a lot heavier. Finally, Bart huffed and walked away.

"You okay?" the kid asked Drake.

"Yeah, thanks," he said finally, still amazed at what had happened.

"I recommend you stay away from Bart. He's always starting something. I'll let Ty know to keep an eye on him."

"You work here?" Drake asked.

"No. Enjoy the rest of your evening." The kid started to leave.

"Hey, can I buy you a drink?"

The kid stopped, facing away. "Not necessary."

"This is my first time here and I don't know anyone," Drake said. Why the hell did he say that? It sounded so pathetic.

The kid turned. "Yeah, I figured you were new 'cuz I haven't seen you around before. You live nearby?"

"Nuh uh, Grosse Pointe."

"I'm Adrian, Adrian Shadowhawk." The kid put out his hand.

Drake shook it. "Drake Radley." *Shadowhawk. Is that like...Indian?* With the back hair and tan skin, he'd thought Adrian was Hispanic.

"So, what do you think of Ling's?" Adrian asked.

"Weirder than I expected."

"That's 'cuz it's theme night."

"Huh?"

"The third Saturday of the month is theme night. Ling picks the theme, but October's is always 'coming out of the coffin.'" He waved his hand at the room. "All the vampires come out for blood."

Weird, but okay. Just party animals having fun. "I like your hair," Drake said, not knowing what else to say. "If I did that to mine, Ethan and Valerie would go postal."

"Ethan and Valerie?"

"The rents."

"Strict?"

"If I was a girl, I don't think they'd let me date until I was thirty. If they knew I was here tonight, I'd be grounded beyond my lifetime."

"So, why *are* you here?"

Drake pursed his lips. "'Cuz they're outta town for the weekend."

Adrian reached for the empty bottle in Drake's left hand. "Let me get you another."

"Sure. Uh, where's the men's room?"

"Over there." Adrian pointed. "I'll order the drinks."

As Drake wandered toward the restrooms, the music shifted to techno again. Maybe the DJ would be playing something else by the time he came back out.

He washed his hands twice, waited until the air dryer stopped even though his hands were dry, checked his hair in the mirror. He could still hear the techno piece playing. A guy with a nose ring and tall hair spikes came into the restroom and unzipped before he'd reached the urinal. Time to leave.

Drake had hardly taken two steps out of the restroom when a woman in heavy vampire makeup rubbed against him.

"You interested in donating?" she asked in a real sexy voice.

A new pickup line? Did she mean, like...sperm donor? "Uh, what did you have in mind?"

"You know, red stuff."

Drake shivered. She creeped him out. She wasn't all that much to look at, and her body had too much on the plus side for his taste.

Adrian appeared from the crowd. "He's with me."

"Uh, sorry, Adrian, I didn't know."

The woman walked away, obviously disappointed.

"What was that all about?" Drake asked.

"Nothing. You wanna go outside? It's noisy and hot in here."

"I guess." Better than hanging around by himself. The techno had stopped, but he figured more wasn't far behind.

He followed Adrian through the crowd. Except they didn't head to the front. Drake tapped him on the shoulder. "Where are we going?"

"Out back, where the smokers go. Ling doesn't allow smoking inside. She's progressive and says soon all the clubs are gonna prohibit smoking inside."

"You smoke?"

"No, but it's a quiet place to talk. If we go out front, it'll cost you two bucks to get back in and they'll feel you up again. Unless that's what you want."

Drake shook his head vigorously. He wouldn't mind if the bouncers were women, though.

They stepped into a sort of courtyard, probably at one time an alley between the buildings. High, stone walls, not that old, enclosed it now. Paving stones covered the ground. The area had three evenly spaced picnic tables decorated like coffins. There wasn't a bouncer out here, but a security camera was mounted above the door. Three guys and two women were smoking. At the farthest table, another couple sat talking and drinking.

"Was that chick trying to hook up with me?" Drake asked.

"Sort of."

"And she thought...you and me...?"

"Here you go." Adrian handed him a bottle and took a drink from his own. "Much better out here. That music's brain-banging me tonight. Too much techno."

"Yeah, techno sucks." Drake bounced his head from side to side and did his rap gestures with his right hand,

"No techno crap;

"Drake digs rap."

"Eminem?"

"That bad boy is my hero."

Adrian knocked fists with him. "I prefer Alternative, like my lifestyle."

Was Adrian gay?

"I'm not gay."

"Huh?"

"You were thinking it. Sorry, I do a little mind reading sometimes." He pointed at Drake's bottle. "'Sides, you don't want to get caught with that inside."

Drake took a cautious sip. *Sweet! Real beer,* good *beer.* "Thanks!"

"No prob. Ling owns a microbrewery and sells her own beer." He raised his bottle. "To a new friend."

Drake copied him. "Yeah!"

"She bottles soft drinks with an identical label—'cept for the small print that's not obvious to a casual observer—so underagers like yourself don't feel uncool."

Drake rubbed one toe of his sneakers over the paving stones. "How'd you know my age?"

"Mind reader, remember?"

"Right." He kicked a pebble. "I won't get in trouble drinking this, will I?"

"I got ya covered long as we're outside and you don't get drunk. You can handle a couple of beers, can't ya?"

"A couple. Why didn't the bartender proof you?"

"'Cuz I know Ling, and he knows I'm over twenty-one."

"You know the owner?" Drake raised his eyebrows.

"Sure. I can introduce you later."

"I'd rather you hook me up with one of the babes," Drake said.

"Most of these aren't your type."

"If they're hot and female, they're my type."

One of the smokers came up to Adrian. He was wearing black leathers and had jet-black, spiked hair, but he was still less goth than most of the crowd. "You wanna do blood later tonight?"

"Not tonight," Adrian said.

"Gimme a call if you change your mind." The guy walked away.

"What did he mean by that?" Drake was surprised the words came out so easily. He wasn't nosy. Maybe it was the beer, but he hadn't even finished one bottle.

"Nothing."

"That's the second time you said that. First was with the goth girl. Do you belong to some kind of cult?"

"Not a cult." Adrian took a drink of his beer. "Let me ask you something. Do you believe in vampires?"

"What?"

"Do you believe vampires exist?"

Drake shifted his beer to his right hand. "I've heard about some goth types who," he shivered, "have these ceremonies where they drink blood. Is that what you mean?"

"What if I told you real vampires existed?"

Drake thought for a moment. No, Adrian was just messing with him, maybe checking his sobriety level. "Like Dracula, you mean—bite your neck and suck your blood, hypnotic eyes, no reflection in a mirror, burn up in sunlight? No way I'd believe those were real."

"Just checking."

Adrian stretched his shoulders back to part his jacket. He touched the silver pendant hanging in front of his white tank top. An oval encircled the word "Vampire" in Celtic script. Adrian bared his teeth. Then he closed his mouth and comically rolled his eyes. "My bad." He pulled a set of false fangs from his jacket pocket and pushed them over his teeth. "Better?"

Joke on the new guy. Okay, he'd play along. "It's sort of cool, but I don't think any self-respecting vampire would have spiky green hair." Drake switched his beer back to his left hand, hefted it to his mouth. "How old are you?"

Adrian removed the fangs. "Twenty-two."

"You look younger."

"We age gracefully. Keep out of the sun, stick to a sensible diet fortified with youthful human blood," Adrian put one finger on Drake's neck, "and don't let your meat loaf."

Drake frowned, then caught on and laughed. "Riiight. Get off often."

"Exactly."

Adrian *said* he wasn't gay, but the guys in his school talked about the stuff that went on in the clubs, how guys picked up guys. He'd figured a lot of it was exaggeration. Maybe not. Maybe he should ditch Adrian and continue on his own.

Drake finished his beer and checked around for a place to dump the bottle.

"I'll take it for you. Ling's strict because she doesn't want to lose her license. She'll kick your illegal ass out and burn mine because I gave it to you."

"I thought you said I couldn't get into trouble. And how would she know you gave it to me?"

Adrian put his index fingers to his temples. "Vamps are telepathic, and she's old enough to be *real* good at it."

This Adrian sure was strange but kinda cool to be around. Unlike the guys in school, Adrian didn't make fun of him for being himself.

"Another beer?" Adrian asked.

Drake spread his legs, rap style, pointed his forefingers at each other.

"Ethan and Valerie

"make *me*," he pointed one finger at himself,

"steer *clear*," he pointed the other finger at himself,

"of the *beer*," and aimed both fingers at the bottles Adrian was holding.

He un-rapped himself. "If they ever smelled alcohol on me, they'd repo something else I don't want repoed."

"Something *else*?"

"My Jeep is locked in the garage because I expressed a politically incorrect opinion in front of one of Ethan's prospective clients." Drake made an "L" symbol with his forefinger and thumb against his forehead. "Ethan wasn't going to get the asshole's business anyway—but that wasn't the point."

"So, how'd you get here?"

"Two guys I know who used to go to my school. They dropped out a couple of years ago and went into business for themselves. They know the whole Detroit scene, so I asked 'em to recommend a place. Jason told me about this dark and dangerous club Downtown. It cost me a twenty for the ride. They dropped me off and said they were going to park the car." He checked his watch. "Forty minutes ago."

"Do you think this club is dangerous?" Adrian asked.

"Nuh uh. Kinda disappointing. Just your basic party goths."

"And you live in Grosse Pointe."

Drake grinned widely. "Home of the rich and shameless. Do you know how late the buses run?"

"Not this late."

"Shit. Guess I'll have to cab it home."

"If you want, I can take you whenever you're ready to leave. I got nothing going on tonight."

"Really?" Drake wasn't sure about being alone with someone he just met, but Adrian *had* fended off trouble twice.

"No prob."

"I wish I'd known about the goth duds," Drake said. "I feel kinda stupid with what I'm wearing."

"You're fine. I'm not exactly goth myself, not with green hair, as you said. Most of the people here are poseurs."

"Have you ever been to the casinos?" Drake asked.

"I go to Greektown all the time. I love to play poker 'cuz with my vamp telepathy, I always win. You play?"

"It's not in my best interest to gamble."

"Not even a friendly friends' game?"

"I'm not exactly drowning in close friends. All the guys I know want serious money so they can buy weed. They only hang with me if I'm paying the tab. What the shit. Beer me!" He took out his wallet.

"No, my treat. Wait here, I'll be right back."

Drake inspected the area while Adrian was gone. A couple more smokers came out and three of the others went back inside. In the shadows at the far end, a young couple he hadn't noticed before caught his eye. The guy had his arm stretched out at the woman, and she held a short plastic tube. He blinked. Was that a needle attached to it? Her other hand grabbed the guy's wrist. Drake flinched when she slid the needle into the guy's arm. *What the fuck? Drugs out here in the open?* What kind of club was this?

A hand tapped his shoulder. "Here's your beer."

Drake jumped and spun around. Adrian held out a bottle. Drake quickly grabbed it in his left hand and took a hefty swig.

"You're a lefty," Adrian said. "Did you know the Latin word for left means 'sinister'?"

Drake ignored him and pointed at the couple. "Are they doing drugs? If the club owner is so strict about alcohol, why does she allow drugs?"

"Ling doesn't allow drugs. The bouncers confiscate them if they find any, and if they catch you doing them, they'll kick your ass out. 'Sides, those two aren't doing drugs. Watch."

The woman now had the plastic tube in her mouth. "She's sucking his blood out?" Drake chugged a third of his beer.

"Uh huh."

"Whoa." Drake shivered, but he couldn't look away. "That's creepy. Isn't it dangerous?"

Adrian shrugged. "Not if you're careful."

Drake couldn't believe Adrian had said that. "Does that happen often around here?"

"Depends."

"On what?"

"On how many vampires are around and how many humans are willing to let them feed."

"Fuck," Drake muttered.

"Don't worry, the vampires won't bother you as long as you're with me." Adrian lifted his bottle and drank.

"What do you mean?"

"'Cuz I found you first, I get first option. It's vampire etiquette."

He pointed back to where the man and woman were. "W-would you do that to me?"

Adrian sighed. "Do you want me to?"

"No!"

"Then you got nothing to worry about." Adrian finished his beer.

Drake chugged the rest of his and held up the empty. "I'm buying, no arguments." He handed Adrian a ten.

Adrian shook his head. "No offense, but I think you should stop at two."

Drake cupped his hand in front of his mouth and exhaled. "Probably right." He checked his watch, not even nine thirty. "But I'm not ready to go home yet."

"You wanna go gambling?"

"I'm eighteen, remember?"

"No, you're seventeen with a fake ID."

"How the *fuck* did you know that?"

"You still don't believe me?"

This was too spooky. No way could Adrian know about his fake ID unless he really could read minds. But that was ridiculous. No one could read minds.

"I can take you someplace where your age won't matter, if you're interested I mean," Adrian said.

Drake looked at his feet. He was a little buzzed, but not so much that he'd do something stupid like go gambling with an almost stranger. Still… "You said you know the club owner. Any chance I could meet her?" That way he could find out if Adrian was really on the level.

"Sure. Follow me."

Adrian took both beer bottles and headed back inside. Some kind of punk music was playing, nothing he'd ever heard. As they wound through the club, it felt more crowded than before. The smells of costumes and makeup and colognes and hair products and leather mingled with the beer and liquor and occasional smells of smoke on the clothing of people he passed.

Adrian put the empty bottles on the bar. They went around it and stopped at the bank vault entrance. Drake could see a slender Oriental woman sitting at a desk inside.

"Hi, Ling. One of your fans wants to meet you," Adrian said.

"Please come in."

"Ling, this is Drake Radley. It's his first time here."

She raised herself from her seat and extended her hand across the desk. He lightly shook her hand. "I am pleased to meet you, Drake. Please have a seat."

Drake waited until she sat before he did. Adrian sat on the edge of her desk facing him.

"How do you like my club?" she asked.

"It's cool." Drake waved his hands over his attire. "I wish I'd known about the vampire theme. I kinda stick out."

"Most of them don't care. I like everyone to be comfortable. I don't have a dress code, except within limits of good taste, of course." She gave him not quite a smile. "I hope Adrian has been behaving himself?"

What did she mean by that? "He saved my ass—my butt, I mean."

"From Bart," Adrian said.

She nodded. "Yes, he can be trouble sometimes. Your last name is Radley? Are you related to Ethan Radley of Radley Biotech?"

Drake's face got warm. "Uh, he's my father. Do you know him?"

"By reputation. I have heard good things about him and his company. We need more businessmen like him to invest in our city and help it grow."

Was she talking about the same Ethan Radley? Feeling uncomfortable, Drake stood. "Well, it was nice to meet you."

"Likewise. Please come back anytime."

"I'm sure I will." Although he wasn't sure he would.

"Tell Stefan to give him a free drink," she said to Adrian.

When they were outside the vault, Drake asked, "Why did she give you that weird look?"

"Probably reading my mind, knows everything I was telling you. She's good at it. She's like a hundred and eighty years old."

What? Okay. This shit was getting way out of control. "So, you're telling me that lady I just met is a vampire?"

"Yup. Let's go this way." Adrian led him past the vault and along the back hallway, past the security office where a guard watched over several video monitors. He opened the door of a room and flipped on the light. It was a storeroom for stage lighting and other equipment. They stepped inside and Adrian pushed the door almost closed. "I promised Eli I'd be more discreet. And I really did try."

"Who's Eli?"

"My watchdog. No, not really. He's my teacher of all things vampire. Here's the deal. I've spilled my guts way too much tonight, but since I've already done it, there's some other stuff you should know. In the basement, Ling has a room that used to be a break room for the bank employees. It's quiet and private. We'll grab your free, nonalcoholic drink from the bar and we can talk without interruptions—if you want to, that is." He pulled a deck of cards from his jacket pocket. "I can also teach you some of my winning poker moves—just a friendly friends' game where no money changes hands." He gave Drake a wry smile. "And no blood leaves your body. If you'd rather go home, I'll drive you or put you in a cab. Whadda ya think?"

Drake didn't know what he wanted. He still wasn't ready to end his night out. He'd just met Adrian, but he seemed okay. "Oh, what the fuck." He got into his rap stance, bobbing his head while he chanted,

"While the rents are away, Drake's gonna play.

"Tonight's my night; I got the right

"to have some fun; it's just begun.

"Ethan and Valerie who?"

He raised both hands above his head and flipped both middle fingers at the ceiling. "*Fuck* you!" He pointed both forefingers at himself. "Drake Radley humbly puts himself into your hands. I am yours to corrupt."

CHAPTER FOUR

Detroit—Friday, October 24, 2003

Adrian turned into the huge driveway of the Radley house and honked the horn. Seconds later, Drake sprinted out of the house and hustled his ass into the Vette.

"Dude, I *so* appreciate you inviting me to your place to meet Eli and picking me up." He did a homey handshake with Adrian, wiggling their fingers against each other's palms and gripping fingertips before releasing.

"'S okay," Adrian said. Drake's hair looked like he'd spent an hour gel-spiking every strand into place. "Nice spikage."

"Thanks." Drake buckled his seatbelt. "I didn't think you'd pick me up until *after* sunset."

Adrian raised a hand to his sunglasses. "What you see in the movies about us not being able to witness the sunset is a load of crap. We just gotta protect our eyes from the light and our skin from sunburn, even in winter. That's why most of us are night people. I was always a night person anyway, so not much changed for me."

Adrian backed the car into the turnaround and pulled out of the driveway. It wasn't that he didn't like Drake. He did. He'd just never gotten so close to a human since he was changed. Humans were fun to hang with, and he did want friends close to his own age, but Eli had said that serious friendships between humans and vamps almost never worked out. Drake had practically adopted him. Too late to back out. They'd gone clubbing twice more since they'd first met at Ling's last Friday. Drake had wanted to go gambling this weekend, but Adrian had to teach him a few things before that.

One thing had led to another. Adrian didn't know why he'd told Drake about Eli's mission to clean up Detroit, either. Two seconds later, Drake volunteered to help with the cleanup effort. Bringing Drake to meet Eli might not have been such a good idea. Well, Eli hadn't said anything directly, but he hadn't been enthusiastic, either.

"Do all of you drive such sweet cars?" Drake asked. He'd said earlier that his father thought a Jeep was a more sensible car, less temptation to do something stupid.

"Most of the ones I know prefer less conspicuous transportation," Adrian said. "I haven't been out of Detroit since Eli changed me, so I can't say what my brothers elsewhere drive."

"It's a primo ride." Drake gave him a high five.

Adrian glanced sideways at Drake and again had second thoughts. *How would Eli react?* For a seventeen-year-old, Drake was cool, but Drake wasn't a vamp, even though he'd stated his desire to convert. Still, they needed help with The Project. Drake was smart, good with computers, and his sincerity wasn't in doubt. *Would Eli refuse an enthusiastic offer to aid his cause? On the other hand, Drake might stretch Eli's open-mindedness.* Adrian turned right onto Holbrook.

"Nice antique neighborhood," Drake said.

"Looks aren't everything. 'Sides, Eli doesn't want to draw attention to us." He turned left onto Oakland.

When they passed three boarded-up, ready-to-collapse houses, Adrian caught pieces of Drake's derogatory thoughts. He wasn't intentionally reading Drake's mind. Drake was projecting them. Humans sometimes did that. They also passed some nice homes, but Drake didn't comment on those. Adrian turned into his driveway. "We have arrived."

Drake peered around the two trees in front of it. "Looks like a crack palace." But he said it with a smile in his voice.

"Helps camouflage us. As far as strangers are concerned, Eli teaches at Wayne State and I'm his nephew. They don't notice that I'm Native American, not African-American."

They got out of the car. Drake followed him across the front yard and up the wooden steps.

"Remember, when you meet Eli, keep it low-key."

Drake smiled and nodded, but Adrian's one-week exposure to Drake Radley told him Drake didn't know the meaning of low-key. Drake would embarrass them both for sure.

He opened the door for Drake. "Eli fixed up the inside sooo sweet! Check it out." Drake stepped inside and started to remove his shoes. "This isn't *your* parents' house. Shoes on."

"Kinda dark, isn't it?"

"Easier on our sensitive eyes. Eli bought this place from some rich guy's estate and had it remodeled." He pointed up and down. "Cathedral ceiling, real oak floors. I love the winding staircase. This way." He walked right a couple of steps into the living room. "We've got a fireplace, a new big-screen TV, and a deadly leather couch. I fall asleep on it all the time."

"You don't sleep in a coffin?" Drake asked.

"I'm not *dead*! In here I like to go barefoot 'cuz you can dig your toes into the carpet. Throughout the house, he's got automatic blinds that adjust to the outside light."

"Adrian, dinner is nearly ready. Is your friend staying?"

The voice came from behind them, and Adrian pivoted around.

Before Adrian could introduce him, Drake turned and thrust his hand at Eli. "Name's Drake, give a shake. Don't be nervous, Drake D. Radley is at your service. And this dude'd be glad to share food with you."

So much for low-key. Adrian watched Eli survey Drake before extending his own hand. When Eli did, Drake gave him a soul-brother handshake.

"Pleased to meet ya, head vamp dude," Drake said.

Adrian grinned sheepishly. "Sorry, Eli. He followed me home."

Drake scowled at him.

"Don't dis me that way,

"I ain't no stray.

"Don't like what I'm about?

"Say the word, an' I'll be peace out!"

Drake was only an inch shorter than Eli and looked him in the eye. "Adrian said you be a big dude with at-ti-tude."

Adrian shrugged. "That's not how I phrased it."

"Exactly how did you phrase it, Adrian?"

"Um...forceful?"

"It's cool," Drake said. "Attitude's a proper thing for a dude like you. Yo, check it out:

"My pa-rents
"they got no sense
"they name me Drake
"it make me quake
"been called a duck,
"but I don't give a fuck.
"Came here with my man,
"A-dree-an;
"don't mean to be rude,
"but when can I be-come vam-pire food?
"Want ya to bury them fangs in my neck.
"Don't make me no vamp re-ject.
"Not here to join no fuckin' choir,
"jus' wanna be a badass vam-pire!"

He bowed fully at the waist, straightened, saluted with both hands, tilted his head left and back, and poked his forefinger into his neck. "Five-star dining."

"You're Ethan Radley's son," Eli said.

"The one and lonely only. A birthright I'll gladly trade to join your crusade."

"You know his father?" Adrian said. The warmth of embarrassment finally left his face. "I forgot, *you* know everything."

"By reputation," Eli said.

During the week, Drake hadn't talked about this father.

Drake took the cue,

"Bi-o-tech is Ethan's biz,
"a big bad company he calls his.
"I seen stuff there that royally sucks,
"and he employs some sick motherfucks.
"Does animal experiments in a major way,
"stuff I'd report to the SPCA."

Drake grinned widely then dropped the smile. "I tried too hard on my SATs—a simple case of you give it your best and you get screwed. When I overachieved, my father used his connections to get me into Harvard. Not *my* choice. But you can't argue with Ethan Radley. He's grooming his son to follow in his sleazy footsteps. Unless I can outsleaze him, next year it's the Ivy Leagues for me. I'd rather watch a PC defrag its hard drive. Adrian says you need help cleaning up Dee-troit, so that's why I'm here." Drake bowed. "Oh great and powerful One, give me a job and save me from Ethan's Evil Empire."

"It's not that we wouldn't appreciate your help, Drake," Eli said, "but this is serious and dangerous business."

"Ethan doesn't appreciate my rap-i-tude, but seeing as you're a hip young African dude—"

"Eli is a hundred and sixty years old," Adrian said.

"Whoa! I hope I'm that well preserved when I'm his age.
"So...give me a bite, I'm ready to fight.
"Vamp me, amp me.
"I'll help my brothers

"slash and trash
"those motherfuckers.
"I'll give you another reason
"why it's my vamp season.
"You don't know the half of it.
"At Ethan's place there's real bad shit
"that's goin' down.
"I wouldn't hang around.
"A new game he plays
"with a dude named Hayes—"

"*Cyrus* Hayes?" Eli said. His eyes went dark.

Drake stretched out his arm, palm down, at shoulder height.

"Small in size,
"blood-red hair,
"and scary blue eyes?"

Eli nodded.

"Who's Cyrus Hayes?" Adrian asked.

But Eli ignored him. "Drake, where did you see Mr. Hayes?"

"At my parents' house. Twice last month he came over late in the evening. He and Ethan went into the study and shut the door. I was in bed by the time he left."

"Drake, I appreciate your offer to help us, but you're better off not getting involved. We'll handle this."

"I'm already in-volved.
"I'm no small chump; I'll give him a lump.
"Not a full bite, not to-night;
"gimme a nip, won't hurt me a bit.
"Just a vamp in training—
"when they feel my bullets,
"they'll think it's raining!

Drake pursed his lips. "If you don't want to fang me, I'll accept honorary vamp status for now."

"Adrian, can we talk in private?" Eli waved him toward the library.

"Back in a few," Adrian told Drake. "Try the couch."

Five steps behind Eli, Adrian sighed heavily. He'd been expecting the lecture. He just didn't know if it would be for bringing Drake here, for telling Drake too much in the first place, or the same old one about consorting with humans again. Probably all three. But, what the shit, why couldn't he have friends and fun? Guys his age needed friends.

Eli slid the pocket doors of the library shut. "I should be angry at you."

"*Should* be? Why aren't you?"

"Drake is right in more ways than he knows," Eli said. "Cyrus Hayes is the *last* person we want in Detroit. Drake's father has no idea of the danger he's put himself and his whole family in."

"Clue me in. Who is Cyrus Hayes?"

"Serious trouble for us and for Drake's family. He's a brilliant and powerful vampire who cast aside his conscience to achieve his goals. Unlike some of us, Cyrus has a totally pessimistic view of humans and sees us as their salvation. This is where he and I strongly disagree. Unfortunately, his methods of achieving his goal are dangerously close to Hitler's. The only difference is that Cyrus doesn't kill humans directly but instead finds ways of helping them destroy themselves. I should have killed him years ago."

Adrian swallowed. "Should have *killed*?"

"Do Drake's parents expect him back tonight?"

"They're out of town for the weekend. Again. They're almost never home."

"Then I want him to stay here for the weekend." Adrian started to ask why, but Eli said, "We'll discuss your unwise actions later." Eli opened the library doors. "Show Drake our hospitality. I have something I must work on in the meantime."

Eli's concern worried Adrian. He sauntered back into the living room to find Drake sprawled on the green leather couch. Drake propped himself up on his elbows, grinning. "Dude, this leather is bumpin' and chillin'. If this were my crib, I'd be on this couch twenty-four seven."

"You'll get that chance. Eli wants you to stay with us for the weekend. After dinner, I'll drive you home to pick up whatever you need."

"Really? I can stay in your house? Among coffins and graveyard paraphernalia? *Chez vampire*, as the French say?"

Adrian gave him the hard stare. "I told you, we don't sleep in coffins. Do you see anything graveyard-like in here?"

"No."

"We have a guest bedroom for you. Just stay out of *mine* at night."

"Why? Do you turn into something ugly and evil? I thought you slept during the day."

"We don't have to. I'm a night person, so I usually sleep in. But when I'm entertaining women, it's not afternoon delight."

Drake grinned. "Women? Plural? Sweet! If you have a spare, send her my way.

"Drake ain't afraid,

"Drake loves to get laid."

He held up his right hand in the Vulcans-from-Star-Trek greeting. "Live long and copulate. How many vamps live in Detroit?"

"A few dozen."

"Why haven't I met any before?"

"You probably did and didn't know it. A lot of them hang out at Ling's Place."

"She's got a sweet body. Does she have a boyfriend?"

"She's too old for you, remember?"

"Older women really give me a bone."

Adrian smacked Drake on the back of his head.

"Ow!"

"You're more of a sex pig than me. Let's go get dinner. Tonight's steak night."

Drake crossed his hands over his chest.

"*Sirloin* steak," Adrian said, "cooked to order by Eli himself. I think he must've been a chef in his former life. We've got chef-like kitchen appliances."

"Sweet. It's usually fast food for me 'cuz Ethan's never home. Valerie's a vegetarian; I'm a meat-atarian." He thought for a moment. "Uh, I don't have to drink blood, do I?"

"Chill! We eat the same food you do." Adrian licked his lips. "Except for our required dietary supplement."

"Any chance I could become one of the *family*?" Drake suggestively stretched his neck.

"If it was up to me, I'd love to have a brother."

"Tell Eli I'm putting myself up for adoption."

No point in telling Drake the reason Eli wanted him to stay with them this weekend, not that Adrian knew why.

CHAPTER FIVE

Detroit—Friday, October 24, 2003

Eli bookmarked his page and shut the book. Not even a good, lighthearted novel was a sufficient distraction. A glance at the wall clock told him it was a few minutes before midnight. He leaned back in his chair and rubbed his eyes.

Adrian poked his head between the half-closed library doors. "Movie's over. We're gonna play a computer game. You okay?"

"I'm fine. Did you put clean sheets on the bed for Drake?"

"Uh huh. Drake says he's not tired yet, but he's so wiped, he won't be any challenge."

Drake came up behind Adrian. "I'll whip your ass."

"Dude, go check yourself in a mirror. Your eyes are burnt."

"That's my fake-out look."

"Don't feel that you have to stay up to keep Adrian amused," Eli said. "He's more than capable of entertaining himself."

"It's okay. I'm practicing my creature-of-the-night skills. Never know when I might have to use them." He waved his hand from side to side. "Thanks for the great dinner. Those steaks were primo."

"You're welcome, Drake. You are always welcome here."

The two left. Eli shut his eyes. He was back in Europe, in the fall of 1906.

***

The dead, and the ones hoping they were, littered the brick streets of the village. This time it was Germany, but he had witnessed the same scene in numerous small towns and villages across Europe and western Asia. Vampires attacked humans, and humans retaliated. Both sides lost, the vampires more so because of their smaller numbers.

Cyrus Hayes stood beside him in the middle of the street, one hand braced on the sword whose point rested on the ground. "This could be a blessing for us," he said.

An incredulous Eli asked, "How is this a blessing?"

"Did Dietrich have you read Thomas Malthus' 1798 essay on population? I expect not. Dietrich is too much the optimist. What a pity. Malthus said that wars, famine, and plagues control the surplus population. 'The power of population is so superior to the power in the earth...that premature death must in some shape or other visit the human race.'" Cyrus swept one hand at the carnage in front of them. "This is population control. Who are we to question the natural order of things?"

Abruptly, Cyrus pivoted, sword point inches away from the belly of the villager behind them.

The man raised his hands. "*Nein! Töten Sie mich nicht!*"

Eli put his hand on Cyrus' wrist. "No, there has been enough death here."

"Apparently he doesn't think so or he wouldn't have snuck up on us with a knife."

"It's not drawn, Cyrus."

The man dropped to his knees. "*Bitte, helfen Sie mir. Mein Sohn—*

Cyrus laughed. "He knows his proper place in our world. As elder, you should feed on him first."

"No feeding, and no more killing."

Eli probed the man's mind. "This man's son is injured. He needs our help," Eli told Cyrus.

Cyrus pushed the sword up to the man's neck.

Eli's hand, still on Cyrus' wrist, tightened and pulled it back. "I said *no*!"

"Your compassion will one day cost you." Cyrus sheathed the sword. "He knows what we are. We're his enemy. He'll kill us as soon as he's gotten what he wants."

Eli helped the man up. "*Wir werden Ihnen helfen. Führen Sie uns zu Ihrem Sohn.*"

As they followed the man, Eli said, "Dietrich is your mentor. Out of respect for him, why haven't you learned his native tongue?"

"He already taught me. Sometimes I speak it with him, but I don't see why I should anywhere else. When we become the rulers of the Earth, we'll tell the humans what language they're allowed to speak with us."

"Most of our elders are German, Cyrus."

"They won't be around forever."

***

Eli opened his eyes and looked at the bookshelves. Too often had the wisdom in them been misapplied, too often had it given way to selfish intent. Back then, Cyrus was forty years old, twenty years a vampire—and already showing a level of intelligence that would make anything possible for him.

Eli leaned forward and reached for the desk phone.

***

Detroit—Saturday, October 25, 2003

When Eli arrived at Ling Lu's nightclub, he found Ling waiting out front, dressed in a silk, burgundy suit with a short skirt, no blouse, and a tailored, tight jacket cut enticingly low. A vintage brooch adorned her left lapel. Black sling-back shoes with three-inch heels and deftly applied facial makeup accented her catlike poise. Ling Lu made men speechless. Even beautiful women caught their breath when they saw her.

He kissed her on the cheek.

"Much improved since last week," she said to Eli. "Come inside. Let's talk in my office." She kept her mind closed to everyone, but he saw her concern.

They twisted their way through the press of leathered and pierced, gothic youth, most of whom had no idea that vampires existed, let alone that they were brushing past two of them.

Ling Lu was an astute businesswoman. She had bought and refurbished the old bank building three years ago. As a club owner, she knew her patrons' expectations and listened to their suggestions, but she never let those outweigh her concern for their safety. Her club's reputation was growing; business was good. Eli noticed her bouncers being especially diligent tonight at checking the patrons and collecting the cover charge.

Ling didn't mind her bouncers taking occasional advantage of their position as long as they accepted responsibility for their actions. She allowed them to admit a few patrons each night without a cover charge. They knew that she knew if they were lying.

She stopped at the bar. "Something to drink?" she asked him. "We've brewed a new beer I think is better than our previous ones. You want to try it?"

"Of course." They were both fond of beer. Though he'd tasted the finest from around the world, hers never disappointed him.

Nothing of human behavior surprised Ling. Eli appreciated that she didn't condone drug use. They both knew she couldn't prevent it. She overlooked casual marijuana use and sharing it in the club, but she drew the line at selling it. The bouncers confiscated anything stronger or more than a small amount; they evicted anyone they caught with drugs inside. In particular, her employees all kept a sharp eye out for drinks being spiked.

She led him into the vault office and closed the inner door. She never closed the outer one and had had the locking mechanism removed to prevent accidents. He hung his coat on the rack and sat in one of the four padded leather chairs. She gracefully sat on the edge of her desk. "I have been thinking," she said. "Your idea is a good one."

"What changed your mind?" he said. "Did something happen? I noticed your security is stricter than usual tonight."

Her expression darkened and she sat in the chair next to Eli. "Three nights ago I saw something that terrified me. At two in the morning, I was here finishing some bookkeeping. I walked out of my office to get a drink, then I stepped outside for some fresh air. A young girl was standing near the street. While I watched her from behind the door, a classy van pulled up. Three young men got out and invited her into it."

He stood, sat back down. "You didn't do anything?"

"I knew her. She's harmless and sells herself to make money for food and rent. The van stayed there. I decided to watch because it was so late and there were three men. I didn't want her getting hurt. If they got rough and she screamed, I would have heard her.

"Fifteen minutes later, she stumbled out, half dressed. The van sped away. I went out to check on her. When I grabbed her to steady her, I saw a fresh needle mark on her arm. Sometimes the women accept payment in drugs, but this one didn't do drugs. Her wild, confused thoughts scared the hell out of me."

"What do you mean?"

"The men were not vampires, yet the girl was developing the bloodthirst."

Ling would know. Most of the vampires in Detroit found their way to her club, and many frequented it. "That's not possible. The infection doesn't work that fast," he said. "She must have already been infected."

Ling shook her head. "This was something else. She had none of the other symptoms. Her mind was racing so much that when I tried to calm her, it was like I had no power."

Ling had strong telepathic powers. He rose and took her hands in his. "What happened next?"

"The girl struggled out of my grasp and ran away," she said. "Before she'd gone a hundred feet along the sidewalk, she collapsed in some kind of seizure. By the time I reached her, she was dead.

"What happened to her, Eli? Has someone developed a drug that turns humans into vampires?"

"'The vices of mankind are active and able ministers of depopulation,'" he said.

"I don't understand."

"It's a line from Thomas Malthus that Cyrus Hayes once quoted to me. Cyrus is in Detroit."

She gasped. "You think he is behind this?"

"It's too much of a coincidence to be otherwise." So much had changed in the hundred years since the Conflict. The same scientific advances that had helped mankind could easily become weapons for whatever plans Cyrus had. Biotech in the hands of Cyrus Hayes scared him more than had the Nazis' vampire experiments. For the first time in their sixty-year history, he saw tears in Ling's eyes.

"Then I will do what I can to help," she said.

He pulled her close and placed his hand on the back of her head, bringing her cheek to his chest. "We will stop this."

Even if it meant a long overdue confrontation with Cyrus Hayes.

CHAPTER SIX

Nine days earlier: Denver, Colorado—Thursday, October 16, 2003

Ben had finally found the courage to drive all the way here, tonight, unlike Tuesday evening when he'd come halfway and turned back. The idea had been gnawing at him for days. When he'd first considered this solution, he'd seen no other option, but that didn't make the decision any easier. From his parked car, he nervously stared out at the Clayton family crypt. Set against the black outline of the Rocky Mountains and the moon casting shadows over it, this scene had more the semblance of a painting than reality.

With his company showing signs of neglect, he'd considered closing it down for a couple of weeks, but how would that help? Work had kept him sane these past weeks. Today, though, instead of going back to the office after lunch, he'd driven around Denver.

A cold, half-eaten burger and fries lay on the seat next to him. The car clock said eleven twenty-eight. Had it really been twelve hours since he'd last eaten? The exhaustion from the stress of the past few days was taking its toll and killing his appetite.

He leaned forward to rest his head against the steering wheel and winced as the barely healed, two-inch gash on his forehead touched it. Raising his head, he delicately pressed the raised scar with the fingertips of his hand. The accident was not his fault, the police report said. He still had trouble convincing himself. Why Jonathan? Why his only son?

Ben wiped his eyes and blew his nose. "There's still hope," he said aloud. Was he making the right decision? And who was he making it for? Himself? Or Jonathan?

Slowly, he pushed open the door and got out of the car. Before he could change his mind, he strode through the uncut grass toward the crypt. The freshly risen moon behind him gave enough light to see. Between the scattered clouds, it cast an eerie light across the stone front of the crypt. To his left a couple hundred feet stood the house that came with the property.

Ben stopped in front of it and Seth's words echoed in his mind. "It's a mausoleum, not a crypt."

"What the hell's the difference?"

"A crypt, from the Greek for hidden, is belowground; a mausoleum, from the Greek for tomb, is aboveground."

"How the hell do you know that?" Ben had asked.

"Because I've been to Europe and seen both."

"As far as we're concerned, you should have stayed in Europe!"

He'd said that when their father was still alive and before—

Ben yelled at the mausoleum. "Damn you, Seth! Why couldn't you have stayed away?"

Two years older than Ben, Seth had always made good grades, had lettered in high school football, and dated any girl he wanted. Seth, the perfect baby, never cried and slept through the night.

Not like colicky baby Ben, who started his existence by making his mother miserable with morning sickness. Ben fussed at everything and didn't know the meaning of sleep. Ben hated football and baseball. *What kind of kid hates sports?* It took him forever to learn to swim. He struggled through his first years in school. He complained about getting Seth's hand-me-downs. Everything had been Seth's first, even the bike that Seth had dinged and dented and scratched long before Ben got it.

Ben would never forget the ice-skating fiasco. Ben was ten years old and their parents told Seth to take Ben ice-skating at the park near their house. While Seth showed off his skating skills, Ben—in Seth's outgrown skates—stayed near the edge of the pond and struggled to keep his balance. Every time he fell down, Seth laughed at him and never bothered to help him up.

"When you're tired of fallin' down, we'll go home, *baby*."

Holding back his tears, Ben shook his head and tried again. He was starting to revel in his triumph when Seth noticed.

"You call that skating?"

Ben ignored him, but a moment later Seth stood next to him.

"Don't be such a crybaby or I'll tell Dad you cried when you fell down."

"I did not!"

"Who's he gonna believe?"

Seth skated behind him and pushed him farther out onto the ice.

Ben scrambled to keep his balance. "You're an asshole!"

"Oooh. Baby Ben used a dirty word. Now we're gonna skate until I say we're done or I'll tell Dad." Seth skated circles around him. Suddenly, he grabbed Ben's hand and flung him toward the center of the pond. Ben's skate hit a rough spot and he went down hard on his back. It took the wind out of him, but he wouldn't ask Seth for help.

Panting, he started to get up. The ice cracked under him and he fell through. The pond wasn't deep, just over his waist, but the water was freezing cold. Seth laughed his ass off while Ben struggled to get a grip on the slippery ice and fought his way out of the water. Too sore to stand, he crawled back to the edge of the pond.

By the time they got home, Ben was shivering miserably. Pretending to care for his brother, Seth wrapped his coat around Ben before they entered the house. The first words out of Seth's mouth when their parents saw them were, "I told him not to go out to the middle of the pond, but he wouldn't listen."

Years later, Ben went to college, worked hard, and graduated magna cum laude. That summer after graduation, he married Margo. A year later, Jonathan was born.

The twelve-by-twelve mausoleum carved from red granite was a magnificent piece of work. When Seth first showed it to him, Ben had asked, "Where did you get the money to afford this?"

"It's my money. Why do you care? You and the family wrote me off."

"You left us no choice, Seth."

As Ben stepped closer, his shadow moved up the metal door and the iron grate protecting it. A bronze plaque with the family coat of arms adorned the center of it. At the top, under the stone arch, the Clayton family name was intricately carved. The irony amused him. His surname meant "mortal." Well, every Clayton buried there so far certainly had been that.

Ben's jaw muscles quivered while his shaking hand retrieved the key ring from his jacket pocket. He unlocked the grate, then the door itself. The two-inch-thick door opened smoothly and silently as he pulled on the lacquered, hammered-iron handle.

The smell of damp stone hung in the air. He took the small flashlight from his left jacket pocket and switched it on. Inside on the floor, he found the oil lantern, a quarter full. He lit it, and closed the door behind him. The short passage had individual tombs on both sides, or plaques if the bodies weren't there. He saw his great-grandfather, grandparents... His parents. He stopped at the end of the passage.

Their grandparents had set up a college trust fund for both Ben and Seth. When dear brother Seth took his half of the money and went to Europe, everything changed. Seth, with the bright, promising future, threw his life down the toilet to party and carouse in Europe, and nothing he said changed their parents' opinion.

On top of everything, the Clayton gene pool didn't have longevity on its side. Everyone buried there died before the age of seventy.

God, things were so screwed up. Ben fell to his knees and pounded his fists against chiseled stone bricks of the mausoleum's rear wall. Tears stung his eyes. This wasn't fair, none of it! Mom and Dad had died just when he was really getting to know them. Now, Seth had come back into his life. And Seth was the only one he could ask for help.

He calmed himself as much as he could. "Okay, let's get this over with."

A duplicate of the family crest was inset on the back wall. Ben wiped his eyes with his sleeve then splayed his fingers and pressed them into the proper spots. First came muted clicks then a soft humming; the stone slab swung open.

Lantern in hand, he walked down the long flight of stairs. At the bottom was Seth's furnished and dimly lit apartment.

"We're at once-a-year visits now, dear brother?" Seth's bass voice sounded almost human. "Isn't it past your bedtime?"

Standing at the bottom of the steps, Ben said nothing.

"It's easier if you come in the back way, you know. I told you I had electric lights and a doorbell installed."

He meant the tunnel that led there from the small house Seth had purchased with the property. Ben hated the tunnel. He was nine when Seth had persuaded him to explore a storm sewer. When the two of them were deep into it, Seth grabbed the flashlight and ran, leaving his younger brother alone and panicked in the dark.

Ben moved forward and held up the lantern. Filled bookshelves lined the large, wood-paneled living room. Beyond that was the kitchen/dining area. The bedroom and bathroom, unseen from here, were off to the left. *Why the hell did he have this place when he had a perfectly good house on the property?*

Seth remained seated at his desk on the right side of the living room, with his profile to Ben. Except for the same dimples and the same shade of brown hair and dark brown eyes, nothing else suggested that they were brothers. Five-nine Ben had unruly hair that no comb could tame, and six-one, athletic Seth had hair that fell into place with a headshake. Once Ben's vision had adjusted to the dim, indirect lighting, he extinguished the lantern and set it down.

Seth stood. He was wearing khaki linen shorts, a white banded-collar shirt, and leather sandals. Ben had seen Seth squander his money, so he surmised those sandals were Italian leather. Seth put a book on the shelf next to him. "What a surprise. I thought my brother vowed never to visit me again."

Without giving Ben so much as a glance, Seth picked up a sword lying on his desk and cut the air twice with it before holding it sideways for Ben to see. "An Imperial German Navy

Sword I recently acquired. I've just finished cleaning and polishing it. A fine piece, don't you agree?"

He replaced the sword carefully on the desk then picked up a pewter goblet. "I was enjoying a fine German wine. Would you like some?"

For a moment, Ben appreciated Seth's rambling because it took his mind off why he'd come here. "Seth..." Ben swallowed. "I want..." He exhaled, feeling emotion rising again. "I need...your help." He heard the nervousness in his own voice.

"*Now* you want my help?" Seth laughed and set down the goblet. "Yes, I said you could come to me at any time, even after you told me I had nothing you could ever possibly want or need. What happened to that self-assured businessman with a prospering business? Did you screw up? And I haven't forgotten your loving reply when I asked if I could see my nephew. 'Stay away from me and my family. I hope you fucking rot in hell.' Did I get that right?"

Ben's jaw quivered as his control slipped away. He saw the question in his brother's eyes a moment before his own clouded. He dropped to his knees, onto the marble floor, doubled over, and sobbed uncontrollably.

"Ben? Ben, what's the matter?" Two strong hands pushed his shoulders back, and Ben found himself looking at Seth, now kneeling in front of him.

"When I first came back here, I tried to apologize to you, but you weren't exactly receptive. I've had time to think over how I treated you when we were younger—"

Ben forced himself to say the words, "Jonathan is in a coma."

"What?"

"A-a month ago, after his soccer game. H-his t-team won. I was taking him for...ice cream... Another driver ran a light, smashed into the passenger side of my car." Fists on the floor, Ben took a deep breath to calm himself. "The doctor thinks he may have brain damage."

"Why didn't you tell me sooner? He *is* my nephew. I could have been there for you."

Ben tilted his head up. "Can you help him?"

"How...?" Realization shone in Seth's expression. "You want me to...change him? You can't be serious."

Ben's throat tightened. "Yes, I am," came out in a hoarse whisper.

"How does Margo feel?"

"She doesn't know..." Ben took several slow breaths.

"Doesn't know what?"

"What you are, or that I'm here. She thinks we're estranged."

"Good God! Have you any idea what you're asking?"

"I want my son back."

Seth helped him up and they sat together on the couch. "More than anything I want to help you—and Jonathan—but I don't know if I can."

"What do you mean?"

"Ben, you've been watching too many vampire movies, and you weren't paying attention when I told you. Vampires are not immortal. We're simply humans infected with a virus that strengthens our immune system and lets us live for hundreds of years."

"But if you changed Jonathan into a vampire, he'd be healed."

"Again, have you any idea what you're asking, what you'd be doing to your son?"

"He'll be alive."

"Becoming a vampire isn't a cure-all. He might recover completely, or partially, or not at all. Or…it could make him worse."

Ben's shoulders slumped. "God, Seth, why did you have to say that?"

"I want you to understand all the risks. The change is physically and emotionally stressful. I've heard of a couple of vampire doctors in Europe. I could contact—"

"No!" Ben found himself panting. "This has to happen now…before I change my mind."

"If Jonathan does revive, he will have to stay with me for several weeks at least, while his body adjusts."

"Absolutely not. You do whatever you do, and I'll take it from there."

"You know nothing about dealing with the change. You won't be able to handle him."

"He's a ten-year-old boy."

"Listen to me. The levels of adrenaline coursing through his body will give him the strength of a grown man, perhaps two, and a new vampire has a raging bloodthirst. Can you handle him when he wants to rip your throat out and drink your blood?"

"Jonathan would *never* do that… You weren't like that, were you?"

"I was delirious, and under the care of someone experienced. I honestly don't remember much of it. One problem is that I have no experience with anyone that young, and I haven't heard of anyone that young being changed. I'd never forgive myself if there were complications. That's why I have to consult—"

"It's *my* decision. I absolve you of any responsibility."

"But it will still be on my conscience, no matter what happens. I do promise that if I decide to do it, and if it works, I'll help him through it, instruct him properly, and teach him safe ways to obtain what he requires."

"About…that. Does it have to be human blood, not animal blood?" Ben cringed at the thought.

Seth unbuttoned his sleeve and pushed it up to bare his arm. "It has to be human. The blood that runs through our veins is missing something that used to be there. That's why we must periodically ingest normal human blood, like an essential vitamin, but we don't require a lot. We don't drain our donors. Of course, I can't speak for all vampires, but I've personally never known one who did that."

Ben hesitated before he asked his next question. "How do you get your blood?"

"In most cities where we live, we have a legitimate supplier who buys blood from volunteer donors and ensures it's free of undesirable contaminants. The donors think it's for research, but really, they don't care as long as they get paid. Drinking blood isn't something I relish. When your survival depends on it, you get used to it."

Ben cradled his head in his hands. "My God."

"I'm also sensing a trust issue here. If you had doubts, why did you come to me?"

"It's devastated Margo, and it's straining our marriage."

"Does she blame you for the accident?"

"No…not directly. The police report said the other driver caused it." He took another deep breath. "But the way she talks about it and looks at me…"

Seth put his hand on Ben's shoulder and massaged the tight muscles. "I want to talk to her. Both of you must agree."

"You can't do that."

"Why not?"

"I told her you were…in rehab…for drug abuse."

"Why would you say that?"

"Because...I didn't want her to want to meet you."

"When I returned to the U.S., I asked nothing from you and even offered to help if you ever needed it. You rejected me, wouldn't let me see my only nephew. That hurt me.

"When Mom passed five years ago, I was out of the country and out of touch. I understood because you had no way to contact me. But when Dad died two years ago, I *was* here, and you didn't bother to call me. If I hadn't seen his obit in the newspaper... Well, that's past and I don't harbor a grudge."

Ben rubbed the corners of his eyes. "I haven't been the kind of father to my son that I should have been. I want another chance."

"You're sure you want me to change Jonathan without Margo's consent? God forbid anything should happen. How would you explain it to her?"

Ben's head nodded, though at what, he wasn't sure. He'd come here with one clear purpose, and Seth had muddied things. "After he's...changed...he won't be any different will he, mentally I mean?"

"He'll probably be more intelligent. The change enhances brain function overall. Let's say I agree to change him. How soon would you want it done?"

Ben already knew. "Sunday evening. Our church has a prayer meeting that Margo goes to."

"Church? When did Ben Clayton put God on his list of business acquaintances?"

"That was uncalled for."

"You're right. I apologize."

"Margo needed more emotional support than I could provide. After the accident, some people from a local church called on us. I suggested she join them. Except to eat and sleep, Sunday nights are the only time she's not at his bedside. He's at St. Mark's Hospital—the best one in Denver—Room 382. I'll meet you—"

"It requires two visits."

"What do you mean?"

"His body must be primed before the infection will take."

"You have to bite him twice?"

"For God's sake, Ben." Seth bared his teeth. "We don't have fangs. Even if we did, bite marks would create suspicion. Without the fangs, we'd rip the skin to shreds. That would really call attention to us. Do you honestly think I'd bite him in any case? Besides, the virus isn't passed by biting. I can stretch the two visits to a week apart, but no longer."

"I'll take care of Margo. You worry about the hospital."

"One other thing: you can't tell anyone except Margo."

"Why?"

"Few vampires live here in Denver, but we travel inconspicuously in human circles. You never know when you might run into one. By changing Jonathan, I'll be breaking a rule among our kind."

"What rule?"

"We're not supposed to change humans without the Vampire Council's consent. Besides, I don't know how to contact them, and I don't know if they'd give me approval."

CHAPTER SEVEN

Denver—Sunday, October 19, 2003

Where the hell was Seth? It was seven fourteen. He was over an hour late, and Margo had said she'd come to the hospital if the meeting ended early.

The heart monitor beeped its steady rhythm. Ben placed his hand gently on top of Jonathan's and watched the slow rise and fall of his son's chest under the sheet tucked around him. "Your mom's praying for *you*. So am I."

Thankfully, Jonathan didn't require respiratory support, a hopeful sign the doctor had said. Except more than a month later, nothing had changed. Ben inhaled the fresh scent of the clean sheets they'd put on the bed after bathing Jonathan earlier today.

Last spring, Margo had mentioned wanting another child. Given how busy he was, he'd said another child in their lives might not be wise. That seemed to mark the beginning of the strain in their relationship.

The door to Jonathan's room opened and Seth entered dressed in an expensive suit.

"Where the hell were you?" Ben asked with more irritation that he should have.

"Getting the results of the blood tests."

"*Whose* blood tests?"

"Mine and Jonathan's."

"How the hell did you get a sample of Jonathan's blood?"

"I came in two nights ago and drew it."

"You did *what*?" Ben exhaled his exasperation. "Why do *you* have to test his blood?"

"Vampire blood is usually fully compatible with normal humans—we're universal donors—but I didn't want any surprises." Seth held up a syringe. "The test confirmed there wouldn't be. I'm going to draw some of my own blood. I'll inject it into Jonathan's ankle vein where the puncture won't be noticed."

"All right!" He sighed. "All right, just do it."

"Lower your voice," Seth said in a raspy whisper, "and keep watch."

Seth removed his suit jacket, unbuttoned the cuff of his shirt, and rolled the sleeve above his elbow. He carefully pulled Jonathan's leg from under the bed sheet. "Watch the door."

Ben obeyed but watched from the corner of his eye. He averted his gaze when Seth pushed the needle into his arm. In the hall, a nurse was headed toward the room. "Someone's coming."

"It's done."

Seth slipped the syringe into his pocket and picked up his jacket as the nurse entered.

Out in the hallway, Ben noticed Seth's eyes were darker than usual.

"Tinted contacts, sunglasses would attract unwanted attention," Seth told him before he asked. "All of our senses are heightened. When the eye doctor dilates your pupils, you know how bright sunlight is painful?"

Ben nodded.

"Imagine that ten times worse. We also sunburn easily, but we don't burst into flames in sunlight."

"Why do you live down under the cryp— the mausoleum, instead of in the house?" Ben asked.

"Don't you think it's more appropriate for a vampire to live under a mausoleum? And just so we're clear, vampires are not undead or the spawn of Satan, although I'm sure you'd argue the latter."

They entered the elevator. "Oh, and the nurse found me attractive," Seth said. "She checked my hand for a ring. Vampire males retain full sexual drive. Jonathan won't be denied that pleasure."

"That's disgusting."

"Sex itself, that vampires can have sex, or the thought of your son having sex one day?" Seth combed his fingers through his hair. "The first phase is done. Next Sunday, same time?"

"That should be okay."

"It has to be. We can't wait any longer, or I'll have to start from scratch. Why don't you go with Margo to church so she doesn't show up here unexpectedly? Your presence isn't necessary."

"My presence *is* necessary, Seth."

"You don't trust me, do you? Believe me, I want him to live as much as you do. I'll give you my cell number, in case you change your mind."

"I won't change my mind."

***

On his drive home, Ben remembered back, when the prodigal Seth had returned from England, four years ago, saying he'd been in school. The shaky reunion between them and their father became emotional when Seth learned that Mom had passed from lung cancer the year before. Ben took him outside and lit into him.

"You bastard son of a bitch! You disappear and leave us no way to contact you? How *dare* you come back and pretend you're torn up over Mom's death."

Seth hung his head. "I had no choice. I contracted a rare blood disease. There's no cure for it, but as long as I take my medicine regularly I should be okay."

At first he'd thought Seth was pulling a bad joke. Later, Seth revealed the nature of the blood disease, but only to Ben. "If you don't believe me, you can stay with me while I deprive myself of blood. I guarantee you'll believe me then."

Ben didn't accept Seth's offer, but neither was he completely convinced of the vampire part. Then Seth vanished again for almost a year.

One day, out of the blue, he called Ben at work and wanted to show him the property he'd bought and refurbished south of Denver.

"What the hell is that?" Ben had asked when he saw the newly constructed mausoleum a couple of hundred feet from the house, with their family name on it.

"It's our family burial place. I got all the necessary permits and I plan to have others of the Clayton family line reburied here…including Mom."

"You're insane! Dad will never agree to have Mom moved."

And Ben was right. Their father refused to have his wife's body moved. Without telling any of them, Seth had the remains of two previous generations of Claytons exhumed and transported here from two different cemeteries, one seven hundred miles away. The family wasn't large. Two had been cremated, one son had died at sea, and a daughter had been buried in Europe with her husband. Seth left them there.

He told Ben this preserved the family heritage. He produced a detailed history of the Clayton family he'd supposedly researched in England. Ben never questioned where his brother had gotten the money to do all of this—and he didn't want to know. After their father's funeral, to keep the peace with Seth, Ben consented to have both their parents' bodies moved there, then Ben decided to open his own business because he was tired of working for someone else.

Within a month, he heard about a building on the market, close to home and for the right price—actually, the price had been almost too good to believe, but he hadn't argued. Four months later, Seth had called Ben to come see his new subterranean apartment. He hadn't seen Seth after that until now.

***

Denver—Sunday, October 26, 2003

At six ten p.m. Ben walked into the hospital room carrying a bag of clothes for Jonathan. Seth was already there, wearing a doctor's white coat.

"How long have you been here?"

Seth glared at Ben. "I'm happy to see you, too. An hour, if you must know. I've already injected Jonathan with my blood."

Ben let out a breath. "You should have waited for me."

"You were late."

"Margo wanted to come with me tonight…and I almost let her." Then he noticed the name badge on Seth's coat. "*Seth Wilson, M.D.?*" he read aloud. "What the hell is that?"

"My first and middle names. Clever, don't you think? Nurses don't question doctors. I do also have a passport in that name, however. Because of our long life spans, we must periodically change identities. Contacts in key government offices, like Social Security and passport, help us out."

"Vampires in the government?"

"Don't you love the irony of that?"

"Cut the crap, Seth."

"I sense an attitude. Did something happen between you and Margo?"

"No. I haven't told her the truth. She's my *wife*, and that's her son, too! I should have talked to her first."

Seth put his hand on Ben's back. "And how would that have helped? Getting upset won't help, and you don't want the hospital staff hearing us and getting suspicious. You came to me. Have faith. Everything happens for a reason. If Jonathan is meant to awaken, he will. Some of my blood is now coursing through his veins. The change is not instantaneous, not like the movies."

"Margo will be here in the morning."

"Let's hope her prayers speed up the process."

***

Ben awoke to voices.

"Are you saying the family isn't entitled to a second opinion?" Seth was talking to a nurse whose back was to Ben.

Ben scooted himself up in the chair and checked his watch: eleven fifty-three p.m.

"No, Doctor," she said, "but this is highly irregular."

"So, the patients in this hospital are entitled to second opinions only during regular business hours?"

"I have to change the IV bag," the nurse said.

Seth blocked her and glanced at the old one hanging next to the bed, still a quarter full. "You're early." He held out his hand; she gave him the bag and left the room, not happy.

"What's going on?" Ben asked.

"Typical hospital officiousness."

Ben looked over at his son. "How is Jonathan doing?"

"No change yet. I gave him another blood sample for good measure. Go back to sleep. You might find the spare bed more comfortable."

"I won't get back to sleep."

***

Ben heard muted voices drifting through the haze around him. Where the hell was he? The hospital? Why was he in a bed? He opened his eyes and waited for them to focus.

"I'm...thirsty," a voice said.

He still couldn't see anything but dim white. Then he realized he was on the spare bed in his son's hospital room and someone had drawn the curtain around it. He lifted his wrist to check the time. *Too dark to see.* He fumbled for the backlight button. The blue glow showed him five sixteen a.m. *Monday morning already?*

He sat up and opened the curtain. "Seth? What's going on?" He pushed the curtain fully aside and moved closer.

His son's bed was tilted up halfway. Seth held a plastic cup a third full of a dark-red liquid that Jonathan was sucking through a straw. "Jonathan?"

"I was going to wake you as soon as he finished," Seth said.

"When did he...?" Ben asked, choking back his tears.

"A little while ago," Seth said.

Jonathan finished with a slurp. Seth picked up a cup of water and let Jonathan sip from it. "Easy, son."

Ben pulled a chair up next to the other side of the bed and cupped his hands over his son's. Young fingers moved against his. Tears flowing freely, Ben leaned over and kissed his son on the forehead.

"Daddy, I wanna go home."

CHAPTER EIGHT

Detroit—Monday, October 27, 2003

From his upper-floor executive suite in the Hilton Windsor, Cyrus Hayes studied the Detroit night skyline. Eli Howard was the only unpredictable element in his plan. Under most circumstances, eliminating that element would be the best solution.

In this case, that action would generate ripples with far-reaching effects and threaten the integrity of his plan, and likely disrupt it in even more unpredictable ways. He hadn't spent decades developing and analyzing this plan to have it fail. Safeguards, even multiple layers of them, offered protection, but they couldn't ensure certainty. Cyrus Hayes wanted certainty.

"Sir, we were wondering when we might expect—" a confident male voice behind him said.

Cyrus spun around and fixed a vitriolic stare at the man who had interrupted his thoughts. "Might expect *what*?"

"The research, sir. We're anxious to begin the research. We have a new idea. It's an innovative—"

"And when did you plan on showing me the proposal for these new ideas?" He encouraged innovation, but only as long as they remembered who was in charge.

"Proposal?"

"Have you forgotten that all research projects must be approved by me first?"

"No, sir. We merely thought—"

"No, Doctor Bergmann, you *assumed*. *As*sumption leads to *pre*sumption, which I tolerate less than I tolerate humans!" Bergmann paled. "Be thankful you are not human, Doctor. Do not forget the three of you serve at my pleasure and only as long as you continue to produce the results I require."

Bergmann was trembling slightly. "My apologies, sir. We did not intend to question your authority nor to offend you." He managed a weak smile. "While keeping our minds busy, we came up with something we thought would please you. Of course, we can present it to you formally."

"How pleased will I be, Doctor?" Cyrus said, returning the smile.

Bergmann relaxed his shoulders. "It's the eye drops. We believe adding an alpha methyl group to the endorphin analogue will slow its metabolism and thus enhance the withdrawal effects to make them more unpleasant, so the user will be much less inclined to go 'cold turkey' as they say."

"How would this impact the production schedule?"

"It's a simple, chemical modification. The limiting step in production occurs after it, so we anticipate no net effect once production has begun."

"How soon can you test the modification?" Cyrus asked.

"As soon as we have laboratory space...and test subjects."

"The laboratory space you will have two weeks from today. As for test subjects, you already have three available."

Bergmann didn't grasp the meaning immediately. "Sir? You expect us to test the product on ourselves?"

"You have the antidote."

"You never told us to develop—"

"In that case, I suggest you exercise your collective brains over the next few days as if the duration of your life expectancy depended on it."

Bergmann opened his mouth to speak and Cyrus pointed a finger at him. "Don't arrogantly believe that you three constitute the only research team in my service." *Always have backups.* "Do you have something else to share to further demonstrate your inadequacies?"

"N-no, Mr. Hayes."

"Good. In that case, I expect you will put forth an extra effort to restore my confidence in your abilities. Don't disappoint me again, Doctor Bergmann."

Overconfidence led to mistakes. The panic to fix an unexpected problem often resulted in irreparable damage to a design. With having to juggle so many variables and hostile elements, only meticulous preparation would ensure the success of his plan. While as close to perfection as he could currently make it—even including multiple contingencies to account for his own premature death—no plan was ever perfect.

One final contingency allowed for complete failure of all other aspects, except the last piece of it was not yet in place, and he had no way of knowing when it would be ready. It depended on uncovering certain secrets. Once he found those in possession of the information, he'd enjoy the challenge of convincing them to relinquish it.

CHAPTER NINE

Denver—Monday, October 27, 2003

Seth stood next to the bed of his nephew, asleep in his underground sanctum. The sedative-laced blood would keep him quiet for a while.

After Jonathan's revival in the hospital, use of his telepathic powers on appropriate hospital staff had ensured Jonathan's discharge proceeded smoothly. Convincing a protesting Ben to pick up Margo had been slightly more difficult, but Ben had acquiesced in the end. He'd even given Ben a cover story for Margo that they were going to talk to a specialist who had just moved into the area. More important, he'd cautioned Ben not to tell her why they were going somewhere other than to the hospital.

Jonathan's unexpected behavior had *not* been part of his expectations. The boy shouldn't be craving blood this soon. At first he'd thought perhaps adult vampire blood was too potent for a ten-year-old and he'd given Jonathan too much initially. But that didn't explain why the boy's mind resisted his telepathic suggestions. This development worried him. For all the things his mentor had not taught him—what with dying suddenly and unexpectedly—he *had* taught Seth about the differences in suggestibility of the human mind at various ages. Teen minds were the most resistant. Prepubescent and later-adult minds were the most pliable. For whatever reason, young Jonathan was an exception, and the boy's resistance was increasing rapidly. At this rate, Seth wouldn't be able to control him much longer. He needed answers and help.

A name came to mind, one his mentor had mentioned, a good man he'd said, someone who wouldn't refuse to help. Would Eli Howard's phone number in Detroit be listed?

***

Ben parked in front of the house on Seth's property. Margo had finally run out of questions, but he expected a new round of them shortly. She noticed the mausoleum as they passed it.

"Maybe the property belonged to his family," Ben said. Fortunately, with the angle of the morning sun, she hadn't seen the Clayton name on it.

They walked up to the cedar-sided house. Ben rang the doorbell. Seth, wearing his white doctor's coat, opened the door. "You must be Mr. and Mrs. Clayton," he said. "Please come in."

Ben hadn't been inside since Seth bought the property a couple of years ago. The house itself was only forty years old. Despite being unoccupied, the place was surprisingly clean.

"Forgive the sparse furnishings. I had to move here earlier than I anticipated, so my office isn't ready. We'll talk in the living room."

A set of steps to Ben's left led up to the second story, where Ben remembered two bedrooms, a bathroom, and an open space twice that size, which had probably been a play area for the kids—or maybe grandkids—of the former owners.

A hallway led straight back to the rest of the house. The vestibule and hallway floors were new hardwood. The last time Ben had seen him, Seth had mentioned maybe renting the place out. Obviously, he hadn't.

Ben started to ask where Jonathan was and thought better of it. His nerves were enough on edge. Anything he said would no doubt be a mistake. *Would Seth use his vampire telepathic abilities on Margo, the way he'd done to the hospital people?* They had discharged Jonathan as if he'd been there for nothing more serious than a cut requiring a couple of stitches.

The decent-sized living room had a couple of older pieces of furniture. Heavy curtains covered the windows, and two floor lamps lit the room. Jonathan was sitting on the couch.

Margo ran to her son and hugged him ferociously. During the teary reunion, and amid her cries of prayers being answered, something puzzled Ben. Where was that uncontrollable, bloodthirsty vampire his son was supposed to turn into? Jonathan was behaving like a normal ten-year-old, and nothing suggested he'd just awoken from a month-long coma.

Ben pulled Seth aside in the hallway, out of Margo's hearing. "When can we take him home?"

"I told you, Jonathan's change is just beginning. Even after it's complete, you will have some issues to deal with. For one, he won't be able to attend a regular school."

"Why the hell not?" Ben said in an exaggerated whisper.

"Ben," Margo said abruptly from the living room, "did you know about this?"

"How the hell am I supposed to answer her?" Ben said, still whispering, but louder than before. "I'll be right there, honey," he told Margo.

"Take Jonathan into my apartment for a snack, while Margo and I talk," Seth told Ben. "Here's the key to the small refrigerator next to the regular one. Inside you'll find some bottles of blood. Give Jonathan the one I've labeled as his. It contains an herb to make him sleep, which is best for him. Give him a juice glass full, no more. He can play video games or use the computer or watch television, but he'll be sleepy soon after he drinks the blood. Just make him comfortable. I'll bring Margo down in a while."

Ben took his son to the kitchen then down into the empty basement with a tiled floor. The tunnel lay a few feet beyond the steps, off the laundry facility. He found the light switch, flipped it on, and opened the door. They made their way along the narrow, two-hundred-foot-long cinder block tunnel.

"This is a cool place," Jonathan said.

Fully waterproofed or not, Ben still didn't like it. With his son next to him, it didn't creep him out so much. He kept thinking about the cost of having it built in the first place, to say nothing of the landscaping above it to hide that it had been dug out.

They reached the heavy metal door at the end.

Jonathan pulled Ben toward the refrigerator. "I'm hungry."

Ben unlocked the refrigerator. His hand lingered over the bottle marked for Jonathan. It contained a sedative, Seth had said. No way was he going to drug his son. Instead, he picked up one of the other bottles. When he turned around, Jonathan had put a regular-sized glass on the table. Ben opened the bottle, suppressing his gag reflex while he poured half a glass. He saw his son's pleading eyes and filled it. Jonathan smiled. Ben resealed the bottle and locked it away.

"Do you want something else to eat?"

"P.B. and J with grape jelly." He took a big gulp from the glass and swallowed, then he licked his lips at Ben. "I like this better than what Uncle Seth gave me earlier."

Blood was blood. *How the hell could Jonathan tell the difference?* He checked the cabinets for the sandwich makings. *It's "Uncle Seth" already? Have they gotten to know one another that fast?* Ben glanced over his shoulder. Jonathan finished his drink, tilting the glass up to get every drop.

"I'm gonna play on the computer. Uncle Seth said I could. Bring me my sandwich with a glass of milk."

Not even, "please."

Ben brought Jonathan the sandwich and milk, then sat on the couch next to him. What had he done to his boy?

***

A loud noise woke Ben. He'd been watching Jonathan at the computer and must have fallen asleep. But Jonathan wasn't there now. "Jonathan?" He scooted up—not in the kitchen, either. Groggy, he pushed himself off the couch and checked the bedroom and bathroom—both empty. He checked the kitchen again. *Oh, shit!* The tunnel door was open, and the lights were on.

He spotted Jonathan halfway down the tunnel, running. Ben sprinted after him. Jonathan had made it up the basement stairs and into the farmhouse before Ben caught up and grabbed him by the waist.

"Let me go!"

Despite paying regular visits to the gym, Ben struggled to hold onto his boy. Jonathan kicked backwards into Ben's groin. Ben doubled over and Jonathan scurried away.

A couple of moments later, he heard his son's voice, "Ow! You're hurting me!"

"Then quit fighting," a calm Seth said.

"Promise you'll feed me! A *lot*... Ow! I'm gonna tell Daddy."

Seth entered holding Jonathan horizontally around the waist with one arm while the other handcuffed Jonathan's wrists behind his back. Jonathan struggled fiercely.

"Seth! Put him down!"

"You want him to run away again?"

"Give him to me!" Ben said. As he approached, still in some pain, Jonathan viciously kicked him in the thigh, narrowly missing his groin. Ben grabbed his boy's ankles and squeezed them together.

"I'm telling Mommy!"

"Go right ahead," Ben muttered.

They carried Jonathan back into Seth's apartment and put him in a kitchen chair. "Now sit there!" Ben said.

Jonathan folded his arms defiantly. "I'm hungry. Feed me now!"

Ben sat next to his son. *What the hell is going on with Jonathan?*

Seth removed two bottles from the small refrigerator. "You're not used to following instructions, are you, Ben?" He poured three-quarters of a glass from one bottle, not the one Ben had used earlier. Seth opened the other bottle and poured a small amount from it into the glass. He set the glass in front of Jonathan, who grabbed it and drank greedily.

What a hell of a Monday, and it isn't even half over. "Where is Margo?" Ben asked.

"Up in the house. Why don't you bring her down here?"

"Does she even want to talk to me?"

"Of course she does. She's more upset that you didn't trust her enough to ask her first than with what you did. She's a lovely woman, Ben. You should pay more attention to her."

Ben started to respond but didn't. Seth was right.

"I'm tired," Jonathan said. "Can I go lay down?"

"Of course," Seth told him. Jonathan shuffled off.

"He won't be able to attend a regular school," Seth began, "because, as his body changes, daylight will become uncomfortable to his eyes. He'll require a doctor's excuse to wear sunglasses in school. We could work around it, but his classmates would tease him constantly. What would he tell friends? That he's a vampire? You don't want to put him through that ridicule. I've also encountered a problem I can't deal with. I've decided to take him to someone in Detroit—"

Ben gritted his teeth. "*You* decided? You never mentioned taking him out of state."

"Jonathan will be under the care and tutelage of a well-respected man in the vampire community. He'll have years of private schooling from someone who is himself a university instructor."

"You expect Jonathan to go to Detroit? And stay there for *years*? That is *not* going to happen. Even if I allowed it—which I won't—and Jonathan wanted to go—which I seriously doubt he will—how would I explain it to Margo?"

"She and I already discussed it. She agrees it's best for Jonathan. Were you aware he has been having some difficulties with school?"

"Why didn't she tell me?"

"Apparently, you're never home long enough to have a meaningful discussion. She's been helping him, but she's been considering private tutoring. And with her being ten-weeks pregnant—"

"What? Margo is not pregnant!"

"She hasn't told you?"

CHAPTER TEN

Detroit—Tuesday, October 28, 2003

Adrian had just finished loading the dishwasher with dinner dishes when the doorbell rang.

"Ling. What a pleasant surprise. What are you doing here?"

"I must speak with him concerning his latest unwise decision."

"Which one would that be?" Adrian asked.

"The young man he's going to be mentoring," she said.

"Oh, that decision. He just got back from teaching his class. He's in the library. Mind if I join you?"

"Please do. This affects you as well."

"Let me start the dishwasher and I'll be right in."

When Adrian returned from the kitchen, Eli and Ling were in the living room. He made himself comfortable in the recliner, anxious to see her pick on Eli instead of Eli picking on him.

"You agreed to take on this kid and be his mentor?" Ling said. "Don't you have enough to do already? Is Detroit even a safe place for him with Cyrus here?"

"He didn't even consider that I might be jealous," Adrian interjected.

"Are you?" Eli asked.

"Just kidding. It'll be sweet having a little vampire brother."

"You never stop disregarding the rules, do you?" Ling said to Eli. "One day the Council will call you to task for your indiscretions."

"I know the rules and when exceptions must be made."

Adrian thought Eli sounded a bit annoyed, so he avoided mentioning how it was okay for Eli to break the rules but not okay for anyone else to break them.

"Do you?" she said.

"I'm taking Jonathan on so he'll learn the correct vampire way. He could be the next generation of our plan for helping humankind."

"Not that you listen to me, but I didn't agree with your decision to change Adrian, either."

"He still needs some work," Eli said, not looking at him.

Adrian growled.

"If you are to be a big brother," she said, "you must reconsider your own lifestyle and set a good example. The places you frequent aren't safe for a young boy, even if he is a vampire."

"I won't let Eli down."

"Adrian will help me tutor the boy," Eli said. "Seth Clayton said his nephew is highly intelligent."

Adrian twisted his lips thoughtfully.

"I don't mean gambling, Adrian."

"What? He's gotta learn sometime, so he doesn't get taken advantage of, I mean."

"It will be your responsibility to see that he doesn't."

Adrian perked up. "I bet he'll love Drake's rap!"

Eli pondered that. "A brother would be good for Drake as well. He'll be a good mediating influence against your impulsive behavior. You and Drake can share responsibility for young Jonathan."

Adrian grinned. "Sweet."

"Seth told me his nephew loves video games. I've seen how you and Drake challenge each other. Include Jonathan in your contests."

"You got it!"

"I don't know what he's bringing with him. He may need a new computer."

"I'll build him one, with all the latest gadgets and add-ons." He rubbed his chin. "Could get expensive."

"Let me know what you need. And while you're around him, stay off the porn sites and steer him away from material inappropriate to his age."

Adrian gave Eli a pouty frown. "Is there *anything* I do you don't know about?"

"You don't hide your thoughts well, particularly the randy ones."

Ling put her hand to her mouth to smother her laugh.

Adrian's neck grew exceedingly warm. When he was really embarrassed, he turned traffic-light red and even his tan skin didn't hide it. "Aw, why'd you have to say that in front of Ling?"

"She's a worldly woman."

"That does it! I'm moving into my own place!"

"He's teasing you," Ling said, "and you should respect him enough to know he will never intrude into your personal privacy."

"But—"

"He's teaching you good judgment," she said. "He's never interfered in your personal life, has he?"

Adrian shook his head. "Not really."

"And you know from Eli's past that he can keep secrets."

That piqued his curiosity. "What secrets?"

"You've been his mentor for five years and you've never told him about your life before you were changed?" Ling said.

"It's not like I haven't asked him, either," Adrian said. "He's just not the gut-spilling kind. All I know about his mysterious past is how he fought in the Big Conflict. Oh, and he helped start the Council."

Still looking at Eli, she said, "You should tell him." Her gaze shifted to Adrian. "You're an intelligent young man, Adrian. Have you never considered why Eli teaches a class on Black History?"

"Not particularly, other than he's Black."

"He *lived* through the period. In the South."

Adrian stared at her. "But...Blacks—African Americans I mean—were *slaves* in the South, weren't they?"

"Yes, and before he was changed, Eli was a runaway slave."

Adrian's mouth dropped open. "Fu— Shit."

"Let's go for a walk," Eli said to him, "just you and me."

"I'll remain here and have some tea if you don't mind," Ling said. "I want to hear what Adrian has to say after you return."

"Might be a while," Adrian said. He would rather have stayed here at home, but Eli preferred walk-and-talk lectures, long ones. He grabbed his jacket from the closet and slipped it on over his hoodie while Eli put on his leather coat.

They walked at least ten minutes before Eli said anything. Sometimes Eli said he liked to let the mood settle in.

"Everyone believes we've come a long way since the time of slavery," Eli said.

"Yeah, a lot's changed since then, hasn't it?"

"The world has changed; culture has changed. Attitudes, sadly, have hardly changed at all. I saw firsthand how Blacks dealt with being set free, how they created their current problems by giving in to the same badges of self-pity that many slaves carried. Today's leaders of Black America claim racism is as bad now as it was in the antebellum South." Eli gave a brief laugh with a touch of bitterness in it. "They have no idea."

Adrian had never seen this side of Eli before and didn't know what to think of it. A light rain started to fall. He pulled up the hood of his sweatshirt and continued to listen.

***

Eli's mind drifted back to when his only goal had been to escape his master and become a free man in the North and to the one thing in his life he still regretted. He let the sadness fall around him and settle in while he picked out the memories one by one, put them in order.

Eli Howard had been surnamed after his first slaveholder, a kind man, unlike his cruel, second owner.

The image of his beloved brother's mutilated and lynched body snapped vividly into his mind.

On that March night in Mississippi, when his life was about to change, a twenty-one-year-old Eli ran as fast as he could, trying not to trip or make too much noise. Dead leaves sounded like broken glass under the soles of the worn shoes his sister had given him. This was his first escape attempt. For the moment, he was doing well.

Dogs. Men's voices. He stopped and hid behind a huge tree. The cool night air made him shiver while he listened carefully, hearing nothing but night sounds. He was ready to move on when he saw what he thought was an older slave.

"Boy! Ova here," a voice said. "Gets yoself away from dat tree."

He was afraid at first, but then he followed the voice. When he got to where he thought he'd heard it, no one was there.

Bewildered, he walked away slowly. Strong hands grabbed him from behind and yanked him to the ground. He looked up into the eyes of a wild man. Teeth ripped into the corded muscles of his neck. Eli tried to scream, but the shock of what was happening had tightened his throat. All that came out was a hoarse gurgling. The man's mouth sucked at his neck. Struggling in vain, growing weaker by the moment, he soon passed out.

For what seemed like days he fell in and out of consciousness, with no idea how much time had passed. He thought he glimpsed the man again. He recognized the taste of blood in his mouth, from the times his second master had beat him. But he wasn't being beaten now.

When he finally came fully awake, it was daylight. He squinted against the intense brightness. He lay in an old, dark barn, in the shadows, but even the small amount light filtering in hurt his eyes.

A wave of fierce hunger passed through him; his body began shaking. He crawled into a horse stall and cowered against the old straw, shivering and sweating. He'd never felt so sick, yet so hungry. Was he dying? He wanted to go outside, to see where he was. He crawled toward the door, more by feel than by sight, because of the brightness. Even through closed eyes, the light was almost unbearable. He knew most of the farms nearby. If he could just get one quick glimpse, he could figure out where he was.

He opened his eyes, then immediately slammed them shut and dug his fists into them. *How could light be that painful?* He fell backwards, rolled over with his face down in the dust and his palms pressed over his eyes. Keeping them squeezed shut, he crawled back into the darkness.

The day lasted forever. Slowly, his sight recovered—he thanked the Lord for that—but he still had the strange sickness. At least he hadn't gotten any worse, and he hadn't died.

Night arrived. His need for food drove him out of the barn. Thin clouds veiled the moon, but he saw as if a full, clear moon lit the night. A new feeling arose in him, different from anything he'd ever felt.

A rabbit hopped across the grass. *Food.* He raced after it and caught it easily. Without a thought, he ripped off the skin and sank his teeth into its warm, bloody flesh. That satisfied his stomach but only slightly eased the sickness.

He walked through the night until dawn approached. He found a small cave to shelter him from the daylight, and he slept there with no fear of being caught. Dark dreams of revenge plagued his sleep. More than once he awoke terrified.

The sickness returned. Worse. Except it wasn't any sickness he'd ever experienced. This was more of a craving for something he couldn't name. Late the next night, he found his way back to his master's house, completely dark inside at his approach. He crept inside and located the bedrooms. The moonlight shining through the windows enabled him to see perfectly. Before he realized what was happening, Eli slaughtered first the master, then the wife, then the six-year-old son. The scent and taste of their blood removed his inhibitions and drove him onward; the screams faded into the background.

He went last to the room of the daughter, a twenty-two-year-old woman, cowering on her bed against the headboard. She had caused the death of his brother Jonas: first castrated, then hanged. She'd refused to admit she had seduced him.

She screamed when he entered her room. He grabbed her, dragged her off the bed and through the other bedrooms to see the dead bodies of her family until she became hoarse from screaming.

This one he wouldn't kill. He wanted to curse her, as he had been cursed. With his sharpest fingernail, he slit the side of her neck and drank the blood that trickled out until she fainted. He left her there, to recover, he hoped, and to remember his face among the horrors for the rest of her life.

He exited the house through the front door, leaving it open, and blended into the night.

The rain had stopped by the time Eli finished his story to Adrian. On the drive home, Adrian remained silent.

Eli rubbed the right side of his neck. Though no longer apparent to the casual observer, one hundred and forty-four years later, he could still feel a trace of the scar where the vampire had ripped into his flesh.

***

Adrian opened the door ahead of Eli. He should say something. "I'm sorry, Eli."

"Why should you be sorry?"

"For not appreciating all you've done for me."

"I believe Ling will want to talk to you. I'm going to bed." Eli hung up his coat and headed upstairs.

Adrian went into the living room where he found Ling sitting in a chair, waiting.

"You appear different than before you left," she said.

He sat on the edge of the couch. "Not that I remember it much, but was I ever that bad when I changed?"

"Eli helped you through it."

"I never thanked him."

"Make him proud of you, Adrian. That's all the thanks he wants."

"Uh, Eli didn't say what happened to the slaveholder's daughter. Did he ever find out?"

"Eli researched her some years ago. She has two great-great-grandchildren. Eli set up an anonymous trust fund for the college education of their children. That's all I know."

***

Denver—Tuesday, October 28, 2003

Just past sunset, Ben and Jonathan sat in the backseat of Seth's Cadillac as they drove into Jefferson County Airport.

"We're taking a private plane," Seth had said when Ben asked why they weren't headed to Denver International.

"With one stop for refueling, we should be landing at Young International Airport, east of Detroit, in under seven hours and well before dawn. Young isn't Detroit's main airport, either. It caters to private and cargo planes. An Adrian Shadowhawk will meet us."

"Uncle Seth, you promised I could fly the plane," Jonathan said.

"It's a private plane and I know the pilot," Seth said.

Whether Ben liked it or not, Jonathan was getting to know his uncle.

Forty minutes later, they arrived at the airport, parked the car, and got onboard the plane, an executive model Cessna Caravan, Seth told him. Besides the pilot and copilot seats, it had two pairs of facing seats with tables between them—plus a mini-fridge, coffee maker, and microwave.

Seeing the plane otherwise empty, Ben asked, "Where's the pilot?"

Seth climbed up into the pilot's seat and put Jonathan next to him. "What the hell is going on, Seth?"

Without looking at Ben, he said, "On behalf of myself and my nonexistent crew, welcome aboard Seth-Air. Please fasten your seat belt and enjoy the flight."

Ben flopped into one of the two front-facing seats, cinched his seat belt, and laughed his head off.

CHAPTER ELEVEN

Denver—Tuesday, October 28, 2003

So, Seth had a pilot's license and owned the plane? Just when Ben thought he finally knew his brother, Seth'd pulled this surprise.

Following their refueling stop, Jonathan, who had been sitting in the copilot's seat, came back to see him. "I'm hungry."

"You ate before we landed."

Jonathan grinned. "Can I taste *yours* to see if it's as good as Uncle Seth's?"

Ben didn't know whether to feel insulted or horrified.

"Ben, I have cold cuts in the frig," Seth said over his shoulder.

Jonathan ran up front and jumped back into the copilot's seat, feet tucked under him, facing Seth. "I want blood."

Seth did something with the controls then turned to Jonathan. "Go back with your father."

"You can't make me."

"Ben, give him one of the drink bottles in the frig."

Ben retrieved one and handed it to his son.

"Not that crap!"

"Jonathan! You will *not* talk that way to your uncle."

Jonathan bared his teeth at Ben. "You can't stop me." He pointed at Seth. "And he can't either."

"Ben, in my shoulder bag is a small bottle. Give him that."

Ben fished it out. Jonathan grabbed it and quickly unscrewed the cap. Looking into the bottle, he frowned. "It's not full."

"It's a special treat," Seth told him.

Jonathan took a sip. "Sweet! I bet you put something in it Daddy wouldn't approve of." He finished it and threw it back at his father.

"If you fasten your seatbelt, I'll let you fly again," Seth told him.

"Sweet."

Seth smiled. For once, Ben found it reassuring. A half-hour later, his son was fast asleep.

"What was in the bottle, Seth?"

"A sedative that's completely effective—and safe—for vampires. I'm told it works with our enhanced brain chemistry, which Jonathan is showing far too soon."

"Vampire knockout drops?"

"I suspected he might get out of control in the plane when I wouldn't be able to do much about it. He'll sleep for a while and be manageable when he wakes up, until it's out of his system. Strap him in one of the rear seats and recline it. You should get some sleep yourself. You're pretty ragged." Seth looked over at his brother. "You made the right decision, Ben."

***

Detroit—Tuesday, October 28, 2003

"Hi, I'm Adrian Shadowhawk." Ben shook the hand of the kid who met them at the airport.

Jonathan had woken up during the landing. Adrian led them to a black-on-black Chevy Impala, not new but kept in mint condition. Ben sat in front; Seth and Jonathan got in the back.

"This is Eli's car," Adrian said. "My Corvette wouldn't fit all of you."

"May I ask how old you are?"

"Twenty-two."

"And you're a vampire?"

"From fangs to toe."

"Vampires don't have fangs," Ben said.

Adrian turned away for a moment then gave him a broad, fang-filled smile. "Who told you that?" Looking straight ahead, Adrian said, seriously, "I'll buy your son a set of fangs so he'll fit right in."

Had Ben made the right decision?

They headed out of the airport and turned onto an expressway labeled I-94. Wanting to make idle conversation, Ben asked, "Do they call this anything besides I-94?"

"Edsel Ford Freeway. All the freeways here are named after famous people of Detroit. Detroit history isn't one of my keen interests, but I think Edsel was one of Henry Ford's sons."

A little while later Adrian exited the expressway. The sign read, *John R/Woodward.*

"You want a tour of the city at night? I'd be happy to show you Detroit's finest casinos and strip clubs."

"We'd better get Jonathan to Eli's," Seth said.

"Suit yourself."

When they arrived, Adrian took Jonathan's two stuffed suitcases from the trunk and carried them effortlessly inside. "Eli, we're here!" he called out. "This way." He led them into the living room. "I think Eli changed me 'cuz he had a deprived childhood and wanted a younger version of himself around to live vicariously through. He also enjoys keeping me out of trouble."

"Is that so, Adrian?" said a deep voice behind them.

"Whoa. I thought you were in the library."

Eli Howard was not what Ben expected. Given that this was Detroit, a tall, muscular black man shouldn't have been a surprise. He gave Ben a hearty handshake. "Welcome. I'm Eli Howard."

"Ben Clayton."

Eli squatted. "This fine young man must be Jonathan."

"Are you a vampire?" Jonathan asked.

"Yes, and so is Adrian."

Jonathan's question took Ben by surprise. Who told Jonathan about vampires? He certainly hadn't.

Eli stood. "Adrian made an excellent beef stew for dinner. Would you like some?"

"I'm famished," Ben said, "and coffee if you have it."

"Adrian, would you mind?" Eli said.

"No problem. I'll show Jonathan his room, too."

Adrian led him off.

"May I call you Ben?" Eli asked.

"Please."

"Come into the living room and make yourselves comfortable."

Eli had a nice house, homey. Ben hoped Jonathan would be happy here.

Seth and Ben sat on the couch. Eli sat in a chair opposite them. "Seth has told me everything, including your concerns. First, to allay your fears, your son will be in a loving and caring environment. Adrian lives with me and will help watch over him. Jonathan will have whatever he needs, plus many of his wants. I do know how to say no, so he won't be spoiled. Nor will we attempt to compete with you for his affection. We will be his friends and extended family, nothing more."

Ben found Eli's words reassuring. "How much is this private schooling going to cost me?"

Eli gave a puzzled look first at Seth then at Ben. "Nothing. I'll provide his room and board. Whenever you and your wife wish to visit, I have plenty of space for you here."

"My wife will want to visit him soon."

"For the first few months, it's probably best if you don't, until he adjusts, but I'll leave the choice up to you and your son."

"Can he come home for summer vacation?"

"He should remain here. Depending on his progress, he might be able to go back to Colorado for a few days during the summer if he wants. I must admit that I've not dealt with a situation like this before."

"But Seth said—"

"What I mean is, we rarely see a new vampire his age. Most young ones are in their teens or early twenties, and they have often been abandoned or orphaned."

"You have a lovely house," Ben said. "How safe is it? I mean, Detroit is—"

"I will protect him as if he were my own son. Being a vampire has some added risks, but your son will develop special skills that will more than outweigh the disadvantages. I'm sure Seth has told you that our average lifespan is considerably longer than yours."

"How long will he stay the size he is now?"

"Vampires grow normally until they're out of their teens, then our aging slows. That's why Adrian looks like a teen. I was changed at twenty-one, and I'm one hundred and sixty now. In vampire years, I'm in my mid-thirties." He handed Ben a card. "Here's my cell number and my email address. Contact me anytime. I'll email you weekly reports."

Ben chuckled nervously. "A vampire with a cell phone and an email address?"

"We're still human, although some vampires won't admit to that."

Ben studied the email address. "You have your own web server?"

"Adrian's idea, to maintain our privacy. He's the computer expert."

"Jonathan used my PC at home. If he wants one of his own, let me know the cost and I'll reimburse you."

"Dad, Adrian has the most wicked stuff I've ever seen!" Ben turned around as his son came running up to him. "He's got a shitload of sweet video games." Ben squatted and hugged him. "Thanks for bringing me here!"

Adrian came into the living room. "Hey, little man, if you wanna play those games, you gotta watch that language."

Ben mouthed, *Thank you*, at Eli and Seth.

***

After dinner, while Ben and his son stayed with Adrian, Eli took Seth walking along Woodward Avenue. "Who was your mentor?"

"Gerrick."

Seth watched Eli's eyebrows rise. "I never knew he had an apprentice."

"It was sort of an accident. Back when I was young and stupid, I wasted my college trust fund trekking through Europe. I never made it past Great Britain. Late one day, hiking across the British countryside, I came to this quaint little village. I needed lodging for the night, so I went to the inn. The friendly male and female patrons insisted on buying me drinks. They got me drunk faster than I expected. I remember erotic contact and a whispered dare to let a vampire drink my blood. In my aroused and drunken condition, I would have consented to anything." He looked at the floor. "As I said, I was young and stupid, and they clearly did more than feed on me. The next morning, I woke up to this distinguished gentleman standing over me. Someone had called him about me.

"He took me all over Europe and showed me its wonders, the things I'd wanted to see originally. He had tutors for me. I earned my degree, got some medical training, and learned to fly a plane. I had time and money to do anything and everything. Then he died unexpectedly, before he got around to teaching me about being a vampire. He did tell me a little about the Council, but not how it works."

"The Council deals with all matters concerning the known vampire world," Eli said.

"The *known* vampire world?"

"It's their term. I find it amusing."

"Do they keep a census?"

Eli smiled. "Not that I know of, but they maintain accurate records of the ones they know about. I'm sure there are many they *don't* know of. Some hybrids escaped the Nazi experimental facilities and disappeared."

"What do you mean?"

"The Nazis wanted to create a vampire/human supersoldier. Most of the experiments didn't survive. I heard our people were searching for them, but I don't know the outcome. I have kept out of their matters for many years. Did Gerrick tell you why the Council was formed?"

"To unify and protect our kind."

"That's partly true. It came in the aftermath of the Great Vampire/Human Conflict in 1905, one of the most shameful acts our kind ever committed."

"Gerrick never told me that."

Eli frowned. "He indeed neglected your education. But you and I have a kinship. My mentor, Dietrich Etter, was also Gerrick's mentor."

"Gerrick never told me who mentored him. Isn't Dietrich the oldest living vampire?"

"As far as we know. He serves as the Council's advisor. I met him in 1885 in New Orleans. Because of the political chaos there, we could roam the streets in relative safety without being noticed. Between 1880 and 1905, New Orleans was to vampires what San Francisco today is to homosexuals."

Seth smiled.

"I'm sure Gerrick taught you that humans have always feared us and to keep what you are hidden. Except in rare circumstances, and despite modern enlightenment, it must remain that way."

"The conflict you mentioned, what was that about?" Seth asked.

"The Industrial Revolution in Europe brought improved communications. Groups of militant vampires claimed their relative anonymity would vanish as human cultures grew closer. They grew suspicious of what humans might do, given the opportunity. They convinced others that fear among humans would increase and that vampires would eventually be hunted on a large scale. Their solution: kill off humans before they killed us off. They attacked towns and cities across Asia and Europe.

"Thousands of humans were murdered, and hundreds of us died. Dietrich, myself, and several others finally stepped in. He personally killed many of our kind before we again established tentative order among us." Cyrus Hayes came to mind. "I regret that the peacekeeping attempt had its dark side. Some among us became overly exuberant in eliminating the rebels. We created the Council to prevent such a conflict from arising again. Many vampires suffered personal loss, and some of those harbored deep hatred of humans for decades afterwards. Even today, distrust of humans runs high among our European brethren."

"I feel ashamed for not knowing all this," Seth said.

"Don't be. Most of us are ashamed it happened, so we don't discuss it much. I was called on to act against our own kind, not something I am proud of having done."

"If you don't associate with vampires now, what do you do?"

"I never said I didn't associate with them. For a long time, I have simply avoided involvement in the decision-making. A few days ago, that changed."

CHAPTER TWELVE

Detroit—Thursday, October 30, 2003

From the window seat Rebecca Goodman peered out the tinted bay window of Ysabel's library. Vibrant reds, yellows, and oranges fluttered on the trees. The wind caught several leaves and spiraled them to the ground to join the ones already there. She'd never seen the Japanese maple more beautiful in its coat of rich crimson. Nearly every house had Halloween decorations in preparation for tomorrow night when ghosts and witches and pretend vampires would be out to collect treats.

Detroit's Sherwood Forest neighborhood had a Norman Rockwell aspect. Ysabel's mansion, the last house on the block, sat two hundred feet from the street. Arm-in-arm an older couple strolled past on the sidewalk, enjoying the sunny day. How many years had they been together? What would the world be like when she looked their age? Would she be with someone then, or alone?

Across the room, at an oversized mahogany desk, sat her employer, Ysabel De La Cruz, poring over a speech she'd give to the Council tonight, which Ysabel called The Board as if it oversaw a large corporation.

Rebecca admired her. Ysabel was a woman of unmatched beauty, poise, sophistication, and kindness. No one would suspect this petite, black-haired woman of being three hundred years old.

Despite Ysabel's perfect posture and the fluid motions in her arm while she wrote corrections by hand on the printout, her dark brown eyes and otherwise perfect complexion showed the strain. Ysabel rose from her chair and strode along the uncarpeted path around the room's perimeter. With her hands behind her back, she skirted the old-fashioned library ladder that stretched twelve feet to the ceiling rail along the mahogany bookshelves.

As she passed the bay window, Rebecca asked, "Would you like a cup of tea?"

"That would be wonderful."

Ysabel's English, as impeccable as her appearance, gave no hint of her Mexican birth and upbringing. Her home, however, told the story. The walls, the furniture, and the accessories, all tastefully reflected her heritage.

Rebecca rose from the window seat and crossed the room to the archway leading from the library. Her shoes clicked on the hardwood flooring and fell silent on the Persian carpet. Again on hardwood, her shoes clicked until she stopped at a small serving table where, ten minutes before, Fiona had placed a pot of fresh tea. Rebecca poured a cup of the lightly fragrant Darjeeling and carried it on a saucer to Ysabel.

Ysabel relaxed as she sipped the tea. "How are your online classes at the University of Phoenix coming?"

"I'm enjoying my Human Resources class. It's a lot of work, though. Accounting is difficult for me."

"If you want a tutor, I'll see that you get one. I've not said often enough how proud I am of you."

She still found it difficult to accept that a woman like Ysabel had taken in someone who ran away from home at sixteen, was raped by three young men, and after she was changed, the rage inside her made her kill anyone she fed upon.

"I saw the good buried deep inside you," Ysabel had told her more than once. "You are no longer that person. Many of us have things we're not proud of in our past. We cannot forget them, but we can learn to overcome and grow from them as you have."

And Ysabel never put their kind above humans. To her, vampires—nonhumans as she sometimes called them—were just a different race.

Ysabel set her tea on the desk and indicated the chair next to it. "Please sit for a moment."

Rebecca sat.

"I've had troubling dreams lately," Ysabel said.

"What kind of dreams?"

"Premonitions perhaps, a foreboding." A wistful expression passed over her face. "Enough of this talk. You can help me tonight. I want you to attend the Board meeting with me."

Ysabel was one of the most stalwart and independent people she knew. Ysabel didn't need anyone's help, especially hers. "I'm honored, but how I could help?"

"They want me to sign off on a proposal I'm against and that no good can come from. Of course, I will refuse, then they will call for a vote. Knowing at least one person there supports me would mean a great deal."

"I know you'll persuade them."

"I'd like to believe they will listen to me, but I fear Dietrich has already persuaded them to vote his way. If so, they'll pass the motion over any objections I may voice. Still, I must try."

"What time is the meeting?"

"Ten o'clock, downtown. In return for helping me tonight, I want you to take tomorrow off."

"That's too generous," Rebecca said.

"You deserve it."

"I'd like to be here tomorrow night to see the trick-or-treaters in their costumes. I bought extra treats because we nearly ran out last year." Ysabel's house was a popular stop.

Ysabel laughed. "Are you wearing the same costume?"

"Of course." The Wicked Witch of the West.

"Then I'll wear mine again." Toto, the dog. "The children loved us."

Ysabel barked while Rebecca cackled, "And your little dog, too," as they both handed out the treats.

For just a moment, Ysabel's smile faded. "Is something wrong, Ysabel?"

"No, not at all."

"What should I wear for the meeting tonight?"

"The others will no doubt be dressed somberly for the occasion. Let us surprise them." Her smile returned. "You wear something bold; I will wear something from my country. Their reactions should be interesting."

"What do you want me to do at the meeting?"

"Take notes for me."

"What kind of notes?"

"The reactions of the other members. As an outsider, you'll see things I will not. Give me your honest impressions. Do not attempt to read them telepathically. They would consider it an insult. They won't be expecting me to bring my assistant because I have never brought one before. That will doubly surprise them and perhaps put them off their guard. I need every advantage I can get."

Ysabel had made her feel welcome among their ranks, had boosted her self-esteem, and always valued her opinion. Never before had Ysabel asked for her help with Council business.

***

Rebecca was waiting outside her downtown apartment building when Ysabel's silver Mercedes pulled up, with Ysabel driving. Rebecca got into the car.

"I'm so glad you chose that suit. The color is perfect on you," Ysabel said. Rebecca had worn her rust-colored pantsuit and adorned it with a light blue scarf.

"If you don't mind me asking," Rebecca said, "where is your chauffeur tonight?"

Ysabel laughed. "I enjoy driving, and I think this is a night to be unconventional. Fasten your seatbelt. I feel daring."

They headed to the downtown Detroit office building where Ysabel rented the entire tenth floor. From there, she ran her import/export business. She'd begun simply with Mexican jewelry and clothing. Now she also dealt with artwork and furniture. A few years ago, she expanded her business to Middle Eastern and African items to meet her customers' requirements.

"If you want to practice your speech, I'd be happy to listen," Rebecca said.

"I appreciate that, but I haven't divulged the content of my speech to you on purpose because the Board members are powerful telepaths. I can't risk them gleaning information from you beforehand. You're exceptionally skilled for your age, but you won't be able to block them from reading you. To gain an advantage, they will ignore our rules of individual privacy."

Ysabel's driving skills made the half-hour trip seem like it only took ten minutes. A young male valet came up to the car. He bent down to look in the open driver's side window. "Good evening, Ms. De La Cruz, Ms. Goodman." He helped Ysabel from the car then quickly went around to do the same for Rebecca. Ysabel tipped him, and he saluted with three fingers. "Have a pleasant evening, ladies!" He jumped into the car and drove it to the executive parking area beneath the building.

As they entered the building, Rebecca's excitement grew. Ysabel's importance and power among their kind made her feel honored. She hoped this would be the first meeting of many she'd be invited to. She would prove her worth at this one.

"Dietrich will be here," Ysabel said.

"If he's so powerful, why isn't he a Board member?"

"That was his choice. As the Board's Adviser, he wields more power through influence. He'll be sitting opposite me."

They'd arrived early and had a few minutes to spare, so they headed to Ysabel's private office on the tenth floor. Down the hall, the conference room was open and the lights were on. Raised voices, some bordering on anger, came from the room.

Ysabel shut the office door behind them and bid Rebecca to take a seat. She appeared concerned as she sat behind her desk. "Before we go into the meeting, I must give you some information."

***

Ysabel entered the conference room promptly at ten p.m., as scheduled. Rebecca followed, her eyes straight ahead as Ysabel had advised. Four of the nine Council members were standing. And arguing. They fell silent and slowly sat. All heads followed Ysabel in her green and gold Mexican wrap. Ysabel strode past them to take her place at the opposite end of the oval table.

By human standards the room was dimly lit. One long wall held a picture window. The heavy curtains were open and afforded a clear view of the Detroit skyline. Rebecca could feel the inquisitive thoughts of the men. The power radiating from them amazed her. She also detected their stress. She took the vacant chair to Ysabel's right.

Along each side of the oak table sat four of the men. Ysabel had predicted they would all be wearing dark-colored, single-breasted suits, and that most or all of them would be watching her, not Ysabel. Rebecca focused on the gray-haired man seated at the far end.

"Ysabel, did we not decide this meeting would be closed?" Dietrich said. His German accent was strong, yet regal, his voice smooth and unemotional, despite the tense atmosphere.

"Rebecca Goodman is my personal assistant. I have asked her to take notes for me." Ysabel scanned the Board members then returned her gaze to Dietrich. "I suggested a closed meeting."

Dietrich's smile faltered.

"Brethren," Ysabel began, "thank you all for coming. The loss of our former headquarters in World Trade Tower Two in New York was unfortunate. Until we establish a new permanent headquarters, we will rotate meeting sites as previously suggested by Dietrich and agreed upon by all of you. I hope you will find this facility comfortable. This being our first gathering since then, I received a request from one member to observe a moment of silence for our losses during that tragedy."

Rebecca bowed her head along with Ysabel. Although she didn't know which member it came from, she read a strong sense of sorrow from one.

"Now, let us come to the main topic of this meeting." Ysabel's tone was businesslike and borderline cold. Rebecca poised her pen to take notes. "It is a fact that we share this planet with normal humans. They are a part of our existence and we of theirs. They are the dominant species; we are the aberrations. It is a fact that currently we cannot survive without them. We have a combined three thousand years of living—and wisdom—in this room. Most of us have experienced a significant amount of recent human history. While we can point to incidents of hatred on both sides, humans are not our enemies. It is also a fact that by current biological definitions of species, we are human." Ysabel paused.

Rebecca continued writing. With only the slightest of head movements, she scanned the members' facial expressions as discreetly as possible and noted her observations. Two bore scowls. None were smiling. The corners of Dietrich's mouth twitched as if he wanted to say something.

Ysabel had said that none of the other eight Board members would speak to the issue tonight. They had discussed everything at length through phone calls and letters. Dietrich had called the meeting, and this was Ysabel's opportunity to present her final arguments before the vote.

Ysabel continued. "Contrary to the rumors you have no doubt heard, I am not opposed to the research."

From the corner of her eye, Rebecca noted an arched eyebrow on the member to Ysabel's right.

"I understand the intent is to find ways to overcome our...disabilities. I am in favor of cooperating with human and nonhuman researchers to study the differences between the two biological variants. What I *do* oppose is covert and nonconsensual experimentation. We have no right to treat our human brethren that way."

A sharp intake of breath came from the member sitting on Dietrich's left. Ysabel glanced at the member. Few vampires agreed with her viewpoint of humans and vampires as racial cousins.

Ysabel stared at Dietrich. "We formed this Board to correct our past mistakes. Let us learn from them and seek cooperation between our two groups. I am not suggesting that we reveal ourselves to the world at large. Caution is prudent. The circle of contacts we now have can slowly and cautiously be expanded as necessary. Both our groups can benefit from cooperative medical research, but it must be *voluntary* and *open.* I ask you to consider the wisdom of this. Vote against the current proposal and let us then draft a new and less hastily wrought one."

"Our survival depends on these experiments," Dietrich said. "Humans have abilities we lack and which we need to survive. They will not cooperate with us, Ysabel. We will take only those who won't be missed, the outcasts of human society."

"That is unacceptable!" She dropped her fist onto the table. "No matter how careful we are, trouble will result. We all were around when the Nazis experimented on our kind. They murdered dozens in their zeal to create a German supersoldier. Let us not follow their dark path. We share tenancy of this planet, and we must respect every form of life on it. Our long lives enable us to observe generations of cultural change. From this, we gain the perspective to act responsibly."

"Ysabel, you of all should be in favor of these experiments. Becoming a vampire denies our women the ability to conceive children. We understand your desire to keep the balance, but what have humans done for us? You speak of our responsibility, yet humans have come dangerously close to destroying their own planet on several occasions, and they will keep trying. Do we wait until they ruin the earth, or do we step in and take charge and create one unified species?"

Ysabel fixed her stare on Dietrich. "No matter how you try to justify an immoral act, it is still immoral, and it walks a path next to the one Hitler's people walked."

"Hitler's people were insane zealots," he said.

"What has changed that we should sanction such experiments now?" Ysabel asked him. "How are we any different if *we* perform them? Have you forgotten those experiments? Some of the subjects were so badly mutated and mutilated, they begged us to put them out of their suffering."

Rebecca gasped and looked up from her notes. She'd never heard this before.

"Now, Ysabel, there is no need to bring up the past that we had no control over," Dietrich said. "These experiments will be carefully supervised. The subjects may suffer some discomfort, but our goal is to ensure no permanent injury to them. When we are done, we will compensate them. They will be better off afterwards."

"How will they be better off, and what gives us the right to decide for them?"

Dietrich stood and braced his arms on the table. "We are vampires!" Quieter, he said, "Because we're superior."

Rebecca glanced up at Ysabel, unobtrusively she hoped. Ysabel stared emotionlessly at Dietrich.

"If we call ourselves superior, that is an even more compelling reason why we should be protecting, not exploiting them, Dietrich."

"Then you agree that we are superior to humans?"

"Not at all." She scanned the members then came back to Dietrich. "You have not persuaded me. If no one objects, we will take the vote."

"A secret ballot," Dietrich said.

"Rebecca will collect the votes and read them aloud. 'Yes' will be a vote for the proposed experiments: without the humans' knowledge or consent. 'No' will be a vote against that proposal. If the motion does not carry, we will amend it and vote again, and so forth."

Dietrich held up a pack of three-by-five cards. "These are preprinted with 'Yes' and 'No' to avoid recognition of handwriting. Circle your choice." He passed the blank cards down both sides of the table and sat. "Of course, as Board Adviser, I do not vote." He smiled confidently at Ysabel. "You will vote if there is a tie."

The members circled their choices and folded the ballots. Rebecca tried to hide her nervousness, but what did that matter now? She knew nothing the members would find useful. Ysabel's persuasive speech would convince the members.

"Rebecca, please collect the ballots and count them," Ysabel said.

One by one she opened them and read each aloud, separating them. "Yes, yes, no, no, yes, yes, no, yes: Five yeses, three noes." She raised her head at Ysabel. "I'm sorry."

"The motion passes," Ysabel said without looking at her. "You have your experiment, Dietrich."

"It is not *my* experiment. It is *our* experiment, one that will benefit every vampire, especially young ones like Rebecca. I will personally supervise the execution..." he smiled at his choice of words, "of the experiments."

***

Rebecca stood with Ysabel on the roof of the office building. The starry, moonless night seemed to capture Ysabel's mood. She had adjourned the meeting following mundane business and suggestions for a new headquarters. Some of the previously silent members had spoken to that.

"I am disappointed you haven't introduced me to your lovely protege, Ysabel," said a suave, German-accented voice behind them.

Without turning, Ysabel said, "Dietrich Etter, Rebecca Goodman." Her voice had an uncustomary chill in it.

He walked around in front of them, lifted Rebecca's hand, kissed it. "Ysabel has praised you on many occasions, so much so I have tried to persuade her to loan you to me for a time. You are everything she said you were. Did she tell you it was I who recommended her to be head of the Council?"

"No."

"Ysabel has neglected some things, a compelling reason why you should study with me. What have you to say to that, Ysabel?"

"That would be Rebecca's decision. She and I will discuss it."

"I can ask no more."

"I don't see why I chair the Board, Dietrich. You're the one who runs it. You determined the outcome of this vote before tonight's meeting."

"On the contrary, you do not give yourself enough credit. You wield more power than you believe. Before your speech, I had seven certain 'yes' votes. Your words persuaded two and almost one other. I erred in requesting a secret ballot. That nearly cost me much hard work." Dietrich's brief half-smile acknowledged Ysabel's efforts.

"I hope you do closely monitor the experiments," Ysabel said. "We would both regret their getting out of control."

"They won't get out of control, dearest Ysabel. Now, I plan to tour your city on my first visit here and see what Detroit has to offer. I will also visit an old friend."

"Eli Howard," Ysabel said.

"Yes. I was his mentor, and I am ashamed we have not seen each other in more years than should have passed. *Wiedersehen, meine Damen.*" He bowed his head sharply and did a curt about-face.

Ysabel stared out across the city and said nothing until after he departed. During their brief chat before the meeting, Ysabel made it clear that, despite the Board's wishes, she couldn't allow these experiments to take place. They required close supervision, closer than she suspected Dietrich would give them.

"Do you wish to study under Dietrich?" she asked Rebecca.

"No, ma'am. I'm sorry you lost the vote. You and Dietrich seem to have a rough relationship."

"We were close friends for eighty years—"

"I'm happy to hear that."

"We've been contentious for the past twenty."

"Oh... Why do we have a Board if Dietrich makes all the decisions?"

"Dietrich is correct in one thing. I've neglected your education about a dark time in our history."

"The Nazis?"

"No, that wasn't our doing. I refer to a time before that, when we let our passion override our rationality. As the Industrial Revolution gained strength in Europe, some zealots among us saw the separation closing between us and our human brethren. The zealots set in motion plans to deal with the perceived threat. Random attacks began in 1905 throughout European cities and towns. Today, they would be terrorist attacks. Many deaths occurred on both sides. In late 1906, Dietrich gathered influential and respected members of our kind and created the Board to protect us from ourselves. That first Board drafted our Code of Conduct."

"I thought the Board was much newer."

"Even then, the attacks continued, although with decreased frequency. The Board created a police force empowered to kill only when other means failed. Did you know that?"

"No."

"Creating the Board solved the immediate problem. Then something happened that few nonhumans and perhaps a handful of living humans know the truth about. You have studied history. What event precipitated World War I?"

"A Serbian dissident assassinated Archduke Francis Ferdinand."

"That dissident was one of us."

CHAPTER THIRTEEN

Detroit—Saturday, November 1, 2003

Eli rang Ysabel's doorbell. "Eli Howard to see Madam De La Cruz," he said to the maid.

"Please, come in, Mr. Howard. It's a nasty night out there. You should have an umbrella. May I take your coat?"

"Thank you."

She hung it on a wooden rack in the vestibule. "Madam De La Cruz is in the library. Please follow me."

Eli followed the maid down the short hall and to the right. "Madam, Mr. Howard is here." To him, she said, "May I bring you something to drink?"

"Whatever Ysabel is having."

"Tea, sir."

"Tea is fine."

Ysabel rose and walked quickly across the room to give him a warm embrace. He bent slightly forward. "Eli, my old friend, it is so good to see you again. It has been nearly a century since we last spoke in person."

She hadn't changed at all.

"Have our lives become so busy that we can't see one another more often?" she said.

"You are more beautiful than ever," he said, "but dressing up for me was not necessary."

"For my business, I must keep up appearances."

Her smile still enchanted him. On Ysabel, even casual attire was stunning. The dark teal suit against her swarthy complexion gave her a regal appearance. She had that quality in common with Ling.

"And you are still as handsome as I remember, Eli." She pointed to the two facing Duncan Phyfe sofas, with rich burgundy velvet fabric, black walnut frames, and black leather arms. "Please, sit."

He waited for her to be seated, then he sat on the other sofa.

"I understand you teach at Wayne State now," she said.

He smiled. "You've been checking up on me."

She lifted her teacup from the table. "Have you not done the same with me?"

"Only to find out that you were doing well."

"If I hadn't been?"

"Dearest Ysabel, I would never have let you falter."

She smiled. "Nor I you. In the past, we accomplished good things together. I respected your wish to divorce yourself from our affairs, but I did want to know how you were keeping yourself."

A black and white cat padded into the room and jumped onto the sofa next to Eli and rubbed against him.

"Pax likes you," Ysabel said.

Something pricked Eli's mind.

"He's a vampire cat, one of five known to exist in the world. He's been with me nearly sixty years."

"I'd heard the rumors, but I never believed them. Is he telepathic?"

"Empathic. We sense each other's moods. He tries to cheer me up when I'm troubled. I think of him as my familiar."

Pax meowed then curled up next to him on the couch.

"And he trusts you," she said.

"Interesting. Now, what is this matter you called me for?" he asked.

"When I called, you said you were going to call *me*. That raised my curiosity. What has caused you to break your longtime silence?"

"A newly made vampire who requires my intervention."

"When does Eli Howard consult anyone before he acts, least of all me or the Board?"

Ysabel sat straight-backed while he told her about Seth and Jonathan. As he finished, the maid brought the tea and placed it on the table between them.

"Thank you, Fiona," Ysabel said. Ysabel leaned forward. "She has been with me for thirty years, but she is very religious and has never been comfortable around our kind."

She sipped her tea. "Seth Clayton acted for the right reasons," she said. "I do not blame him, although not all of the Board would agree. It will be our secret." Her wry smile radiated her inner warmth. "I'm glad he contacted you. You will be a wonderful teacher for young Jonathan."

She held her teacup out toward Eli. "But this is not the reason you wanted to see me, is it? A simple matter of our rules, the rules which you counseled Dietrich to propose that the Board adopt and which you yourself constantly bend, is hardly important enough to bring the reclusive Eli Howard out of his hermitage."

"Hermitage?" He chuckled, then picked up his cup and drank.

She studied him. "It's a serious matter, isn't it?"

"Dietrich paid me an unexpected visit a few nights ago," he said.

"He came here for Board business. Why should a visit from your former mentor be unexpected? Or serious?"

"We haven't seen each other in over forty years, yet our conversation consisted of cordial small talk, as if our last meeting had been only a few weeks ago. He struggled to conceal his thoughts from me. What's going on, Ysabel?"

Her expression mirrored the dark one he'd seen in Ling the other evening at the club. "It's why I called you," she said. "The Board just voted on a proposal that scares me. They sanctioned experiments on humans of the same kind the Nazis did, which we abhorred."

"Can't you stop them?"

"I tried. Dietrich was the one most in favor."

"Dietrich?"

"I don't understand why he's changed his viewpoint. This could start the Conflict of 1905 all over again, only worse than before." She sipped her tea.

Eli mediated over his own teacup for a moment. "How can I help?"

"Dietrich used the old argument of wanting to overcome our disabilities and convinced a majority with that shallow logic. He's concealing something. Perhaps you can uncover the truth. He trusts and respects you. Convince him of his poor judgment before this goes further."

Now, it made sense. He would talk to Dietrich, but he already suspected where this came from. "Cyrus Hayes is in Detroit," he said.

The teacup trembled in her hand, and the tremor moved to her lips.

"That's the connection," he said. "That's what has changed."

The doorbell rang. From the corner of his eye, Eli caught the maid heading to answer it. Moments later, a young woman's voice said, "I saw a car in the driveway. Does Ysabel have someone with her?" He didn't hear a reply.

"That would be my assistant, Rebecca," Ysabel said to Eli. "She has been with me for five years."

A slender blonde with blue eyes and pale skin stood at the library entrance carrying a portfolio. "I didn't mean to disturb you, but you asked for these papers."

"Please come in. I'd like you to meet Eli. He is an old friend."

Eli stood as the woman approached.

"Rebecca, this is Eli Howard. Eli, Rebecca Goodman."

"*The* Eli Howard? I have heard good things about you from Ysabel, Mr. Howard." Her pleasure in meeting him was apparent.

He found that amusing, given that Ysabel and he had had no contact for decades. He caught a brief glimpse of Rebecca's thoughts. Apparently, he wasn't at all what she expected. "Please call me Eli. I'm pleased to meet you." He took her hand and kissed it. More surprise registered in her thoughts.

"I'm certain Ysabel has exaggerated."

"I don't think so," Rebecca said.

Ysabel's expression told him that he'd let his repressed thoughts escape and Rebecca read them. "You should have come last night, on Halloween," Ysabel said by way of distraction. "Rebecca and I both dressed in costumes to greet the trick-or-treaters."

He couldn't imagine either of them in costume.

"Rebecca and I will be a few minutes, then you and I will continue our discussion. Please make yourself comfortable."

If Rebecca had caught his thoughts, she'd know he hadn't felt this way toward a woman in a very long time.

***

New Orleans, Louisiana—May 1884

Eli remembered every detail. For twenty-five years he'd wandered the backwoods of Alabama, Georgia, and Mississippi: hating, feeding, killing. Alone.

He'd tried to understand fully what had happened to him, what all the changes in him were, why he could hear better than he'd ever heard before, why he heard voices in his head when people were nearby. If his reflection in moonlit water didn't lie, he hadn't aged in those twenty-five years, nor had his appearance changed.

He'd heard whispers on the lips of his victims and in places where he stayed too long: blood-drinker and vampire. Was that what he was?

He remembered stories his elders told to frighten children into behaving, stories of beasts who were cursed to live in the shadows of night and drink the blood of men. Why had God cursed *him* at twenty-one years of age? What horrible thing had he done to deserve damnation? Had his brother's shame also fallen upon him?

Eli never forgot he had killed his slaveholder's young son, an innocent boy. Sometimes he'd wanted to take his own life for that, but wasn't suicide a greater sin? He had so many questions and no one to answer them.

He had avoided cities on his journeys, but now he stood, with a tied pack of extra clothes in hand, outside the great city of New Orleans. He saw other Negroes there. He'd heard all slaves were freed. This city called to him, as if something waited for him here.

In the past twenty-five years he'd killed, or wanted to kill, every white person he'd seen, not fearing anyone. For the first time since he'd become a blood drinker, he was afraid, not of men, but of what answers he might find to his questions. He entered New Orleans wearing the same style of country clothes he'd always worn, which he stole to replace what wore out.

The streets at night were wondrous with buildings and gas streetlights. Some of the lights weren't lit, but it didn't matter. He kept himself in shadows in case any of the people could tell what he was. He'd learned to be selective with the voices in his head, realizing they were men's thoughts. Here, if he let the thoughts in, were so many that he found it difficult to concentrate on any specific one.

Some of the people he passed didn't give off the scent he'd learned to associate with humans. Down one alley he saw two men feeding—as he himself fed—on the blood of two young girls. No one cared. Except for the one who changed him, whom he'd only glimpsed, he'd never encountered another of his kind.

Was someone watching him? He glanced over his shoulder. Across the street stood a woman with curly hair, wearing a laced-up, black and white striped dress, a white feathered hat, and a red shawl. She carried a fan and drawstring purse. She stared back at him.

When he turned back to face the alley and the men, he still saw the woman in his mind. Even though he wasn't looking at her, he sensed her walking toward him.

"You can join them," a soft voice behind him said. "You are one of us."

He turned. It was the same woman. "Who are you?"

"I am Sophie Benoit," she said, pronouncing her last name *ben-wa*. "You are new to my city."

"How do you know what I am?"

"I can read your thoughts, and you can read mine if I let you. You can tell I am not human, no?"

He tilted his head. He did feel something different.

"You are so green it is *pathétique*."

Somewhere in his past, he'd heard an accent like hers.

"I am French," she said. "Did the one who changed you not teach you anything?"

"Changed?"

"That is how we refer to being made into a vampire."

He shook his head. "He cursed me, then left me."

She laughed, but not unkindly. "You are not cursed. Sophie will teach you. *Suivez-moi*."

He didn't understand her words, but he understood the gesture to follow and lowered his head. "Y-yes, ma'am."

She put her hand gently under his chin and raised his head. She was nearly a foot shorter than him. "You are not a Negro. You are a vampire. Others of your race will fear you. And you bow your head to no one, not even to one of us."

She was the most beautiful white woman he'd ever seen. Now that she was so close, the moonlight and streetlights revealed her chestnut hair, kind eyes, a beautiful smile. He noticed the long string of pearls around her neck

"You are not alone, *mon cher.* Thousands of us live in the world. You must lose your fear when among those of our kind. We are not savages like humans believe, but you must also learn to defend yourself from them. They know how strong we are and fear us. When they attack, they come in large groups."

This new information astounded him. "How old are you?"

"It is not polite to ask a woman her age. Only because you are *jeune et très beau* will I tell you. I am one hundred and twenty years young. I was changed in 1785 in Paris, France. It is good you are here. I will show you New Orleans. Many wise vampires come here to educate young ones like you. You will have the opportunity to learn from elders who are hundreds of years old. First I must get you some proper clothes and teach you to stand proudly, as one of us."

They walked along Royal Street and into the nighttime crowds of humans. He would later learn the names of all the streets. For now, he was an innocent child, amazed at the splendor of this newfound place. All of his senses came alive. Sights and scents, more wonderful than he'd ever experienced, flooded over him. More amazing, a beautiful white woman walked at his side and treated him as her equal.

"Where are you taking me?" he asked.

"*Chez moi.*"

He was confused.

She laughed. "To my house. You need a place to stay, *non*?"

"Yes."

He didn't remember all he saw or how long they walked, but they came to a place of many magnificent buildings. "This is Storyville," she said, "where the sporting women live. For us, New Orleans is *une bonne ville.* There is so much crime. The officials and the police—*les poulets* we call them, the chickens—are like dogs who so stupidly chase their *queues.* Men's *queues* always lead them to Storyville." What a sweet laugh she had.

He would learn later what all this meant.

She took him inside a building finer than his slaveholder's plantation house. The carpet was thick; fine draperies adorned the windows. He rubbed his hand over a deep-red, velvet-textured wall. A crystal chandelier, larger than he'd ever seen, hung in the center of this room. "This is *my* sporting house, *les filles à ton service,*" she said. "Women to serve you."

He saw women everywhere, many beautiful women. Some wore full dresses, others were half-dressed. A number of them were alone, a few were talking to men, still more were escorting men out of the room. He didn't see any others of his race here.

One woman came up to them. "Madam Sophie, is he your new servant?"

He avoided looking at her bare breasts.

"He will serve me," she said. She took hold of his chin and turned his head back at the woman. "Do you not like what you see?"

"She is..."

"Naked? *Oui.* What is wrong with a beautiful, naked woman?"

"N-nothing."

Sophie laughed her sweet laugh again, then she led him up a grand stairway. At the top, she opened a door. "Here is my room."

If possible, the room was more elegant and luxurious than downstairs. The bed, covered with pillows, was large enough for three people. Inside the fireplace to his right a roaring fire heated a huge kettle. In front of that sat a bathtub for two people. He'd only seen its like once before. Next to the tub was a wooden toilet.

She'd been holding his hand and now let it go. "Wait here." When she returned, a Negro woman much darker than he was accompanied her. "This is Elba, my maid."

"What you lookin' at, boy?"

"His name is Eli," Sophie said, "and you will not speak to him that way again. Prepare my bath then leave us."

"Yes, ma'am." Her tone was chilly. On the plantations, he'd known skin color sometimes mattered among Negroes.

Sophie took his clothing bundle and tossed it on the floor. She bid him sit on the bed while she disappeared behind a dressing screen. He watched Elba use a wooden bucket to dip water from the fireplace kettle and fill the tub. He marveled at the crystal oil lamps that lit the room. Some were mounted on the walls; others sat on tables.

Elba finished and left. When Sophie came from behind the screen, she wore a thin, green, silk robe, open in front. "Do you like what you see?"

She had unfastened her hair so it now touched her shoulders. The robe fell open next to her nipples. A string of pearls around her neck hung halfway down her breasts. His gaze drifted down past her stomach. She paused in front of him then walked around the room dimming the lights and glancing playfully at him.

Now that he understood what was about to happen, a memory of his brother Jonas flashed through his mind.

She came over to him. "*Mon pauvre petit*, I am so sorry for you. Do not be afraid. No one will do that to you here." She placed her hands on his cheeks; her eyes smiled at him. "Sophie will not let them."

She pulled him to her and kissed him lightly with her moist and wonderfully warm lips. "It is time *pour l'amour.* Take off those old clothes."

He didn't move.

"For your bath, *mon chou.* Do you take a bath in your clothes? We will burn the old ones and I will buy you fine new ones."

She stood up with him while he took off his cotton shirt. She ran her hands over his chest and shoulders, down his arms, squeezing his firm muscles. Her hands slid over his chest; her palms brushed his nipples.

He shivered.

"You like how Sophie touches you." Again she pulled him to her. Her lips came to rest gently on his. He opened his mouth; their tongues touched. Before he realized it, or could stop her, she had untied the rope holding up his pants. In cooler weather, he would be wearing long johns underneath, but those were in the bundle on the floor.

She took a step back and took in his nakedness. "*Mon dieu! Quel cigare.*"

He dropped one hand to cover himself. She pulled it away. "*Mais, non.*" Sophie pursed her lips then formed them into a tiny smile. "Do not hide what makes you beautiful." She led him to the bathtub. He lifted one leg to step in. "*Un moment.*"

Next to the tub, a small table held several jars. She opened one, liberally sprinkled scented flakes into the water, then vigorously mixed them with one hand to stir up bubbles.

"*Maintenant le bain.*" She gestured for him to enter the tub.

He lowered himself into the foam and soothing warmth. Most of his bathing had been in cold streams and lakes.

Sophie knelt beside the tub and ladled water over him with her hands. Why did being bathed by this white woman distress and arouse him at the same time? He shouldn't be here. He braced his hands on the edge of the tub to stand.

She put a hand firmly on his shoulder. "It is my turn, *mon chou.*" She slid the robe off her shoulders. It fell to the floor as she stood and stepped into the tub, facing him. He took in the fullness of her beauty.

The curve of her hips, her creamy skin and golden chestnut hair, the fullness of her breasts with their caramel-colored nipples and the pearls draped between them, all drew him into her spell. She put her hands beneath her breasts and held them out to him.

He hesitated. She leaned into him. The scent of her skin made his reservations melt away. He took a firm nipple between his lips, massaged it, gently bit it.

She moaned. "*Oui*, you are learning fast, *chou chou.*" She guided his hand to her warmth. While his fingers explored it, her throaty moans encouraged him to continue.

Before he realized it, she'd knelt in the tub and had taken him into her mouth. He shivered at the touch of her lips playing over his erection. Her fingers pressed underneath the base, stiffening him more. His body jerked; he gasped. Her tongue played over him, cruelly teasing. She brought him to the brink many times, yet never allowed his release. The torment drove him wild.

Unable to endure any more, he lifted her out of the tub and carried her to the thick rug in front of the fireplace. He knelt before her, and brought one hand to the center of her pleasure. He swirled his fingers through her soft hairs, at first touching only them, tormenting her as she had tormented him. He probed for her pleasure spots, delighting in her moans.

He leaned forward to take in her sweet fragrance. Her hips thrust forward when his tongue went where his fingers had been.

"Mmm." Her body went limp. He rose to catch her, kissing her hard, and held her against him.

She brought his erection to her swollen opening. Rubbing herself with it, she said, "*Baisez-moi.*"

They fell together in front of the fire. She straddled the tip of his erection and lowered herself. She moved on him with aching slowness.

Deep inside him the tremors began and intensified.

She clenched herself around him. Her moans drowned out his. She shuddered, cried out again. Her powerful spasms pulsed around his erection. Moments later, he cried out and exploded inside her. His body shook repeatedly with his release. He held her tightly until her body went limp on top of him.

Their lovemaking moved to the bed. When their passion had exhausted itself, they fell asleep. He was still inside her when they woke the next morning.

In the days and months that followed, they often went out after their lovemaking and fed their blood hunger together.

He learned to speak fluent French.

That December, New Orleans hosted the World Cotton Exposition, which lasted until the beginning of June. Eli and Sophie saw its wonders together.

He had lived with her for a year in New Orleans when she said he was ready to have a mentor. She was sad because he was the first vampire in four decades she had carried on a relationship with. She had taught him so much. He wanted to learn more from her, but he trusted her to do what was best for him.

In July 1885, in the middle of a sultry summer night, Sophie took him into a dimly lit café. A regal older man sat there alone sipping tea.

"Is this the one?" he asked her. The man gave him a critical appraisal. "He is different from the last."

"Yes, he is Eli Howard." To Eli, she said, "Dietrich Etter has come from Germany seeking a student. He has agreed to be your mentor. You should feel honored."

"He is ready," Dietrich said. "You may leave us now. When I have finished with him, I will return him to you."

"I will see you soon, my love," Eli whispered to her.

"Not so soon," she said.

"I don't understand."

"You will be with Dietrich for the next ten years, perhaps more."

Eli was completely lost in that moment and grabbed for her. She backed away. "Ten years to a vampire is like one year to a human. Go with Dietrich. We have an eternity to share when your training is over."

Sophie walked out of the café. Although she could hide her thoughts from him when she wanted to, this time she didn't, and he felt her sadness.

Then she was gone.

"Young man, you will realize that being a vampire can be lonely," Dietrich said. "You didn't ask for this new life, but you are one of us now and must accept that. It won't be an easy life, nor a safe one. Enjoy your last night in New Orleans. Tomorrow we will board a ship."

"Where are we going?"

"To Europe, to England and France and places you've heard of but never thought you would see. I will introduce you to your European and Asian brothers and sisters. Then we will travel to Germany, where my home is. I will make you into the educated man you must become. I will teach you things many vampires never learn."

Dietrich would teach him the vampire side of his new life; Sophie had taught him the human side.

***

Detroit—Saturday, November 1, 2003

Seeing Rebecca made him longingly remember Sophie's youthful, pale skin and golden chestnut hair. He owed her so much for refining him so he could get a mentor. She taught him how to walk and talk and dress properly. While Rebecca sat next to Ysabel, engaged in business and turned away from him, neither of them could see the moisture clouding his eyes.

Making love with Sophie had been beyond anything he'd ever imagined as a human. He cherished these memories because he never saw Sophie again. He has not loved a woman that way since.

"Thank you for stopping by, Rebecca," Ysabel said.

Rebecca rose from the sofa. He also rose.

They exchanged glances. "It was a pleasure meeting you, Eli," she said. "I'm sure I'll see you again."

He watched her leave. He was still staring after her when Ysabel spoke.

"I thought I knew Eli Howard. I've learned something new today. Yes, it's *that* obvious, Eli. Perhaps your visit here was predestined. Sophie must have been a special woman."

"You read my thoughts?" He felt himself blushing.

"You were *projecting* them. It's not like you to lose control that way. It wouldn't surprise me if Rebecca picked up on part of them. Her powers are strong for her age." Ysabel gave him a warm, understanding smile. "May I ask what happened to Sophie?"

He'd come here to share his vision with Ysabel and to voice his concerns about Cyrus. He hadn't expected buried emotions would resurface. Ysabel had already seen a part of his soul. He might as well tell her the rest.

"She had moved back to France when New Orleans became unsafe. In 1906, near the end of the Conflict, when it spilled over into France, Cyrus Hayes sent a group of his men there—counter to my orders—to deal with rebel factions, human and vampire. I found out later he'd also ordered his men to dispose of any vampires not actively fighting for us. Sophie was among them."

CHAPTER FOURTEEN

Detroit—Monday, November 3, 2003

Ethan Radley's office phone bleeped twice—the security desk in the front lobby. *Finally.* Ethan pressed handsfree. "Radley."

"Mr. Radley, Mr. Hayes is here."

"Have him brought up to my office."

"Right away, Mr. Radley."

Damn demanding clients think they own you. Million-dollar contract or not, he hated customers who thought their money was better than anyone else's. Ten o'clock at night for a business meeting? What the hell did Hayes have against regular business hours? Normal people, if they weren't at home, went to a casino or club to enjoy themselves. Still, he couldn't afford to lose such a lucrative contract, not when Hayes said it could yield more.

Ethan got up from his desk and went to the window of his sixteen-hundred-square-foot office on the fourth and top floor. He really wanted an office twenty or more floors up, with a stunning aerial view, but none of the office buildings in Troy, Michigan were that tall, and even then he'd still be seeing a sleepy-quiet city that had nothing worth the view anyway. Downtown Detroit had some spectacular aerial views—at that height the less-spectacular parts of the city disappeared. He sighed. Low property taxes; low crime; affluent neighborhoods; free parking for him and his employees—that was worth something. His chauffeur and personal limo made his late meeting slightly less annoying.

Cyrus Hayes. Nothing fit the mental image Ethan had formed of him. He was five-foot-six and slender. That almost comical flame-red hair couldn't be natural. Those spooky, deep-blue eyes had to be contact lenses. The first time they met, he'd had to repress the desire to laugh. Yet something about him commanded respect bordering on awe.

"Come in!" Ethan said in response to the knock on his office door. He continued facing the window.

"Mr. Hayes, sir," the voice said.

"Thank you, Craig."

The security guard left. Hayes strode forward. Ethan walked around the desk to shake his hand.

Damn. For a small man, he has a grip like a vise.

"Ethan, how are the preparations progressing? Have the security arrangements I requested been implemented? I plan to bring my people in the first of next week."

Ethan still hadn't placed Hayes' slight accent—possibly somewhere in the British Isles.

"I apologize for the lateness of our meeting. Being a businessman, you can appreciate the constraints of a busy schedule. I'm sure the size of our contract will ease the inconvenience."

Smug clients annoyed him. The million dollars Hayes offered up front had caught his immediate attention, but nothing beyond that had been discussed or put in writing, only the suggestion of more. Hayes flashed a sinister smile that gave Ethan an eerie feeling that Hayes knew exactly what he was thinking.

"Well, Ethan?"

"Nearly everything is in place. Given the…sensitive nature and circumstances surrounding your research, I had my security chief reevaluate the backgrounds and psych profiles of those we selected to assist in your program. We found two of the men have been under some family stress lately, so we decided their involvement might pose an unnecessary risk. We found one replacement among the previously rejected candidates."

"This concerns me, Ethan. I don't like surprises. My schedule has no margin for error. Nothing must interfere. Have I made a mistake in placing my trust in you and your company?"

"Not at all, Mr. Hayes." *Damn. Not only annoying, but insulting!*

"There are other companies with equal or greater expertise in the areas I require. I selected yours for its location, inconspicuous yet still visible, hiding in plain sight."

Hayes had said the project was a military contract: countering biological warfare coupled with AIDS research. *Military. Biological warfare. AIDS.* Those keywords clawed their way through Ethan's thoughts for a moment until the promised millions of dollars once again restrained them.

But he, Ethan Radley, not the customer, was in charge and he would stay in charge.

"Then you should appreciate my position and that I must maintain control over my work. What I'm paying you should be sufficient to answer your questions." Hayes' sinister smile reappeared for a moment then vanished.

Ethan shivered. It must be his body language. Hayes couldn't be reading his mind. "Regarding that, Mr. Hayes. To date we have not discussed any monies beyond your initial payment."

"Five million, Ethan, likely double that, more if the project goes as well as I anticipate. If you recall, one clause in the contract specifies that I do not expect you to pay for any of my particular requirements out of pocket and I will advance any sums required. Have I violated any part of that?"

Ethan shook his head.

"Then I expect you to honor your part. My men will arrive late next Monday evening. Are their accommodations ready?"

That had been another strange request. Hayes' three researchers were to be housed on the premises. Ethan had suggested, "There is an excellent residence inn nearby. I can arrange a shuttle—"

"That's not acceptable. I'll pay whatever additional sums are necessary for the renovations to your building. I want a security lock on their quarters, accessible only to them and myself."

However Hayes wanted to spend his money, Ethan wouldn't argue. He had the perfect place. The basement had a small gym and exercise facility, with bathrooms and showers, that he and his employees could use. Several currently vacant rooms also existed down there, one of which used to be a lab. It had heat and plumbing. Converting it into suitable sleeping quarters hadn't been difficult.

"They will be ready, Mr. Hayes. Will there be anything else tonight?" Ethan fought to keep the annoyance out of his voice.

"We are done for now," Cyrus said. "You may call your driver to take you home. Stop by a pub on the way. You're too tense." He took several brisk strides toward the door, then stopped abruptly and looked over his shoulder. "Don't think you have any secrets from me, Ethan. There's nothing you do or *think* I don't know about."

Damn arrogant son of a bitch.

"Including how many times you've cursed me tonight."

***

Detroit—Wednesday, November 5, 2003

Adrian had just stepped inside his house and was hanging up Drake's and his jackets when Eli came down the stairs.

"I was going to call you," Eli said, with a slight annoyance in his voice. "You did remember that I'm meeting with Dietrich tonight and you're watching Jonathan?"

"Got it covered," Adrian said. "I went to pick up Drake. When I told Jonathan I knew a rapper, he wanted to meet Drake. We'll play video games together, too. You got a minute before you go? Drake wants to ask you something."

"I'll be in the library."

"We'll grab a couple of Pepsis and be right there."

Carrying their unopened cans, Drake and Adrian entered the library.

Adrian popped his can open and went over to sit next to Jonathan, who was absorbed in his book.

"Have a seat," Eli said to Drake. "What can I do for you?"

"It's about my Jeep."

"The one your father locked up because of your bad behavior?"

"Uh huh."

"Yes, Adrian told me."

"I need your advice," Drake said. "I figured out a way I can get it back. Ethan has this big 'work ethic' thing. If I had a job where I needed wheels, I'm pretty sure he'd rescind the punishment."

"Doesn't your father have a limousine and chauffeur?"

"He's got a lot of things."

Eli steepled his fingers in front of him. "Which he doesn't share with his son."

"Exactly."

"So he bought you the Jeep."

"Uh huh."

"What kind of job do you have in mind?"

"Helping you and Adrian and Ling clean the scum out of Detroit."

"I've told you—"

"Yeah, I know, it's too dangerous for me. There's gotta be *something* a willing dude can do to help."

Adrian smiled to himself. Eli could read all of Drake's thoughts if he wanted to. But Eli didn't probe minds uninvited unless absolutely necessary. Or so he said. He continued to watch them intently. Next to him, Jonathan flipped a page. Adrian glanced sideways. *Greek Mythology? Was Eli making him read that, or had he picked it up on his own?* Whichever, he must really be into it because he flipped another page and it looked like he was reading, not just browsing the pictures. Adrian drank his Pepsi.

"You want this job to be something your father will approve of," Eli said to Drake.

"Which means it'll be sucky for me."

"Not necessarily. What if you were helping a professor at Wayne State?"

"That'd be stellar! You teach there, don't you?"

"Yes. Would you be willing to work as my assistant: grading papers, typing up the tests, perhaps an occasional bit of legwork? It'll be mostly mundane work, nothing of major consequence, but work that needs to be done. And you will be helping me."

"Uh, I guess so... Sure. That's sounds cool... But doesn't the university, like, have to hire me, and don't their wheels run in ultra-slow motion? It'll take *weeks* before I see my first paycheck. At that rate I'll be lucky to get my Jeep back before Christmas."

Adrian took another drink of Pepsi, swirling it in his mouth so it fizzed over his teeth.

"You are correct, but I would pay you myself from a business account set up for when I have to appear official."

"Vampires R Us?"

Adrian snorted involuntarily and Pepsi blew out his nose. *Shit!* He grabbed the box of tissues on the corner of Eli's desk.

"Spaz monkey," Jonathan muttered while Adrian wiped and blew his nose.

"That's enough out of you."

Jonathan snickered and went back to his reading.

"Is there a problem, Adrian?" Eli said.

"Just a little accident." He wiped the drips off his chin.

"Adrian will pick you up tomorrow night," Eli told Drake. "I'll have a paycheck for you then."

"Wow. Thanks."

"When you have your Jeep back, you *will* be doing work for me at Wayne State, some of it there, part of it may be here. This is an advance I expect you to earn."

"I *really* appreciate it, but isn't there some way I can help you and Adrian?"

"I'll give that some thought. No promises."

"I understand."

Eli stood and went over to Jonathan. "How do you like that book?"

"It's sweet. Can I keep reading it?"

"Of course, but wouldn't you rather beat Adrian at video games?"

Adrian snarled.

"Sure."

"I'm leaving in a few minutes. I'll be back later." Pointing at Drake, he said, "Have you met Drake, Adrian's rapper friend?"

"But he's *white*."

Drake walked woodenly over to them with both forefingers rap gesturing.

"Don't matter what skin

"I'm in." He put a finger against his head.

"In *here's* a dude's

"at-ti-tudes."

Drake stuck out his left hand, palm toward Jonathan.

"Pleased to meet ya, new vamp dude,

"long as ya remember I'm not food!

"Five me." He gave Jonathan a high five.

"Behave for Adrian and Drake," Eli said.

"I will, Uncle Eli." He grinned evilly. "I'll only beat Adrian a little. Maybe I'll let him win *one* game."

Adrian smacked Jonathan lightly on the back of the head. "Be good and I'll let you have Drake for dessert."

Drake clasped both hands around his neck and stuck out his tongue. "No way!" he croaked. Then Drake relaxed his hands and grinned at Eli. "If he snacks on me, will I become a vamp?"

"I may be out late," Eli said.

***

Eli gazed across the Detroit River at the hazy Windsor skyline. A damp November chill, left by today's on-and-off rain, hung in the air. He cinched his leather coat around his waist. The many emotions struggling inside him tonight added to his discomfort.

This was his favorite spot for mediation. The present and the past coexisted in the river's flowing waters. Here, he remembered better times in Detroit, when promises for a bright future seemed endless. He shut his eyes, braced his hands on the metal railing, and let his thoughts drift back. Images beckoned to him, lost in history and recalled today by few, from eighty years ago, before the rise and sprawl of architecture, when the old trolley buses patrolled the streets of Windsor. Last year, at Detroit's three-hundredth anniversary, he'd attended the dedication of the two bronze monuments to the Underground Railroad. The one in Hart Plaza he'd stopped at on his way here tonight showed a group of slaves with a white man pointing toward Canada. Its mate, half a mile across the river, welcomed those slaves with uplifted arms. A century and a half ago, Detroit had brought hope to escaped slaves like him. Decades later, visionary giants made their dreams of a better life come true here.

He tucked the memories back in their beds. Detroit's heart was beginning to beat again. Its soul, the part he wanted to revive, still lay buried.

Cyrus Hayes' presence in Detroit unsettled him. Cyrus' presence anywhere foreshadowed trouble. Here, it could unravel the city's recovery. *Where did the Council fit into all this? Surely Cyrus was influencing their recent decisions, but how deep did Cyrus' influence run?*

"Good evening, Dietrich," Eli said, still staring at the water.

"Your senses are as sharp as ever, Eli. It is a shame you chose to abandon your talents."

With his hands still on the railing Eli looked at his former mentor. Dietrich's regal features and bold jaw line were slightly more gaunt than he remembered. "I haven't abandoned them. I've simply directed them differently than you wanted."

"Still contentious after so long. Despite our lack of correspondence, I have kept up with you. I'm glad you took my advice and became a teacher. Still, I would have preferred hearing about your accomplishments firsthand."

"I didn't think you cared."

"When Sophie brought you to me, I saw promise in you underneath the unschooled rawness."

"You saw someone you could manipulate to your own ends, and were disappointed when you discovered you couldn't."

"You were too much your own man. The years have been extremely kind to you, as healthy and robust as ever. Come visit me in Europe. There are many things I would like to show you."

"Why is Cyrus here?"

"For not having seen one another in so long, should we not be catching up, as you say, and discussing more pleasant topics?"

"I have spoken with Ysabel. It takes a great deal to disturb her, but you have managed to do it. What are you planning, and what is Cyrus involved with?"

Dietrich's jaw muscles tensed, his tone chilled. "I thought Eli Howard preferred to keep himself isolated from the affairs of our kind. When did that change?"

"When Cyrus arrived here." Eli heard the bitterness in his own voice.

"Is this a personal concern, Eli?"

"You taught me to put personal concerns aside in favor of the greater good. 'Memories of the past give rise to emotions that blind us. The past cannot be changed. Accept the present, embrace it, and mold your future with it.' Were those not your exact words of guidance to me?"

"Cyrus is here to help us fight for our survival."

Eli narrowed his eyes. "If he told you that, he's lying. Where he walks, death prowls not far behind. Many things have indeed changed in the past century. Cyrus is not one of them. If you believe he has, then you have ignored your own advice. You've also conveniently forgotten that we formed the Council to foster a peaceful coexistence with humans." He pointed a finger at Dietrich. "Now you advocate exploiting them? When did *that* change?"

Dietrich's lips trembled slightly and his gaze shifted away from Eli for an instant. "When 9/11 happened. As a teacher of history, you can't have ignored it."

"I haven't." Eli thrust his hands into his coat pockets.

"We formed the Council for *our* benefit, not for theirs." Dietrich cast a glance across the water. Silence fell between them. "It is damp and chilly out here," Dietrich said abruptly. "Could we not find a warmer place to continue what is likely to become a lengthy conversation? At my hotel perhaps, where I can show you my hospitality. I have the Presidential Suite at your Ritz Carlton. My hired car and driver are waiting nearby."

Eli bowed his head at him. "As you wish." Was Dietrich starting to experience the frailties of old age? He had never revealed his exact age, only that he was in his mid-thirties when changed. From historical clues picked up when Dietrich was mentoring him, Eli guessed him at over four hundred. If so, in human terms, Dietrich was in his seventies.

"I stopped by your home before I came here tonight. I hope you don't mind? Adrian said you'd already left. Is the Council aware of your two new charges? I was puzzled about seeing the young human who was with them."

Reluctant to say too much, Eli chose his words carefully. "He is a friend."

"We established the rules for a reason, Eli. You are setting a dangerous precedent in letting your students consort with humans."

Not as dangerous as the one Dietrich was setting. He'd also thought it best not to tell Dietrich that the young human was Drake Radley, whose father owned the company Cyrus was doing business with. In all likelihood, Dietrich was not aware of the extent of Cyrus' business dealings here or anywhere. For the moment, he was more interested in learning what had brought Dietrich and Cyrus together. The last he knew, the two were traveling in different circles and had tacitly agreed not to let those circles intersect. Dietrich would not be forthcoming in that regard. Tonight's game of strategy might prove interesting.

A short while later, they entered Dietrich's hotel suite. Neither had spoken during the short drive. "It is comfortable," Dietrich said.

Eli noted the grand piano. "And pricey," Eli said.

"But aren't all American hotels? If one has the means, should he not indulge himself?" Dietrich called room service to order a bottle of Beaujolais Fleurie.

They sat opposite one another.

"This has become a critical period for us. Most of the humans who were alive during the Great Conflict are now dead. After you left Europe, we sought out records of the event and destroyed them. We recently discovered that we overlooked some. These documents have come to the attention of several covert groups around the world, who have in turn passed the information to certain government officials in the United States and China. Speculation about the significance of the documents has led to covert investigations. We are fortunate these two countries still distrust one another. Cooperation between them would escalate the problem for us."

Eli straightened. "What is the exact nature of this problem?"

"Given the anxieties from 9/11, accusations and fears are suggesting we are in league with terrorists and plotting a new wave of attacks on a scale unlike any the world has seen before."

"Do these officials believe in vampires?"

"Not at first. The topic did not come up. Other factions are working to convince them of our existence and to find a credible way to demonstrate that we are a threat."

At the knock on the door, Dietrich said, "Come in." A young, room-service waiter entered. After he opened and poured the wine, Dietrich tipped him generously.

Dietrich sipped his wine. "Not an expensive wine at all—unfortunately. I've developed a fondness for it. Wonderfully fruity, and best drunk new." He savored it for a moment. "Cyrus is here to help us, Eli. I presume Ysabel told you about the Council's vote?"

"Yes."

"Despite our longevity and powers, we are still mortal. Weapons kill us as effectively as they kill humans, and far fewer of our kind exist. With a concerted effort, they could obliterate us from the Earth. Several covert groups are already organizing against us. One thing hampers them."

"Which is?"

"We're good at hiding. It will take them a while to organize and find us, but they will not give up."

"We can increase our numbers the old way," Eli said.

"You are not that naive, Eli. We cannot do it fast enough without attracting attention. Even with a concentrated program of training, the new vampire is mentally too vulnerable. But I need not tell you this. Cyrus is seeking a way to alter the change. His research team is seeking a way to create our kind quickly and safely."

Like the girl who died outside Ling's?

"Too long have we been subservient to humans. We have reached a turning point. Our time is now. Or it is never."

Eli drank his wine, saying nothing.

"You know I'm right, Eli. The cause of the 1905 Conflict would be an interesting topic in one of your classes, would it not?"

Eli poured himself another glass. The 1905 Conflict indirectly resulted from the Industrial Revolution. Now the world had entered the Technology Revolution. Dietrich's thinking mirrored that of militant vampire factions in the early twentieth century. Had Dietrich become so pro-vampire that humans no longer mattered and had become a simple fact of life?

"You really believe humans will begin to hunt us?" Eli said.

"Once they learn of our existence, can you give me even one reason they would not?"

Eli set his glass on the table next his chair. "Cyrus Hayes can't be trusted."

"He has changed from when you last saw him, Eli."

Not for the better.

"Nevertheless, I have not told Cyrus that you live here. If he finds out, it won't be from me."

Eli stood and put on his coat.

"My driver will meet you in the lobby. I'll be in Detroit for several more days. I would like for us to talk again."

Eli didn't see any point to another meeting.

CHAPTER FIFTEEN

Detroit—Friday, November 7, 2003

On his way back from taking Drake home, Adrian had decided to stop at Ling's Place. Maybe she could give him some advice. Clutch in, he revved the engine before shutting it off. *When you own a Vette, you're morally obligated to show it off.*

He checked his watch—twelve thirty a.m., no longer Thursday—and headed inside. Tyson the-one-man-football-team waved him by. Ty had been with Ling for several years and was working on his Masters degree in engineering.

On his way to the office, Adrian lingered a moment to appreciate the two scantily dressed dancers next to the DJ station. The DJ was on break. Adrian waved and smiled. The girls liked to be appreciated. The tightness in his jeans assured him that he fully appreciated them.

He poked his head into Ling's vault where she was counting out the night's proceeds. "Evening, Ling."

She kept counting and said, "You must be bored tonight, Adrian."

"How so?"

"You only come here this late when you're bored." She stopped counting. "But it's always good to see you."

He removed his brown, bomber jacket. "I'm not bored. I've been thinking over some stuff and I wanted to talk to you about it." Adrian thrust a thumb behind him. "'Course I appreciate the scenery, and you've got some of the best." He grabbed the chair next to her desk, pulled it around in front, and plopped himself down.

She jotted something on a pad, then folded her arms on her desk. "Thank you. I appreciate the compliment. How can I help?"

He scooted forward and braced his elbows on the desk with his hands under his chin. "I need counseling. I'm going downhill fast. My best years are already behind me."

"Why do you say that? You are a handsome, virile, young man. I understand you have no lack of women in your life."

"Yeah, that's true. But I mean…as a vampire I'm a total loser. Eli's disappointed in me."

"What makes you think so?"

"Well, I've been like this for five years, and I can't even do a little thing like conceal myself from him. Jonathan, the kid he just took on, is ten years old. He's only been a vamp a couple of weeks, and his telepathic powers are on the fast track. Real soon, they'll be stronger than mine, and I'll be yesterday's news, discarded trash, a has-been vampire. It royally sucks!"

"Not all of us develop in the same way or at the same rate."

"That's what Eli says. And I'm supposed to be the kid's big brother, teach him stuff. How can I do that when he's smarter than me? He reads some serious shit."

"From what Eli tells me, you are far from stupid, Adrian."

"The kid whips my ass at video games. *That's* embarrassing. On top of that, Eli's trying to make me old and wise. I don't see a future in that, either. I'll stick with young and stupid."

"Would you like a beer?" she asked.

"Gonna take more than one beer to cheer me up."

She pressed a button on her intercom and one of her waitresses came in a few moments later. "Which beer do you want, Adrian?"

"It's a Heineken night."

"Three Heinekens, please," Ling told the waitress.

While they waited, Ling placed the money in a cash box and locked that in a small safe inside the vault. She'd had the vault's main lock disabled when she transformed it into her office.

The beers arrived. She gave two to Adrian. "I think something else is bothering you."

Adrian sighed and took a pull on his beer. "Eli's idea to clean up Detroit. He's got you, me, and him. Three of us fight all the ugliness Detroit has to offer ain't a poker hand I'd bet on."

"You underestimate Eli."

"Not him, *me*. You know, sometimes I wish hadn't been changed into a vamp. It's gotten me in trouble too often."

"More trouble than if you were a normal human?"

"Well, since Eli still considers me his student, he gives me a monthly stipend—"

"An allowance, you mean," she said.

"*Stipend.* Kids get allowances. I also have my own credit card I'm responsible for. But the stipend is a generous amount and it leads me down the path of sinful gambling."

"By your own admission, you always win because you use your telepathic skills. How is that bad?"

"I take other people's money unfairly."

Ling cracked a smile. "Have you ever taken money from someone who truly needed it?"

Adrian rubbed his chin, fingering the trace beard he hadn't shaved off today. "Well...not really."

"Eli has told me about your strip poker games."

He covered his neck with his hand, hoping to hide the blush he felt rising.

"Your Robin Hood attitude in donating the lost clothing is a noble one. Eli is very proud of you."

"But he's always picking on me!"

"No more than any father would pick on his son."

"He's not—"

A scream came from down the short hall and around the corner to his right. Adrian shot out of his chair. Another scream. He ran to the girls' dressing room.

A half-naked Latina girl, with traces of white powder around her nose, convulsed on the dressing room floor. A second girl stood against the wall, hand over her mouth, shaking. "S-she only did one line."

Adrian took out his cell to call 9-1-1 but put it away before he did. The EMTs didn't respond to calls from clubs, not quickly anyway. That Ling's Place wasn't a strip club didn't matter. He knelt by the girl. "Go get Ty," he told the other girl. She didn't move. "Now!"

She ran out.

Adrian was wrapping the girl in a coat when Ty rushed in, with Ling following. "Carry her to your car and take her to the hospital."

"Right away, boss."

"You go with Ty," Ling told the other girl, "and call me to let me know her condition."

Ty picked up the stricken girl while Adrian went ahead to open the side door that led to a small lot for employees only. The other girl followed them.

"Thank you for your quick action, Adrian," Ling said to Adrian. "This way, she has a chance." She dabbed her eyes with a handkerchief. "Detroit Medical Center is less than two miles away. Ty will get her there quickly and safely."

Adrian had never before seen an emotional side to Ling.

"Let's go inside," she said. "It's getting cold."

Back in the office, Ling sat behind her desk.

Adrian settled uneasily into his chair. He finished his first beer, stuck his finger into the bottle's neck, and balanced the bottle on his knee. Staring at it, he asked, "Are you going to fire her for doing drugs?"

"She has a younger sister she's helping support. She needs the work. I hope this scares her into stopping the drugs. I will let her keep her job if she agrees to go for counseling, which I will pay for. Tonight you proved you are not worthless as a human, either, Adrian," she said.

He raised his head.

"You will make a good big brother to young Jonathan. Listen to Eli's advice."

Adrian set the empty bottle on the desk and opened his second one. "That slave stuff about Eli shocked me. What else is he hiding?"

"Why not ask him?"

"He won't tell me."

"Have you asked before?"

"Well…no. I…never knew there was anything to ask." He took a hefty swallow of the beer.

Ling leaned forward. "Now you do."

"I don't understand why he's never told me."

"Because he's waiting for you to ask him," she said.

"He told you that?" Adrian took another drink of his beer.

"Yes. Do you want something to eat?"

"Pizza smothered with everything." Ling's was the best, but the kitchen was closed now.

"Is Pizza Hut okay?" she asked

"Yeah, crispy crust soaked in oil."

She picked up the phone, pressed a number in speed dial, and ordered two large, which amazed Adrian. "Thank you," she said into the phone. She hung up and smiled at him. "Twenty minutes. You're not the only one who enjoys pizza."

"I guess I'll help Eli fix this broken city," Adrian said. "Drake wants to help, too."

"You must protect him. He's the age you were when—"

"—When I made a bad decision."

Ling's phone rang. Ty. They'd gotten the girl to the hospital, and she was going to be okay. "You have a good heart, Adrian," she said. "Eli expects you to make mistakes. He's only trying to save you from making some of the ones he made."

He finished his beer.

"Would you like another?" she asked.

He thought for a moment. "Uh. . .I'd better do near beer."

"A wise decision. Shall we get it together?"

She came around her desk and joined him. Halfway to the door, he asked, "When did you meet Eli?"

"That would be 1943. But it's a story for another time perhaps. Know that your life isn't the only one Eli Howard has saved."

When they got to the bar, Adrian noticed a different bartender. "Where's Stefan?"

"He took the night off. His sister and her husband wanted to go out, so he offered to babysit his three-year-old niece."

They sat at the bar in silence, waiting for their pizza and watching the patrons slowly clear out for the night.

An hour later, on his way out, he said, "Thanks for the advice."

"My pleasure, Mr. Shadowhawk." She winked at him.

Outside, sitting in his car, he wondered what having a normal human existence might have been like for him. His first thirteen years of living in South Dakota had been pretty good—until his parents were killed in that car accident.

CHAPTER SIXTEEN

Detroit—Friday, November 7, 2003

With his first paycheck from Eli in hand, Drake knocked on the door of his father's study. On Friday nights, normal adults relaxed at the end of workweek. Not Ethan. When he didn't work late, he was out of town. *Given this once-in-my-lifetime exception, why not take full advantage of the situation?* What did he have to lose?

Ethan had come home shortly before seven; Drake had already eaten dinner. He'd learned years ago that Ethan Radley didn't like to discuss his day—or his son's day, or anything for that matter—at dinner.

"Come in," said the cold voice.

"Got a minute, Dad?" Calling Ethan Radley 'Dad' insulted fathers everywhere, but he was in a precarious position with his father and didn't want to screw up again.

"Is it important, Drake? I'm rather busy." Ethan was writing on pieces of paper scattered all over his desk.

Busy on a Friday night? Give me a fucking break. "Just take a couple of quick minutes," he said.

Ethan looked up from the papers on his desk. "Have a seat." He went back to his work.

"I've been thinking how I could better spend my spare time. I saw this ad in school from this dude, er, professor who teaches history at Wayne State and is looking for an assistant."

"Wayne State? You're going to Harvard next year."

"Yeah, I know. This is an internship for a senior taking AP History, a chance to get a taste of college. I made an appointment to talk to him."

Ethan perked up. His father was *paying attention* to him?

"That was good initiative on your part. And...?"

"We talked and he offered me the job. It's ten to twenty hours a week, depending on my schedule, grading papers, typing up exams, preparing handouts for his class. Maybe some library research, too."

"You've cleared this with school? I don't want anything to jeopardize your academic standing or your entry into Harvard."

"No problem. I only have four classes, and I'm way ahead in all of them. Besides, Christmas break is coming up."

Ethan pondered this information. Should he show his father the paycheck yet? No, better to wait for a reaction. Too much initiative was just as bad. Ethan Radley liked believing he was in control and that everything was either his idea or the direct outcome of one of his ideas.

"Well," he finally said, "your recent attitude had begun to worry me. Your mother suggested it might be senioritis, so I decided to see how things developed. You've pleasantly surprised me and restored my faith in you. When would this job begin?"

"Uh, it sort of already did."

"Oh?"

Had he overstepped? "The professor had other interested applicants. He said he really wanted *me*, but he needed a quick decision. I didn't want to lose out on such an excellent opportunity, so I said yes."

Ethan's stoic expression revealed nothing. Drake hoped his father hadn't detected the myriad—he liked that word—of lies.

Finally, his father cracked a faint smile. "I've tried to teach you to recognize good opportunities and to not let the important ones slip away. I believe you made a good decision."

What a fantasy world his father lived in. When had Ethan Radley taken time to teach his son anything except blind obedience? Or did he prefer obeisance? Okay, now for his last surprise. Drake rose from his chair and handed his father the check from Eli. "Here's my first paycheck."

His father examined it, then frowned. "This isn't from the university."

Drake smoothly delivered his rehearsed explanation. "It's from the professor's personal business account. He's paying me directly. He said the university's red tape wasn't worth all the time he'd spend to get through it, especially since I'll only be working with him a few months, until I start school next fall. He'll show the university the record of payment to me and he'll get reimbursed."

"I see. This check is rather generous for an internship. Don't disappoint him." His father said it as if he thought Drake didn't deserve it and probably wouldn't come through. Nothing his son did was ever good enough.

"I won't. Um, one other thing. Is there any chance I could get my Jeep back? The buses aren't reliable, and cabs are expensive."

Ethan held the check in front of him before handing it back. "Since you took the initiative to find a job, the least I can do is restore your transportation privileges. I want you to have a safe way to get to and from your job. With winter coming and since it's been in the garage for a month, make an appointment with my mechanic to have it checked and to be sure it's ready for winter. Tell him to bill me for it… But since you're earning a paycheck, I expect you to pay it back."

"Fine."

Ethan glared at him and Drake realized he'd answered with more attitude than he should have. "That's fair. Oh, one of my school friends wants to study bioengineering in college next year. Is it okay if I give him a company tour one day this week after school?"

"That's fine," Ethan said. He sounded annoyed at having had too much of his valuable time taken away. "Tell security to call me if they have any questions. Don't forget that your actions and behavior reflect on me as well. Don't screw it up."

"I won't, Father."

Ethan went back to his work. Drake quietly left the study and headed up to his room.

Calling Ethan Radley "Dad" earlier was just *wrong*. At least "Father" was accurate in the biological sense. Although sometimes Drake wondered if he'd been grown in a test tube instead of in his mother's womb.

Drake went into his room and shut the door. *Transportation reinstated. Commence Black Ops.* He took out his cell phone to call Adrian.

***

Detroit—Monday, November 10, 2003

In his newly returned Jeep, Drake went to pick up Adrian.

Adrian answered the door wearing his sunglasses.

"You sure this is gonna work?" Drake asked.

"All I need is server access, which we'll get today. Come on in while I grab my jacket and gear. Got your backpack?"

"It's in the Jeep."

In the heavy, late-afternoon traffic, it took over an hour to get to Troy. At four thirty, nearly sunset, they pulled into the Radley Biotech parking lot. Drake grabbed his backpack from the backseat.

"Hi, Drake. What brings you out here?" Pete the security guard said. Drake had hoped Pete would be on lobby duty. The company was twelve years old. Pete had been here nine years and knew all about the strained relationship between father and son.

"Pete, this is Adrian, one of my classmates. He wants to study biochemical engineering in college next year. Dad said it'd be okay if I gave Adrian a tour. He said to call him if you had any questions."

"No problem. Kind of late in the day, isn't it?"

They already had a perfect cover story. "Adrian has a full class schedule and a part-time job evenings and weekends, so after school is the only time he could make it."

Pete studied Adrian. Fortunately, Adrian did look young enough to be in high school. "Biochemical engineering, huh? I hope you have good grades. I hear it's a competitive field."

"Straight As," Drake said.

Pete nodded at Adrian. "You're Native American."

"How'd you guess?" Adrian politely said. "Most folks think I'm Hispanic."

"We get a lot of different nationalities come through here. I've made it a hobby guessing what they are. Okay, print your name here on the form and sign at the bottom. Drake, you sign the line below his name."

Pete took the form and checked it over. "Shadowhawk. What tribe are you, if you don't mind me asking?"

"Lakota."

"I'm glad Drake's found a friend. Good luck in college." Pete handed Adrian his temporary visitor's badge. "Sorry, but I have to check the backpack."

Drake knew the routine. Check what's going in and what's coming out.

"What's this?" Pete asked, picking up the bubble-wrapped circuit board.

"It's a new video card for Drake's PC," Adrian said. "I gave it to him in school today. Drake, give me your car keys and I'll put it out in your Jeep."

"It's okay," Pete said. "I'll mark it on the log and it won't be questioned when you leave, in case I'm not here. The night guard comes on at six thirty. Okay, step through the metal detector." He pointed at the archway Ethan had installed a couple of years ago. When they were on the other side, Pete handed Drake the card.

When he was past the guard's desk, Drake let out a small sigh of relief. "What would you have done if he'd wanted you take it out to the car?"

"I telepathed him. He wasn't gonna hassle you 'cuz you're the owner's son."

They'd agreed that Drake really would give him a tour of the building and talk to some of the lab people. Pete was a cool guy, so he wouldn't be a problem, but they wanted their asses covered in case Ethan checked up on him. Drake's badge admitted him to most places. The only ones he couldn't access were the biohazard labs and a couple of restricted areas. They weren't interested in those anyway.

At five forty-two, having completed their bogus tour, Drake took Adrian to the third floor. He pressed his badge against the access pad next to the security monitor room. The lock buzzed open. Racks of equipment, TV monitors, and metal cabinets filled the ten-by-fifteen room. A rolling cart in the middle held a toolbox. Test equipment and coils of wire littered a narrow bench along one of the smaller walls. All the security monitors plus the lobby desk and security office hooked into this room. The guards didn't monitor from here because the cluttered room had no place to sit comfortably—no place to kick back and relax on the job.

In this room, the security server and a PC were connected to the company's network. The PC gave Adrian access to it.

"You really a hacker?" Drake asked.

Adrian grinned. "When I want to be."

"Does Eli approve?"

"Eli says I'm responsible for my own actions, which means know what you're doing and how to cover your ass. You're sure no one will come in here?"

"I've only seen the techs come in when there's a problem. It's not a high-security room because I guess they figure everything is protected with passwords. I guess that's not a problem for you."

Adrian smiled evilly. "Not usually."

"If anyone comes in," Drake said, "I'll pretend to be showing you around, like in the labs. I thought you asked some great questions on the pretend tour. I didn't know what the hell you were talking about, but the lab guys did. Did Eli teach you that stuff?"

"Eli made me read and study in my early vampire days. You've seen his library. This biotech shit is cool, and there's a lot online. *Please* don't tell anyone I'm a geek. It would ruin my party-guy reputation and my sex life. Chicks don't want geeks." He held out his hand. "Give me that network card."

The bubble-wrap package actually contained two wireless network cards nested back to back. Drake unwrapped them, then handed one to Adrian. The second was a decoy. In case another guard examined the package, there'd be the one they supposedly brought in. As they'd hoped, Pete hadn't opened it for close inspection.

Adrian installed the card into one of the computers.

Pete knew the workings of Radley Biotech more than he let on to most people. Drake had learned from him about the camera Ethan had installed in his office a few months ago. "Doesn't Ethan, like, legally have to tell people he's recording them?" Drake had asked. Pete reminded him that notices were clearly posted around the building that the premises were monitored. Drake had rolled his eyes at that.

"So, how does this work?" Drake asked Adrian.

"You're probably better off not knowing, in case we're captured and tortured."

"Dude, we're already in this together."

"Okay, here's the tech-challenged explanation."

"I am *not* tech challenged."

"Okay. Your father's employees can access their company email from outside."

"So?"

"I'm hooking the video line from the camera in your father's office to the email server."

"Won't everyone be able to access it then?" Drake asked.

"No, because I'll configure it with a password only we know. When I finish here, we'll be able to activate the camera and monitor it from home."

"Sweet."

"There's only one possible glitch." Adrian pointed to a piece of equipment. "That's an expensive, tapeless recorder with a RAM drive and hard drive, to make changing videotapes unnecessary. It creates a problem for us. I have to disable the recording function. If your father tries to use it, it won't work. I checked the hard drive. It's blank except for an initial test when it was installed. He hasn't used it yet, so I think we're okay. When we're done with our nefarious activities, I'll reconnect it and they'll never know the difference."

"You hope."

"Hey, I'm a vampire. I'm supposed to live large and dangerous."

Drake laughed.

"Once I configure the IP addresses and set the password, we'll be good," Adrian said.

At six ten, they were back in the lobby. "Did you see everything you wanted to?" Pete asked them.

"Sure did," Adrian said. "This is one sweet place. Drake said maybe his dad would give me a job when I graduate college."

Drake took Pete's expression to mean, *Not a fucking chance in hell.* He opened his backpack. Pete touched the bubble-wrapped package and checked it off on his sheet. "Thanks for letting us in, Pete. Have a good evening."

"You, too, Drake. Oh, your father is still here, working late as usual."

No surprise there. "Too bad you can't tell the night guard not to come in, lock my father in the building, and go home right now."

Pete gave him a knowing smile.

On the way to the Jeep, Adrian said, "You should be careful who you say stuff to."

"Pete's cool. He knows how it is. Last April my school had this field trip and I'd forgotten to get the permission slip signed. Mom wasn't home, so I called Ethan. Because he poured money into the school's sports program, they knew him and would've accepted his word over the phone. Ethan told Pete to tell me he wasn't in. So, I had to stay at school and couldn't go on the field trip. Getting the picture?"

"How could a father do that to his only kid?"

"Okay, I'm not one to hold grudges for long—I only held that one for three months. I decided to show him I cared even if he didn't. His birthday is July 2, and it was on a Wednesday. I copped a peek at the day planner on his desk at home. He had a two-thirty meeting marked 'important' so I knew he'd be in his office. I wanted to surprise him by taking him to lunch. When I got there, I asked Pete to buzz him. Once again, kind, considerate Ethan told Pete to tell me he was out of the office. Yeah, Pete understands perfectly."

They got into the Jeep. Drake put his seat belt on and started the engine. "You sure this'll work?"

"You doubt the skills of Adrian Shadowhawk, Master Hacker?"

Drake chuckled. "Never." He backed out, hooked his hands over the steering wheel, and burned rubber out of the lot, throwing Adrian back against his seat.

Once on the expressway, he clamped his left hand on the steering wheel and used his right to gesture. "Check this out:

"Yo, Ethan dude,
"you're 'bout to get screwed;
"we're gonna find
"what's on your mind."

He ended with a firm, upward thrust of his middle finger. "Whadda ya think?"

"That it's probably too late for father and son to consider joint counseling."

When they got back to Adrian's house, they tested the system.

"Very extremely sweet," Drake said.

***

Detroit—Tuesday, November 11, 2003

Veteran's Day. Official school holiday. Ethan went to work; Drake drove to Adrian's, a safer place to spy from than from his own house. Adrian's home computer room, which Adrian called Hack Attack Central, was a twelve-by-fifteen room painted dark red. Opposite the door, an L-shaped table attached to the walls ran the full length of one long wall and half of a shorter one. Shelves held software, CDs, books, and an assortment of computer parts and circuit boards. A closet contained two spare monitors. The wood floor let Adrian slide his rollered chair freely along the long table where his three PCs and two servers were more or less evenly spaced. The shorter side table served as his workbench. Adrian kept this room tidy, unlike his bedroom.

Lunchtime came. They were scarfing deep-dish pan pizza when Ethan's hot female administrative assistant entered the office pushing a small cart with covered dishes. Drake and Adrian drooled all over their pizza. She rolled the cart in front of the desk, uncovered the dishes, then left.

"Where's he get steak?" Adrian asked.

"The company cafeteria. Wednesday is normally steak day, but it's Ethan's company, so he gets whatever he wants whenever he wants."

"Want another Pepsi?" Drake asked.

"Sure."

Nothing else happened for the next hour. Ethan's admin returned for the cart. "Don't forget your appointment with Mr. Hayes at nine this evening," she said before she left.

Drake and Adrian gaped at each other. "And we've got a front-row seat," Drake said. "Un-fucking-believable."

***

At eight thirty that evening, Drake sat tensely next to Adrian as they watched the progress bar creeping across the bottom of the nineteen-inch flatscreen monitor for the third time. Two previous attempts to connect to the security server at Radley Biotech failed.

Drake chewed on a fingernail. "What's wrong?"

"Stay frosty," Adrian said. "Internet traffic is usually heavy in the evenings. If it doesn't work this way, I can force it through a lower priority path. Not to worry. We'll get in." Suddenly, the progress bar flashed all the way to the right and the connection established. "See?"

For the next half-hour they watched Ethan seated at his desk, working at his PC. He jumped at the electronic beep of the desk phone. His fingers danced nervously over his keyboard. The phone rang again. Ethan pressed a button. "Yes?"

"Mr. Hayes is here, Mr. Radley."

"Send him up."

"Do you want him escorted?"

"Of course not! He has full security clearance."

"Yes, sir."

"What's up your father's butt?" Adrian asked Drake.

"Dunno. Pretty tense even for Ethan Radley. Guess we'll find out. Cyrus Hayes is really bad news, huh?"

"Bad enough that Eli's scared of him. Remember that first night you were here? Well, Eli didn't tell me any of the details, but there's definitely some dark history between them. He let it slip that he should've killed Cyrus years ago when he had the chance."

"Whoa. That's some serious shit. I got the impression Eli was the peaceful type."

"Me, too. Eli and I need to schedule a serious one-on-one. I'm finding out there's a lot of stuff—"

"Shhh."

"Good evening, Cyrus," Ethan said. "What's on your mind?"

Drake detected a hint of sarcasm, but Ethan's fingers twitched the way they did when he was nervous or upset.

"I wanted to inform you of new arrangements. On Friday, we will begin using human volunteers in my experiments."

"What kind of experiments?"

"I'm not at liberty to divulge the details. The volunteers have signed waivers and have been given assurances of humane treatment."

"What does this have to do with me?"

"They will be staying here, so I need a room for them." He handed Ethan an envelope. "Here is a list of requirements plus money to cover the additional expenses."

"This was not part of our agreement."

"Our 'agreement' says I am paying for the use of your facilities and the rental of space. It put no limits on what I could or could not do within that space."

"It's out of the question. We aren't authorized to do experiments on humans in this facility."

"It's not a request. If you're concerned, I suggest you implement additional security measures to prevent anyone from finding out. If you wish to rescind our agreement, I'll expect reimbursement of the entire sum I have paid you to date."

"Less the cost of renovations to my building," Ethan added.

"*All* of it. If you check the wording and terms of our contract, it states that should you renege before the completion of its term, I'm entitled to the return of all monies paid, as a penalty. I'm surprised your lawyers didn't advise you of this clause, but you didn't let your lawyers read it, did you?"

Ethan's face grew red.

"They would have advised you not to sign it. You won't dare take the case to court because you can't afford to have it known what kind of experiments you allow to be conducted here. I have more resources at my disposal than you can possibly imagine, Ethan. I can disappear without a trace, and if you decide to pull out of our agreement, your company will become the target of a government investigation faster than you can possibly imagine."

The redness and rage in Ethan's face were so great that Drake expected his father might have a heart attack at any moment.

"Do we have an understanding, Ethan?"

Ethan nodded slowly.

Cyrus pointed at the envelope, still in Ethan's hand. "Please see to my requirements." Cyrus walked to the door. With one hand on the knob, he said, "One more thing. I will be staying here to observe, at least for the next few days."

Pulling a handkerchief from his inside jacket pocket, Ethan wiped his forehead.

Drake's heart raced, and his breathing sped up.

Adrian put a hand on his shoulder. "You okay? Seriously, your face looks like a vampire just drained you."

"Dude, we gotta *do* something."

"*We* do nothing except tell Eli. You stay away from Cyrus Hayes. Good friends are hard to come by. I don't want to lose the best one I've found so far."

Drake blew a loud breath out through his mouth. "I don't want to lose me either."

CHAPTER SEVENTEEN

Detroit—Friday, November 14, 2003

Adrian stood inside the entrance of Ling's Place and scanned the dancing patrons. Femme Fatale, the regular DJ, was making them happy with her music and her body. All the changes in his life lately had kept him busy. Having no time for a dishonest game of poker was one thing, but the three weeks of abstinence threatened his sanity. He unbuttoned his Navy peacoat and slipped through the crowd to the bar while casting lustful glances at the female patrons.

"Evening, Adrian," Stefan the bartender said. "Soft or hard?"

"Huh?"

"Drink. What'll you have?"

"Red wine."

"Really? I thought you were a beer person."

"Really."

"You okay?"

"I'm fine."

Stefan put up a glass and poured the wine into it. "On the house."

Adrian dropped a five into the tip glass.

"Thanks."

Drinking his wine, he noticed Ling's vault office was open. He didn't see her inside. What she'd said last time came back to him. Did Eli really think of him as a son? *No way.* Eli had too much baggage in his past to have parental leanings. More like a guidance counselor: helpful and supportive. Except, in his heart, Adrian knew better. Just as he'd known Ling was right when she'd said it.

All week he'd been thinking over the recent revelations. He'd never seen Eli so spooked as when Drake had mentioned Cyrus Hayes being in Detroit. And Eli had saved Ling's life at some point? He thought he knew Eli, but it was turning out he didn't know shit. Hell, in the past month he'd gone from a stay-out-all-night, do-as-he-pleased, getting-laid-often, party animal to…a responsible, stay-at-home, big brother? *Shiiit.* No wonder he wasn't getting any.

"See that dancer?" Stefan had returned and was pointing at the dancer next to the DJ. She was the one who had been in the dressing room last week, the one who'd screamed for help. "She told me she'd like to wrap her lean legs around you and screw your brains out."

Adrian choked, and wine spewed out his nose. "Fuck!" He grabbed a bar napkin and blew his nose hard into it. What was this new thing with him and beverages out his nose? He coughed several times.

"Sorry about that, man. You okay?"

"Yeah." He held up the wine-stained napkin. "You don't want to know what snotting red wine feels like." He wiped his nose with a fresh napkin. "Pepsi is worse. Take it from someone who's recently done the comparison."

Stefan laughed. "I bet Bacardi one-fifty-one would beat them both. It's on me if you want to check it out."

"Fuck, no! She didn't really say that, did she?"

"Naw. Just bustin' on you. Seriously, she did ask me to thank you, said it was nice to see someone care." He put up another glass of wine and went to wait on a customer.

Stefan's remark had certainly changed his mood, increased his heart rate, and sent blood rushing into all the right places. Was it warm in here tonight, or just him? He shed his coat and put it on the empty stool beside him.

He hadn't decided if being a vamp was a plus or a minus for his sex life. On the one hand, he was twenty-two years old with a sex drive still in its horny teens. On the other hand, he was twenty-two years old with a sex drive still in its horny teens. He drank his wine and watched Stefan serving his customers. He had been with Ling a couple of years and pretty much kept to himself. They talked from time to time, and recently he had asked what it was like being a vampire. Since all bartenders were part counselor, he thought being telepathic would be great for business.

Screams came from behind him. "What the fuck?" He leaped off the barstool. Smoke billowed from the coatroom near the front entrance, but he didn't see any fire. The music stopped and minor panic ensued as people pushed and shoved. A male voice came over the speakers, "Everyone, please remain calm and head to the emergency exits." More shouts and screams. "*Please remain calm!*" But panic had already spread through the place. The bouncers were doing their best to move people outside.

Then he spotted a couple flailing about in the coatroom. He pushed through the crowd and reached them seconds later. He grabbed a coat from the room and threw it over them. "Get down. I'll get you out." He'd almost cleared the entrance to the room when something exploded behind him. Heat swept over his back. He pushed the couple the rest of the way out of the room. More screams came from farther away.

With a loud whoosh, frosty mist sprayed across his back. "I got them," a voice said as someone took the couple.

"Get another extinguisher in here!" That was Stefan.

Adrian looked up to see Ty with a second fire extinguisher. The sprinklers in the coatroom finally activated and finished the job.

Stefan spun around to assess the room. Then he helped Adrian up and tugged him toward the bar. "Come on, let's get you tended to."

Adrian grunted and winced. "Shouldn't we evacuate?"

"Fire's out." They went around behind the bar. "Get that shirt off!" While Adrian unbuttoned it, Stefan grabbed a clean towel and soaked it under cold water.

The club was nearly vacant, and someone had shut off the sprinklers. Interesting that only the ones in the coatroom had activated. Stefan carefully took off Adrian's ruined denim shirt, bent him forward, and gently laid the wet towel on his back.

Adrian arched his back. "Ah!"

"That hurt?"

"Just cold." Hunched over, he took a deep breath. "Feels good." He heard sirens outside.

"Lucky you weren't wearing a T-shirt. Peeling that off might have been painful." He plugged the bar sink, dumped in some ice, and tossed in two more bar towels. He pulled the towel off Adrian's back. "This will feel *really* cold." He laid on a fresh, icy one.

Adrian gasped. "Fuck!"

"Cold?"

"I'll be frozen soon. Aren't you supposed to put grease or ointment on burns?"

"Nope. That slows the healing. Ling made me take a class, as a condition for hiring me."

"I'm glad she did."

Stefan carefully lifted the towels, inspected the burns, and put on a fresh, cold towel. "Do you want to go to the hospital?"

"What do you think?"

"It's mostly first-degree, with a couple of small blisters. Since you guys heal fast, I say you'll be fine in a couple of days. But if you want to go wait in the emergency room for a couple of hours so they can tell you the same thing…"

"I'll have Eli check me out." Adrian managed a smile. "He's my health insurance. Any idea what happened?"

Stefan looked around the club. "I don't think it was an accident, if that's what you mean."

"You see Ling anywhere?"

"There." He pointed at the front entrance.

Eli had arrived, with Jonathan, and was talking to Ling. Adrian waved to catch their attention.

A few minutes later, an impatient Jonathan had dragged Eli over to the bar. Seeing Adrian's cloth-covered back, he looked worried. "Are you okay?"

"What happened?" Eli asked.

"Adrian decided to play hero," Stefan said. "Check his back."

Eli lifted the wet cloth. "It's nothing serious. It'll be tender for a few days. Take some aspirin or Advil if it bothers you."

"I'm tough," Adrian said. "So, how did you get here so fast?"

"Half an hour ago, I received an anonymous email warning me to stay out of certain matters that are not my concern. It mentioned there would be a demonstration. I had a feeling it might be here. Can you trace the email?"

"Probably," Adrian said. "Drake can help me."

"Be careful about involving Drake. His father's connection to Cyrus Hayes could put him in danger. Ling is going to hire two bodyguards, and I think you should sign up for martial arts training."

"Sweet," Adrian said. "Maybe Drake should have it, too?"

"I'll pay for him if he's interested."

"And me," Jonathan said.

"Wouldn't Jonathan be safer back with his parents?" Adrian said to Eli.

"No, here I can protect him, but I'll expect your help."

"Do we know yet exactly what happened?"

"The fire marshal found a spent smoke grenade and traces of a stun grenade, normally not dangerous, but it must have gone off right behind you and burned your back."

"There is no serious damage," Ling said. "We'll have everything cleaned up by Monday night."

"Whoever planted them knew how to circumvent your security," Stefan said.

"Yes, my bouncers rarely search the women."

"This place is so cool," Jonathan said. "Will you bring me here sometime?"

"Sorry, bro, you gotta be eighteen to party here." Adrian gritted his teeth as Stefan put a fresh, cold cloth on his back.

"Who would do this?" Ling asked.

"I'll bet serious money it's Cyrus Hayes," Eli said.

CHAPTER EIGHTEEN

Detroit—Saturday, November 15, 2003

The doorbell startled Eli. After a sleepless night, he'd been grading papers most of the day in a futile effort to distract himself from worrying about other matters.

"Good evening, Eli," Drake said. "How are you tonight?"

"I've been better."

"Something wrong?"

Adrian came down the stairs in his sweats.

"I'll let Adrian tell you."

Drake checked his watch. "Dude, how come you're not ready? The movie starts in half an hour."

"Sorry, man, I forgot to call you. I was sleeping all day and just woke up a couple of hours ago. Some nasty shit happened at Ling's last night. First, a smoke bomb went off in the coatroom, then there was a small explosion that caused a fire. Deliberate. I got some burns on my back."

"Dude! You okay?"

"Yeah. No worse than a nasty sunburn. I'm healing."

"Anyone else hurt? How bad was the damage?"

"No one else hurt, and no major damage."

"Who'd do something like that?"

"Eli's had me checking it out. That's why I forgot to call you. Business before pleasure." Adrian rolled his eyes at Eli. "The email came from somewhere in New York City. I'm having trouble finding out any more."

"You've been at it since you got up. Take a break. You and Drake go enjoy yourselves, and come at it fresh later. Jonathan will be awake soon. He concentrates on his lessons better when you're not here."

"He's asleep, too?" Drake said.

Adrian nodded. "I couldn't sleep last night, so he stayed up to keep me company. We didn't crash until nearly sunrise. 'Cuz of my back, you'll have to drive. Want to take my Vette?"

Drake beamed. "You'd let me drive it?"

"Why not?" He said to Eli, "Thanks for letting me go. We'll probably grab something to eat. I've got my cell."

They left and Eli returned to the library. The email had come from New York? Who in New York knew his email address? As he sat at his desk, a new email arrived.

Next time I will hit closer to home.

Why was this happening? This wasn't Cyrus' style, at least it didn't used to be. Or had a new enemy, one he wasn't aware of, entered the scene? Other than Ling, Adrian, and Drake, no one knew about his desire to clean up Detroit—which was still in the thought stage—and he hadn't shared that with either Ysabel or Dietrich. So, he doubted the warnings had anything to do with his Detroit reform idea. The only thing that made sense was Cyrus saw him as a serious threat to whatever he was doing or planning.

"When are you gonna take me out to have some fun, Uncle Eli?"

Eli looked up. Jonathan, wide awake, entered the library in his pajamas.

"I'm tired of staying here. When am I gonna learn to be a proper vampire? When do I get to hunt humans like Adrian does?"

"What?"

Jonathan approached the desk. "Adrian gets to feed on humans and I never do."

"Now, slow down. Is that what he told you?"

"Well, sort of."

"What exactly did he tell you that he does at night?"

"He says he goes out and plays with humans."

Eli laughed. "He goes to the nightclubs and gambling casinos, which you're too young for. Sometimes he plays poker with his friends. That's what he meant."

"He says he snacks on humans and hangs out with Goths."

"Adrian needs to be more careful with what he tells you. Do you know what Goths are?"

"Uh huh. I checked them out on the Internet. They're pretty weird, like a religious cult."

He really didn't want to discuss this with Jonathan, but complete trust between them was essential. "Let's go into the living room." They sat together on the couch. "Stop me if you don't understand something. Okay?"

Jonathan did a double thumbs up. "'Kay."

"Some Goths, not all of them, are into religious cult behavior, but most simply want their own identity and to be part of a group that accepts them. They dress in black, wear dark eye makeup, and listen to certain kinds of music to be different. Unlike many Native Americans and African Americans and other ethnic groups—"

"And vampires?"

Eli smiled. "Of course, and vampires. All of those already have a racial and cultural identity. The Goths create their own."

"That's what one website said."

"Do you understand it?"

"Sort of."

"Well, there's nothing wrong with wanting your own identity, but like anything else, you have to do it for the right reasons. Sometimes troubled teens get into the Goth culture, and from there they may get into drugs and into trouble with the law and worse."

"I read that, too."

Jonathan surprised him with his knowledge, but the boy didn't yet have the wisdom to understand all of what he was reading. "Adrian met this one group of Goths that practices a blood ritual every full moon," Eli said. "It's nothing really. I told him that he shouldn't associate with them."

"What do they do?" Jonathan asked.

"They drink each other's blood."

"How do they do that?"

"Adrian says they prick their fingers and each one sucks a few drops."

"That's all?"

"That's all."

"Bo-ring."

"That's what Adrian said, but he tells me that they think it's cool having a vampire with them to witness the ritual," Eli said. "Hey, how about you and I go out tonight? To a mall, perhaps?

"Sure! Will you buy me some Goth stuff?"

"I think you're too young for that."

Jonathan thought about that. "Maybe just *one* thing?"

"No."

"I need some new sneakers. Can I take blood from someone at the mall?"

"No, Jonathan. Before we go out, you need to understand some things. Before you became a vampire, did you know vampires really existed?"

"No..."

"And do you understand that we're nothing like the vampires you've read about or seen in the movies or on TV?"

"I guess so."

"I'm going to have a long talk with Adrian later about what he's telling you and how he behaves. For one thing, the humans he hangs out with are a small group, and he's known them for a while so they understand what we are. But there are people out there who will hurt us because they *don't* understand. That's why we have to be careful. If you were still a human and just found out that vampires were real, would you trust them not to hurt you?"

Jonathan thought about that. "Probably not."

"Good. Don't forget it. We are a lot more human than those vampires in movies and in stories and legends. The best way to protect yourself is to act like you did before your uncle changed you. Act like you're no different than anyone else. Understand?"

"Yeah. I wish you were my father."

"You have a father."

"Yeah, but he never lets me do cool stuff."

"Do you want to eat here or in the mall?"

"Your food's better, but eating mall food is fun. I'm glad I still like human food."

"Go get dressed."

Jonathan ran out of the library.

The Council prohibited changing humans indiscriminately for this reason. Children presented special problems because their cognitive development hadn't reached the analytical stages. Although Jonathan's change on the surface had been surprisingly mild, the subtle emotional changes had to be monitored.

He'd deal with the boy's feelings for his father later. Adrian, at seventeen, had been a challenge, but Eli was able to deal with Adrian as a teacher to a student. With Jonathan, he had to be a parent, and he had no experience with that. Ling had helped with Adrian, but she also lacked experience with young children. As for Ysabel, she had had a family long ago, when the world was very different. He'd talk to Adrian and they'd work through it together.

Eli shut his eyes and exhaled through his mouth. The past few days had brought too many unexpected surprises.

***

Eli and Jonathan arrived at Twelve Oaks Mall a little past seven. Because mall lights were too bright for their eyes, at home they'd found a pair of Adrian's sunglasses that weren't a bad temporary fit for Jonathan. They went to buy sunglasses first then had pizza.

During their walk through the mall to buy sneakers, Eli sensed Jonathan's growing hunger for human blood and hoped he wouldn't have to exercise control over the boy for that.

Outside a sports store, Jonathan stopped cold. "No! I don't want to go in here!"

"Why not? You like to play soccer."

"I *hate* it! I hate all of it!"

The memory of his accident? "Let's go sit down." He found some benches out in the mall with no one around them. "Do you want to talk about it?"

"No." Jonathan folded his arms and rounded his lips in a typical little boy pout.

"If I'm going to understand, you have to tell me what the problem is." He waited for Jonathan to decide when to respond. Reading the boy's mind would breach the growing trust between them.

Something else was puzzling. A few minutes ago, when Jonathan's emotions had burst forth, he'd felt a surge of telepathic power from the boy. For being changed only three weeks ago, his power shouldn't be developing this quickly. Apparently, the normal development rules didn't apply to someone his age. Dietrich would know the answer or could suggest someone who did, but the less contact he had with Dietrich right now the better, at least until he had more information and learned the source of the mysterious email. He didn't believe Dietrich carried the blame for any of the recent events, but he wasn't completely divorced from them, either. Lately, Dietrich's discretion had been faltering.

"I wanna go home now," Jonathan said.

"We still need to get sneakers for you, but if you want to leave…"

"Can I have my own computer?"

"Doesn't Adrian share his with you?"

"I only get to use it when he's not home."

"But he has more than one."

"He won't let me touch those. They're dedicated to other stuff, he says."

"I can have Adrian build you one."

"He's too busy."

"There's a Dell store here. Let's see what they've got—on one condition. I'll be having you study some things online, and you have to promise to do your homework first. Okay?"

Jonathan gave him a thumb up. "I can live with that. Are you gonna have Adrian put in parental controls?"

"Yes, for now anyway. But that doesn't mean we're restricting what you can learn. I don't want to stop you from learning about anything. There are many ways to present a subject. Things on the Internet are not always presented appropriately for someone your age. I want to be sure you're seeing things the best way for you. You can come to me with questions anytime. I'll always do my best to explain. Parental controls are not foolproof, either. If they're blocking a site you think you should have access to, or if you're seeing something you aren't sure you should, let Adrian or me know."

Jonathan smiled. "That's fair."

They decided a laptop would be best, being portable. That way Jonathan could use it anywhere in the house. Eli bought a Dell Corporate laptop with a D500 Centrino processor, the best in the store. But Jonathan should have something to make him feel more independent, something Adrian did not yet possess.

A half-hour later, they exited the mall's new Apple store, and Jonathan was the proud owner of an Apple iPod. "This is sooo sweet! Adrian will love using it."

"You'll share it with him?"

"'Course. He's my big brother." Jonathan admired his new acquisition. "'Sides he's gotta show me how to load music into it." He tilted his head up. "Thanks, Uncle Eli." Jonathan hugged him.

Eli bought him a giant chocolate chip cookie and found a bench for them to sit while Jonathan ate it. "Jonathan, I'd like you to try something for me. When any kids come near us, tell me what they're thinking."

"How am I supposed to do that?"

"Just concentrate. Vampires can read minds. It may be too soon for you, but I want you to try."

A young boy eight or nine and his mother walked by. "He's mad at his mother because she won't buy him a new video game," Jonathan said. "She told him to ask Santa Claus." He grinned. "This is cool!"

Next came a young man and woman. The woman was pushing a stroller with a baby girl in it. Eli read the man's thoughts too late and hoped Jonathan hadn't picked those up.

"I can't tell anything from the baby," Jonathan said. "She's too young. The man isn't happy about the baby."

"How do you know that?" Eli asked tentatively.

"You really want me to say what he was thinking?"

With the boy's power developing this fast, such things were unavoidable. He'd guide Jonathan the best he could. "Tell me."

Jonathan blushed. "I'm not supposed to say that word."

"It's okay. You're not saying it yourself. You're just repeating his thoughts, no different than if you were reading out loud from a book."

Jonathan signaled Eli to lean closer and whispered, "He said, he wished he'd used a condom before he fucked her that one time."

"Do you know what that means?"

Jonathan blushed more. "Sort of."

"And it embarrasses you."

"Uh huh."

"Did you learn a lesson from this?"

"That I gotta be careful when I read thoughts?"

"Yes. And what else?"

Jonathan scrunched up his face. "I'm not sure."

"Always remember that people's thoughts are private. Would you want someone reading yours without your permission?"

"No."

"Remember that if you want people to respect you, you must respect them." Eli checked his watch. Twenty minutes before closing and a telescope later, they left the mall.

"Thanks for all the cool things, Uncle Eli."

"I'm glad you like them. I'll add astronomy to your science studies."

"Sweet."

On the way home, Eli asked him, "Have you ever heard of the Museum of Science and Industry in Chicago?"

"Yeah! They have a real German submarine there. I read about it last year and asked Mom if Dad would take me."

Jonathan's sadness hit him. He decided to read the boy's thoughts this time. Jonathan had overheard his father say it was a waste of time, and it wasn't healthy for a kid to sit in front of a computer all day. He should be outside playing.

"If you'd like to go there, it will be your Christmas present."

"Really? You mean it?"

"It's a promise."

"Can Adrian and Drake go, too?"

"If they want to."

Chicago was a five-hour drive from Detroit, and the museum wasn't open in the evening. Figuring out the logistics would be relatively simple. Getting Ben Clayton's permission for the trip might require more effort.

***

"It's a good night to observe the moon," Eli told him when they arrived home. Other than a few clouds, the sky was clear, and the moon was nearly three-quarters full.

"You set up the telescope and I'll go try out my laptop," Jonathan said. "When Adrian gets home, he can help me with my iPod." Grabbing the PC, he hurried up the stairs and disappeared into his room.

Eli carried the telescope into the library. First, he checked his message machine. One call. From Ysabel. She asked him to call her back tonight. That could wait. With Jonathan occupied upstairs, this was a good opportunity to call Ben Clayton.

"Ben Clayton."

"Mr. Clayton, this is Eli Howard."

"Is something wrong with my son?"

"Jonathan is fine. He's occupied at the moment, and I thought we should talk."

"Sorry, I forgot that your kind works at night." The edge in Ben's voice went away. "How is he doing?"

"Adjusting quickly to the changes in him. As I told you during your visit, we have little experience with ones so young. I do have some concerns, however."

"I thought you said he's fine—"

"Physically and emotionally, yes. Psychologically he harbors some resentment toward you."

"What the hell does that mean? I'm his *father*. He loves me."

He could hear Ben's rapid breathing over the phone. "A father should guide his son, Mr. Clayton. You pushed him into doing things he didn't want to do."

"How dare you question my parenting!"

"Mr. Clayton, I am questioning nothing. I am stating fact. Your son resents that you forced him to play sports and discouraged him from pursing his own interests."

Ben said nothing immediately. His breathing rate increased then slowed. "That's what Margo told me. I guess I didn't listen."

"It's natural for fathers to have certain expectations for their sons," Eli said.

"I suppose he blames me for the accident, too."

"Not that I can tell."

"You can get inside his head like Seth can, right?"

"Yes. He's a good boy and extremely intelligent, probably more than you give him credit for. That brings me to the other reason I'm calling. Did you know he's keenly interested in science?"

Ben sighed. "I guess I did."

"Then I'd like your permission to take him to the Chicago Museum of Science and Industry."

"My God. Margo said he wanted me to go...and I said it was a waste of time. What have I done to him?"

"Nothing that can't be remedied, Mr. Clayton."

"I'm losing my son, aren't I? I suppose that shouldn't come as a surprise. In my heart, I knew I'd lost him."

Time to stop this downward spiral. "Mr. Clayton..." And no more formality. "Ben...you cared enough for your son to give him back his life. You made a difficult decision, not one most fathers would have contemplated, let alone gone through with."

"I almost didn't."

"But you did make the decision, and you did it out of love for him. Jonathan will come to understand and appreciate that."

"So, where does that leave us, Mr. Howard?"

"First, I'd like you to call me Eli. I want us to be friends. Jonathan is starting to see me as a surrogate father. It's not what either of us intended, but it's happening nonetheless. He already calls me 'Uncle Eli' and thinks of Adrian as his older brother. Here is my immediate suggestion: give me your permission for the trip to Chicago sometime in December. I also want you to join us there, to show him that you approve and you recognize your past mistakes."

"December is a busy time for me. Couldn't we make it after the first of the year?"

"Ben, if your business is more important than your son, then I'll respect that and won't bother you further. When you contacted your brother, you put Jonathan's life on a new path. Walk that path with him now or you may never catch up."

Ben's breathing became more erratic. A long pause followed. "I want to go with him to Chicago." He sniffed back the emotion Eli had heard building in his voice. "Let me know when."

"As soon as I've made the arrangements."

"Tell Jonathan I called...and that I love him."

"I will do that, Ben." Eli hung up the phone.

The wall clock in the library said five past ten. He opened the telescope box and took out the parts and directions. By ten thirty he'd finished with it. Jonathan was still upstairs, so he called Ysabel.

"I just received some distressing news," she said. "Last Saturday, one of the Board members, Hobart, died in his home in Germany. I'm still upset over it. Would you mind coming over here tonight? Rebecca is at her house studying and I don't want to disturb her."

Despite her fragile appearance, Ysabel De La Cruz was a strong individual and not easily upset. In her words, he heard something more, something she clearly didn't want to discuss over the phone.

"Young Jonathan is with me," he said, "and Adrian isn't home."

"Then I will come there. One hour?"

"I will be expecting you, Ysabel." In the meantime, he'd take Jonathan outside to use his new telescope.

While Eli had busied himself downstairs, Jonathan had tried out his laptop and already researched the current night sky. Together they set up the telescope to shield it from the streetlights, not that his street had enough of those working to be bothersome. They checked out the lunar craters first. Jonathan wanted to look at Orion. He zeroed in on the giant red star Betelgeuse and then the Great Nebula in Orion's sword.

When Ysabel drove up, the three of them went inside.

"It's a pleasure to meet you, young man," Ysabel said while Eli hung up her coat.

"Ysabel is an important lady, Jonathan. She's head of the Vampire Council."

"Sweet. Can I go back outside?"

"Let me know when you're done so I can bring in the telescope. We don't want anyone to steal it."

"I will, Uncle Eli." He darted out, leaving Eli to close the door behind him.

"Uncle Eli? He calls you that already?" Ysabel said. "How long has he been one of us?"

"Three weeks."

"How did he get through the bloodthirst rage so quickly?" she asked.

"He never developed it, only the normal bloodthirst. That has puzzled me."

"I've heard reports that the young ones are affected differently."

He showed her around his house, made her some tea, then they went into the library. "Now, what has upset you? I sensed you didn't want to discuss it on the phone."

"Given the events surrounding the Board—what we discussed previously—and now this, I can't be sure my phone is not being tapped. I said that one of the Board members died. That's not the whole truth. He was murdered."

"Murdered? How?"

"In a covert and sinister way. Another Board member, Jurgen Dengler, is a doctor who also lives in Germany. He performed the autopsy. The cause of death appeared to be a stroke."

"Vampires aren't susceptible to strokes," he said.

"That's what Jurgen said. When he performed a blood analysis, he found the human factor we require to keep us alive almost completely absent from Hobart's blood, despite there being adequate fresh blood in his home. Analysis of *that* blood showed it was tainted with a chemical that poisons a vampire by making him die of blood starvation. It also makes said death excruciating."

"I am so sorry, Ysabel. Do we know why Hobart was killed?"

"I surmise it's because he cast a dissenting vote against the experiments. You know of Gerrick's death a few years back, correct?"

Seth Clayton's mentor. Eli nodded.

"Gerrick died the same way as Hobart. Only after Hobart's death did we realize Gerrick had also been murdered."

"Who would murder Gerrick?"

"Jurgen wondered if perhaps he was a test subject."

He told her about the incident at Ling's Place last night.

"I fear this is the work of Vampires, Inc.," she said.

"That group no longer exists." Ysabel and the Council had given Cyrus and him permission to create it late in the Conflict to handle problem vampires. "When the Conflict ended and the problems had been handled, we decided to dissolve it."

"Cyrus convinced us to retain Vampires, Inc. as a small, covert police force for emergencies. We kept its continued existence a secret from you and all except the Board and a few others. Gerrick knew." She looked directly at Eli. "I regret not telling you, but you made it clear you did not wish to be involved. We haven't used it since World War II and all but forgot the group still existed. I believe Cyrus has secretly increased its membership and is using it for his own purposes."

"His personal hit squad, you mean. He must be stopped."

"I could not agree more," she said. "Unfortunately, the Council will not dare to act against him."

He heard cars outside and someone come in the front door a few minutes later. Adrian appeared at the library entrance.

"Did Drake go home?" Eli asked him.

"Yeah. Did you know there's a telescope outside our house?"

"I bought it for Jonathan tonight. Isn't he with it?"

"I didn't see him."

"Maybe he came in to use the bathroom." Although he hadn't heard Jonathan come in.

A few minutes later Adrian returned. "If he's in the house, he's hiding really well. I can't sense him, either."

Neither could Eli. Twenty past midnight. Where was Jonathan?

CHAPTER NINETEEN

New York City—Saturday, November 15, 2003

Adam Mathews entered the northwest corner of Union Square Park at Broadway and 17th Street. He loved New York City. He'd been born here; he'd been homeless here; he'd robbed people on the streets here. When he thought about it, like now, the first seventeen years of his life hadn't been so bad. He'd answered to no one and to nothing, not even to the conscience discarded somewhere along the way.

Two days ago he turned thirty-three. He'd been born on a Friday, a lucky day for him. And sixteen years ago, he'd been reborn. Today, he wasn't homeless; he still robbed when he was bored; for fun he sold drugs; for profit he killed people. Life was good.

He owed his rebirth to one man, his lord and savior, Cyrus Hayes. For reasons he would not reveal, Cyrus had taken Adam in and changed his life. Yet he still had a large degree of freedom, with the unspoken agreement that his personal business would never intrude on or endanger Cyrus'.

He could afford expensive clothing, but he liked high-top sneakers and surplus military coats. This full-length, navy-blue one was Swiss. For forty dollars and change, it kept him every bit as warm as the high-priced coats, even on this chilly, breezy New York evening. Better, it was inconspicuous. In his line of business, he preferred inconspicuous. Adam Mathews didn't need to *look* important. It only mattered that he *was* important.

New York was already embracing the coming Christmas season. His favorite holiday was Thanksgiving. He traditionally celebrated it by killing a human turkey or two who had particularly annoyed him during the year.

His cell phone buzzed under his coat. He deftly pulled it out and flipped it open, one-handed. "Mathews."

"Adam, I have business for you in Detroit. I've already made your plane reservations. My email will provide you with the itinerary, the target's address, a location where you may perform your work, plus some additional instructions. The young man is not to be killed or permanently injured, and I want no permanent marks on his body. Is that clear?"

"Yes, Mr. Hayes."

"If you encounter resistance or interference, you may restrain or incapacitate as you see fit. However, there will be no deaths or permanent injuries to *anyone*, not this time. Is that also clear?"

"Yes, sir."

"I am paying triple the usual amount, which you will receive when the task has been accomplished. If you deviate from my instructions, the entire sum will be forfeit."

"I understand, Mr. Hayes."

"I will be providing everything required and some special items to aid in your activities. Be creative, but exercise restraint. You will have three days, no more. Then you will email the victim's location anonymously to the previous address I gave you. Do you have any questions?"

"No, sir." The call disconnected. He'd much rather kill, but for three hundred thousand, he wouldn't argue. Cyrus had once demonstrated the price of not complying with his wishes. One of his other employees had once deviated from instructions. Hayes had bound the man and slowly drained the blood from his body while vampires fed on it. On the brink of death, the man begged for a second chance.

"You get a second chance only once," Cyrus had said. "Consider this yours."

After witnessing that, Adam always followed Cyrus' instructions explicitly. Yet, despite fearing Cyrus, Adam was drawn to him for reasons he did not understand. Over the years he'd grown to appreciate Cyrus' relentlessness. At one time he would have been content to be a vampire himself, had he been offered that opportunity. Vampires were evil, and evil was something he excelled at.

He'd decided a while back that being a vampire wouldn't be enough. Oh, he'd willingly accept it in the short term. In the long term, he aspired to something greater. Vampires had limitations: they weren't immortal; they depended on others for their survival. Adam was not—and never wanted to be—dependent upon anyone. He wanted to be immortal, and his black heart told him that one day Cyrus Hayes would grant him that wish.

***

Detroit—Saturday, November 15, 2003

Eli, Adrian, and Ysabel stood in Eli's front yard deciding how to locate Jonathan. "He is too young, too newly changed," Eli said to Ysabel. "His mind is still untamed. I shouldn't have left him outside alone. My experience with Adrian should have reminded me of that."

"I wasn't that bad!" Adrian said.

"You were worse, a memory I expect you have conveniently repressed."

Adrian snorted.

"It's my fault as well," Ysabel said. "It should have occurred to me not to leave a young one on his own."

"If I were him, I'd probably go hunting," Adrian said.

Eli glared at him. Nevertheless, it was a logical conclusion about a ten-year-old's sense of adventure.

"I didn't see anyone out when I drove up." Adrian sniffed the air. "I don't smell any humans around. No colognes or deodorants, I mean."

Eli didn't detect any either. The recent passage of humans would hang in the crisp, still, night air.

"You want me to drive you around the neighborhood to see if you can sense him?" Adrian asked.

"That would be best. Ysabel will stay here in case he returns."

Eli gave her his cell number. "Call me if he returns."

She went inside. Eli squeezed himself into Adrian's car. They headed toward Oakland. Adrian turned north there and drove counterclockwise around the block.

"You don't think he was kidnapped?" Adrian asked.

This neighborhood was better than most, but neither was it completely safe. Eli had no idea what Jonathan would do if kidnapped. "His mental powers are strong enough that Ysabel or I would have heard his thoughts if he'd been in danger," Eli said. Although he had not completely convinced himself of that.

Adrian widened his circle to the next block and continued spiraling outward.

Two blocks south, Adrian hit the brakes. "There he is!" Jonathan was walking in the direction of their house. Adrian jumped out of the car and rushed up to him. "Bro, where ya been? We were worried." He hugged Jonathan.

Eli came up behind them.

"I'm sorry, Uncle Eli. I got lost."

Eli squatted. "It's all right," he whispered. "You get in the car with Adrian. I'll walk."

Ten minutes later, Eli was carrying the telescope into the living room.

"Are you gonna take away the things you bought me?" a teary-eyed Jonathan asked.

"Do you think I should?"

"Probably."

"Let's sit and talk." Eli caught Ysabel's smile.

Jonathan sat next to him. "If you take away my iPod, can Adrian still use it?" he asked, wiping his eyes.

"You bought him an iPod?" Adrian said

Jonathan sniffled. Eli handed him a Kleenex. "Why did you leave the yard?"

"Two human teens walked by our house while I was looking at Mizar—that's the binary middle star in the Big Dipper's handle." He wiped his nose. "They were thinking about breaking into a house. I followed them to see if I could scare them off, and I kind of got lost."

"Did you stop them?"

"Uh huh. They came to a dark house and started up the sidewalk. I hid in the bushes and made noises and threw some rocks at the sidewalk. They got scared and ran."

Eli ruffled Jonathan's hair. "I'm proud of what you did, but what if they had attacked you?"

"I didn't think of that."

"In the future, come get me or Adrian." He caught Ysabel's approving nod from the corner of his eye. "Why don't you show Adrian your new laptop?"

"You got him a laptop, too? You never buy *me* cool toys."

"What do you call the Corvette?"

"Necessary transportation." He hurried out of the living room and bounded up the stairs two at a time. Jonathan followed.

"They'll make me old faster than I should be," Eli said to Ysabel.

Sadness clouded her eyes. "I would gladly trade that for the joy of having two fine boys like them. Could I trouble you for some tea?"

"Of course." He rose to get it.

"You don't have a servant?"

"I enjoy cooking. When I was in Europe with Dietrich, I had the privilege of learning. I also taught Adrian."

"My maid Fiona won't let me lift a hand in my own house to do what she considers her work. Do you mind if I browse your library while I'm waiting?"

"Not at all."

Eli had just returned with Ysabel's tea when Jonathan came running down the stairs and into the living room. He was panting and smiling the biggest smile Eli had seen on him yet.

"Uncle Eli…can Adrian take me to the mall Monday night? He wants to buy me some accessories for my iPod."

Adrian came into the living room behind Jonathan. "Little bro promised to behave," he said.

Eli narrowed his eyes at Adrian.

"I can handle him."

"Do you promise to stay with Adrian and not wander off?" Eli asked Jonathan.

"I promise."

"All right, you can go."

"Sweet!"

Jonathan bounded back upstairs while Adrian followed at a more leisurely pace.

Ysabel entered the living room from the library, and Eli handed her the tea. "Your library is impressive," she said.

"Smaller than yours."

She sat on the sofa. "You have some excellent first editions."

"I occasionally indulge myself."

"Now, back to less pleasant talk," she said. "What are your plans for Cyrus?"

"He must be stopped."

"I agree. How may I help?"

"By giving me your permission to do whatever is necessary."

"You have mine," she said, "but I believe you'll need Dietrich's as well."

"I will ask him, as a courtesy."

***

Detroit—Monday, November 17, 2003

"Your car's so much sweeter than Uncle Eli's," Jonathan said on their way to the mall. "You won't tell him I said that, will you?"

"No way. Eli's car isn't *un*cool. It's just a different kind of cool, a more mature cool."

"Why doesn't he drive something like a Hummer?"

"We aren't supposed to call attention to ourselves. A Hummer most definitely demands attention. Okay, strap in."

Adrian backed out of the driveway. Once on the street, he hit the gas. The sudden acceleration pressed Jonathan against the seat. The tires squealed.

"Sweet! Did you burn rubber?"

Adrian pulled over, stopped, and backed up a couple hundred feet. "Sure did. Go check it out. Just watch for traffic."

Jonathan got out, checked the street behind them, and got back in the car.

"Well?"

"Sweet. Two tracks. I smelled it, too." Jonathan gave him a high five.

On the expressway, heading toward Twelve Oaks Mall, Adrian did a few zigzag race-car maneuvers to impress Jonathan.

"Can this go over a hundred?" Jonathan asked.

"Piece of cake, but I can't do it here. The poh-leece give you nasty tickets."

"Have you ever gotten any tickets?"

"Not for speeding."

"You got a ticket for parking in a handicapped spot?"

"How did you know that?"

"You're thinking it."

Keeping his eyes on the road, he reached sideways and poked Jonathan in the arm. "*You* stay out of *my* head, 'cuz you'll find things in there you aren't supposed to know about yet."

"You mean sex stuff."

Adrian's neck got hot. "Yeah, sex stuff."

"I already know."

"*Where* did you learn that?"

"Some in school, some from other kids, some on the Internet."

"Your parents didn't use parental controls?"

"I knew how to get around them."

"Well, it isn't polite to read people's thoughts without permission. Didn't Eli teach you that?"

"Uncle Eli had me do it when we were at the mall last Saturday."

"To everyone?"

"Not exactly."

"You and Eli and I will talk later. Unless we tell you to do it, *don't*. You have to respect other people's privacy. Deal?"

"Deal."

"Okay, here's the mall. Are you ready for all the sweet stuff you're gonna get?"

"Uh huh!"

"Wanna buy first or eat first?"

"Buy first, eat, then buy more."

"Good plan."

Having spent more on iPod accessories than Eli had on the iPod itself, Adrian took Jonathan to the food court for pizza. "You want Haagen-Dazs ice cream for dessert?"

Jonathan licked his lips. So did Adrian when he saw the babe who worked there. He squatted beside Jonathan and whispered, "This ice cream is sooo tasty, but it's way overpriced." He hoped Jonathan wouldn't comment on the fact that he'd just spent a shitload on iPod accessories and why would a couple of bucks more matter. "I'll order us two ice cream bars. I want you to think at the nice lady that she should give us one for free because I'm extremely cute."

"Are we supposed to do that?"

"This is a test of your powers, little bro, just like Eli had you test your mind reading."

"I still don't think we should."

"Then we'll do it this way. You make her give us one for free. When she does, I'll tell her that she's made a mistake and pay her for both. Is that okay?"

Jonathan nodded.

"Don't forget, make her think I'm cute."

"You want her to have sex with you."

Adrian's neck got warm.

"Oooh, your face is red."

"You won't tell Eli about any of this, will you?"

"Not if you buy me a new video game and play it with me tonight."

"You're a shrewd lit-tle dude," Adrian said, accenting the syllables and pointing his two forefingers first at Jonathan then at the floor in what he knew was a shitty attempt at rap.

Jonathan scrunched up his face. "Drake does it better."

They finished their ice cream and Jonathan asked him, "Can we be blood brothers? I mean. . . *taste* each other?"

"Umm, I guess it won't hurt. . . Sure. That'd be cool. We'll do it when we get home."

"Sweet." Jonathan frowned. "Uncle Eli won't mind, will he?"

"Nope. We'll do an official ceremony, with candles and everything and ask Eli to say some vows for us and make us swear to protect one another." He gave Jonathan a high five. "C'mon. I owe you some game time."

On the drive home, Jonathan asked, "Can I play my new CD?"

"Sure."

Jonathan put *The Best of Sugar Ray* into the car stereo. Adrian cranked it. Jonathan liked Alternative Rock and hated Techno as much as he did.

Adrian couldn't believe how strong the kid's telepathic powers were for being a vampire only a month. Maybe it was some kind of record. He probably should be jealous, but he wasn't. Jonathan was the little brother he'd always wanted and never had. He'd let nothing spoil their new relationship. Having a video game partner was cool, too. Most of the guys he hung with weren't interested or had the attention span of a two-year-old.

For sure he had to talk to Eli about how to guide his little brother properly. It was his vampire responsibility. Jonathan reminded him of young Anakin Skywalker in *Star Wars: The Phantom Menace*, which came out in 1999, when he was eighteen and less than a year after Eli had changed him. Now that he thought back, Eli had had his hands full with him that year. Adrian cringed inwardly. Oh yeah, he'd been one holy terror.

Well, he'd accomplished two things tonight. No, three. He'd adopted Jonathan as his little brother; he'd taught Jonathan how to get free food; he'd gotten a date with the Haagen-Dazs babe. With any luck, on Wednesday night he'd get laid.

"If Eli asks, just say we went shopping and I bought you some cool stuff."

"He knows when I'm lying."

"You're right. I'll tell him the truth so you won't have to lie or be embarrassed. Big brothers do that for their little brothers." *Like fathers guide and protect their sons.* Shit, Eli was rubbing off on him. He just hoped he could protect Jonathan from this Cyrus Hayes and whatever was going on.

CHAPTER TWENTY

Detroit—Tuesday, November 18, 2003

Drake tucked his Jeep into a visitor's spot in the Radley Biotech parking lot, still unsure why Ethan wanted him here. Last night Ethan had given him a signed excuse to get him out of school at noon. All he'd said was, "I have a meeting with someone important and I'd like you to be there."

Who the hell could it be? Not a college recruiter. Ethan had him all set to go to Harvard, and he still fervently hoped that something would wedge itself between him and that particular school.

Not a prospective employer.

The press for a major breakthrough announcement? A possibility there. Father and son together would go over well with the media.

God help him if it was Cyrus Hayes. Cyrus' vampire telepathic powers would suck the secrets from Drake Radley's tender young brain and Drake Radley would cease his existence as a rational human being.

For a moment he considered going back to school. Instead, he shut off the engine and called Adrian.

"Drake?" a sleepy voice said.

"Sounds like somebody had a long night? Is she still there?"

"You're an evil person if you woke me just to ask that." Adrian sounded more alert. "I was out clubbing, that's all. With Jonathan living here, Eli suggested discretion on my part."

"I need a favor."

"Did Daddy repo the Jeep again?"

"No, and he's 'Ethan' not 'Daddy'. I'm possibly about to march through the Gates of Hell. I'm outside the company, ready to go into his office. He summoned me here to meet someone, and I have no idea who. I want you to monitor us." He told Adrian his speculations. "Alert Eli if it goes south."

"Hang on while I boot up my PC and make sure our spy monitor is still working."

Drake waited.

"We're good. If it's Cyrus, do *not* think about the video camera. He'll know at once and we'll all be screwed. Better yet, when you get in the office tell your father your stomach hurts, school cafeteria slop or some such thing. That way, if it is Cyrus, you can fake a retch and run off to the men's room."

"He's got a bathroom in his office."

"No matter. If it's Cyrus, get your ass out of there and come straight here. It's daytime so he's not likely to follow you."

"Check outside," Drake said. "It's raining."

"Well, I don't think you have any worries. After what your father saw of Cyrus last week, he's not stupid enough to ask you there to meet him."

"Good point," Drake said. "Later, dude."

Drake clipped his cell back into his belt holder, zipped up his jacket, and headed inside. He'd arrived early, so he stopped at the guard's desk to talk with Pete.

"Hi, Drake. Your father said you'd be coming."

"Any idea who the guest of honor is?"

Pete checked his logbook. "Jeffery Thomas."

"And who is he?"

"A local politician running for mayor in 2005. Is your family getting into politics?" Sarcasm tinged Pete's tone.

"I sure hope not. I have no idea why my father wants me here to meet him. What do you know about this asshole?"

Pete put a finger to his lips. "Careful."

Drake leaned halfway over the desk. "You think I give a shit?"

"I know you don't, but I don't want you to get yourself into trouble again. Between you and me, I know this guy and you called it right."

"I promise I'll behave in front of my father, but I can't promise pure thoughts."

Pete looked down at the clock embedded in the desk. "It's twelve forty-five. He should be here any minute." He looked past Drake, out the door. "Unless I'm mistaken, that Cadillac will be him arriving now. Better get up there."

"Just for grins, buzz Ethan and tell him, 'Master Drake is on his way.'"

"For you, I will."

He gave Pete a thumbs up. "Later, my man."

"Got your badge on?"

He unzipped his jacket to show it clipped to his belt and marched to the elevators.

A few minutes later, Drake knocked at the door to his father's office.

"Come in."

"I'm not late, am I?"

"Right on time." Ethan didn't get up from his desk.

"Are you going to keep me in the dark about who's coming?"

"A political hopeful," Ethan said. "Have a seat over there." He pointed to a chair near the corner. "Please stand when he comes in."

"VIP?"

"He asked for an appointment to discuss financial backing. Regardless of what he says, how I act, or what you may think of him, sit quietly and listen. If he asks you any questions, I expect you to respond honestly but with discretion. Do not embarrass me."

"Should I lie?"

"No, but consider your words carefully. A good answer in a difficult situation is, 'That's interesting. I'd like to think about that and get back to you, if I may.' It doesn't offend, and it gets you off the hook."

Ethan Radley, sometime father of Drake Dorian Radley, was actually giving his son helpful advice? Maybe he'd been scared so shitless by Cyrus Hayes that he'd decided to be nice in the time he had remaining, before his world collapsed around him.

Drake thought about that for another moment. *No way, not a chance. This was purely and simply all about Ethan covering his ass so he didn't look stupid in front of his guest.* Drake removed his jacket, put it over the back of the chair, and sat. "Can I ask why you wanted me here to meet him?"

"To observe and to have the experience. In business, we have to deal with local politicians whether we want to or not."

Okay, now it made sense. Like the cocktail parties he despised, this was more of Daddy Dearest grooming him to join the business one day.

The phone bleeped twice. Ethan pressed a button on it.

"Mr. Radley, Mr. Thomas is here," Pete's voice said.

"Have him brought up to my office. He won't require a badge. I'll be escorting him out."

"Yes, sir."

Ethan stood and came around the front of his desk. "Remember what I told you, Drake."

Several minutes later, a guard entered with a black man, and Drake stood. Ethan immediately shook the man's hand. "Ethan Radley. Thank you for coming, Mr. Thomas."

The guard left.

"Thank you for seeing me, Mr. Radley."

"This is my son, Drake," Ethan said. "Drake, this is Mr. Jeffery Thomas, a Detroit mayoral hopeful for 2005."

Drake walked over, his hand out.

Jeffery Thomas shook it vigorously. "*Reverend* Jeffery Thomas, young man."

Drake forced a congenial smile that threatened to break into a laugh at the fluffy hair and sloppy suit, something most folks would donate to the Salvation Army. Did Ethan Radley have a loser magnet inside his body somewhere? And Jeffery Thomas had the worst skin Drake had ever seen. *His parents must not have been able to afford acne medications when he was a kid. Or maybe it's to hide the "L" on his forehead.*

Reverend Thomas flashed a crooked-teeth smile, first at Drake then at his father. "Heir to the throne, Ethan? I *may* call you Ethan, mayn't I?"

Mayn't?

"Do call me 'Reverend.' No need to be formal among friends."

"Make yourself comfortable," Ethan said.

Thomas sat in the leather chair in front of the desk.

"Dad, do you have some paper or a notepad I could borrow?" Drake interrupted intentionally to see Ethan's reactions. His father's eyes narrowed. "I left my backpack in my Jeep. I want to take some notes for my Civics class."

Without a word, Ethan opened a desk drawer and pushed a steno pad to the edge of the desk. His glance reminded Drake to sit quietly in the background and not interrupt again.

Drake leaned forward out of his chair to take the pad then sheepishly retreated back into it. He cast a glance at the security camera. Nothing hinted that it was active. He flipped open the pad, reporter fashion. Pulling a pen from his pants pocket, he poised it over the paper. This baboon would certainly amuse him more than a day in school. He'd use his notes to write rap lyrics to bring him comfort and joy in the coming holiday season.

"Lemme get rih-ght to the point uh mah visit," the reverend began.

At the top of the page, Drake wrote, *Thomas' promises.*

"With our current mayor retirin', Detroit needs strong leadership. Our proud city is in a cry-sis: financially; socially; an' spiritually. Our city is morally bankrupt. 'I lead in the way of righteousness, in the midst of the paths of justice,' Proverbs 8:20."

Drake wrote, *Ass-holiness.*

"Our current leaders have failed us. We're taxed and overtaxed and have nothin' to show for it. We'll lead Detroit into a new era."

Drake wrote, *Into a new era of financial ruin.*

"We'll clean up the crime in our streets, the drugs, the rape, the shootings, the prostitution."

How come he said "we" not "I?"

"Equitable education for all."

Blacks.

"Women should be able to make the choice on abortions. I advocate stronger rights for women."

Drake wrote, *The right to bare breasts.*

"And gay rights and gay marriages," the reverend said.

Drake wrote, *The right to stick it up the reverend's ass.*

"I stand tall for these American freedoms!"

Drake wrote, *I bend over for Americans.*

"Let's be honest, Ethan. Why did you build your company here in Troy? Because the taxes are lower. The current administration offers tax incentives to build in Downtown, but those aren't enough. You feel unsafe in Detroit. What if we could offer you everything you have here and more?"

"More, Reverend?" Ethan said.

"Exactly. With your generous support for 2005, I would be in a position to provide very attractive incentives for you to relocate."

Political favors rear their ugly, pockmarked faces.

"Can I count on your support, Ethan? I'm not speakin' only financially, but I'm askin' you to talk with the other businessmen you fraternize amongst. Convince them that we must share the responsibility for rebuildin' our city."

"I'll give it serious consideration, Reverend."

"An' somethin' else. You might've heard about a cult group gathering strength in our city?"

"I'm not sure what you mean."

"These are not God-fearing individuals, Ethan. Their followers do not worship the Almighty but the one who was cast out of Heaven."

"Satan worshipers? I'm not aware of any such group here in Detroit."

He means vampires. How does this jerk-off know about vampires? Especially when I just learned about them. What was going on here? He'd have to talk to Adrian and Eli about this. Was Cyrus Hayes putting his nose into local politics? If Ethan only knew how deep he'd stepped into the shit.

"They are gainin' strength and threatening to pull our fine city further into sin. Psalm 37:17, 'For the arms of the wicked shall be broken, but the Lord upholdeth the righteous.'"

What's the Bible have to say about strip clubs, which I'm sure are part of his regular nighttime itinerary? How does his pecker stand on those?

The reverend looked over at Drake. "Son, do you have any questions? I assume your father asked you here because you're studying local politics in Civics class so you could get the facts straight from the horse's mouth, as it were. Civics was my favorite subject." He flashed another broad, crooked-teeth smile.

You made it through high school? He noticed Ethan's jaw tense. "No, sir, no questions. I appreciated the privilege of hearing your views."

"Do you agree with them?"

"I'd like to think about that and get back to you, if I may."

"Of course." He held out his business card to Drake. "If you call mah campaign office, they'll send you a brochure explainin' mah position on the issues facin' our city and give you somethin' you can quote."

I'm sure it will contradict everything you said here and make no mention of vampires.

The reverend stood. "I must be goin', Ethan. My schedule is extremely busy. It's lucky I had an opening for you and your son."

I thought you, not Ethan, were the one who called for an appointment.

Crooked teeth again put themselves on display. "Ah look forward to what I'm sure will be a generous contribution from Radley Computers."

Radley Computers? This loser doesn't even know the company's name? Drake snorted, then hoped his father or the reverend hadn't heard him.

The reverend reached across Ethan's desk to shake his hand. Ethan came around it to walk him out. Drake tore off the top three pages from the notepad, folded them into thirds, and put them in his back pocket. He left the notepad on Ethan's desk and his jacket on the chair.

As Drake followed them out, he looked up at the security camera and winked. His father escorted the reverend back to the lobby. Ethan didn't usually accommodate visitors that way. More often he called security to escort them, but he must have figured that would be an affront to the reverend. Which meant his father was considering supporting him.

Pete wasn't at the guard's desk when they reached the lobby because he always took a late lunch. *Perfect.* Drake hastily said, "I've got homework, so I gotta be going." *Places to go and rap to write.* "Thanks for inviting me, Dad." He shook the reverend's hand. "Thanks again, Rev, I learned a lot of cool stuff. Hope you win." He caught his father's expression of disapproval. "Oops, I forgot my jacket. I'll go back up and get it. See ya at home tonight."

Drake hustled himself back to the elevators. He retrieved his jacket and he snuck himself into the security monitor room to call Adrian. "Did you see it?"

Adrian chuckled. "Yup. Saved it so I can burn a DVD. Eli can watch it, and you can use it against Reverend Thomas when you run for mayor of Detroit. With some judicious editing and your rap soundtrack—I assume that's why you were taking notes—we'll be set with our 'Drake Radley for Mayor' campaign. You *will* let me be your campaign manager, won't you?"

"I can't run for mayor."

"Why not?"

"Among other things, I'm not a Democrat. Talk to ya later." Drake flipped his cell shut.

Adrian had shown him how to connect the output from the camera in Ethan's office to a monitor for private viewing. He wanted to see what his father was up to next. He didn't have to wait long.

When Ethan returned, a man in a lab coat was following him. Ethan walked behind his desk, pissed about something. Drake cranked up the volume.

"Mr. Radley, it's about these experiments Mr. Hayes is conducting. A week ago he brought in ten volunteers."

"I know that. Get to the point."

"When they arrived, they all were healthy. Yesterday, five were sick enough to be bedridden. This morning…two of them died."

CHAPTER TWENTY-ONE

Detroit—Tuesday, November 18, 2003

"*Two* of them died?" Ethan said. "Why wasn't I told?"

The guy in the lab coat fidgeted. "Mr. Hayes said you were busy and he'd take care of it."

"Damn it! Whose company is this?"

"Yours, Mr. Radley. But I thought Mr. Hayes was supervising—"

"Mr. Hayes has no say in my company! I expect to be kept informed of *everything* that goes on here, particularly where Mr. Hayes is involved."

"Yes, sir."

"What did the volunteers die from?"

"We don't know. Mr. Hayes refused to let the bodies be examined."

"Get it done. If Mr. Hayes objects, tell him to see me."

"Yes, sir. One more thing you might be interested in, sir. I examined the consent forms for the volunteers..."

Ethan scowled. "My patience is reaching its limits."

"Sorry, sir. The addresses of the volunteers are all the same, a homeless shelter Downtown."

Ethan's face went through a series of expressions Drake had seen only when his father fought emotions threatening to erupt into extreme unpleasantness for all those around him.

"Send Mr. Hayes in here at once," Ethan said through his teeth.

"He sleeps during the day and insisted we not disturb him except for an emergency."

"He *sleeps* during the day? When did that begin?"

"He always has."

Ethan's face reddened. "Wake him."

"He keeps the door locked, sir. We don't have the combination."

"Bang on it until he answers!"

"It's soundproofed at his request. He won't hear us."

"Use a hammer, break the lock, do whatever you have to. Just get him up here. Now."

"Yes, sir." The man spun on his heels and hastily exited.

"What the fuck is going on?" Ethan muttered.

Drake's lips parted in amazement. In his life, never had he heard Ethan Radley use the f-word.

Ethan went to his desk and pressed a button on his phone. A dial tone came out of the speaker. "Am I losing control of my own company?"

He pressed another button, probably a speed dial because, after a pause, a voice said, "Barnes. How may I help you, Mr. Radley?"

Martin Barnes. Ethan's head of security.

"What have you found out about Cyrus Hayes?"

"I know it's been a week since you asked us to check on him, sir, but we've learned almost nothing. His background is a mystery. Cyrus Hayes isn't the name he was born with, neither the first nor the last name, but he's been using it for a long time. We haven't discovered his real identity or background. There's a large estate outside Dublin, Ireland that's been listed in the name of Cyrus Hayes for the past sixty years."

"Sixty years? He's not that old."

"We're thinking the name may have been legally changed in the past, by his father, and that this Cyrus Hayes is a junior or a second. We're still researching him, but a lot of the old foreign records aren't online yet. We did find something else interesting. The name of Cyrus Hayes popped up in connection with global drug trafficking. Would you like us to send someone to Ireland to investigate him?"

"Shit." Ethan didn't say it loudly enough to be heard, but Drake saw it on his father's lips.

"Sir?" Martin said.

"Yes, send someone, very low profile. I don't want Hayes alerted that we're investigating him." He punched the phone off.

"I've got homeless people dying on my premises, and I'm doing business with a drug dealer? I don't need this crap."

Ethan stood and paced back and forth behind his desk. Drake watched for a few minutes before he called Adrian. "Are you watching this?"

"Sure am. I can't wait to see what happens when Cyrus arrives."

Drake heard the office door open. "Uh, show time. Talk to you later."

Ethan stopped pacing. Cyrus approached. Drake could see only the back of his head and the fiery hair that hadn't been combed.

"How may I help you, Ethan?" Amazingly, Cyrus sounded calm.

"Some questions and serious concerns have arisen over your experiments here."

"Ya not be havin' a pleasant day that ya had to disturb me?"

Ethan's startled expression said he'd taken notice of the Irish brogue Cyrus had suddenly slipped into. "Two of the volunteers died, and others are seriously ill. Why didn't you tell me?"

"It not be yer concern," Cyrus said.

"It *is* my concern. This is my company, and I control what does and does not happen here."

"You'll be wantin' to cancel our contract then?"

"I should."

"Because yuv been researchin' me."

"How do you know that?"

"You shouldn't be concerned over my outside business dealings." The accent faded as suddenly as it had begun. "You're already manufacturing drugs for me."

Ethan sank into his chair. "Not the illegal kind!"

Cyrus pulled a chair next to the side of the desk. This forced Ethan to swivel his own chair sideways, and Drake saw a clear profile of the disarming smile aimed at Ethan. "Several months ago, you signed a contract to manufacture a number of custom biochemical compounds for a private research company. Do you recall that?"

Ethan nodded.

"The contract came from me, under another name. Designer drugs, quite illegal, or they will be once their true nature becomes known. Your research people didn't recognize them, so they aren't as good as you believe them to be." Cyrus combed his fingers through his hair with an air of extreme smugness. "Or is it because I've invented a new class of targeted drugs they wouldn't recognize?"

Drake recalled the TV ad, "Parents, the anti-drug." *Right.*

Ethan pressed a button on his phone.

"Security," a voice said a moment later.

Drake closed his mouth, which he'd just realized was hanging open. Ethan had pressed the emergency button on his phone.

"Send four armed officers up here immediately."

"Is there a problem, Mr. Radley?"

"Would I call if there *wasn't* a problem?" He punched the phone off and told Cyrus, "I want you and your people out of here tomorrow. Your money will be returned according to the terms of that contract."

"I warned you before. You need a demonstration."

Less than a minute later, four guards entered without knocking. Ethan stood. "Escort this man to his quarters, see that he gets all of his belongings, then escort him and his men off the premises."

Cyrus laughed. "You are so incredibly naive, Ethan."

Ethan's body jolted; he wobbled. "What the hell did you do to me?"

Two of the guards approached Cyrus from behind. One of them immediately collapsed to the floor. The other drew a Taser and fired. The short, slender Cyrus moved with incredible agility and dodged the Taser darts. With a couple of martial arts kicks, Cyrus had the second guard lying flat on the floor.

Guards three and four rushed him. Number four waved a cattle prod. The third guard fired his Taser. The darts hit Cyrus with no effect. Were vampires immune, or was Cyrus wearing some kind of protective armor under his outer clothes?

Cyrus yanked the wires toward him, pulling the Taser from the startled guard's hand.

"Shoot him!" Ethan said.

The fourth guard advanced with his prod but never got the chance to use it. With his arm, Cyrus knocked the prod from the guard's grasp and dispatched him as efficiently as he had the first two.

The third guard, the largest and most muscular, apparently thought he could take Cyrus down when a Taser couldn't. For the first few moments, it appeared as if he might land a blow on Cyrus. After he missed three times and it became apparent Cyrus was playing with him, Cyrus took control with a series of spins, kicks, and punches that made the guard look like a wuss. His final kick broke the guard's left leg.

Cyrus straightened himself and faced a shaking Ethan. "You get a second chance only once, Ethan. Having provided a small demonstration of my sincerity to keep doing business with you," he swept a hand at the four disabled guards, "I'm willing to give you that second chance to reconsider your decision, on the basis that you had insufficient facts when you chose to cancel our contract. I'm offering you an excellent business opportunity. The work I commissioned comes with no risk to the reputation of you or your company. I assure you that I'm adept at concealing the true nature of my activities. Cooperate, and nothing will be linked to you."

Ethan stared in silence.

"I'll be back at ten this evening. If you still wish to cancel our contracts," he emphasized the plural, "then my several million dollars and I will walk out of here as quietly as we entered. The consequences of such an ill-advised act on your part will not be pleasant. Your company will—I assure you—suffer considerably. The knowledge of what you were manufacturing will become known to the appropriate agencies in your government."

Cyrus executed a sharp about-face and strode out of the office. Drake caught a full view of him as he walked under the camera. If Evil had a face, Cyrus Hayes was wearing it. Despite being in a closed room a floor below, Drake's body was trembling. He had to get out of here. *Oh, fuck.* How was he going to leave without being seen? If he left through the front lobby, Pete would see him. And he'd parked out front. *Rear exit?* The guard there might not know him, but he'd have to show his badge and he'd be recognized.

The security alarm suddenly blared. Drake didn't hesitate. He grabbed his things and headed for the stairway. If he slipped out now, with all hell breaking loose, no one would notice the door alarm on the emergency exit. He leaped down the stairs.

***

On the way to Eli's house, Drake cranked up the heater in his Jeep full blast. The warmth didn't help; his shakes wouldn't stop. He checked his rearview mirror frequently. No one was following him that he could see. No one knew he hadn't left earlier, so he was safe even if Cyrus probed Ethan's thoughts. In any case, Cyrus wouldn't see him as a threat, but he *was* potential hostage material if Ethan didn't cooperate. Moisture trickled from his armpits. After seeing what Cyrus had done, Drake had never been more frightened in his life.

He should've called Adrian, but he'd been too scared. Well, not too scared to call, just too scared to stay in the building while he did. He wanted his ass far away from there as fast as possible.

Whoa, dude. Ease off. The speedometer registered fifteen miles over the limit. *Not cool.* He quickly scanned ahead and along both sides. No cops. Being pulled over was the last thing he needed.

Exit 55, his exit. He breathed a little easier. He'd be at Eli's in a few minutes, the only place in Detroit he'd feel safe at the moment.

As soon as Drake rang the doorbell, Adrian answered. "Why are your hands white?"

"From clenching my steering wheel." Drake was panting. "I scooted out the emergency exit when I heard the alarms."

"That was me. I set them off. Somebody had to do something fast."

"Where's Eli? Does he know?"

"Sort of. He's in the library."

Drake pushed past Adrian. "Cyrus Hayes took out four of my father's security guards," he said to Eli from the library entrance.

"Why were you there?"

Drake told him about Jeffery Thomas and the camera setup. "He's fucking insane. You gotta stop him."

"I plan to, Drake. Are you're sure Cyrus didn't see you and didn't know you were observing?"

"No way he could. Even my father doesn't know." He entered and sat in front of the desk.

"We must keep it that way. Cyrus is a powerful telepath."

"Is that what he did to my father? I saw Ethan stagger right after Cyrus looked at him."

Eli nodded. "Cyrus can disable a man with his mind alone."

"Shit."

"I want you to stay here tonight. Call your parents, tell them you're doing some work for me at the university. Say it might run late and you'll stay at a friend's house. It's not a lie."

"Yeah, that'll be cool with my mom. She knows I keep a change of clothes in my Jeep. Will she be safe?"

"Cyrus doesn't kill for pure pleasure, only for good reason. He's a master manipulator and prefers to intimidate. He knows your father's vulnerable spot is his company. Only if he finds it isn't, will he choose another target. Are you in your father's will to take over the company?"

"Why does that matter? He's talked about me joining the company after college, but if I'm in his will, it's news to me."

"What if you are and Cyrus finds out?"

"How could he?"

"Your father doesn't know what Cyrus is. All it takes is one betraying thought for Cyrus to read."

"Not to worry. I don't want his stupid company."

"What you want isn't the point. What your father intends for you is what matters to Cyrus. The fire at Ling's was a warning to me to stay out of his business. Cyrus knows that in a hand-to-hand battle, I would likely prevail. He knows a direct attack on me is pointless. Once he learns I've chosen to ignore his warning, he'll find other means to persuade me. I don't want you to be one of his options."

CHAPTER TWENTY-TWO

Detroit—Wednesday, November 19, 2003

With his carry-on bag slung over his shoulder, Adam Mathews exited the plane and strode through the accordion tunnel leading to the terminal. Having to be at LaGuardia before five a.m.—in the rain—for his six ten flight had already put him in a foul mood. Having to leave New York City for this pissant place had increased it. The flight had been delayed nearly an hour, and it was raining here. Rain in his great city of New York he forgave. In this shithole, it was fucking unacceptable. Given his mood, following Cyrus' orders to restrain himself would be difficult.

He'd almost reached the terminal when some asshole in a rush from behind tried to squeeze past him. Adam nonchalantly elbowed him hard under his rib cage.

"Hey!"

"Sorry. Didn't see you."

"Next time, *look*, buddy."

Adam squared himself. "You're lucky there's witnesses around," he said with menace in his voice. If this had happened on the street, the man would be on the ground, in pain, and needing a cast or two.

The man glared back and rushed away, rubbing his side.

Too bad he was under contract and a time constraint with Hayes or he'd follow the man to a more private place and deal with him.

He exited the gate area and spotted a man with a sign that said, "Adam Mathews." Limo and driver as promised.

"I'm Mathews."

The man took a photograph from the pocket of his gray uniform shirt and held it next to Adam. "My instructions said to verify my passenger."

Adam glanced at the photo. "Not my best side."

"I'm Joe."

"That your real name?"

"Why wouldn't it be?"

"No reason."

Adam got into the limo. Joe pointed to a case on the seat. "That's for you. I was told you'd know the combination."

For pin numbers and combinations he always used the time of day he was born, in military time, zero-two-fourteen. It was a secure code because his birth records had been destroyed in a fire, and no one else except Cyrus knew it.

"You like living here?" he asked Joe.

"Not particularly. I'm from Seattle originally. Got a good business here, though. Weather's better, more sunshine, but colder. It's supposed to be sunny the rest of the week if you're planning on going out."

Adam nodded to himself.

At the hotel, Joe handed Adam a card with his phone number. "I'm at your disposal twenty-four/seven, pick up and delivery or whatever. They booked me a room at the hotel. For what I'm being paid, I didn't ask any questions."

"Where's a good place to eat?"

"The hotel dining room, if you don't mind the prices."

Why should he? Cyrus Hayes was paying for everything. This seemed too pat, too quick, and it made Adam nervous. This job wasn't his style. Normally, he'd research his target and the location, make sure everything would go as it should. But Cyrus had never fucked him over. No reason not to trust him.

***

When Eli entered the living room with Jonathan, Drake paused the video game he and Adrian were playing on the big-screen . "I promised Jonathan I'd take him to the movies tonight," Eli said.

"What are you seeing?" Adrian asked.

"*Brother Bear,*" Jonathan said.

"Perfect choice, little bro."

"You've got guard duty on Drake," Eli told Adrian.

"Um, I have a date with Haagen-Dazs tonight."

"Ice cream in winter?"

"It's not officially winter for another month, and there's no wrong time for ice cream. But I'm really going for the sweet thing who sells it. I met her at the mall when little bro and I were there Monday."

"Tonight I want you to stay away from humans, Adrian. Please remain here."

"Drake's a human, in case you forgot."

"I don't mind," Drake said. "I'll be fine. If he gets lucky, he can tell me all about it, and I can live vicariously through him."

"He means Adrian might have sex tonight, Uncle Eli," Jonathan piped in.

Eli jerked his head at Jonathan. "I know what he meant." Then at Adrian. "What have you been teaching him?"

"I didn't teach him *anything*, not *that* anyway. He already knows it. Honest!"

"He's right, Uncle Eli. I know all about sex stuff. Can we go to the movie now?"

"You and I will talk later," Eli told Adrian. "Reconsider your plans for this evening. Drake's safety is your responsibility, too."

"She doesn't get off work until nine anyway," Adrian said. "I got a couple of hours."

Jonathan tugged at Eli's leather coat. "Come on, or we'll be late."

Adrian put a hand on Drake's shoulder. "I promise I'll keep him safe. I'll take him with me and he can ride in the trunk on the way back. Enjoy the movie."

After Eli and Jonathan left, Drake punched Adrian in the arm. "I am *not* riding in the trunk!"

"Well, if I put Haagen-Dazs in the trunk, it'd kill any chance of me gettin' lucky."

***

Drake was lounging on the living room couch in front of the TV while Adrian was upstairs changing. He'd called his date. She'd agreed to stop by here after work. The doorbell rang, and Adrian thumped down the stairs. "I'm on it."

Drake checked his Rolex. It was a little past nine. The mall where she worked was over ten miles away. She couldn't have gotten here this fast. He heard Adrian open the door and say, "Who are you?" A loud pop followed.

Drake jerked his head around to see Adrian backing into the hallway. A moment later, a man he didn't recognize appeared and was aiming a weird gun at Adrian.

"Run!" Adrian yelled.

Drake noticed a dart sticking out of Adrian's leg. He jumped up and took several steps toward them. "Who the fuck are you?" The man aimed the gun at him. Drake halted.

With his other hand, the man unclipped something from his belt and sprayed Drake.

"Fuck!" Drake screamed a couple of seconds later when the effects of the pepper spray kicked in. His eyes slammed shut; his face was on fire. He fell to his knees, gasping and gagging, with his hands over his face. *Shit, shit, shit.*

"Rub it in good. Here, have some more." The man sprayed him again. His hands blocked some of the second blast, but now *they* were burning.

"Tell Eli Howard that Cyrus Hayes sends his regards and to have a good evening."

His watering eyes had swollen shut; his lungs were on fire. He couldn't even use his cell phone to call for help. *Fuck, fuck, fuck.*

An eternity later, the front door opened.

"Drake!" Eli's voice. "Jonathan, run upstairs and turn on the shower."

Drake tried to speak.

"Shhh. You'll be all right soon. Keep your eyes closed." Eli's soothing voice calmed him.

Eli carried him upstairs, removed his pants and shirt, and put him on the floor of the shower stall. The cool water spraying over his face felt like it was hot instead of cold and wasn't helping. He reached up to rub it, but strong hands stopped him.

"No. You'll make it worse. Jonathan, in the kitchen cabinet where we keep the spices is an orange box of baking soda. Bring me that, the milk, and a bowl and spoon."

Eli washed Drake's hands three times with a liquid soap. That took away most of the burn. Now it felt like tiny needles pricking his skin. His face felt a little better, too. When the worst of the burn had subsided and he was breathing more or less normally, he said, "He took Adrian."

"I know."

"Hand me the milk," Eli said. Jonathan must have returned. Eli shut off the water. "Lean back, eyes closed. This will be cold."

Very cold. Drake sucked air between his teeth. Eli rubbed one hand over Drake's face and poured on more milk. *Much better.*

Eli told Jonathan, "Put half the box of baking soda in the bowl and mix some milk with it to make a thick paste. Can you do that?"

"Uh huh."

"Drake, I'm turning the water back on—eyes still closed." After a little of that, he said, "Now, blink and squeeze your eyes as you do to create tears."

He followed Eli's instructions. "Fuck!" came out as a gurgle when water ran into his eyes.

"I know it feels worse. Keep blinking." Eli turned off the shower.

"What's gonna happen to him?" Drake asked, able to see blurs of light now.

"Adrian or his kidnapper?"

"Both."

"Let's worry about you first."

"I'll be fine. Go after Adrian."

Eli smoothed the paste on Drake's neck. "Tilt your head back and close your eyes tightly. You don't want this in them." Eli smoothed the paste over Drake's face and eyelids.

"How did you know what happened to me so fast?" Drake asked.

"Close your mouth."

"What if he's gonna *kill* Adrian?"

When he wiped the paste onto Drake's lips, a little got in his mouth. That lovely salty bitter taste he remembered from having his teeth cleaned with that baking soda spray almost made him gag. Drake spit it out. "Ugh."

Eli rubbed more paste over Drake's lips. "Your attacker left the can of pepper spray next to you along with a note warning me to stay out of Cyrus Hayes' business. It said that no permanent harm would befall Adrian. Okay, we'll leave the paste on a few minutes."

After the final rinse, Drake asked, "You believe him?"

"Yes, I believe him."

"How do you know for sure?"

Eli handed him a towel. "The note said I'd be contacted by email in three days about where to find Adrian."

"So, you'll do *nothing* until then?"

"I didn't say that."

"Doesn't Adrian need blood every couple of days?"

"We can survive a week or more without it. Don't touch your eyes. The pepper will still be on your hands for a while."

"Yeah, I feel it."

"Scrub them until it's gone."

Drake blinked repeatedly to force his eyes to focus. They hurt like hell, and everything appeared blurry. "Where's Jonathan?"

While Eli tended to Drake, Jonathan had gone into his room. They found him on his bed. Crying.

Ignoring his own discomfort, Drake sat on the bed and massaged Jonathan's neck.

"Eli will find him, J."

Jonathan threw himself at Drake and hugged him tightly, sobbing. "A-Adrian w-was gonna m-make m-me his b-blood br-brother."

"We'll get him back."

"Jonathan, I need you to help with something," Eli said softly.

He raised his head. Tears streamed down his cheeks. "What?"

"I had Adrian researching someone for me. I think it's the same man who took him. Can you get into Adrian's PC and find out how far he got?"

He sat up and sniffed. Drake grabbed a tissue and wiped Jonathan's eyes. "No one can get into his PC." He wiped his nose on his sleeve and gave Eli a bit of a smile. "Except me. I know his password."

CHAPTER TWENTY-THREE

Detroit—Wednesday, November 19, 2003

"Mmm, what a wonderful meal," Rebecca said. Ysabel usually dined alone, but she had given her maid the night off, and cooked an exquisite dinner. The invitation had been a complete surprise.

"Have you guessed why I asked you here tonight?"

Rebecca shook her head.

"It's five years today that you've been working for me." Ysabel lifted her wineglass. "I toast an excellent employee—and a friend—who has proven her worth many times over."

Rebecca caught her breath. "You are too good to me."

"You have earned it. My business has grown so much that I could not have managed it these past five years without your diligence and hard work."

Overwhelmed, Rebecca felt the warmth rise in her neck as she sipped the fruity Merlot Ysabel had served with the meal.

"You must always believe in yourself," Ysabel said. "You are no longer that lost, young woman I took in. You have a new life full of possibilities. Now, shall we retire to the living room for dessert and coffee? I hope you like chocolate."

"What woman doesn't?"

Ysabel smiled. "Well said."

Walking to the living room, Rebecca contemplated what Ysabel had said. Ysabel was her mentor, and as far as she knew, Ysabel had never mentored another. Had Ysabel not found her, her life could have gone so many other ways, most of them self-destructive. Maybe one day she'd have her own business and be mentoring a young vampire herself.

She pushed Ysabel's words aside. Ysabel would live several hundred years more, and who knew where either of them would be then? She sat on the sofa in front of the fireplace.

Ysabel pointed at the serving cart beside the fireplace. "If you will pour the coffee, I will serve the cake."

Rebecca poured two cups and carried them to the table in front of the fireplace, inhaling the aroma of the dark, French roast on the way. She sat on the couch. Ysabel brought plates with cake on them and joined her.

Rebecca took a bite of the rich, chocolate cake filled with orange mousse and frosted with whipped cream. "Oh, this is exquisite."

"I think it's my favorite. I so love to cook, but I seldom have time for more than simple meals, that is when Fiona lets me in the kitchen."

Fiona was Ysabel's maid, but she believed she should be Ysabel's cook as well. Ysabel had found arguing futile.

Rebecca took a second bite of cake then sipped her coffee. "What does Eli Howard think of me?"

Ysabel looked up. "What do you mean?"

"When he was here before, I got a flash of his thoughts. I don't think he intended to project them."

"You remind him of someone he knew long ago, someone he was once in love with."

"Oh."

"What did *you* think of him?" Ysabel asked.

"He's nice, a bit disarming."

Ysabel laughed. Rebecca hadn't seen her laugh often. "With those thoughts, I suppose he was."

"Now, I confess there is another reason I asked you to join me tonight. Do you remember last month, the night of the Board meeting, I mentioned the troubling dreams I'd been having?"

"I remember."

Ysabel glanced away for a second. "The dreams have gotten worse. I fear bad times lie ahead. Like you, I did not ask to be a vampire. Yet, I owe what I am to people like Dietrich and Eli and to others who are no longer with us. If you don't mind, I'd like to tell you my story."

She always been curious about Ysabel's past, but theirs had been more of a business relationship, and she'd felt awkward asking. "I'd love to hear it."

"I was born in 1676 in a small village in west central Mexico, what is today the state of Jalisco. I'm a mestizo, a mix of Spanish and Indian blood. I had five brothers and sisters. We lived on a farm where I learned, as all Mexican women do, to be a good wife and mother. At seventeen, I married a fine man thirteen years older than me. By the time I was twenty-two, I already had three children: two handsome boys and a beautiful daughter." Ysabel dabbed her eyes with a corner of her linen napkin.

"One day in 1698, I was out trading in another village. My husband had stayed home with our children. During my absence, pirates raided my village. They'd done this to others closer to the coast, but ours was more inland, so we'd previously been spared. When I returned, I found my husband dead, lying next to the bodies of my children. Those women who weren't taken had been raped, and the husbands who tried to fight had been slaughtered. In my grief, I ran and never looked back."

Rebecca felt like she should say something, but she continued listening.

"I wandered from village to village, where I'd work for a meal and a night of lodging. Many nights I wished to die. One day I fell sick, and an older man found me and took me in. I told him that he should leave me, that it would be better for me. He tended me just the same. When I'd recovered fully, he asked me to stay and become his wife."

Rebecca gasped ever so slightly.

"I agreed. Where else could I go? He had given my life back to me. You see, that night, he changed me. 'Now our ages will not matter,' he said. He was a medicine man and taught me the healing arts. You'll find that skill among many of our kind. It's a paradox that we long-lived, nonhumans cherish life more than humans. Yet, I would gladly give up my longevity to be a mother again. I had a dark side then."

"You could never have a dark side," Rebecca said.

"Like you, I killed those I fed on." Ysabel put her hand on top of Rebecca's. "Except in my case, it wasn't anger which drove me. I blamed humans for what I'd become. Had I not lost my family, none of this would have happened to me, I believed. We had a different understanding of our kind then, much of it born from superstition and myth. I thought a simple bite caused the change, so I saw killing my victims as a kindness to them. Death was better than condemning them to be what I had become." She brought her hand to her lap.

"Didn't your new husband teach you otherwise?" Rebecca asked.

"He knew a bite did not always cause the change, but he didn't know why."

"What happened to him?"

"He was a wise man. 'I sense greatness awaits you beyond here, dear Ysabel,' he told me. 'Your destiny is not here with me. Now you must discover for yourself what it is.' He had taught me all he knew and had made me stronger than before." Ysabel put her hand under the silver and turquoise necklace she often wore. "This was his gift to me the night we parted." She smiled sadly at Rebecca.

"When I first met Dietrich in New Orleans in 1880, he already understood the need for training among us. He wanted to bring us into a new age and asked me to help him. Later, we created the Board and I became its head. I proposed a uniform set of rules for us and that we adopt Dietrich's mentoring idea among our kind."

"*You* created the rules?"

"With Dietrich's help. We agreed that humans should not be subject to our indiscriminate feeding and should be given the choice to be changed. And after being changed, they should have a teacher to guide them. For a long time, Dietrich has wanted to bring us into a new age."

"Then why does he oppose you now?"

"I believe he has grown tired of waiting and has let others cloud his judgment. It used to be said that the curse of vampires fell upon the women, not the men, because we cannot bear children. The experiments Dietrich supports and convinced the Board to support are an attempt to overcome the defect that makes our women sterile. That is what he said. I've since learned that Cyrus Hayes, not Dietrich, is leading this movement. I have purposely kept secrets about us from you, but no longer will I do that. A few weeks ago, I had a will drawn up. I've made you the legal heir to my business."

"Me?"

"By our law, you would inherit it anyway, but the laws in the United States often pervert one's intent. If something should happen to me, I want to know it will be in capable hands. I admit that training you and seeing to your education has been a bit selfish on my part. I've been grooming you to replace me."

"You're still young and have many years left in you."

"Perhaps."

"I'm not worthy of such an honor."

Ysabel put her hand on top of Rebecca's again and squeezed it. "The hardships you suffered in your early life have made you worthy." Ysabel gave her a knowing smile. "Who else could take it over? You're the one closest to family I have. You've more than demonstrated your capability. Still, I won't force this on you. If you truly do not wish it, I'll call my attorney and have my will changed. At least promise me that you'll give it careful thought?"

Rebecca sipped her coffee. This had overwhelmed her. "I promise that much."

The phone rang. "Excuse me," Ysabel said. She rose and crossed the hall to the library. Five minutes later, she returned, her face pale. She sat and bowed her head into her hands.

"What's wrong?"

Ysabel didn't answer at first. When she raised her head, the sparkle that usually dwelled in her eyes was absent. "Adrian Shadowhawk, Eli's student—someone kidnapped him this evening."

"Oh, my God!"

"Eli doesn't believe Adrian is in any danger. The kidnapping, he feels, is to make a point. Still, I know he's worried. As I feared, it has begun." Before Rebecca could ask the question, Ysabel said, "My nightmares."

"How can I help?"

"You're a strong woman, Rebecca. Even though you may not realize it yet, your powers are formidable." She forced a smile. "Let's finish our dessert. I have a lot more to tell you, and I regret that I must now share with you the dark times that have tainted our history. I had hoped to spare you the details of this unpleasant topic until another time."

CHAPTER TWENTY-FOUR

Detroit—Wednesday, November 19, 2003

Adrian regained consciousness with his head slouched forward. And the worst hangover he'd ever experienced. Sitting on cold concrete in the dark. Wrists tied behind his back. He figured he was inside because the cold air hovered around him instead of blowing past him.

"How's your head feel, vampire?" The voice echoed slightly, as if in a large, empty space.

He cautiously raised his throbbing head and straightened his back. "It hurts, asshole." A heavy collar encircled his neck.

"Yeah, nice side effect of the tranq," the voice said. "I'm told it's a special mix that takes your kind down faster, keeps you there a long while, and makes waking up a special treat. Did it give you a good buzz?"

"Why don't you try it yourself and find out, fuckface?"

"You're in no position to throw insults, vampire boy."

Intense pain shot through his neck. "Fuck!" He bent his head forward to stretch the suddenly contracted muscles.

"And there's plenty more where that came from if you keep mouthing off. It's an industrial-strength collar with extra-long-life batteries. I've never tortured one of your kind before, a Na-tive American, I mean." He laughed. "You prefer I call you Sitting Bull or Crazy Horse?"

"I prefer not to be here."

"Not an option. Let's warm you up. Let there be light."

With the heavy thunk of a large switch, the orange glow of filaments warming up made the darkness disappear. The lights got brighter. And brighter, until blinding lights surrounded him. They hurt, and squeezing his eyes shut didn't help.

"Don't think you can escape."

Another—stronger—shock from the collar made him arch his back, which refreshed his headache.

"I'd put up 'Dog in Training' signs, but nobody's around to see them. Or care. I bet you're smart enough not to wander too far. Yeah, I know the collar is crude, but there's something about putting an animal collar on a vampire that just makes it right."

He didn't hear the voice after that. The man was nearby, at the edge of Adrian's weak telepathic ability to detect him. Finally the lights went out. The pain in his damaged eyes remained. He couldn't sleep if he wanted to. Even if he were free to leave, he'd be blind until his eyes healed.

"When did you last feed?" the voice said what seemed like a long time later. "Yesterday? The day before? What's it like not to have blood? You're gonna be here long enough so I can watch you suffer."

He hadn't fed on blood for two days. Three would start the discomfort, but he could hide it for a while.

"I hear it hurts real bad. Down deep. You get sick and your body shakes. Then cramps wrack your body. Excruciating pain. You'll have to tell me if it's worse than this—"

The collar zapped him viciously. His whole body twitched for a long time afterwards.

"Dawn's not far away," the man said. "Sleep tight, don't let the rats bite. There's a blanket—if you can find it." His loud laughter echoed in the emptiness and faded into the distance. Adrian listened to the footfalls. They hit what sounded like concrete in some places place and old wood in others.

When he couldn't hear the man or sense his thoughts anymore, Adrian pressed his face against the rough concrete floor. Its coolness soothed his eyes. The musty, old-wood smell of the place, and the echoes suggested an old warehouse. He wiggled his wrists in the heavy handcuffs. No chance he could escape from them. If he had Eli's telepathic powers, he'd be able to make this bastard release him.

Adrian shifted his head to another cool spot and alternately squeezed and relaxed his eyes. "Make them water. They'll heal faster." Eli told him that four years ago, the day he'd decided to go out on a sunny day wearing a pair of sunglasses he thought were cool instead of the UV protective ones Eli had bought him. "It hurts, but it's temporary. Eyes heal fast." Small consolation it was during those several hours of agony.

It scared him that this guy might be working for Cyrus Hayes. Was Cyrus worried that killing him would piss Eli off enough to do something drastic? Was Cyrus afraid of Eli?

Today's cold-and-crappy weather was a blessing. His tormentor couldn't expose him to sunlight. Tomorrow might be another story.

His body started to cramp. He rolled onto his back, wincing when the handcuffs dug into his wrists and tried his best not to scrape himself on the rough floor. He was totally naked, not even briefs. Maybe his torturer hadn't realized stripping him meant he could piss without soaking himself. Wet briefs in this cold wouldn't be comfortable, and he had to piss real bad.

Adrian rolled onto his stomach. *Ouch.* His thigh was sore where the tranq dart had hit him. Maneuvering himself onto his knees with his hands behind his back proved difficult. More than once he scraped his forehead and knees against the floor. Finally, he positioned himself so he could pee comfortably.

He had no idea how long he'd been out or if he was still in Detroit. He suspected he was in some old, falling-apart warehouse. Southwest Detroit, near the Ambassador Bridge to Canada, had its share of abandoned warehouses. Even if that's where he was, not much chance of Eli finding him anytime soon.

He blinked a few times, then kept his eyes open. The cold, dry air hurt just as much. His nightsight let him see blurs of light here and there. Pulling one foot under him, he tried to stand. *Whoa! Bad idea.* His legs were stiff from the cold and his body was still wobbly from the drug. He had no idea how long he'd been unconscious, but if dawn wasn't far away, it must've been three or four hours at least.

He walked on his knees to get away from where he'd pissed, gently so he didn't land on a pebble or a protruding nail or broken glass. Probably best not to go too far. If the man was watching him from the distance, who knew what he'd do if his prisoner tried to escape? Dart him again? Probably not. He wanted his prisoner conscious for torture. The collar was sufficient.

Was there really a blanket here? He tried again to get to his feet. *Success!* This would save his knees, and maybe he could feel the blanket easier.

Okay, Adrian, do this logically. If you can hack into PC networks, you can find a blanket on the floor of an empty building in the dark. Do it in a pattern. Start from here and walk in a widening square. He cautiously felt ahead with his toes. *Wet there.* He stepped over it and continued his search. So far, no shocks from the collar.

He remembered Drake, hearing him scream, and hoped his friend was okay. *Oh, shit.* He'd smelled pepper spray just before he passed out from the tranquilizer.

Well, he'd been kidnapped close to nine, and Eli would have come home shortly after that and found Drake. Eli had good doctoring skills. He'd have Drake fixed up real fast. But Drake would be worried about *him.* Not that Eli wouldn't be. He didn't want to be this sicko when Eli found him.

He found the blanket. With his feet, he felt over and around it to be sure the asshole hadn't put something unpleasant on it. Stepping near what he judged to be the center, he carefully lowered himself to one knee.

Thinking about Drake took his mind off his own situation. He could imagine far worse pain that what he was in and hoped his captor wasn't that inventive. He could imagine how painful pepper spray would be on his cold, naked skin with no way to wash it off. Maybe, if he didn't resist, he'd make it out of this without permanent injuries.

Despite the warning about rats, he doubted any lived in here. Didn't they like warmer, closed spaces? He lay down on the blanket, rolled himself up in it. Shivering. At least the lights had kept him warm.

***

With a towel wrapped around him, Drake shouted down from Eli's upstairs hallway, "I'm going to help you find Adrian. On the double, my friend's in trouble!" Even after thirty minutes under the shower, his face and hands still prickled. His eyes felt like they'd been sandblasted.

Eli had been ignoring him for the past ten minutes, but finally appeared at bottom of the stairs. "You are not going out tonight, Drake. I put the spare clothes from your Jeep in the bedroom next to Adrian's. If you want to help, put them on and come down to Adrian's computer room."

Drake got dressed. He sniffed his arms before he put on his shirt and wrinkled his nose. Eli had made him wash with lemon-scented dishwashing liquid. A few minutes later, he joined Eli and Jonathan in Hack Attack Central. Jonathan was seated at Adrian's PC; Eli stood behind him. Jonathan sniffed the air and snickered. "You smell weird."

Drake ruffled Jonathan's hair. "Lemon fresh. How ya doing?"

"Great. Can I tell him, Uncle Eli?"

"Tell me what?"

Drake pulled up a chair next to Jonathan.

"You know that email warning Uncle Eli got about Ling's Place? Well, Adrian tracked the IP address to a guy who lives in New York. It's kinda technical. I can explain it later if you want."

"Get to the point, dude," Drake said impatiently.

"The guy's name is Adam Mathews. He's a hit man."

A chill shot through Drake. "A *hit* man?"

"Apparently," Eli said, "he does Cyrus' dirty work."

"And he's the one who took Adrian?"

"We think so."

Drake's hands were shaking. "A h-hit man's got Adrian?"

Eli put a reassuring hand on his shoulder. "Adrian will be okay."

With his heart racing, Drake turned his head around to face Eli. "How the fu— how the hell can you be sure?"

"Cyrus is warning me to stay out of his business. If he wanted Adrian dead, his man wouldn't have bothered with an abduction, and you'd probably be dead as well. Cyrus knows how much he can push me before I'll go after him, which he doesn't want."

Drake stared. "So, Adrian's not important to you?"

"Adrian is *very* important to me. Cyrus wants to make a point with me, not start a war."

"You're gambling Adrian's life on that assumption?" Drake pointed at Jonathan. "And you're not worried about your big brother?"

"Uncle Eli won't let anything happen to him. 'Sides, Adrian's tough." But Jonathan's eyes told a different story.

Drake gritted his teeth. "You knew about this *freakin'* scumbag coming here and you didn't do anything? I'm only seventeen and *I'm* smart enough to figure out he didn't come to Detroit to see the sights! I expected someone your age would be smarter."

"I know you're upset, Drake, and no, I did not know about it, but you have to trust that I know what's best in this situation. The last thing I want is for Adrian to come to any harm. I know how Cyrus thinks. He will have set limits on what he lets Adam do."

"Yeah, right. He's a *vampire*. He won't give a shit what Cyrus says." Eli's glance warned him about his language.

"According to our research, Adam is a human. My age *has* made me smarter, Drake. For us to interfere with the present course of events might well push Adam beyond the limits Cyrus has set. I don't like the situation any more than you do. Consider this: Adam arrived today, but his return flight to New York is on Saturday. He already has Adrian. If his goal is to kill Adrian, why stay so long?"

"How about torture first, *then* kill—like in the movies?"

Eli shook his head. "We also know he's staying at the Ritz Carlton Hotel."

"What'd you do, *Google* him?"

"Adrian hacked into hotel and airline records," Jonathan said. "See?" He brought up a website that advertised an exterminator. "This is his website."

Drake tilted his head back at Eli. "I thought a hit man always covered his tracks. Sounds to me like this guy wants to be found."

"Cyrus sees all humans as expendable," Eli said. "I'm guessing he is targeting me but isn't aware of Adrian's hacking skills. Cyrus also knows I'm an acknowledged pacifist and that I wouldn't kill Adam if I found him."

"So, that's why you're not doing anything, because you're a pacifist? You're a vampire!"

"Vampires are human, Drake, not superheroes. There's no way we can find Adrian if Cyrus and Adam don't want him found. Cyrus thinks he's manipulating me. He's hoping I'll get worried enough to do something irrational. I refuse to oblige him."

"You really believe they won't harm Adrian?"

"Yes, I truly believe that. Despite my reputation now, Cyrus knows I *can* kill"

Drake's anger rose again. "I don't give a fuck what you do. I'm going to find Adrian."

"I can't permit that, Drake."

He had walked only a few steps before his muscles stopped responding. The effect lasted just long enough to convince him that Eli meant what he said. "But he's my friend!"

"And he's like a son to me. I called Ysabel and Ling. Ling has some street connections who can watch for suspicious activity. That's the best we can do for now."

Drake sat. "This really sucks."

Eli again put a gentle hand on Drake's shoulder. "Yes, it does. I know you won't be able to sleep. Why don't you and Jonathan play a game you can take out your frustrations on?"

"What should I do about school tomorrow? I only have three classes. I can skip those, but I have a test on Friday," Drake said.

"If you feel well enough in the morning, you should go to school. You can't do any more here."

"What are you going to do?"

"Search my soul," Eli said. "In a way, this is my fault."

"How is it your fault?"

"Do you remember the first night Adrian brought you here?"

"Yeah."

"And do you remember when Adrian and I went into the library to talk?"

"Uh huh."

"I told him I should have killed Cyrus many years ago, when I saw the evil he was capable of."

"Adrian told me you said that. Why didn't you kill Cyrus?"

"My mentor, Dietrich, wouldn't give me permission."

"Why did you need his permission?"

"Because I respected him then."

"And now you don't?"

"It's not that I don't respect him. Cyrus has led Dietrich astray and he doesn't see it. I'm praying he learns before it's too late."

"Too late for what?"

"Cyrus Hayes has access to technology that, had it been available in Hitler's time, Hitler could have easily taken over the world, and Cyrus is much more intelligent than all of Hitler's men combined. He wants to eliminate our dependence on human blood. Once he does that, humans will be irrelevant to him."

CHAPTER TWENTY-FIVE

Detroit—Thursday, November 20, 2003

A sharp tug of his hair brought Adrian awake. "Get up, vampire," the rough voice said. "I see you found the blanket."

He must have slept, finally. His eyes had healed some, but he didn't expect to enjoy it for long. The lights were coming on again.

"A sunny day ahead. Maybe you'll get a little tan. Or a lot of tan." He laughed. "Don't know why you want to live in such a shithole of a city. New York's so much better."

This must be Cyrus' New York connection.

"I brought you a doggie dish with food and water. Don't try anything. I got some other darts."

Something jabbed into his right thigh. A moment later, his leg began to burn. A lot. "Fuck!"

"That's a small sting." The man yanked it out, but it didn't make any difference. "It'll get worse before it gets better. Lasts a while, too. Try to run and I'll use a big one. It'll have you crying like a baby. If that and the collar don't stop you, I can tranq you, but watching you sleep isn't much fun for me."

Fuck! His leg was on fire. He wished the man *would* tranq him. That way he'd get some rest. The headache would be a small price to pay.

It seemed like many hours before his leg finally stopped giving him major grief, but it was still swollen and hot. Of course, now his attention focused on the lights. That brought up other questions. Where was the man when he wasn't talking to him? How did he keep watch and not get bored? If he were doing this, he'd use a portable video camera. And how did the man stay warm in this cold? He hadn't heard a generator running, but there had to be electricity somewhere to power the lights. The man probably had a space heater, maybe even a PC.

No matter how much Adrian tried to think about other things, the blinding lights kept him reminded of where he was and what was happening to him. His bloodthirst finally kicked in, so now he could figure out how long he'd been here. For him it took close to three full days for the onset of the symptoms. He knew exactly when he'd last fed, two days ago, so he'd been here close to a full day. It felt a lot longer, though. Hiding the bloodthirst symptoms wouldn't be too hard for a while. The other pains gave him something to concentrate on, but tomorrow his tormentor would get the full show.

***

At school on Thursday, one of Drake's classmates asked why his face was all red. "Some girl was showing me this pepper spray she got and it went off by accident."

"Dude! That must've been awful."

"Wasn't fun."

Right after school, he stopped by his house, with sunglasses on to hide the redness still around his eyes.

Valerie was unusually talkative, but didn't question the sunglasses. "Drake, do you know what's going on with your father?"

"Why should I?"

"You were with him on Tuesday."

Right. Reverend Thomas Day.

"When he came home that night, he didn't eat any dinner and went right into his study," she said. "Last night he didn't come home at all."

"Not a clue. Call him and ask. Oh, I've got work to do for Professor Howard at Wayne State tonight. I'll be staying with my friend again."

"Are you all right, Drake? First your father is acting strange, and now you."

"Yeah, Mom, I'm fine. It's just that close to Thanksgiving, my teachers pile on the work. Maybe 'cuz I'm a senior, this is their last chance to harass me. I probably won't be home Friday night, either." He held up his gym bag. "I grabbed some extra clothes and my toothbrush." He hated lying to her, but he didn't have a choice.

"You're not staying with a girl, are you?"

"No, Mom. It's a couple of guys."

She shot him that questioning look.

"*Friends.* I promise I'm not gay. I like girls." He gave her a quick kiss on the cheek. On his way out, he muttered, "They just don't like me."

Driving to Eli's house, he wondered why he'd kissed his mom. He couldn't remember the last time he had.

***

Detroit—Friday, November 21, 2003

Shakes and cramps from bloodthirst wracked Adrian's body.

"Must be miserable being a vampire," his tormentor said.

After another session under the lights, Adrian couldn't see. He imagined the sadistic smile. "Why are you doing this to me?"

"Because I enjoy it. Because I can. Because I got paid real well to do it."

Adrian's muscles spasmed. He retched. Eli had taught him control. When his torturer left him alone—which wasn't often—he could stave off some of the suffering, but this asshole knew his business well enough.

"I think we'll change your accommodations."

The man crammed him into a small cage. On top of everything, Adrian was blind and weak from lack of food and inadequate sleep. Even if he had the strength, resistance would have led to additional suffering.

He couldn't straighten his legs fully, not even on an angle. From outside the cage, the man yanked Adrian's head back and pulled open an eyelid. Cold drops landed in one eye. Then in the other. Adrian prepared himself for the worst, but…the drops *soothed* his eyes. In fact, they hadn't felt this good before the lights. He blinked—even better. Why was the asshole being nice to him?

"Enjoy. The sun will be up in a couple of hours, and I put your cage in a spot where you can appreciate it. The blanket's gone, so don't bother looking for it. Oh, I forgot. You can't see." He grabbed Adrian's hair, yanked his head back, and sprayed something up both sides of his nose. "This'll kickstart the drops." He laughed cruelly as his footfalls retreated.

After several minutes not only did his eyes feel great, but his whole body did too. He didn't even mind the bloodthirst.

Chills then hot flashes coursed through him. *Okay, here it comes...* But this was more like an adrenaline rush. Kinda like cocaine. He'd done a little coke before he met Eli, but it wasn't anywhere near this good.

Waves of intense pleasure—sexually arousing pleasure—rolled over him. *What the hell?* He was rapidly getting an erection. *What the fuck?* He'd never sprung a bone like that, never been horned up and ready to blow so fast. What the hell had this guy given him?

"Really like that, do you?" the man said.

He'd been with enough women that he'd learned how to control himself, but this was something else. His heart pounded; his breathing became ragged. His body was fast approaching the point of inevitable release. His bloodthirst and all his other discomforts faded into the background as the sexual energy built and released itself with fantastic force.

"That's impressive." Through Adrian's sexual haze, the voice seemed distant. "Never seen a guy shoot that far. I wonder if Guinness has a category for that." He laughed raucously. "Must be really embarrassing with someone watching, too."

Humiliating, swirled through his sexual high.

"I'm supposed to report on how well the drug worked. Guess I'll report a mind-blowing success. Too bad it only works on vampires. We'd make a fortune selling it on the streets."

***

Friday, November 21, 2003

A bright day greeted a groggy Adrian as he came down from his high and slowly realized he'd been staring into the daylight. His legs were cold. And wet. Besides the other, he must have peed on himself.

"Ready for more?" the familiar voice said.

His eyelids were spread open one at a time, and the cool drops fell into them.

His torturer didn't use the bright lights again. Maybe he realized the eye drops took away the pain and the lights warmed his body. The periodic shocks from the collar continued. At first, they hurt a lot, but soon his bloodthirst agony made them not matter. He lost track of time.

"Have to leave." A long zipper unzipped; Adrian heard things being put into a box.

"Enjoy the sunny day. I know I will. I left the eye drops for you. Don't waste them. You'll understand why soon enough." He laughed.

In the distance, a car door opened and closed. The car started, then it drove away. *A trick?* As much as his rebelling body would let him, he stretched out his mind but couldn't detect the man.

He got onto his knees and put his head down. Feeling around the cage, he located his food and water bowls. He maneuvered his head over them and sniffed. At least he hadn't peed in them. His stomach was queasy from the bloodthirst. The cold air didn't help. He retched twice and yanked his head away from the bowls, vomiting the minimal contents of his stomach onto the ground. He leaned over his water bowl and lapped up some to rinse the foul taste from his mouth. He spat that out and drank again.

His hand touched a small bottle with a rubber bulb on top of it, next to the bowls. The eye drops? He had no way of knowing. Might be something nasty. Maybe the car driving away was a ruse and the sadist had set up a remote video camera to watch him cause himself more pain. But his eyes were hurting, and the drops had helped before. The bloodthirst made him retch again. This time he managed not to vomit.

A new sensation rose in his body, on top of the others, a deep craving. Like being horny. A frustrated horny. A having-been-teased-to the-limit horny. His breathing increased to a slow pant. The drops had made his bloodthirst go away for a while. Before he thought any more about it, he grabbed the bottle and squirted some drops into both eyes.

Sooo nice. He carefully recapped the bottle then lay down on his back, hands up to shield his face from the sunlight. The warm sun on his naked body was so sweet. His mind drifted into a peaceful place.

***

Detroit—Saturday, November 22, 2003

Drake was asleep on the living room couch when Jonathan began whaling on him. "Wake up! We got an email about Adrian." Drake's eyes popped open.

Jonathan yanked him off the couch and dragged him toward the library. "Hey! You're giving me rug burn!"

Jonathan stopped pulling. "Hurry up."

Drake got to his feet and stumbled along behind Jonathan into the library. Eli was sitting at his PC. Drake came around to look at the screen. The email read:

You will find him in a warehouse at West Fort and West Grand.

Drake's heart raced. "Where is that?"

"Southwest Detroit, near the river."

"When did this come in?" Drake asked, scarcely able to stay calm.

"Five minutes ago."

He jerked his head at the wall clock: ten fifteen. "What are we waiting for?"

"You drive my car," Eli said and handed him the keys.

"We're outta here!" Drake grabbed the keys and was already in the car and revving the engine by the time Eli and Jonathan joined him.

Fifteen or twenty minutes later, they arrived at a group of old buildings. "Which one?"

"The email didn't say."

"Must be a dozen of them," Drake said. "How the fuck are we gonna find him?"

"Watch your language in front of Jonathan."

"Sorry."

"Drive slowly around the area, close to the buildings. If Adrian is conscious, Jonathan or I may be able to pick up his thoughts."

"What if he's *un*conscious?"

"I know you're worried, Drake, but this is our best chance to find him quickly."

"Okay, I'll try it your way."

He'd driven by several buildings when Eli pointed and said, "He's in that one."

Drake slammed on the brakes, jumped out of the car, and ran toward the warehouse as fast as he could. Though it was dim inside, it only took him a few seconds to spot the cage bathed by the morning sun coming through the many broken windows. He reached the cage, panting hard. "Adrian?"

Adrian lay on his side, curled up in fetal position, not moving. His skin was dark cherry red. The cage had a combination lock. Drake grabbed the bars and tugged to drag it into the shade.

Strong hands pushed against his back. "You'll scrape his body on the concrete and make his injuries worse." Eli pointed to the collar on Adrian's neck. "And we want to disable that first."

Jonathan came over to the cage. "I disconnected the perimeter fence."

"Let's all lift and carry it out of the sun," Eli said.

They had just set the cage down when Jonathan spotted a piece of paper on the floor where the cage had been. He picked it up and read it.

Here's the combination.

While Jonathan opened the lock, Drake said, "That's sick, giving him the combination when it wouldn't do him any good with the collar on."

Eli removed his leather coat. "Jonathan, you're the smallest. Crawl in and wrap this around him. Be careful you don't rub it against his skin."

Adrian groaned while Jonathan wrapped him. Drake was relieved to see him alive.

"We're lucky it wasn't cold enough to give him frostbite. Being in the sun probably prevented hypothermia," Eli said. "Jonathan, help me roll him over."

As Jonathan nodded, Drake noticed his tears. Eli put his hands under Adrian's shoulders while Jonathan bent over and lifted Adrian's feet.

Drake noticed the small brown bottle clutched in Adrian's hand. "What's that?" he asked.

"Bring it along," Eli said.

When they had Adrian clear of the cage, Eli carried him to the car and laid him on the back seat with his legs bent. "I'll drive," Eli said.

"You sure?" Drake asked.

"Sit in the front with me. Jonathan will ride with Adrian."

A few minutes later, Drake asked, "Everything okay back there, J?"

"Y-yeah."

Drake chewed on his lip and said to Eli, "I said I wanted to be a vampire. Now I'm not so sure. He'll be okay, won't he?"

"Adrian has been though worse in his life."

From the back of the car, between his rhythmic sobs, Jonathan kept repeating, "Please don't die."

CHAPTER TWENTY-SIX

Detroit—Saturday, November 22, 2003

Eli carried Adrian into the house and up the stairs. Drake followed him.

"He's gonna be okay, isn't he, Uncle Eli?" Jonathan said from close behind.

"Drake, pull down the blankets and the sheet."

Jonathan helped him. Adrian shivered while Eli laid him on the bed, carefully unwrapped him from the leather coat, and put the sheet lightly over his naked body. "Do either of you want to stay with him?"

"I do," Jonathan said.

"Drake and I will be back shortly."

Outside the room, Drake asked quietly, "Why is he shaking like that? Shouldn't we take him to the hospital?"

"He's suffering from severe bloodthirst and exposure. I know a human doctor who specializes in our kind. I'll call if necessary, but I don't think it will be."

Drake followed him downstairs.

Eli went into the kitchen and to the special refrigerator for their blood supply. "He can have my blood if it'll help," Drake quickly said.

"I have enough here, but thank you for the offer." Eli opened the refrigerator.

"Holy shit!" Before when Adrian had shown him this, he'd seen half a dozen blood packs. Now it held twice that many. "Why so much?"

"We have three mouths to feed."

"Where do you get it all?"

"From regular donors that I pay well for their services. Come."

Eli went back upstairs with a blood packet. "How's he doing, Jonathan?"

"He's real bad."

Eli propped Adrian's head up with pillows. Within a few minutes, Adrian was slowly sucking the blood through a tube.

"Wouldn't an IV be faster?" Drake asked.

"It's less effective. We only do it when the vampire is unconscious."

Ten minutes later, Adrian's shakes had subsided, but he still whimpered around the tube he was sucking on. When he tried to push the sheet off, Eli folded it back just below his waist.

"Can't you take away his pain, Uncle Eli?"

"Now that he's had the blood, I can help him." Eli took the blood tube away and concentrated. Adrian's body visibly relaxed.

"How long will it take him to recover?" Drake asked.

"I've dealt with his bloodthirst. The burns aren't serious. It's winter and he wasn't exposed that long. If this had been summer, his skin would be blistered." He carefully lifted one of Adrian's eyelids. "I'll call the doctor to prescribe some cortisone eye drops."

That reminded Drake of the small bottle he'd taken from Adrian. He took it out of his pocket and examined it. *Oh, shit.* He showed Eli. "This bottle Adrian had—the label is from Radley Biotech. Where did he get it?"

"We'll find out. Don't lose it." Eli held it near the heavily shaded lamp next to Adrian's bed. "A better question is, why did he have it?"

***

Later, downstairs, Drake talked with Eli while Jonathan stayed with Adrian. "What's your plan? You gonna find this Adam Mathews? His flight schedule said he wasn't leaving town until tomorrow."

"That's my intent."

"So, whatcha waiting for?" Drake tried to sound casual, but what if Adam got away?

"I don't want to leave Adrian yet. His well-being is more important at the moment. Adam Mathews will pay for what he did. You can trust me on that."

Eli took Drake into the library and examined the bottle. "I need to find out what's in this. My guess is Adam Mathews used it on Adrian, but until he's lucid, I can't ask him."

"Why would my father's company insignia be on the label?"

"Most likely because your father's company manufactured it."

"Evil Ethan's Empire doesn't do drugs," Drake said, pleased with his assonance and alliteration skills.

"Do you know what this code on the label means?" Eli asked.

"I try to know as little as possible about Ethan's company."

"Is there someone you trust whom you can ask? If I'm right, this is Cyrus Hayes' doing, and your father probably knows nothing about it. If it's something addictive, I'll want more information so we can figure out how to counteract it."

"I know several of the research guys, but the only person I really trust is one security guard. He wouldn't know or have access to that info. Ethan once told me they keep database records of everything they make. Maybe we could hack in."

"That's Adrian's department. Right now, he can't."

Shortly after dinner, Drake went upstairs to Adrian's room. Jonathan had refused to leave the room and parked himself in a chair next to the bed. "You doin' okay, little bro?"

Jonathan rubbed his eyes on his sleeve. "Uh huh."

Drake massaged the back of Jonathan's neck. "Eli says he'll be fine."

"Why did they hurt him like this?" Jonathan sniffled.

"Because they're bad people."

"Hey," Adrian said weakly.

"Dude! You're awake." Drake ran downstairs to get Eli.

Eli checked Adrian over then said he had to go out to take care of some business and to call if they had any problems.

Drake pulled up a chair. Adrian sounded in good spirits even though he looked like shit. His eyes were swollen, and his fierce sunburn made Drake cringe.

"Help me sit up," Adrian said. "Real easy. Hey, little bro, some cold ice cream would taste great. Would ya mind gettin' it for me?"

Jonathan beamed. "Sure!"

"And some for Drake."

"Sounds tasty. Thanks, J."

"Take good care of Adrian while I'm gone," Jonathan said.

"I promise."

With Jonathan out of the room, Adrian said, "What happened to that little bottle I had when you found me?"

"Uh, I gave it to Eli. It's on his desk in the library. What's in it?"

"Special eye drops. Any chance you could bring me that bottle?"

"Why?"

Adrian reached out and put a hand on Drake's knee. "Please?"

"Not until you tell me why."

Adrian sighed. "It's a nasty drug, and he hooked me on it."

"We gotta tell Eli."

"Well, he's not here." Adrian's breathing got heavy and rapid. The sheet tented below his waist. Adrian bent his knees up.

"Dude, are you throwing a bone?"

"It's the drug. Shortly after you use it, you get horned like you've never been horned before, and it doesn't go away. It keeps going until you— Okay, here's the problem. After you get off, you're on this fantastic high for a couple of hours. Then you get horned all over again, but in a different way. It's like if you don't have sex right away, you'll go out of your mind."

"Can't you just…uh…take care of it yourself?"

Adrian inhaled deeply and blew it out through his mouth. "Tried that in the cage… I couldn't make it happen, like something was stopping it." He took another long breath. "You know…how a guy's…gotta wait a while afterwards…before he can do it again?"

"Sort of." Drake's face got hot. "Remember, I'm only seventeen. My experience is…limited," he said.

"Still a virgin?"

"I got laid once."

Adrian inhaled and exhaled slowly. "You want to get off, but you can't get relief no matter what you do. You have to use…the drops…again." He wiggled on the bed and winced. "Shit…these sheets feel like…sandpaper." He was panting.

"You don't look so good."

"Get me the…drops… Please?"

"When did you last use them?"

"Early…this morning…'fore…you…found me…sun was…beginning to burn." He put his hand on his chest.

Jonathan came in carrying a tray with three huge dishes of chocolate ice cream. He looked at Adrian then at Drake. "What's wrong?"

"Nothing. Feed him some ice cream. I'll be right back."

***

"Mr. Mathews' room please," Eli asked the desk clerk. This was also Dietrich's hotel, surely a coincidence. Dietrich likely wasn't aware of Cyrus' activities or of Adam's presence here, if he even knew who Adam was.

Eli appreciated that Adrian had also hacked the New York State DMV records to get a photo of Adam. There'd be no mistakes. He knocked on the door of Adam's room.

"Who is it?" the voice on the other side asked.

"Cyrus Hayes sent me."

With his telepathy, Eli knew Adam was peering back at him.

"Hayes didn't mention anyone was coming, Mister…"

"Radley."

Adam hesitated.

"I made the eye drops," Eli said.

Adam opened the door. "I expected—"

"A white man? That is statistically unlikely in Detroit."

"Come in, Mr. Radley."

Eli entered and locked the door behind him, standing in front of it.

"I was just going to dinner." Adam's attire consisted of a black dress shirt, no tie, and navy slacks. And he matched his photo: six-three and a very healthy husky. "Care to join me?" Adam walked to the bed, where a navy blazer lay beside an open suitcase.

Eli moved toward him. "I had hoped to catch you before you ate."

"Those eye drops are something else. If they worked on humans, you'd make a fortune."

"I'm not Mr. Radley, Adam. My real name is Eli Howard."

Adam paled. Reacting instantly, he reached into the open suitcase and withdrew a dart gun, aimed, and fired. In that last fraction of a second before it struck, Eli snatched it from the air and threw it back, narrowly missing Adam on purpose. Adam dropped the gun and charged.

Eli's telepathic burst made him stagger.

"What the fuck?"

Eli grabbed him around the neck. "I do not appreciate you injuring—and torturing—my friends."

Held in Eli's grip, Adam regained his composure. "You can do what you want to me, but you'll answer to Hayes for it."

"Mr. Hayes doesn't care about you. You are his pawn, serving his immediate purpose. At his whim, you are expendable." Eli knew that, in his heart, Adam Mathews must know it as well. "You think we're all evil. Cyrus Hayes is evil. I am not. I am, however, determined to get some answers I suspect you're not going to give me willingly. Am I right?"

Adam put on a stoic face; Eli read his deepest fear.

"Mr. Mathews, please remove your shirt."

Adam didn't move. Outwardly, he exuded confidence. Eli ripped the shirt off, then physically forced Adam onto his knees. Still holding Adam around the neck, with his other hand Eli took the bloodletting tube from his coat pocket. Using his teeth, he pulled the cap from the sterile needle then jabbed it into Adam's jugular.

Adam's neck muscles corded while he tried to pull his head away. Pressure on the nerves at the base of his neck convinced him of the futility of escape. Eli put the open end of the attached plastic tube in his mouth and started to suck.

Fear took over. Adam began to tremble. "Stop, please stop," he said just short of sobbing. "I don't want to die this way."

Eli removed the needle. Pressing two fingers over the wound, he telepathically relaxed Adam. "You won't die today, not by my hand. I'm not the killer you and Cyrus are," he said around the tube in his mouth. He sucked out the residual blood and dropped the tube. "Consider this a demonstration that I could easily kill you. Remember it before you attack anyone associated with me again. Tell Cyrus that his tactics and menials will not deter me."

Forty-five minutes after his arrival at the hotel, Eli walked out of the Ritz Carlton. He waited for the valet to bring his car, tipped the man, wished him a good evening, and drove calmly home.

At six twenty, carrying two large pizzas liberally topped with the boys' favorites, Eli unlocked the front door.

Drake appeared at the top of the stairs. "We didn't expect you back so soon."

Eli set the pizza boxes on the small table inside the front entrance. "How is Adrian faring?"

"Right now? He's feeling pretty good."

Eli came up the stairs. "I expect he is."

"So, what happened with Adam?" Drake said. "We had a pretty good idea what you were going out for."

Eli continued into Adrian's room and immediately went over to Adrian. He took a small bottle from his left coat pocket and put it on the nightstand next to the bed. "Here's another bottle of drops for your continued pleasure until I can find out how to counteract your addiction. I picked up eight more from Adam, all he had."

"Oops, he knows," Drake said behind Eli.

"Appreciate it," Adrian said with a lopsided grin.

"What happened with Adam?" Drake asked again.

"I expect none of you have eaten dinner, so I brought everyone's favorite pizza."

"Okay, we're hungry," Drake said, highly annoyed, "but won't you tell us *something* first?"

"I accomplished four things tonight."

"Like?"

"First, I forcefully probed Adam's mind for useful information. Second, I returned his can of pepper spray."

Drake's mouth dropped open. "You *returned* it?"

"After I emptied it over his face and bare upper body."

Drake grinned. "Very sweet! And..."

"I stuck a dart into his thigh. It caused him significant pain and had him spewing invectives at me."

"Outstanding," a mellow Adrian said.

Drake raised his eyebrows. "What's the fourth thing?"

CHAPTER TWENTY-SEVEN

Detroit—Saturday, November 22, 2003

Eli removed a full blood packet from his coat pocket. "For Jonathan and Adrian," he said, "I brought dessert, courtesy of Mr. Mathews."

Anxious to know the details, Drake quickly brought TV trays and an extra chair into Adrian's bedroom so they could all eat and talk. "Aren't you going to tell us what happened?" Drake asked when Eli didn't spill his guts.

"Enjoy your pizza first."

They draped a cloth napkin under Adrian's chin so he wouldn't slop pizza on himself where wiping it off his sensitive skin would be uncomfortable. Watching Adrian having to eat more daintily than usual made Drake mad at himself for not protecting his friend. But what could he have done except make matters worse for himself and Adrian? He didn't even want to think what would have happened if Jonathan had been here. The whole thing was so fucked up.

With a mouth full of pizza, Jonathan asked, "Did you kick his butt?"

Drake waved his hands. "Mmm huh. I bet he used his supertelepathic powers."

"I handled him," Eli said. "What I did to Adam Mathews tonight was for the three of you, not for myself and not for revenge. He needed to understand that I will protect those close to me and I won't be intimidated. Now, we must discuss the matter of your safety."

"Whose safety?" Drake asked.

"All three of you will be leaving Detroit on Monday."

"Nuh uh, I'm staying." Drake stared directly at Eli. "You can't make me leave."

"This is not open to debate."

"Where are we going?" Adrian asked.

"Chicago. I promised Jonathan a trip to the science museum."

Drake's mouth fell open as Adrian said, "You're not serious."

Eli met Adrian's astonished gaze. "I'm going to sneak the three of you out of town. Airline flights can be traced—like you did with Adam. Driving you all to Chicago is the best way."

"Why will we be safer there?" Drake asked.

"I'll call Seth Clayton, Jonathan's uncle, who owns a private plane. He'll pick you up in Chicago and take you to Denver afterward. It'll be nearly impossible for Cyrus to trace you, assuming he's interested in trying, and Jonathan can visit his parents for Thanksgiving."

"When are we coming back?" Drake asked. "I have school next week and a big test in my history class."

"You'll come back when it's safe," Eli said.

"If I miss that test, I'm screwed."

"Your safety is more important. I'll handle your teachers if necessary. I'm taking every possible precaution. Once Adam Mathews recovers and contacts Cyrus, none of you will be safe here. I plan to keep Cyrus distracted. Unfortunately, my probe of Adam Mathews' mind revealed nothing of use. As I expected, Cyrus kept him ignorant." He asked Jonathan, "Would you like to see your father and mother?"

Jonathan shrugged. "Yeah, I guess so."

"For the moment, though, none of you is going anywhere. Drake will stay here until we're ready to leave. Jonathan is also a possible target. I've enough things to worry about without adding the three of you to my list. Adrian, by the time we get to Chicago, you'll be healed enough to protect Drake and Jonathan. Later tonight I'll call Ling, Ysabel, and Dietrich to come over for a conference."

Adrian held up a bottle of eye drops. "What about these? I'm still addicted, and the supply is limited. If we stay until Tuesday, I might be able to learn some useful information about them."

Eli seemed intrigued. "What's your idea?"

"Well, Drake's father's company manufactured them. There must be records. Right, Drake?"

"Yeah. Anal Ethan keeps records of everything."

"While you were gone, Drake and I talked about it," Adrian said. "It has to be an inside job, and Drake's the only one who has access."

"It's too dangerous," Eli said.

"Not if we do it during the day, late in the afternoon," Adrian said. "We know Cyrus sleeps then. He won't be expecting us. Drake goes in supposedly to see his father, except he sneaks into the security monitor room instead. I'll be in contact by cell phone and talk him through it. Then he leaves, and no one is the wiser."

"What if he's discovered? Did you consider that?" Eli asked.

"You'll drive out there with him and stay in the car while he goes in. That way, you'll be there in case anything goes wrong."

Eli thought that over. "I'm impressed with how well you've thought this through."

"Thanks. Jonathan stays here with me. You can have Ling come over and bring one of her bouncers if you want bodyguards for us. We'll be safe, Drake will be safe, and you'll get the information you want. Win-win."

Drake had been bobbing his head back and forth between them during their conversation.

"All right. Does anyone have any questions or anything to add?" Eli asked.

Jonathan, who had been silent, quietly raised his hand. "Can Adrian and I have that dessert you brought us now?"

For the first time since Drake had known him, Eli laughed heartily.

"Before that," Adrian said, "I made Jonathan a promise." He patted the bed next to him. "Come up here and have a seat, little bro." Jonathan, somewhat puzzled, got onto the bed. "Before this nastiness happened, I told him that he and I could become vampire blood brothers. We want you and Drake to be our witnesses."

***

In the library, Eli stared at the telephone. Adrian was sleeping; Jonathan and Drake were in the living room. He never expected the stopping of a rape a few weeks ago would be the catalyst to change the life he'd been living, nor that his initial, noble quest to fix Detroit would become a fight to protect Ling and Adrian, the two people who were family to him. He also hadn't expected two new responsibilities, a human and a vampire, to enter his life: Jonathan Clayton and the lost and lonely—but likeable—Drake Radley. Was he no more than the idealistic dreamer Ling had said he was? But Ling had never been the optimist when it came to humans. He was sure her undisclosed past had influenced her in that regard. His idea hadn't failed. Outside forces intervened before he'd had a chance to start. The plan still made sense.

The sounds coming through the closed library doors suggested that Drake was letting out his frustrations on whatever game they were playing. He didn't have to read Drake's thoughts to know he'd felt totally helpless during Adrian's kidnapping. Despite their short-term acquaintance, Drake regarded Adrian as a trusted friend and had fiercely resolved not to let anything happen to him or Jonathan, who had acquired two brothers, not one.

Therein lay one of Eli's concerns. He was directly responsible for Adrian and Jonathan and indirectly responsible for Drake. Ironically, the threats to their safety resulted from his own past action or inaction. If he'd disobeyed Dietrich all those years ago and acted on his instinct to kill Cyrus when he should have, none of this would be happening now. Even more ironic, he'd helped create the police force, the one they nicknamed Vampires, Inc., to rein in the warlike vampire factions. Those factions had been dealt with long ago. Yet according to Ysabel, Cyrus now controlled the group and was apparently using it as a covert, terrorist organization to wreak havoc on humans: definitely Cyrus' style.

Then there was Adam Mathews. He was an anomaly. Assuming Cyrus still hated humans, what had persuaded or convinced Cyrus to use one for his work? A hundred years ago, by any standard of the time, Cyrus Hayes had been a cold and calculating genius. What skills had he acquired since then and how far had he pushed himself toward achieving his diabolical goal of world domination by vampires?

Back in 1905, when the world was a smaller place and the technology cruder, a terrorist group couldn't inflict the damage one could today. Nine-eleven amply demonstrated the power of a *human* organization. That kind of power and organization controlled by a twisted genius like Cyrus Hayes was too horrible to imagine. The potential devastation would be far worse than the 1905 Conflict. Cyrus Hayes had to be stopped.

Cyrus wasn't his only worry. Complacency among their kind was another enemy. He'd let that sin creep into his own life as well. Dietrich and the Council had seriously fallen prey to it. Could he convince them of the danger before it was too late?

And where did the wild-card, mayoral candidate Jeffery Thomas fit into this already convoluted situation? How had Thomas come to know about vampires in Detroit? It couldn't be a coincidence. The Detroit vampires were a discreet lot overall, even given Adrian's occasional gaffes. He doubted Adrian's and Jeffery Thomas' circle of friends had any common links. Was it further meddling by Cyrus? If so, why? Nothing they'd uncovered about Jeffery Thomas suggested he posed a serious threat to them. What did Cyrus have in mind? Harassment? Misdirection?

Ling was coming over later. She had wanted Ysabel to join them, and Ysabel asked if Rebecca Goodman could come as well.

"Given my feelings toward her the last time we met," Eli had said to Ysabel, "is that wise?"

"She is involved and concerned. It is precisely because of your feelings that she should be with us. The two of you should talk in private after our meeting."

He assented, even though he'd feel uncomfortable. This time, he'd be more discreet about controlling his thoughts.

"Call Dietrich," Ysabel had said.

"I don't want Dietrich with us."

"I agree, but call him, feel him out on the issues."

Dietrich had made his support of Cyrus' plans clear. Less clear was his relationship with Cyrus. How could he not see what Cyrus was doing? Or had he realized the truth and was covering or protecting himself? Not even Dietrich was safe if Cyrus saw him as an enemy.

He dialed Dietrich's hotel room. Dietrich didn't answer. He didn't leave a message. Then he called Ysabel. She had no idea where to reach Dietrich, and Dietrich didn't believe in cell phones. As Eli hung up, he hoped Dietrich hadn't become another one of Cyrus' victims.

CHAPTER TWENTY-EIGHT

Detroit—Sunday, November 23, 2003

Drake wandered downstairs a little past eleven in the morning. He found Adrian on the leather couch watching TV and wearing only a pair of silk boxers.

"Hey," Drake said. "Should you be out of bed?"

"Hey," Adrian said. "Why not? I feel okay."

"Dressed like that, I mean."

"I should be able to dress any way I want in my house, right?"

"Even naked?"

"Naw. It's not polite to brag."

Drake laughed. "How long you been down here?"

"Couple of hours. Couldn't sleep anymore." Adrian had a satin-covered pillow propped behind him. "'Sides, the leather feels good on my skin."

"You look a lot better than you did last night. Whatcha watching?"

Adrian paused the DVD. "*Farscape*, first season. They finally released it late last year. I missed some of the first episodes, so I was catching up on commercial-free entertainment."

"Sweet."

"You're a fan?"

"Aeryn Sun—Claudia Black—is a bootylicious babe," Drake said.

Adrian sighed and discreetly folded his hands over his groin. "Let's avoid that subject. Remember the eye drops? I'm trying to avoid lustful thoughts."

"Sorry, I forgot. I hope Eli finds an antidote soon. It's gotta be embarrassing 'specially when you can't wear anything to hide it." He pointed at the TV. "Mind if I watch with you? Whenever Ethan catches me in front of the TV, he says I should be studying, even if I'm done with my schoolwork, or watch stuff that's relevant to my life."

"Like, more down to Earth?"

"Yeah, History Channel and Discovery Channel—and the news." Drake let out a heavy sigh. "I wish I could stay here next year, in Detroit I mean, instead of going to boring Harvard. What's wrong with Wayne State? It's an excellent school."

"But you don't have any say in it, do you?"

"Exact-a-mundo."

Adrian scooted up a bit to give Drake room to sit. "Your father wants prestige attached to your name."

"The way things are going for him, prestige won't be worth shit. Maybe he won't be able to afford Harvard."

Adrian lifted one hand and touched his fingers lightly to his sunburned chest.

"You doing okay?"

"Still tender. You recovered from the pepper spray?"

"Yeah, but it put me off spicy foods for a while. Say, I'm starving. Too bad I can't cook or I'd make you breakfast."

"Jonathan loves toaster pastries. There should be a supply in the kitchen."

"Sounds good. He won't mind if we dip into his stash?"

"Eli just did shopping. I'm sure he stocked up."

"You want red stuff drizzled on yours?"

"No red stuff. I'm set for a while. Then we can watch *Farscape* until little bro wakes up. He usually sleeps past noon on the weekends."

About one thirty they'd just finished watching their third *Farscape* episode, when Eli and Jonathan came downstairs.

Jonathan ran toward Adrian, arms spread as if to hug him. Drake grabbed him around the waist. "Don't touch."

"I'd appreciate it if you put on more clothes," Eli said to Adrian.

"They chafe too much. How about PJs?"

Eli nodded. "I'm going to fix lunch. Jonathan, would you like to help?"

"Okay."

They went into the kitchen.

"A year ago," Adrian said, "I bought these silk boxers 'cuz I thought women might find them sexy. I bought a pair of silk PJs, too, but I've worn them exactly once. My women prefer me naked."

Adrian went up to his room, walking slowly, and came back five minutes later in his PJs. After lunch he spent the rest of the afternoon in his computer room while Drake and Jonathan watched *Farscape*.

During a break, Drake went to check on Adrian. "How's it coming?"

"Shitty." Adrian pounded his fist next to the keyboard. "I can't get past the fucking password."

"What password?"

"The one for Radley Biotech's files."

"Why didn't you say so before?"

"And your point is?"

"I know it. Ethan always uses the same one." Drake wrote down *DorianGrey* on a pad. "My middle name, Dorian, came from the Oscar Wilde story, but Ethan spells the password G-R-E-Y instead of with the 'a' like it should be. He said that would confuse hackers." He grinned at Adrian. "I guess it worked."

Adrian balled up a fist.

"Dude, you didn't ask."

Within a few minutes, Adrian had found the files they wanted, but… "Shit. They're locked to outside access. I thought I could do it all from here. I guess you still gotta do the secret spy thing and go in there tomorrow."

"I'm ready." But Drake was nervous.

"Let's hope you don't run into Cyrus," Adrian said.

Exactly *why* he was nervous.

***

Detroit—Monday, November 24, 2003

Late that afternoon, in a light snowfall Drake and Eli drove out to Radley Biotech.

Drake stopped at the security desk to say hi to Pete.

"You've been visiting here a lot lately," Pete said.

Pete didn't seem suspicious, but best to justify his recurrent visits. "Ethan and I are trying to patch up our father-and-son relationship," he lied with a tilt of his head. "Well, at least *I* am. I'm not all he wanted in a son. Even if I was Superboy, he'd find a reason to be disappointed. I figure I'll be in college next year and won't see him except on vacations. Still, I'm his only kid, sole heir to the Radley fortune or whatever. My mom has been pushing me to make peace with him."

"Probably not bad advice."

Pete was forty-two. When he was around Drake's age, Pete had lost his father in a motorcycle accident. He'd said he wished they'd talked more.

"I heard you had some excitement here last Tuesday," Drake said. "Some kind of fight?"

"They hushed it up real fast. Two of the guards went to the hospital, one with a couple of broken ribs, the other unconscious. I only found out when they asked if I wanted to chip in for a get well card and gift. Neither one is back to work yet."

Pete motioned for Drake to come closer. "Rumor says one of the lab guys went postal, but I didn't see anyone being escorted out, so I don't know what really happened. Besides the two guards who went to the hospital, two others went out on leave. We got some contract temps in to replace them. My boss advised me not to ask any questions. I don't think he knew the details either. If you know or find out anything, you probably shouldn't tell me."

Pete straightened and leaned back. "They've upped the security. Make sure you keep your badge in plain sight."

He'd been wondering how they were going to explain away Cyrus' outburst. "Do you know if my father's busy?" he asked Pete.

"I haven't seen him since he came in. Normally I don't pay much attention except to say good morning, but he came in an hour earlier than usual, with shadows under his eyes, like he hadn't slept for a couple of days. He's had no visitors today, and Mondays are usually busy for him. Is he okay?"

Drake shrugged. "You see him more than I do. Later, Pete."

Interesting. Ethan always came to work in control and ready to conquer the world. Well, he didn't have time for Ethan's problems. People he cared about were depending on him. "Work fast," Adrian had said. "In and out, like rabbits fucking."

He headed to the elevators and got off on the top floor, where Ethan's office was. The front desk could monitor the elevators. Not that he thought Pete would check on him, but if they'd increased security, Pete would be expected to keep a close watch.

He took the stairs down one floor and strolled to the security monitor room. His badge buzzed it open. Once inside, he called Adrian's cell phone.

"Bunny one in position and ready to screw," Drake said when Adrian answered.

On the other end, Adrian coughed and cleared his throat. "Don't ever do that again while I'm eating."

"Do what?"

"Make me laugh."

"How was I supposed to know?" Drake pictured Adrian spewing lunch all over himself.

"Get serious," Adrian said. "The longer you're there, the more chance of being discovered."

Drake logged in at the console. Adrian talked him through locating the files. As soon as he found them, he hung up with Adrian. They didn't want to chance that someone walking by would hear voices and come in to check.

Adrian had given him two USB drives. He plugged in the first one. When that download finished a couple of minutes later, Drake checked his watch. He'd been in the building twenty minutes already. He called Adrian again. "Yo, done with one, on to more fun," Drake said.

"Make it fast. Remember, Eli is waiting in the parking lot. We don't want someone to get suspicious about him sitting in his car so long."

"Right," Drake said. He swapped USB drives. "Be done in a few."

"Hang on the phone. I'm gonna check in with Eli." Adrian used their house phone to call Eli.

Meanwhile the download completed. Drake slipped the second USB drive into his pants pocket and put his cell on speakerphone while he restored the PC to its logon screen.

"Okay, Eli hasn't seen anything suspicious. Just hurry," Adrian said.

Drake heard the door to the room open. He grabbed his cell and quickly took it off speaker.

"What are you doing in here?" a voice said.

Oh, fuck. "Security's here," Drake said into his cell a moment before he flipped it shut.

"Turn around slowly, hands away from your body."

Drake followed his instructions. "I'm Drake Radley," he said. "My father owns this company and pays your salary, so don't do anything you'll regret."

Drake knew most of the guards by sight, but this one was younger than most, probably one of the temps Pete had mentioned. Eager to impress.

"Who were you talking to?" the guard asked.

"My mom, Valerie Radley, the wife of the guy who owns this company and is paying the fat salary you're enjoying."

"It's not that fat," the guard said.

Drake gave him a sheepish smile. "Maybe I could put in a good word for you with my father."

"Unclip your badge and hand it to me slowly."

Worth a shot. Drake complied.

"Does your father know you're here?" the guard asked.

If you say 'no', he's gonna call someone and that someone will call Ethan. If you say 'yes', he's gonna escort you to Ethan. Either way, Ethan finds out. He was so screwed. Wait, there might be a way out of this. This guard didn't know him, so…

"Okay, my father doesn't know I'm here yet. Here's the story. I stayed with a *friend* over the weekend, and wasn't home. I just got out of school for the day," Drake continued. "I was on my way to my part-time job, so I wanted to stop by to say hello to my father. You know, maintain a good father-and-son relationship?" *Drake Radley is gonna rot in hell.* "Now, I bet you wanna know why I was in *this* room?"

The guard sort of nodded and raised his eyebrows at the same time, in a weird way. "Well, I know it's a private room where almost no one goes. I figured it was a good place to call my…" He did the quote thing with his fingers as he said, "…*friend* to say what a nice time I had last night."

"You told me you were talking to your mom."

Shit, how much more obvious did he have to be? Drake smiled sheepishly. "Okay, I lied about that."

The guard half smiled. He'd finally caught the implication of a female friend. Just when Drake thought he might get away with it, the guard said, "I'd better take you to your father." He gave Drake back his badge.

"Great. I'd appreciate the escort. First, can you give me a quick moment to call my *friend* back? Just take a minute. So my *friend* knows I wasn't being rude when I hung up the call?"

"Make it fast."

Drake redialed Adrian. "Hi. Sorry I had to hang up before. A security guard came in and thought I didn't belong here. I'm going to see my father 'fore I head off to work with Professor Howard. I'll call ya later."

"Message understood. I'll be watching," Adrian said.

Drake closed his cell and smiled. "Thanks. Appreciate it. Shall we go see Oz the Great and Powerful?"

The guard gave another of his weird facial contortions, not understanding the slam. The guy was maybe mid-twenties and had a heavy tan, with black hair liberally gelled down and back, a gym fanatic judging by the athletic size shirt he was wearing. The small black letters on his gold nametag read, *Jeremy.*

Ethan's office. The moment of truth. At least Adrian would get to see it all. Jeremy stopped at the secretary's desk, and she buzzed Ethan.

Let him repo my Jeep. I'm free, white, and seventeen. He had a job now. He could save up and buy his *own* Jeep.

Jeremy ushered him into his father's office. "Sorry to bother you, Mr. Radley. I found your son in the security monitor room. He said he was authorized to be in there, and was coming to see you, but with the new security directives, I thought I'd better escort him."

Nice professional speech. This guy knows how to suck up. He'll go far.

Jeremy left.

Drake had been in his father's office dozens of times, but never before had it been so dark. It was almost spooky with the blinds closed and the lights dimmed. He'd gotten used to the low light levels in Eli's house, but Eli's house was bright compared to this.

Behind the desk sat a version of Ethan Radley he'd never seen before. Pete had understated his appearance. His father's sunken eyes and the creases around his mouth had aged him ten years in a few days. He looked like total shit.

Staring at his father, Drake sat. Ethan's eyes focused on the top of his highly polished desk lit by two overhead spotlights. "What were you doing in that room?"

"Talking to someone on my cell. I was coming to see you when it rang. It was one of my friends, so I ducked in there because it's quiet."

Ethan raised his head. "That's down on the *third* floor."

"Yeah, I was taking the *stairs* up—it's good exercise for the heart, you know."

Ethan rose slowly from his chair and walked over to the small bar in his office. He poured himself a shot of something and downed it. "Drake, I'm not in the mood for any of your shit today. Why are you here?"

Ethan Radley said "shit" to his son? Hell must be experiencing an ice age. Drake sat back in the chair and crossed his arms. "Because I wasn't home all weekend, I thought I'd stop by to say hello to my loving father. And as a reward, I get hassled by your ass-kissing security squad out spying on innocent citizens. Oh, I forgot. I'm not an innocent citizen. I'm the boss' kid so I get hassled even more."

"What is your problem today, Drake?"

"*I* don't have a problem, at least I didn't until I ran afoul of your Protectors of the Realm."

"Drake..."

Here it comes.

Ethan stared at him. "If you came here to argue about something, I don't have the time or the energy for it right now. Please leave. We'll discuss this at home." He poured himself another drink.

"That's always your answer for everything. 'Later, Drake. We'll talk about this later, Drake.' I'm tired of *later*!"

"That's enough." His father's voice lacked the authority it usually had.

What the fuck is going on with him? He said that without even a hint of a threat behind it. Drake put his feet up on the desk. "What say we kick back and have a little shouting match? It's been a few weeks. I kinda miss it."

"You're an ungrateful little prick."

"That's right, blame the kid, like you always do."

"I've given you everything—"

"Now *that's* more like the *loving* father I remember from the past seventeen years. Right, you've given me everything...*except* your love."

Drink in hand, Ethan returned to his desk. He put the glass on the desk, sat, then braced his elbows on the desk and rested his forehead against his fingertips. "Drake, I really don't want to argue with you. Not now. I've done something stupid, or rather, I became involved in something that's gotten out of my control, and my attempt to fix it has made matters worse."

"I'm sure you'll get through it." Drake tried to spike his words with sarcasm.

Ethan massaged his forehead. "This isn't something I can 'get through.' An unwise business deal has gone very bad."

"Okay, so you're having some financial problems. That's not the end of the world." Then Drake saw the fear on his father's face. *My God, he means Cyrus Hayes. Did something happen between them that I missed?*

His father put his fingers on his temples. "It's more than that. All I ever wanted was a good life for my family. No matter what you think, I do love you. I know I haven't shown it, not for a long time. I let my ambition get out of hand and didn't realize what I was doing to you and your mother. Worse, I'm afraid for both of you. I've put you both in danger, and I don't know how to protect you. Or if I can."

"That's okay," Drake said, "I can take care of myself." He took his feet off the desk and pushed himself to his feet. "Email me when you get your life sorted out and I'll see if I can work you into my busy schedule." He headed to the door.

"Drake...please don't leave yet."

"In case you haven't figured it out, Cyrus Hayes is bad news."

He slammed the door behind him.

On the drive back, Eli asked him, "Is everything all right?"

"No prob. Just glad I'm outta there."

Eli didn't say anything more until they got back to his house and were headed inside. "Adrian called me and briefed me on the conversation between you and your father. He recorded it. You should watch it with me."

"Why would I want to?"

"Because I'm asking."

First Ethan, now Eli? "*Fine* with me."

"Drake..."

"Yeah?"

"Drop the attitude."

Adrian took the USB drives and headed into his computer room with Jonathan while Drake and Eli watched the recording in the living room. When it was over, Eli said to him, "I'm disappointed in you, Drake. What you said to your father was beyond cruel."

"Like why should I care? He's learning what the receiving end feels like."

"Your father knows he's in serious trouble, and that his family might be in danger."

"So? What was I supposed to do? Give him a big hug and say, 'Everything's gonna be all right, Dad'? I don't think so." Drake stood to leave.

Eli put a firm hand on his shoulder, pushed him back down, and held him there.

"Hey!"

He grabbed Drake's chin firmly and forced Drake to look at him. "You need to change your attitude, young man."

"Who the fuck you think you are? My father?"

Drake clenched his neck muscles, trying to move his head. Eli's thumb and forefinger dug painfully into the sides of his jaw. "Ow!" Eli's icy stare frightened him.

"Cyrus Hayes is a ruthless man. He thinks nothing of killing someone—anyone—who gets in his way, vampire or human. Your parents, your father *and* your mother, are potentially in his path of destruction. Whether or not you acknowledge it, your father did help raise you."

"Barely," Drake said through a mouth being squeezed sideways.

"He provided for you; he has tried to ensure that you have a home and a good life. He may not be the ideal father in your eyes, but he is still your father."

Releasing his grip on Drake's chin, Eli ejected the disk from the DVD player and handed it to Drake. "I suggest you watch this again before you pack your things."

Drake's heart thumped in his chest. "You're kicking me out?"

Eli put one hand on Drake's shoulder and gave it a firm, but not uncomfortable, squeeze. "Have you forgotten that tonight we're leaving for Chicago?"

"Oh."

"I'll do everything in my power to protect your parents. It's my sincere hope you won't have to attend their funerals, regretting the last words you spoke to your father."

Adrian stepped into their line of sight. "Sorry, didn't mean to interrupt, but I just found something important in those files Drake copied."

"Tell me," Eli said.

"Well, I found the records for the eye drops, but nothing about an antidote. It looks like they've already made hundreds of bottles. Other 'substances' are listed as well. The files tell what they're all for in great detail." He looked directly at Drake. "Your father's company—probably unknown to him—is manufacturing illegal drugs. If this information gets into the wrong hands, like to the feds, your father will be in a shitload of trouble, and probably be facing criminal charges."

CHAPTER TWENTY-NINE

Detroit—Monday, November 24, 2003

Eli glanced into the rearview mirror at Adrian and Jonathan in the backseat playing an adventure game on Jonathan's laptop. Adrian had bought him two extra battery packs so they could play uninterrupted. They'd left Detroit an hour ago, on their way to Chicago. Before leaving, Drake had called his parents.

Adrian's addiction to Cyrus' eye drops concerned Eli. The one withdrawal attempt resulted in severe, migraine headaches. Several rounds of vomiting later, Adrian begged for the drops. Eli refused to let him try withdrawal again until they learned more about the drug's effects. In the meantime, the current supply of drops would last a couple of months if Adrian used them judiciously.

Drake sat in front listening to the new iPod he'd bought himself with the money from his job. The teen had a lot of anger. He carefully concealed his intellect beneath his rebellious exterior. This trip would help him channel his anger to more productive uses and let his hidden side come out. Eli had expected that Jonathan, not Adrian, would be the catalyst. Drake's desire for a sibling, preferably a brother, was clear. Adrian and Jonathan had bonded immediately, but Jonathan also adored Drake. The feeling was mutual. The night Adam Mathews abducted Adrian, Drake had shown deep concern for Adrian's well-being. Underneath those feelings, Eli had read a sense of relief that Jonathan hadn't been home at the time. In his heart, Drake had adopted Jonathan as his brother. This trip would bring them all closer and reassure Jonathan's parents. Although Jonathan communicated with them regularly by email and phone, this was his first visit back home since being changed.

He looked askance at Drake. For the moment, the teen was content. He tapped Drake on the shoulder and waited for him to pause his iPod. "Are you getting sleepy?"

Drake nodded.

"Adrian, please hand Drake a pillow."

"Thanks," Drake said. He stuffed it into the corner between the seat and window and resumed his iPod music.

"Keep the noise down back there," Eli said.

"Uh, huh," Jonathan said. "No, you gotta go *here*," he said to Adrian.

Eli smiled to himself. Having these fine boys in his life was a privilege. At all costs, he'd keep them safe.

Last night's tense meeting with Ysabel, Ling, and Rebecca replayed in his mind. He'd fought to focus on the immediate matters and had avoided Rebecca. Ysabel kept giving him subtle warning glances. Ling also noticed and more than once nodded at him.

"Dietrich has gotten so caught up in Cyrus Hayes' lies and exaggerations that he no longer sees the truth," Ysabel said. "There is no doubt we're in some danger from humans, but Dietrich doesn't realize Cyrus has stirred up the trouble."

"Can't you tell him the truth?" Rebecca asked.

"Dietrich is beyond listening to me. For too long we've distanced ourselves from the human world." With a gentle smile, Ysabel pointed at Eli. "That one has been equally guilty until recently. He is our prodigal son. I thank him for returning to us."

Eli felt himself blush.

"You were drawn into the Great Conflict in China against your will," Ysabel said to Ling. "I respect and understand your choice to live a peaceful life in the United States. I regret once again drawing you into something not of your choosing."

"Before the fire at my club, Eli had asked for my help in cleaning up this city. He is difficult to refuse. I pondered carefully before I consented to help him."

Ysabel straightened and regarded each of them before she spoke again. "We established the Board to provide unity among our kind. It seems that Cyrus now indirectly controls the Board, and I fear he will soon have direct control. I have become a figurehead. It may be time for another to take my place."

"No!" Rebecca interjected.

"Vampire society is at a crossroads," Ysabel said. "We need a stronger, younger one to lead us."

Eli heard the desperation in Ysabel's words. She never referred to their kind as vampires, always as nonhumans. The stress had already affected her.

"Ysabel, the Board needs you," Rebecca said.

Ysabel shook her head. "What use am I if they won't listen to me? I have a successful business I enjoy running. Lately it has been demanding more of my attention. As my capable assistant, you well know that."

"But you have led for so many years."

"I'm not ready to abdicate my position quite yet. I will not do so unless asked to or until a worthy replacement steps forward, but I wanted you all to know my feelings. We are in a new century. Our continued survival demands that we change our thinking accordingly."

As always, Ysabel had spoken with wisdom, but Eli worried about the consequences of those changes. He had one last question for her. "How will you deal with Dietrich?"

"I don't know." She rose from her chair. "We must be going. Ling has to go back to her club to close up; Rebecca and I have some business to take care of before tomorrow. Eli, I thank you for your hospitality."

He knew her coldness reflected her frustration. He escorted the women to the front door and retrieved their coats from the closet before he walked them out to Ysabel's car.

Before she got in, Ysabel had said to him, "Perhaps Dietrich will listen to you?"

***

Detroit—Tuesday, November 25, 2003

On the way back to Detroit, Eli felt good that he had accomplished at least one thing in Chicago. At first, he'd been apprehensive about Jonathan seeing his father again, but that had gone well. Seth, Ben, and the boys enjoyed the museum. Because they could see only half of it in one day, they were staying overnight in Chicago to see the rest tomorrow. Seth insisted on paying for the hotel. Then they'd fly to Denver on Wednesday night.

Ben stayed close to his son, asking questions about Jonathan's new friends and how he liked Detroit. Eli didn't fully understand why Ben took an instant liking to Drake. On the other hand, Drake was trying hard to impress Ben.

Jonathan showed his father the new laptop and the iPod. "I hope you thanked Mr. Howard for them."

Jonathan puzzled over that. "Oh, you mean Uncle Eli. I did."

"We miss you. We're glad you're coming home for Thanksgiving."

"Me too," Jonathan said.

"You're not giving Mr. Howard any trouble, are you?"

"Nooo."

"How's your schoolwork?"

"Uncle Eli gives me all As."

"Only because you deserve them," Eli said.

Later in private, Ben said to Eli, "I'm glad he's made new friends. Is he really doing okay?"

"He's bright and anxious to please."

"He doesn't resent me?"

"He did initially, but the memories of his good times with you have pushed the bad ones aside. You haven't lost him, Ben, and you never will."

Ben sighed. "Seth and I have talked a lot. I wanted to understand my son's new life and to resolve my own issues with my brother."

Given all the upsets in his life in the past couple of months, Eli was glad at least some things had worked out well. He wanted to hope that everything would. As soon as he got back to Detroit, he'd talk to Dietrich. This time he wouldn't mince words.

***

The doorbell rang a second time at Ysabel's home. "I'll answer it, ma'am," Ysabel's maid, Fiona, said as she passed the library.

"Are you expecting someone?" Rebecca asked.

"Not that I know of."

Rebecca had come there at Ysabel's request to discuss recent events. Ysabel had just switched the topic to Eli Howard before the doorbell rang.

"May I help you, sir?" they heard Fiona say.

"Is Ysabel here? I wish to speak with her."

"Is Ms. De La Cruz expecting you, sir?"

"I don't believe so."

"Ms. De La Cruz is busy, but I'll ask. May I tell her who's calling?"

"I'll announce myself."

"Sir—"

A moment later, a short, red-haired gentleman wearing a long woolen coat entered the living room. "Ysabel, how good to see you again."

"You are not welcome here, Cyrus," she said.

Cyrus...Hayes? Rebecca's hands trembled in her lap.

"I'm sorry, ma'am," Fiona said behind him. "He forced himself past me."

"It's all right, Fiona. Go back to whatever you were doing."

"Yes, ma'am."

Ysabel rose from the sofa. "Why are you here, Cyrus?"

"Ysabel, it has been so long since we last saw each other. Am I not allowed to pay you a visit?"

"I doubt that you're here for a social call, Cyrus."

He held out his hand, palm up, at Rebecca. "Who might this charming lady be?"

"She is my assistant, and we were discussing business. Again, why are you here?"

He looked over at Rebecca. "Ysabel never did like small talk." With his hand now pointed toward Ysabel, he said, "Please. Sit." She did. He remained standing and panned his head around the library. "A charming house." He faced her. "You and I have business to discuss."

"I am not interested in whatever you have to say, Cyrus."

Rebecca, looking at Ysabel, started to rise. "Would you like me to leave?"

"No. I'm certain Mr. Hayes will be leaving shortly and anything he has to say concerns both of us."

"Quite so," he said. "All right. Since you insist, I'll come to the point of my visit. A crisis is coming. Our race is being threatened. As we speak, humans are plotting to hunt us down. I do not intend to let that happen. I want your support for whatever action is necessary."

"I am not a fool, Cyrus. The only threats that exist are ones *you* have deliberately created. Nonhumans have peacefully coexisted with humans and can continue to do so."

"Dear Ysabel, why do you persist in seeing us as less than what we are?"

"We *are* human. Our best action is to reveal ourselves to them, to help them understand who and what we are, and to show them that we pose no threat."

"You would have us subjugate ourselves to *humans*!" He said it with such violence, nearly spitting the last word, that it startled Rebecca.

"That will happen only in *your* mind, Cyrus. The Council intends to forge a beneficial relationship with them."

Cyrus laughed raucously. "Relationship or sustenance? Ysabel De La Cruz still lives in her naive fantasy world. The Council is not inclined to such an impossible dream. I, not you, control them now. Humans threaten our existence now more than ever. With six billion of them in the world, they outnumber us a million times."

"We were all human once."

"And we've risen above their pitiful weaknesses. Humans had charge of the world and they have made a mess of it. Now it's our turn." He gestured toward the hallway, at where Fiona had been. "You defend the pitiful weaklings, yet you recognize their place as our servants."

"Fiona is not my servant; she's my employee."

"An arguable distinction. Dietrich is also afraid for us. He agrees with me."

"Only because you deceived him. You told him the experiments were for our benefit."

"I *convinced* him that they were our best course of action. You'll benefit as well. If I'm successful, you'll be able to bear children. I know you both long for that day."

Rebecca didn't like how this meeting was progressing. She feared for Ysabel, for them both.

"Not at the cost of harming humans," Ysabel said. "I intend to tell the Board and Dietrich the truth. We will stop you, Cyrus."

He laughed. "The Council members are doddering fools stuck in a past they never really belonged to, and you, my dear, are a powerless figurehead."

"You're insane to think you have any chance of succeeding."

He laughed again. "Those who fail to recognize my genius have called me insane. Live in your delusions while I conquer the weak and mold the vampire race into the rulers of this world. I have resources you can't even imagine. I will succeed, and those who oppose me will be eliminated. Hobart and Gerrick opposed me."

Rebecca gasped. *Cyrus killed them?*

"We know about the drugs you're making and selling. We will stop that as well."

Sarcasm tinged his laughter. "What resources have you at your disposal to accomplish that? You are such an idealist, Ysabel. As long as humans are willing to buy, why should we deprive them of their pleasures? It's ironic that their money funds our research, which we will use to subjugate them. A new age is dawning for us. It's a shame you won't live see it." From under his coat he withdrew a large gun with a silencer. "In a small way, I almost regret what I must do."

Cyrus aimed it at Ysabel; the gun popped loudly. Ysabel's mouth opened and her eyes widened. Two more shots came from Cyrus' gun. Red stains formed on the front of her blouse. Her expression of surprise collapsed; her eyes shut and she slumped away from Rebecca onto the sofa.

Cyrus pulled the body onto the floor. A moment later, he withdrew a machete from under his coat and swiftly and efficiently severed Ysabel's head from her body.

Rebecca swallowed her scream.

Cyrus straightened himself. When he stared at Rebecca, she trembled and prepared to die. He wiped the blade with a handkerchief, then tossed the handkerchief onto the floor and slid the machete back into its sheath under his coat.

"The beheading was unnecessary," he said with indifference. "She was already dead, but the Council must understand my sincerity in this. Our kind *will* rule the world."

Breathing rapidly, Rebecca watched him exit the living room. The front door clicked open then shut.

Pax the cat ran into the room and halted. He sniffed the air before padding over to investigate. He looked up and gave a long, mournful meow. She knelt beside him. He lay there on the floor, mewing.

A scream from the living room entrance startled them both. Fiona stood horror-stuck in the hallway. "Oh, sweet Savior, no!"

Rebecca rose, squared her shoulders, and went to comfort Fiona. Then she'd call Eli Howard.

CHAPTER THIRTY

Detroit—Thursday, November 27, 2003

Four people sat around the dining table in Eli's home. He'd insisted Dietrich sit at the head. On the wall behind him hung the Mexican flag. Rebecca and Ling sat across from one another on either side of Dietrich. Rebecca's eyes were red; a deep sadness emanated from Ling. Dietrich's face was impassive now. Last night had been another matter. Eli had never seen him so visibly shaken and struggling to contain his thoughts and emotions. At some point between then and now, Dietrich had composed himself, but he made no attempt to conceal the traces of conflict that simmered inside him.

Dietrich pushed back his chair and stood. "Through Eli's kind hospitality, we are here to share our grief at the passing of our beloved Ysabel. It is appropriate that we do so on the American day of Thanksgiving, in the country where she made her home. We owe her much for unselfishly giving of herself to us. Let us bow our heads in remembrance of Ysabel Maria De La Cruz. Eli, will you offer a prayer?"

Dietrich had surprised him yesterday by suggesting this gathering and asking him to say a prayer. He'd struggled with the words for many hours last night. He didn't consider himself religious. With all the death and violence he'd seen in his life, he'd never found any religion particularly comforting. In other times and places he'd grieved over the deaths of his brother Jonas and his beloved Sophie, but he hadn't prayed for them. He wanted to believe an afterlife existed. If anyone deserved it, Ysabel did.

The words welled up in his heart. "Heavenly Father, we thank you for Ysabel and for blessing us with her presence. The trials you put her through strengthened her and gave her the wisdom to lead us. We will miss her." He tilted his head heavenward. "Be at peace, Ysabel. If you are watching, pray for those left here who will carry on your work."

Dietrich nodded his approval and said "Amen." He held up a bottle of wine. "This is a German port I had flown here from my estate in Germany late yesterday. The vintage is 1880, the year I first met her. I invite you to partake of it with me."

He opened the bottle and poured, first for Rebecca, then for Ling, Eli, and himself. He lifted his glass. "To you, Ysabel, for enriching our lives, for your stalwart presence among us, and for your vision of our future." They drank together. Dietrich sat, and the caterer served the traditional American Thanksgiving meal. Eli had offered to cook, but Dietrich insisted he not.

Before dessert Dietrich said, "Ysabel and I often disagreed on what was best for us. In the past, one would either convince the other, or we would reach a compromise. The recent vote on the human experiments was the first time that didn't happen. I forced the Council to decide for us, and I swayed some of the votes. Although I believe she knew this, she played fairly and relied instead on her own powers of persuasion. She nearly won.

"I wish now I had listened to her. I knew her heart was speaking, yet I ignored it. As long as I have known her, her heart has never been wrong. Instead, I listened to Cyrus Hayes, who said this was for the good of all vampires.

"I also know that in the end, the vote would have made no difference. Cyrus didn't require our approval. He manipulated me into manipulating the Council to believe his ideas were a boon for us all. I learned recently that he had begun the experiments on his own even before the vote. He believes our rules don't apply to him."

"You did what you thought was right," Eli said.

Dietrich shook his head. "I thought Cyrus offered a new hope at a price we could all live with. I knew what he was. I let his false promises misguide my zeal, and it has cost us dearly. We have a German proverb: *Kommt Zeit, kommt Rat.*"

"With time comes insight," Eli said.

"You have remembered your German. For me, the advice of the proverb came too late."

"I won't let you accept the blame alone."

Dietrich lifted his glass to Eli. "Neither will I let you blame yourself. Decades ago, when it came to dealing with Cyrus, you followed my wishes not to act against him."

"Had I known, I could have stopped him," Eli said.

"And perhaps added your own death to the tragedy."

"Last Wednesday, Ysabel and I had dinner together," Rebecca said. "She shared with me the details of her life before. Ysabel had a premonition this would happen. I should have told someone." Rebecca lowered her head.

Ling quietly rose from her chair, walked around the table, and knelt beside Rebecca. Putting an arm around her, Ling said to Dietrich, "What will the Council do?"

"We are having a meeting tomorrow. They will all be attending the funeral on Saturday."

Ling looked at Eli. "What will *you* do?"

***

Detroit—Friday, November 28, 2003

Eli called Adrian in Denver with the news. Adrian had met Ysabel only once, but he'd want to know.

"She's dead? What happened?"

"Cyrus Hayes happened," Eli said.

"This keeps getting worse, doesn't it?"

"Do you want to attend her funeral tomorrow?"

"Is it safe for me to travel?"

Eli heard the concern in Adrian's voice. "If you want to come, we'll make sure it is."

"Well, the problem is everyone here will want to know why I'm leaving. We came here because Detroit wasn't safe, and now I'm going back? Not a good idea. J and Drake are having a fun with J's parents. I don't want them worrying about me."

"J?"

"Yeah, that's what Drake calls him now. Since you call him by his regular name, and I call him little bro, Drake wanted his own nickname. Drake's the only one allowed to call him J, 'cuz it's a rap name and Drake's a rapper."

"Everything's good there?"

"We're all enjoying the holiday, so I don't want to bring it down with bad news."

"My wisdom is finally rubbing off on you."

"Yeah, Adrian Shadowhawk with a conscience kinda sucks. I'll tell everyone you called to wish us Happy Thanksgiving. See you soon."

Dietrich took care of the funeral arrangements and kept Ysabel's death out of the local news media. Eli appreciated his efficiency. Ysabel's lawyer, a human, understood fully what she was and worked with equally impressive efficiency to handle the legal aspects, even the death certificate. Rebecca would send a notice to Ysabel's clients, advising them of her untimely death from a heart attack and that she, Rebecca Goodman, would take care of all business matters for the time being.

After the service, they would ship Ysabel's casket to Mexico. Dietrich had arranged to bury her on the land where the village of her birth had stood.

***

Detroit—Saturday, November 29, 2003

They scheduled the evening service at a funeral home near Ysabel's neighborhood. Dietrich would preside over it, which surprised Eli because Dietrich was an avowed atheist.

On his way there, Eli picked up a tearful Fiona. "Thirty years with her, now I've no job." At first she hadn't wanted to go. Being deeply religious and despite working for Ysabel, vampires made her uncomfortable. But she owed it to Ms. De La Cruz to be here, she'd told him.

When they arrived, Dietrich, Rebecca, and the seven Council members were already present and talking among themselves. Eli introduced Fiona, then he caught Rebecca's attention and exchanged brief thoughts with her.

"Don't worry about your job, Fiona," Rebecca told her. "I inherit Ysabel's house. Your longtime service to Ysabel means a lot to me. I could use help keeping it up. I'd like you to stay on with me, but I'll see you're taken care of no matter what you decide."

Eli sensed Fiona relax a little.

Dietrich signaled Eli to gather everyone into the chapel for the service. As soon as everyone was seated, a tired-looking Dietrich walked to the podium.

"The Ysabel De La Cruz most of you knew was different from the Ysabel De La Cruz born in Mexico over three hundred years ago. She was a woman of peace and of great strength among us. In the dark times of the Conflict, she found the courage to act impartially and in the best interests of our kind. While she led the Council, she did not neglect to forge a life for herself. She established a successful import/export business and became wise in two worlds: human and vampire."

He tilted his head heavenward. "Dearest Ysabel, over the past decades, your insight and wisdom have guided us. Among all of us, you were the most worthy to lead and the most gentle soul I ever knew. May eternal peace be yours." Dietrich had temporarily lost his atheistic proclivity.

Rebecca spoke a few words, as did Ling and Eli. At the end of the service, the Council members together laid a wreath of orchids over Ysabel's closed casket.

After the service, Dietrich approached him. "Ysabel didn't deserve this death," Eli said.

"No. Over the years, one thing Ysabel and I always agreed on was our respect for you. She spoke often of first meeting you in 1906, near the end of the Great Conflict. You were a mere seventy years old. It impressed her how the older vampires already respected you. She saw great wisdom and a great future in you. You disappointed her when you divorced yourself from us to follow a solitary life on your own."

"I wanted time to understand myself."

"For that reason I suggested you become a teacher. Yesterday, during my meeting with Council, we spoke of Ysabel's wish regarding her successor."

"Rebecca would be a fine choice for the job," Eli said. "Ysabel was grooming her for it."

"We were aware of that. One day she will be ready, but Rebecca wasn't her first choice. Ysabel wanted *you* to lead us, and the Council members are unanimous in that. Will you accept?"

Eli didn't hesitate before saying, "Only if Rebecca is my second."

Dietrich laughed. "Ysabel also wished that. The unexpected opening on the Council resulting from Hobart's murder, we will offer to Rebecca."

Eli was glad to see Dietrich in better spirits. He was unsure how to take this unexpected series of surprises. "There is something I must do first."

"Cyrus Hayes has returned to his estate in Ireland," Dietrich said. "You have my permission to deal with him."

CHAPTER THIRTY-ONE

Denver—Sunday, November 30, 2003

Adrian's cell phone woke him. Why had he chosen that obnoxious ring tone? And who the hell was calling him at eight on a Sunday morning? He rolled over in bed, fumbled to retrieve it from the bedside table, and noted the incoming number. He'd managed to adjust his sleep schedule while here in Denver with Jonathan's parents, but he'd been up until four in the morning playing board games with Jonathan and Drake. He needed sleep. "Yo, Eli. 'Zup?"

"How is it going there?"

"Hang on a minute." Adrian quietly got out of bed and walked into the hallway outside Jonathan's room.

"Sorry, I didn't want to wake Jonathan. Been kind of emotional for everyone, for Jonathan in particular. We had Thanksgiving dinner at his parents' house. I helped his mom with the cooking. He's excited he's going to have a baby brother or sister in June..."

"Is there a problem?" Eli asked.

"Not exactly. He's started having bad dreams."

"About what?"

"I don't know. He won't tell me. I talked to Seth and he wonders if it's a delayed reaction to his change."

"Perhaps. Well, the three of you can come home now."

"Drake's gonna be disappointed with that. He started enjoying himself once I got him to stop worrying about his AP history class. Apparently, he has an 'A' going in it."

"I didn't know he cared that much for school."

"That's the impression he gives his parents. In some ways, he's more of a nerd than I am."

"In what ways?" Eli asked.

"He's only been laid once."

Eli sighed. "I hope Jonathan didn't hear you."

"Little bro is sleeping, which I should be doing. You did wake me, you know."

"Tell Seth to bring you back to Detroit tonight, to Young International. I'll have a limo waiting for you."

"You're not picking us up?"

"I'm going out of town."

"Where to, if I may ask?"

"Dublin."

"As in Ireland? What you wanna go there for?"

"It's where Cyrus Hayes is."

"Oh... Oh, shit!"

"It's necessary, Adrian."

"Now I've got you to worry about?"

"I'll be fine, but please don't tell Drake or Jonathan. When you get back to Detroit, Ling will stay at the house with you. See that Drake gets to and from school safely, although I don't foresee any problems."

"Can do, will do. And *please* be careful."

"Trust me, Adrian. There is no need for you to worry. I'll see you in a few days."

Adrian went back into the bedroom. *Don't worry?* How could he not?

"Who was that?" a sleepy Jonathan asked.

"Eli. He says we're going back to Detroit tonight."

"Shit. Do we gotta?"

Adrian glared at him.

"What? Drake says 'shit' all the time."

"He does not," Adrian said.

"He *thinks* it."

"Why are you reading Drake's thoughts? We've warned you about a person's privacy."

"Sometimes I can't help it. You won't tell Uncle Eli, will you?"

"Only if you promise to let him help you control your telepathy. It's gonna get you in a lot of trouble otherwise."

"I promise. What's Uncle Eli up to?"

"Nothing. He has to go out of town on business."

"Where's he going?"

"I can't tell you."

"I'll read your mind."

"No, you won't, because I can block you."

"Not always."

Adrian glared at him again. "If you try to read my mind, I'll take away your iPod. Understand?"

Jonathan nodded slowly.

"Okay, let's go wake Drake."

Jonathan gave him a high five. "You rhymed. Let me wake him. That'll piss him off."

Adrian pointed at the nightstand next to Jonathan's bed. "I'm really wantin' that iPod, little bro. It's gonna feel so sweet clipped on my belt."

Jonathan pursed his lips. "Will you make me breakfast? I want blueberry pancakes."

His favorite. "I think your mom will want to fix you breakfast, but I promise to make some when we get back. We'll eat, then Drake and I will take your stuff to the airport and load it in the plane."

"Drake and Uncle Seth can do it. Uncle Eli said you're supposed to stay out of the sun until you're all healed."

"I'm healed, my eyes are anyway. Heavy clothing and sunglasses will be more than enough protection for the short time I'm outside."

Jonathan had a lot of shit he wanted to take with him. Fortunately, the plane—and Eli's house—had plenty of room for everything. Seth promised to take them all on a vacation sometime to see the Grand Canyon, and Adrian talked him into a trip to Las Vegas in the spring.

By the time Seth and Drake and he had finished stowing the second load in the plane, it was midafternoon. A concerned Ben was sitting in the living room when they got back.

"Where's J?" Drake asked.

"In the bedroom… Crying, I think."

"What's wrong?" Adrian asked.

Ben shut his eyes. "Maybe you can talk to him. He won't listen to me."

Adrian took off his sunglasses and headed to Jonathan's room. "Little bro?" Jonathan had his face buried in the pillow.

"M-my mom…h-hates me."

Adrian sat on the bed and put his hand on Jonathan's back. "No, she doesn't."

"Sh-she th-thinks…I'm…a…m-m-monster."

What the fuck is going on? "Wanna tell your big brother about it?" He rubbed Jonathan's back and shoulders to calm him then lifted the boy off the pillow. Adrian rested Jonathan's head on his shoulder and gently hugged him. Drake came to check on them. "Any idea what this is about?" Adrian asked him.

"Ben doesn't know, either. I was in the kitchen talking to his mom while she fixed lunch. A few minutes later, he ran to his room."

"You stay here," he told Drake. Adrian marched into the living room and confronted Ben. "What the fuck did you do to him?"

Ben matched his stare. "How dare you accuse me!"

"I *dare* a lot things. Remember what I am."

"Calm down, Adrian," Seth said. "I'm sure it's just a misunderstanding."

Adrian stared at Ben. "Tell me, and it better be the truth."

"Margo isn't coping well, seeing him again and watching you move his stuff out. She thinks she's losing him. I'm sure being pregnant isn't helping."

Seth shrugged. "First I've heard about it."

Ben raised his head, completely lost.

"Be right back," Adrian said. He went to the bedroom and dragged a reluctant Jonathan into the living room. "Give your dad a hug."

"I don't want to."

Ben's shoulders sagged.

"Drake, go bring me his iPod from the bedroom," Adrian said.

Jonathan tilted his head up at Adrian. His expression said, *You wouldn't.*

Adrian nodded twice and pointed at Ben. Jonathan didn't move. "iPod," Adrian said to Drake, who went to get it.

"I know everything's screwed up, but none of this is your fault, sport," Ben told his son. "If I didn't love you, I'd never have asked your Uncle Seth to turn you into a vampire. He gave you back your life. I'll always be grateful to him for that. It's just that your mother misses you. You're our son, always and forever." Ben stretched out his arms. "We love you."

That did it. Jonathan leaped into his father's arms and hugged him fiercely. "I love you, too, Daddy."

"I promise we'll come see you on your birthday, at Thanksgiving, and at Christmas, and whenever I can get away. Now, let's go talk to your mother."

***

"Is there anything you need?" Ben asked Jonathan when they were ready to leave.

"I'm good."

"You email me if there is. Okay?"

"'Kay."

Ben shook Drake's hand. "It was a pleasure meeting you. Thanks for being Jonathan's friend. You're always welcome to visit." Ben put his arms around Adrian, who felt a little awkward. "You, too. Thank you for being his big brother."

"Not a problem, Mr. C."

Ben released his grip. "I know you'll take good care of him."

Adrian ruffled Jonathan's hair. "Always."

"Dad, Adrian's got this sweet colored hair gel he's gonna let me use when we get back."

Adrian looked down at Jonathan. "When did I say that?"

"You were thinking it. I gotta say bye to Mom." He ran off.

"I still wonder if I did the right thing," Ben said.

"He's happy, and he's alive," Adrian said. "What more is there?"

Ben shrugged. "Are you happy you became a vampire?"

"Yeah, but I was kinda out of options at the time."

On the drive to the airport, Drake asked Adrian, "I bet you can't wait to get back and play with your computers."

Adrian sighed. "Yeah." He wished Eli hadn't told him where he was going.

CHAPTER THIRTY-TWO

Dublin, Ireland—Monday, December I, 2003

When Eli last visited Europe, commercial airlines hadn't existed. Time being critical, he'd chartered a private jet to Dublin. It also accommodated his preference to fly at night.

"Eli Howard?" Eli nodded at the pleasant Irish voice that greeted his exit from customs. "Quinn Connor at yer service." Someone Dietrich trusted and who wasn't in Cyrus' camp.

Eli set down his bags to shake Quinn's hand. Rough and roguish, with dark eyes, dark eyebrows, and spiked, dirty-blond hair. Frayed jeans that had nearly worn through one knee, a black T-shirt, and a denim jacket cemented the image.

Quinn gave him the once-over. "Have ya known Dietrich long?"

"He was my mentor."

"That be quite an honor. The old German gets hisself around." Quinn gave him a wry smile. "We've met on several occasions. I once visited his estate in Germany. Come on, I'll drive ya to me humble home so we can chat a bit. Cyrus, he won't be leavin' soon."

They headed to the short-term car park. "How do you know he won't?" Eli asked.

"There be a lotta activity at his mansion since he got back, comin' and goin'. He ain't bein' one to trust leadership to anyone 'cept himself, and we think he's plannin' somethin' big."

"Who is 'we'?"

"The Irish nightfolk. That's what we call ourselves here, an inside joke when fraternizing wit' humans. Most of 'em don't know about us a'tall."

"It's no different in the U.S."

"Well, we keep a close eye on himself, we do. Cyrus Hayes—you know that not be his birth name?—mostly kept his business away from here. He didn't wanna draw attention. Lately, his drugs have found their way into the local population. The suspicious deaths have got the Garda takin' notice."

The Irish National Police.

"Some of us are concerned they'll discover our existence. We've a large population of nightfolk here in our beautiful country, a discreetly peaceful lot—" He grinned. "Most of the time. We be likin' to keep it that way. I'm the designated leader and spokesman here for twenty years now. Not ready to give it up neither."

They arrived at Quinn's car and put Eli's one suitcase in the back. "Sometimes we go pub-crawling with humans. When they're totally pissed—drunk, as you Americans say—we maybe have our way with them." Quinn angled his head and shrugged with his hands held palms up. "Don't ya know we be just a bunch of party animals." He clicked the auto locks open. "Get in and I'll show you me humble cottage in Maynooth."

The airport lay six miles north of the city, and Maynooth lay west of there. With daylight more than an hour away, Eli's nightsight let him enjoy the scenery—even through the tinted car windows. Nearly thirty minutes later, Eli was admiring Quinn's old Maynooth cottage next to the Royal Canal. "Humble" understated the place.

"Do ya like me place? I figured, why hoard me money when I can squander it on a property like this? 'Course this is my secret vampire place. I keep a small apartment in West Dublin to show off to me human friends."

Quinn showed him to the guest bedroom decorated in Danish modern. "I got the sword Dietrich said you wanted. Nothin' else?"

"Cyrus wears body armor," Eli said.

"Wears it as undergarments when he goes out," Quinn said. "What good's a sword against that?"

Eli put the edge of his hand across his throat.

"You're good enough to do that?"

Eli nodded and Quinn's eyebrows rose.

***

That evening before sundown, Quinn drove Eli to Cyrus' estate to show him some of the beautiful countryside during the half-hour drive. On the outside, the estate was just another mansion among the many in County Kildare. A new motorway ran not a hundred yards from Cyrus' eight-foot-high boundary wall.

"Too beautiful for the likes of Cyrus Hayes to be spoilin' it," Quinn said. "This area's grown over the years. When Cyrus was born, most of it was farmland. As ya can see now, it's a suburb of an American-style metropolis. Wouldn't mind it m'self, stud farms nearby an' lines of trees with mists that rise in the mornin'. We're gettin' lotsa out-of-town folk movin' here, like from Poland and Lithuania. Orientals and Africans, too. Love that foreign food." Quinn grinned. "Ya sure 'bout doin' this?"

Until Eli told him, Quinn hadn't heard of the recent deaths of Ysabel and Hobart. Quinn knew that Cyrus sold drugs, but he didn't know about the nasty designer ones Cyrus had come up with.

"There's no one else to do it," Eli said.

"Then let's be gettin' ya to your destination."

They drove up to the estate house and stopped. There was one car parked in the driveway. "This not be a good sign," Quinn said. "Where are all the others? He runs Vampires, Inc. from here. Unless they all be out on a killin' spree we haven't heard about."

"Cyrus is here, and he knows I'm coming," Eli said.

"Surely ya can't feel his thoughts this far away."

"I know he's expecting me."

"I wish ya luck, my friend. I'll drive a little distance away and wait for ya."

"I'll call you when it's over." Eli got out of the car, then reached into his coat pocket and handed Quinn a slip of paper. "If you haven't heard from me in six hours, call Dietrich and tell him I failed." He retrieved the scabbard and sword from the backseat and strapped it on under his leather coat.

"Part of an old Irish blessing says, 'Until we meet again, may God hold ya in the hollow of his hand.'"

Quinn drove away.

Eli stood in front of the estate. The house itself was less than a century old. The plot it sat on had been in Cyrus' family for nearly twice that long. Cyrus Hayes never attempted to hide his background from other vampires, only from humans—Irish born in 1866 and changed at age nineteen by a female prostitute. He bragged about it. Eli walked up to the front door and pressed a button for the door chime.

A century ago, when Cyrus was already out of control, he'd asked Dietrich, "Cyrus is more dangerous than those we fight against, and he's doing more harm than good. Let me eliminate him."

"Don't let your emotions blind you. I know he's overzealous, but he's helping end the Conflict. In any war, there will be casualties. This is a war for the survival of our kind. If it's not quickly brought under control, we stand to lose the most. The longer this goes on, the more it will remain in human memory and we will never be safe again. For now, we need Cyrus. I'll ask him to temper his fervor."

Kommt Zeit, kommt Rat. Wisdom came too late. For Sophie, for Gerrick, for Hobart. For Ysabel.

The light above the door came on. A traditional and very British butler opened it. "Yes, sir?"

"Is Mr. Hayes in?"

"May I tell him who is calling?"

Eli pushed past him into the vestibule. The butler vainly attempted to stop him. "Where is he?"

When the butler didn't reply, Eli probed his mind. Cyrus was here alone. His men had departed over the past few days.

Eli removed his leather coat and hung it the cloakroom attached to the vestibule. "Take me to Mr. Hayes."

The butler saw Eli's sword and hesitated.

"Or I will find my own way."

Eli found Cyrus in a spacious, windowless room at the back of the estate house. Wall sconces around the room held ten small spotlights aimed at the stucco ceiling. Except for an old-style, slate blackboard on the far long wall, the walls were bare. He had a laptop open in front of him.

The butler cleared his throat. "You have a visitor, sir."

With his right side toward Eli, Cyrus sat at the left end of a long table with eight chairs along each side of it. He didn't look up. "Come in, Eli." He dismissed the butler. "I wondered if you would have the audacity to come here." He stood. His tailored, black, velvet coat struck him at mid-thigh. He gestured at the sheathed sword. "I assume that's not a fashion statement."

"You threaten the good of vampires and humans."

Cyrus threw his head back and laughed. "And you've appointed yourself supreme judge. The last time you set yourself against me, Dietrich forbade you to kill me. Have you finally learned how to make your own decisions and summoned up the courage to act?"

"I have Dietrich's blessing. Murdering Ysabel made him see the truth. He'll no longer listen to your lies."

"No matter." He took a step forward and walked slowly along the table, with his right side toward Eli. He put a hand on the back of each chair he passed and stopped one chair short of the center. "Dietrich's time is past; a new age is coming." He spread his arms. "Imagine a world where humans serve us, and we don't require their blood to sustain us. Vampire blood lacks four factors that humans possess. My researchers and I have identified and isolated three of them. We're on the verge of perfecting a synthesis. After that will come gene therapy to permanently resolve the problem. Once we identify and synthesize the fourth factor, humans will be irrelevant. This is no lie."

"They will fight back."

"Then I will eliminate all who do."

"The several *billion* humans on the planet won't go away that easily, Cyrus."

"Oh, I won't kill them all. I find a planet without humans an attractive thought, but they do have value as entertainment—and slaves. You of all of us should appreciate that, having been a slave to them before you were changed. With selective breeding and biochemically engineered drugs, control of their population and temperament won't be a problem."

"Do you also tell your followers that only those vampires *you* deem fit will share this new world with you and you'll kill those you see as weak?"

Cyrus took a step forward. He parted his coat and braced his hands on his waist. He stood less than ten feet from Eli. "I believe I forgot to mention that." He laughed.

"You told Dietrich the perceived threat was from humans."

"Oh, it's not *perceived.*" Cyrus arched his back and brought his right hand around behind him. He stretched his neck from side to side then centered his gaze on Eli. "It's very real."

Eli met his stare. "Only because you've been feeding lies to key elements in world governments about a new terrorist threat. No doubt your people have been convincing any who will listen of the existence of vampires."

Cyrus' face registered mild surprise. "Maybe I've not been discreet enough. In anticipation of your arrival, I sent my people where you won't find them. They are quite safe and will continue their tasks whether I'm with them or not. I am more prepared than you can possibly imagine."

"We'll find them and eliminate them."

Cyrus studied him. "I believe you'll try. Do you have the courage and strength to fulfill what you came here for?" Cyrus studied him. "My powers have increased since we last stood together a century ago."

A telepathic outburst touched Eli. He blinked.

Cyrus registered surprise once again. "So have yours. I underestimated your determination. So, it is the two of us. Alone. How shall we begin? A duel? I don't have a sword."

"What you severed Ysabel's head with will do."

"A machete is not a dueling weapon. There is another way to settle our differences." From behind his coat, Cyrus quickly drew a gun and fired at Eli's chest.

The body armor did its job. Eli barely flinched. While taking two strides toward Cyrus, he drew his sword, swept it upward and to his right, striking the gun and disrupting Cyrus' second shot. Before Cyrus could alter his aim, Eli's left hand joined his right on the sword's hilt. Moving one more stride forward, he swung the blade back across the shoulders and through the neck of his enemy. Cyrus' head fell to the floor, eyes open; his body collapsed beside it seconds later.

The butler rushed into the room, alternately looking between the body and the head on the floor and the sword Eli had pointed at him. He snapped to attention. "I am your servant. Do you wish me to call anyone for you, sir?"

"No, and I mean you no harm. I'll take care of his body."

Eli called Quinn on his cell phone.

"I'll be there in a few minutes," Quinn said.

***

Quinn studied the body. "You weren't lyin', and now he's lyin' on the floor."

Except for Cyrus' laptop, a search of the estate yielded nothing of importance. They found no records of Cyrus' business dealings on the premises. Eli knew enough from Adrian's computer advice not to attempt to access the PC himself. He'd let Adrian handle that.

As far as the butler knew, Cyrus kept all of his records in electronic form. He showed them a basement room, where Cyrus kept other PCs and the fireproof wall safe for backup disks. The PCs were gone; the safe was open and empty. If he had a secret vault elsewhere in the house, the butler had never seen it. Neither had he seen any important-looking papers around.

The butler said he'd take Cyrus' car, if they didn't mind. He knew someone he could stay with for now. Eli and Quinn let him go.

"Do you know who inherits the estate?" Eli asked Quinn when they were outside alone.

"Not sure, but I could arrange a pretty bonfire and we could have a grand time."

"I have a different kind of fire in mind," he told Quinn.

CHAPTER THIRTY-THREE

Detroit—Tuesday, December 2, 2003

A seriously worried Jeffery Thomas sat behind the desk in his downtown campaign office. "How the hell did this happen?"

Taylor, his campaign manager, stood before him. "We have no idea, Reverend."

"*I'll* tell you how! We got a spy in our midst. You find out who leaked to my opponent, and I'll fire his ass!"

"In the meantime, Reverend, I recommend a press conference ASAP, for damage control. Do you want me to arrange one?"

"Tomorrow afternoon. At my church."

"Is that a wise location?"

"In a House of God, I expect the press will behave themselves better. Now, get out so I can write my speech." *Damage control, my ass. I need disaster recovery.*

Ethan Radley was embroiled in some kind of drug scandal and *he*, Jeffery Thomas, had been linked to it. How had his opponents found out so fast he'd approached Radley for campaign contributions? Someone close to them, who knew where he'd solicited funds, must have leaked it. Worse, he hadn't even gotten any money from Radley! Few of the suburban businesses had agreed to support him, and those who did hadn't been exactly generous with their contributions. This didn't bode well at all.

***

New York City—Tuesday, December 2, 2003

In his Upper Manhattan, New York apartment, Adam Mathews had been sitting in front of his computer since before midnight. He'd finally gotten all that fucking pepper spray washed off. After three fucking days!

But right now he was happier than he'd been in over a week. In his hand he held a piece of paper, one of two items that had arrived in a FedEx package from Cyrus last Friday. The paper contained a password. The other item was a serum vial, like doctors gave you shots from, with a note to put it in a very safe place.

Cyrus had called on Saturday to verify he'd received the package. After that, Cyrus was supposed to call him every day between eleven thirty and twelve thirty at night, New York time. Unless he received instructions to the contrary and if no call came on his cell phone for two consecutive days, Adam was to assume Cyrus was dead. Further instructions would then follow.

Adam received a call on Sunday night. Monday night, no call. Here it was eleven fifty-six p.m., Tuesday night. Still no call. Adam's heart raced and continued to do so until the time on the clock turned twelve thirty-one.

He went to his refrigerator for a beer. Fifteen minutes later, he got up for another. One a.m. arrived.

Cell phone clipped to his belt, Adam left his penthouse apartment, making sure he set the burglar alarm and locked all three locks before he headed out for a prime steak dinner and a light drunk. After that, he'd get laid.

***

Detroit—Wednesday, December 3, 2003

For once Adrian didn't mind the five a.m. call on his cell phone. He'd just gotten to bed an hour ago, following a long game session with Jonathan.

"Yo, Eli. I hope these early-morning calls won't become a habit." Adrian wouldn't give him the satisfaction of knowing how very glad he was to hear Eli's voice.

"I'm an hour out of Detroit. I should be home by six thirty."

"Tell me you didn't wake me up just to tell me that."

"I have Cyrus' personal laptop with me. I want you to do whatever it takes to retrieve the information from it as fast as you can."

Adrian was suddenly more wide-awake than he wanted to be. "You got it, boss." Eli hated when he called him boss, but he deserved it for calling so early and putting him through mental anguish for the past couple of days.

Dragging himself out of bed to use the bathroom, Adrian found a wet-haired, towel-wrapped Drake exiting from it. Since they'd gotten back from Denver, he'd been staying here at night.

"Morning," Drake said. "You look like shit. You and J were up all night video gaming, weren't you?"

"Yeah."

"Why aren't you still in bed?"

"Eli just called. He's on his way back. He's bringing a laptop he wants me to hack into." He hadn't told Drake or Jonathan where Eli had gone.

"S-wee-t. I'll play hooky so I can watch."

"You go to school. I'll fill you in later."

"Uh, I might not be here tonight," Drake said. "My mom called last night. She and Ethan want to talk to me. She sounded worried."

***

Over an earlier-than-usual breakfast for Adrian, Eli related the details of his Ireland trip.

"So, where's this PC?" Adrian asked.

"In my suitcase. There's something I want to show you first." Eli opened the small carry-on bag beside him on the bench of their kitchen breakfast nook and put a plastic snap-top bowl on the table. He pried off the lid.

"You emptied out the ashtrays in Cyrus' house?" Adrian said.

Eli went to the refrigerator where they kept their blood supplies and from its freezer took out a smaller plastic container. He opened that in front of Adrian. Inside, on several chunks of ice, were two thumbs.

Adrian's mouth dropped open as it dawned on him what the ashes were. "You *cremated* him?"

"I kept the thumbs in case someone wants verification that Cyrus Hayes is really dead."

"Who has a record of his fingerprints to check against?"

"The Vampire Council. They have mine as well."

Adrian thought about how best to ask his next question. "Wouldn't it have been easier just to bury him?"

"It would have. I expect his followers will label him a martyr. We can't prevent that. I cremated him so there would be no gravesite they could make into a shrine. Quinn wanted to burn his estate house. I convinced him that might cause a war. We're considering a better use for the property."

"What's that?"

"A school for vampires, possibly a training academy."

***

Adrian opened the cover of Cyrus' laptop and plugged the USB drive loaded with his hack tools into it.

"Are you pissed I won the game last night?"

Adrian snapped his head around at a smirking Jonathan standing in the doorway of his computer room. "Oh, hi, J. You surprised me."

Jonathan smacked him on the back of his head. "Only Drake gets to call me J."

"No, I'm not pissed at you. You won fair and square."

"Sweet. Whatcha doin'?"

He told Jonathan the full story. "So, I'm getting ready to power up Cyrus' laptop to see what goodies I can extract from it."

Jonathan sat next to him. "Can I watch you screw up?"

Adrian snarled. "Watch the smartass comments, little man."

"Be nice or I'll tell Uncle Eli about the girl you had in your room while he was gone."

"I did not!"

"Did too. I heard her moaning."

"For your in-for-mation I was watching a video, and don't going looking around for it."

"Nuh uh. I heard live action."

"Wrong!"

"The spare TV is still in the guest bedroom." Jonathan put a finger from each hand on his forehead and stared at Adrian. "I was on the other side of the wall."

The little shit read her thoughts through the wall?

Jonathan nodded once. "Your face is *so* red."

Adrian tried to smack him, but he ducked. "She really liked what you were doing to her."

Adrian let out a long sigh. "Make you a deal. I'll let you help me crack this PC, if you forget about what went on in my room that night and you agree to move into the other bedroom down the hall so I can have more privacy. You're too young to be hearing that stuff yet."

Jonathan rubbed his chin in a thoughtful way.

"What *else* do you want?"

"A girl for Drake."

"So you can spy on him, too? No way, you little pervert!"

Jonathan's mouth drooped. "Not for *that*. He's lonely. He's never had a girlfriend."

Adrian ruffled Jonathan's hair. "No promises, but I'll see what I can do. Grab a chair and park yourself next to me. I'd better get to work before Eli comes in and threatens to chop my nuts off."

"I bet that'd hurt a lot."

Adrian cuffed him gently on the ear.

With Jonathan seated next to him, he made sure his USB drive was firmly plugged in before he powered up the laptop. "Watch closely while Adrian Shadowhawk's magic PC debauchery program handles the nasty password protection."

He waited, but he didn't see a password prompt. *Why would Cyrus not have protected it with a password?* And Windows was taking longer than normal to boot up.

"Shit."

"What's the problem?" Jonathan asked.

He pressed CTL-ALT-DEL to check the running tasks. The email program was running. "Fuck me!"

"Oooh," Jonathan muttered. "You must've screwed up extra bad."

Adrian nodded slowly at him. "Big time, little bro, big time."

CHAPTER THIRTY-FOUR

New York City—Wednesday, December 3, 2003

When Adam awoke, Brandi had his morning erection in her capable hands. She crawled under the covers. Her wet, warm mouth became part of the action. Brandi knew how to wake a man properly. He folded his hands behind his head on the pillow. That way he'd be less tempted to claw her back like he did once. It cost him double the next time. Of the three girls he used from the agency, Brandi was his favorite, his addiction. She drove a man insane. Why pollute your body with drugs when women like Brandi existed?

She teased him again with her lips. "Ready, lover?"

It was a warning, not a question. She got on top and took him to heaven.

An hour and a shower later, he sat down to check his email. With a thousand of his dollars in her possession, which she'd more than earned, Brandi had gone to please another of her exclusive clients. He shivered. *Lucky guy.*

Unlike most of the women he'd been with, Brandi improved with age. She didn't need sex toys, either. Her body was one giant sex toy. He'd been with her four times, and she was still finding new pleasure spots on him.

He clicked his email program. *One new message. From Cyrus?* It had no subject line.

Open the attachment, it said.

If Cyrus was dead, how could he be sending an email? Didn't emails send right away? They weren't delayed like regular mail. It did mention the password, though. An outsider wouldn't know about that. Well, he'd paid a guy enough to be sure no harm came to his PC. The guy had installed some kind of special outside backup that ran every day in case his PC did die.

Adam clicked the attachment.

A white box labeled "Enter Password" popped up. He pulled out the piece of paper from Cyrus and typed in the thirty-character password. *Error*, it read. *Fuck.*

He typed it again. This time a new window opened.

Adam, if you are reading this, I am no longer alive, or else I am severely incapacitated or a prisoner and my PC is not under my direct control. This message sent automatically if I did not enter a private code within the previous forty-eight hours. I assure you that I would not do it under duress. Regardless of my actual state of being, you are to assume I am dead, and you are to act in accord with the instructions herein.

What the fuck? Adam had to read that part again. Okay, now he understood. Why couldn't Cyrus write in simple English?

At the end of this message is the number for a Swiss bank account containing ten million dollars. It is yours to spend as you wish. Make dealing with Eli Howard a top priority, but I recommend caution in exposing yourself.

Agreed! The first thing he'd do is find Eli Howard and teach him not to fuck with Adam Mathews. But what if Howard had killed Cyrus? Would Howard come after him next? Is that what the warning meant? On the other hand, why should he care if someone killed Cyrus?

Employer or not, he was a vampire. Sure, he enjoyed spending the money Cyrus paid him, but he'd also been smart enough to bank some for his retirement years. He had a nice nest egg already. On the other hand, ten million more would let him hire someone else to fix Howard. He'd be safe...but then he wouldn't have the pleasure of watching Howard suffer in person. And he didn't trust anyone else to do the job.

The email continued:

A certain Reverend Jeffery Thomas is running for mayor of Detroit in 2005. I have made Mr. Thomas aware of satanic elements in his city that will require his attention once he is elected. I did not mention specifics or name names. Reverend Thomas would be a good place for you to begin to establish yourself in control. With generous campaign contributions to ensure his election as mayor, you would be in a position to control him. I have also planted seeds of distrust in his own organization. He should be very open to your offer of support. His phone number is included at the end of this email.

Politics? Adam thought about that for a moment. *But why Detroit?* New York was larger and more powerful. Adam rubbed his chin. *Because Howard is in Detroit. Howard must be the key.*

In addition to you, an elite group worked for me to handle larger problems requiring less delicacy. One of them will contact you. This brings me to the bottle of serum. It is my gift to you, my most trusted employee.

Trusted? Adam laughed out loud. Cyrus Hayes trusted no one. Still...

While this serum will give you the immortality you desire, the side effects are most unpleasant. Use it only if you have no other choice.

What'd that mean? Was this serum his longtime wish come true? And what did the side effect thing mean?

Do not disappoint me, Adam. Remember that revenge upon Eli Howard is only one small part of my grand plan. I recommend you transfer the ten million to another bank as soon as you finish reading this, before Eli Howard finds it. He may now be in possession of my computer.

Adam immediately picked up his cell phone and made the necessary calls.

Having secured his newly acquired wealth, he went back to the email to figure out some things that still puzzled him. The serum was the first puzzle. Would it change him into an immortal vampire? Cyrus hadn't said that, not directly. If the serum could do that, why hadn't he used it on himself? He'd still be alive. Unless he wasn't really dead. Cyrus knew how to vanish. He'd done it before.

Cyrus also didn't grant any wishes except his own. Weren't dead celebrities sometimes referred to as immortals? More likely the serum granted eternal rest, not eternal life. Cyrus hated humans for the most part. Why would he trust his life's work to one? Adam wasn't naive; he wasn't indispensable to Cyrus, nor did he come up to Cyrus' standards of intelligence. No, Adam Mathews was a high-paid lackey, kept alive only to serve Cyrus Hayes. Or was he?

Over the years, Adam had learned how to slip in and out of anyplace, how to keep himself hidden. He did his job, and he was gone. His victim was happily—or unhappily—on his way to the afterlife, if such a thing existed.

The recent job on the Shadowhawk kid had left a bad taste in his mouth. More now than before, Adam was certain Cyrus had neglected to warn him on purpose about how Howard would react.

That brought him to the second puzzle: why was that? Did Hayes want Howard to come after him? If so, why? Adam rarely took any job personally. This had become personal.

For the past sixteen years, he'd let Cyrus use him for one reason: the money. Before tonight, he'd had nearly two million in his bank account. Now, he had twelve. That was a lot of money, but fucking lottery winners won more. He was certain Cyrus had a lot more somewhere else for some sinister purpose.

The third puzzle: Cyrus had mentioned an elite group—assassins no doubt, probably some of them vampires. Why would they contact him? He didn't have anything they would want, did he?

Adam retrieved the vial of serum from his wall safe where he'd put it for safekeeping. *Safe*keeping. He'd made a joke. Holding the bottom of the vial in his fingertips, he swirled it. The milky pink liquid rolled around inside.

Was his future in that tiny bottle? It was only half full. The instructions didn't say how much to use. Was it enough for more than one dose? After he was a vampire, maybe he could turn Brandi into one and have an eternity of fantastic sex with her. He hoped vampires could still fuck. He'd rather go to hell and suffer pain and torment there than spend a fuck-free eternity anywhere else.

Then he remembered those eye drops he'd given that vampire kid. Yeah, vampires could still get off.

But Cyrus had never given anything away for free. The more Adam thought about that, the more he doubted the serum was anything good. More likely it was a vicious and painful poison with no antidote. Cyrus would be laughing inside his grave. No way would Adam Mathews become the target of his last act of torture.

Still, he wasn't about to turn down a real chance to be immortal. Well, he'd think about it later.

The email had ended with:

Make my vision a reality, Adam.

Cyrus had given him one vision already, and it was a true religious vision. First he'd take a walk, have lunch: a juicy steak or a couple half-pound burgers with everything. Red meat recharged his sex drive. Too bad Brandi wasn't available tonight. Hell, he was in such a good mood, he might even toss a twenty into the cup of a homeless guy along the way.

Then he'd call Reverend Jeffery Thomas' holy number.

CHAPTER THIRTY-FIVE

Detroit—Wednesday, December 3, 2003

Jeffery put on his best winning smile, walked onto the chancel of his church, with Taylor following him, and took a seat behind the pulpit. Taylor stepped up and raised his hands for the crowd to quiet down. Among the dozen reporters, Jeffery had strategically placed some of his own people.

"Ladies and gentlemen, Reverend Thomas has prepared a statement. We ask you to remember that this is God's house and to let him read his statement first. Then we'll entertain your questions. I give you the Reverend Jeffery Thomas."

Cameras flashed as Jeffery stepped up to the pulpit. He scanned the audience, feeling comfortable and in control. More cameras flashed amid murmurs. If hostility had a smell, the sanctuary stank with it—vultures everyone, out for carrion to feed on. Well, he'd disappoint them.

He narrowed his gaze at them. "Friends," he said. *Best to win them over first.* "Durin' my campaign for mayor of Detroit, I want to be honest and forthright. I will not tolerate corruption in my ranks. I trust my staff members, but if anyone breaks that trust, I'll promptly dismiss them. Before me or mah staff approach anyone for campaign support, we carefully check their backgrounds. Ethan Radley was an upstanding member of the community, and we were convinced he and his company were above reproach.

"We were shocked to learn otherwise. I trust you won't blame us for what Mr. Radley clearly went to great lengths to hide. Let me assure you that to date, we have *not* received any funds from Mr. Radley, only his promise of such. Further, we will not accept any contributions from him or his company. Our books are open for your examination."

So far, so good.

"I hold to my campaign promises. I'll clean up our city physically and morally. I'll see our people properly fed. I'll see our children properly educated. I'll reduce crime and *eliminate* the drugs which are a danger to our children. Ah was *stunned* to hear ah had a contributor who sold drugs to our youth! No, mah friends, that be *sin*. Psalm 39:1, 'Ah sin not with my tongue; ah will keep my mouth with a bridle, while the wicked is before me.'"

At least two of them were nodding.

"I've instructed my staff to screen every one of our contributors. Lemme tell you how sorry ah am this happened. I've been in fervent prayer and have asked God's forgiveness. Now, ah ask *your* forgiveness."

An, "Amen," came from somewhere in the audience, one of his people no doubt.

"My opponents attack me at ev'ry turn." He lifted and spread his hands, raising his head as he did. "'O my God, ah trust in Thee; let me not be ashamed, let not mine enemies triumph over me.'" He looked back at the audience. "I will not back down from these false allegations. They want to attack me because I'm a proud African American, like eighty percent of our fine city, like some of you in the audience, but ah refuse to make this a race issue. I'm runnin' my campaign under the banner of cleanin' up Detroit from dark elements threatenin' the safety and security of *all* Detroiters." He placed his hands on the pulpit. "Now, I'll gladly answer your questions."

Several raised their hands. Taylor fielded the reporters' questions and pointed first at one particularly antagonistic local newslady. *Good. Show 'em we're not afraid.*

"Reverend, have you ever used drugs?" she asked.

He'd smoked pot as a kid. Hell, who hadn't, but none of those five friends who knew about it were around to tell the tale. Two moved away years ago, two died in a car accident, and the last died a few years ago from a drug overdose.

"The body is God's temple, and mine has been sanctified."

***

Back in his office, Jeffery Thomas was congratulating himself on the press meeting when his phone rang. He reached for it then stopped. Let his secretary get it. That's the job she'd volunteered for. He didn't want to talk to any more media people right now. The press had bought his speech, and he'd skated through that press conference by the skin of his teeth.

His secretary appeared at his open office door. "A gentleman on the phone wishes to speak with you."

"Who is he and what's he want?"

"He wouldn't give his name, but he said he wishes to make a *large* contribution—those were his exact words—to your campaign."

"It's some reporter. Tell him I'm not interested."

"I don't think he's from the media, Reverend Thomas. He said to tell you that his offer is seven figures."

Jeffery got lightheaded. If this was legitimate, he couldn't afford to refuse it. "I'll take the call."

"Line one, Reverend." She left.

His hand shook. He picked up the phone and pressed the button. "This is Reverend Thomas. Who am ah speakin' to?"

***

"This is Reverend Thomas," Adam heard the voice on the other end say. "Who am ah speakin' to?"

Adam put on the most professional voice he could muster. "My name is Adam Mathews, Reverend Thomas. I believe someone spoke with you recently about certain subversive elements growing in Detroit."

"I'm listenin'."

"I have large sums at my disposal, and I'm prepared to contribute whatever is required for you to be elected." Adam didn't hear a reply. "Reverend Thomas?"

"Sorry, had to clear my throat. I'd be pleased to accept your generous support, Mr. Mathews, but you do realize we have some legal limits on such contributions."

"Let me handle the details. Tell me where to direct the money. I'll see it arrives safely and secretly at its destination. There is one stipulation, Reverend. This will create a partnership between us. In return for my seven-figure contributions—"

The reverend coughed.

"—I'll expect your full cooperation on certain matters."

"I wish to make it clear that I'm a nonpartisan and will do what's best for my city, Mr. Mathews... But I'm sure I can make adjustments to accommodate your wishes."

And your pockets. "That's all I'm asking. Detroit needs to be cleaned up. I want to help you do it. Do you believe in vampires, Reverend?"

"Mr. Mathews, for your generous support, I'll believe in whatever you want me to."

"That's not what I mean, Reverend. I'm talking real vampires, the kind who feed on human blood. They are in your city, and their population is growing."

For a long time Jeffery Thomas was silent. "You're not joking?"

"God's honest truth, Reverend. That's something you should be familiar with. When the time comes, I'll convince you of their existence. They exist all over the world. I'm sure you can imagine the political position you'll be in as the one who reveals their evil existence to interested parties in high places. Your political career won't stop at mayor."

Again the reverend hesitated. "Are they Satan worshipers?"

"What difference does that make?" Adam asked.

"A holy war is easier to wage."

"They're Satan worshipers. I'll be in touch, Reverend."

"Thank you, Mr. Mathews."

Yep, Adam was ready to step into the world of political corruption, to become the user instead of the used.

He flipped the serum vial over and back and stared it. If it took a while to put himself in power, so what? If Hayes hadn't lied, Adam Mathews was holding eternity in the palm of his hand.

***

Eli entered Adrian's computer room where Jonathan and Adrian had camped out all day. "Any progress?" Eli asked.

Adrian put his hand on Jonathan's head. "Sort of."

"And?"

"Have a seat." Adrian's stomach growled. It was dinnertime.

Eli pulled up a chair.

"Good news and bad news."

"He means *real* bad news," Jonathan said.

Adrian glanced sideways at Eli but couldn't read anything in his expression. Taking a deep breath, he brought up a file on the screen of his own PC. "I copied the files and made a CD backup, in case of an accident." Adrian gave Jonathan a warning shake of his head. Still looking at his monitor, he said, "There's lots of good stuff in here. That's part of the good news. The other part is there's no antidote for the eye drops."

"How is *that* good news?"

He swiveled his chair toward Eli. "Because there's none required and apparently it was planned that way to keep people addicted. I have to suffer through withdrawal, like we tried before. After I puke my head off for three or four days, I'll be cured. I'll go cold turkey when I have four days free and want to put myself through total agony again." He grinned at Eli. "I know I should do it as soon as possible, before I run out of drops and don't have a choice. Okay, on to the rest. The first part of the bad news is none of the files were a problem to access."

"Why is that bad?"

"It's like Cyrus wanted us to know what he'd done." He swung his chair back toward his desk. "Now here's the *really* bad news."

CHAPTER THIRTY-SIX

Detroit—Friday, December 5, 2003

Adrian found Eli in the kitchen tossing a salad for dinner. Drake and his parents would be here soon for dinner. He sat at the small table in one corner of the large kitchen. "Are you upset with me?" he asked Eli.

Eli didn't turn around. "Why should I be?"

Adrian sighed. "I couldn't hack that Swiss bank account number fast enough?"

"The money was probably gone before we saw the email. I'm impressed you decoded it. Doing it in less than a day impressed me even more."

"And I let that email send to Adam in the first place."

"You did your best, Adrian. You couldn't have known about his little trick."

The timer rang. Eli opened the oven and took out a dish of scalloped potatoes. He set it on a trivet on the counter. "Is there something else on your mind?"

"No. I'm just wallowing in self-pity."

"Tomorrow evening I have a meeting with the Vampire Council. I'd like you to attend."

"I thought it was only for members."

"You're an invited guest. You performed a valuable service by accessing Cyrus' data files. I want the Council to recognize your contributions, and I think you should meet those stodgy rule makers in person."

Adrian's face got very warm. "You won't tell them I said that, will you?"

Eli chuckled. "Hardly." The doorbell rang. "Ah, right on time. Go welcome our guests while I finish up."

As he exited the kitchen, Adrian heard Jonathan bounding down the front stairs and glimpsed him running past the living room. By the time Adrian got there, Jonathan had already opened the front door.

"J!" Drake said and leaned over to hug him. "I missed ya."

"Only been two days."

"I can still miss ya, can't I?" Drake straightened. "Mom, Dad, these are my good friends Adrian Shadowhawk and Jonathan Clayton. Guys, these are my parents, Ethan and Val."

Jonathan waved at them. "Hi. Did Drake tell you I'm a vampire, too?"

"Dude, slow down. Yeah, I told them, but I don't think they believed me."

"That's okay, I guess," Jonathan said.

"Adrian's a Lakota Indian," Drake said.

Adrian stepped forward and shook their hands, Mrs. Radley's first. "I'm glad you came. Let me take your coats then we'll head into the dining room. Eli's fixing dinner. Would you care for a drink before?"

***

Adrian finished the last of his chocolate cream pie and waited to see what Eli had planned next.

"Superb dinner," Ethan said. "You're a fine cook, and you remembered my wife is a vegetarian."

"My pleasure, Mr. Radley."

"Please call me Ethan and call my wife Val." He gave Drake a sideways glance. "Our son does."

Drake smiled sheepishly. "I'm trying to break that habit."

"When Drake told me about vampires, I was skeptical, to say the least."

"As in, he didn't believe a word," Drake said.

Ethan put his napkin on the table. "All right, I have to be honest. I didn't believe him until he reminded me of Cyrus Hayes. I understand Mr. Hayes has been...taken care of?"

Eli nodded. "Yes, he has, which brings me to why I invited you here tonight."

"May I say something first?" Ethan asked.

"Please do."

"I really don't see how you can help with the federal charges against me for illegal drug manufacture. At this point, I don't know if they have a case, but even if they do and I claim I didn't know what Hayes was doing, it's my company. Ignorance is not an acceptable legal excuse."

"I can almost guarantee Cyrus made sure they would have a strong case, Ethan. He was an intelligent and cunning individual."

Ethan sighed. "Well, my lawyers have told me that without proof Cyrus Hayes was involved, they don't have much of a defense."

"Didn't you have a signed contract?"

"His signature is a scrawl no one could decipher. I've had a couple of meetings with a federal representative. There is no proof of a connection between the Cyrus Hayes, who resides—er, resided—in Ireland, and me. I'm out of options." He pointed at Drake. "My son claims you can work miracles. I'm skeptical, but I'll listen."

"Miracles?" Eli said to Drake.

"Adrian says he's seen you work small ones."

Eli faced Ethan. "As I understand it, the charges are against you individually as well as your company?"

"That's the confusing part. They're claiming I kept my people in the dark so they wouldn't know what they were doing and I would be solely responsible. Why would the government want to destroy the company and put all those people out of work yet still say my employees are innocent of any wrongdoing?"

"Cyrus bribed at least one federal prosecutor. I know it, but I can't prove it."

"He promised he'd destroy me if I backed out of the contract." Ethan let out a long sigh. "He's a man of his word."

"Drake says you have a background both in research and business management. Is that correct?" Eli asked.

"Yes, but what does it have to do with my problem?"

"More than you can imagine, Ethan. If you will allow me to handle the details, I have worked out a mutually beneficial solution to your dilemma. Have you ever been to Germany?"

Ethan's eyebrows raised in curiosity. "No, I haven't."

That piqued Adrian's interest as well.

***

Detroit—Saturday, December 6, 2003

Adrian followed close behind Eli and Rebecca as they entered the building where Ysabel had rented space. The Council members were waiting for them in the conference room. Feeling the pressure, Adrian ran his fingers under his collar and muttered, "I don't see why I had to wear a dress shirt and tie." This was punishment for something, but he didn't have a clue what it was.

Dietrich met them. "We're ready for you." He took Rebecca's hand and kissed it. "Ysabel would be proud."

"Thank you, but I'm not sure why I've been invited," she said. "I'm honored to be among you again."

Adrian glanced at Rebecca. *Hmmm, she doesn't know why she's here, either?*

Dietrich shook Adrian's hand. "My congratulations to you, young man."

I get congratulated for dressing up?

Adrian counted four empty chairs at huge conference table, one at the near end and three at the far end, including the head chair, which would be for Dietrich, the new leader of the Council. The seven men in the room stood when Dietrich entered with his guests and led them to the far end.

"You and Rebecca take the two chairs on my left," Dietrich said to Eli. "Adrian, please take the chair on my right. Now, everyone, please be seated." He remained standing behind the head chair. "Before we come to the purpose of this meeting, I ask that we spend a few moments in silence, to reflect and pray if you wish, for our departed Ysabel."

Adrian felt so out of place. As the youngest one in the room by far, he didn't belong or fit in here. He had no interest in what the Council did.

After an unexpectedly long silence, Dietrich said, "To business." He turned to Eli.

The next few minutes blurred together for Adrian. Dietrich announced that Eli would be the new Council head. He said Rebecca would fill the vacant eighth position. Then Eli, standing in front of the head chair said, "Sitting on my right is Adrian Shadowhawk. He has been my apprentice for the past five years. Because of his efforts, we have discovered new information about our kind. Adrian learned Cyrus had secretly been compiling a database of all vampires on Earth, dead and alive. The files go back several hundred years and include considerable information: their background; who changed them; who mentored them; aliases; past and present locations; date and place of death; human and vampire relatives. We found a reference to a list of over three thousand names, yet the file itself contained only several hundred. This suggests a more extensive database exists somewhere. Other records we found mention surviving human/vampire hybrids from the Nazi experiments."

Adrian heard a couple of gasps in the room.

"Therefore, my first act as Council head, is to appoint Adrian Shadowhawk as my official administrative assistant and to put him in charge of setting up and maintaining a secure, worldwide computer network for the Council."

Adrian's open mouth went dry. *Shit!*

Eli winked at him as he shook his hand and said softly, "You even get paid for it."

Adrian had no idea what to say, so he stood, bowed to the members, and sat again.

"Isn't he a bit young and inexperienced for such an important responsibility?" one Council member said with evident concern.

"If you know of anyone among us who boasts skills superior to his, I'll make it a joint appointment."

"His executive powers allow him to make this appointment without requiring our approval," Dietrich said. "I'm sure Eli would still appreciate your vote of confidence in what I know is a well-thought-out act."

"But of course," the questioning member said. One by one, the others added their affirmation.

"Adrian will also be assisting with research and investigations," Eli said. "Several battles lie ahead of us. Cyrus Hayes deliberately raised awareness of our existence among humans. Those of you who believe our darkest days are behind us are deluding yourselves. If we are to have a future, we must ally ourselves with key individuals among humans."

"They'll seek us out and slaughter us. It's happened before," another member said.

Eli addressed him. "Only because *we* began those hostilities in 1905. That's why we must establish trustworthy contacts in various world governments and work discreetly with them."

"They'll never trust us, no matter what we do." The other members started to murmur among themselves.

"Gentlemen, please! You appointed me to lead you. I intend to do so in a way that will ensure our safety and will benefit *both* sides. We have new enemies. I can't deny that. We must find them and stop them, or the 1905 Conflict will become trivial in comparison. This will not be easy, and I must have everyone in agreement if we are to prevent disaster."

***

On the way home, Adrian sat next to Eli in the car, arms folded, staring out at the light snowfall. "You could've warned me!"

"Are you unhappy with my decision?"

"No... Yes." Adrian snorted. "Shit, just chop off my nuts now, 'cuz Adrian Shadowhawk, vampire hacker extraordinaire, will have to do everything legal instead of sneaky like before."

"Who says you do?"

"The Council," he said between his teeth.

"I head the Council. I'm giving you free rein, tempered with your good judgment, to do what you believe is best."

"...Oh."

"Oh," Eli said.

They stopped at a traffic light and Adrian asked, "So, you got any other surprises for me?"

"Perhaps." The light turned green.

When they arrived home, several cars filled the driveway. As soon as Adrian stepped into the house, Jonathan ran at him and hugged him around the waist. "Way to go, big bro!"

"Hey, J. Thanks."

Jonathan rubbed his chin thoughtfully at Adrian. "Only Drake's supposed to call me J." He bobbed his head. "But I'll let you this time."

Drake came up and cross-shook Adrian's hands. "Congrats on making the big time."

"Was I the only one who didn't know about this?"

"Eli swore us all to secrecy."

Jonathan hurried off.

"Where's he going?" Adrian asked.

Drake put one hand on Adrian's back and coaxed him forward. "For the food. There's munchies and drinks in the dining room, but the way J is sucking them up, they won't last long."

Jonathan was already piling a plate with food when they entered the dining room less than a minute later. "That's his second," Drake said.

Adrian quickly loaded a plate of his own and grabbed a Pepsi.

"Did ya hear *my* good news?" Drake said.

"What's that?"

"My parents are gonna let me skip Harvard and go to Wayne State." He panned one hand in front of his face. "Doctor Drake Radley. Has a nice sound to it, don't ya think? I'll make sure I avoid Eli's history classes, though. I've seen his exams. They're killers."

"You can't avoid history, Drake," Eli said, coming up behind him.

"Does that mean I get to be a vampire?"

"Make your mother proud of your academic accomplishments, and I may consider it for your graduation present."

"Sweet!"

"Not so fast, young man. I didn't say yes, only that I'll think about it. Your parents are entitled to a say as well."

Eli walked away.

"Only until I'm twenty-one!"

Adrian and Drake chatted for a while before they headed into the living room. Jonathan sat on the couch, chowing down.

Drake whistled and pointed out Ling standing with Rebecca and Eli in front of the fireplace. "Dude, check her out." Ling's traditional Chinese attire hugged her slender body. "Think she's too old for me?"

"Definitely."

Drake sighed.

"Let's join them," Adrian said.

Rebecca was telling Ling about her new position. Adrian said to Eli, "You revamped the Vamp Council. What's the other surprise you hinted at?"

"Rebecca and I are moving into Ysabel's house."

"Whoa. You're shacking up? Isn't this a bit sudden?"

Rebecca blushed.

"We're sharing the house, Adrian, nothing more. Jonathan will be living with us."

"But, what about *this* place? Where am I gonna live?"

"You said you wanted your own place. Try not to trash it."

"Oh...*shit.*"

***

Detroit—December 31, 2003

The Detroit News reported:

Tragic death of Troy businessman

Ethan Radley, owner and president of Radley Biotech, was found dead late last night near the Detroit Riverwalk. Said a police spokesman, "The mutilated body, identified as Radley's by his family, had been shot multiple times."

No motive has been given, but investigators are calling it a drug-related crime. Radley was recently charged with manufacturing illegal drugs at his company. Local police are cooperating with federal investigators, who refused to comment.

Mr. Radley lived in Grosse Pointe and is survived by his wife and son. A private memorial service will be held at a later date.

***

Detroit—Monday, January 5, 2004

Shortly before nine a.m., Valerie Radley strode confidently through the front doors of Radley Biotech and into the lobby. She paused to unfasten her wool overcoat, revealing a tailored, navy skirt, white blouse, and lemon jacket. It had been a while since she was last in here, but nothing had changed. The marble floor tiles and plate glass windows were immaculate, as Ethan insisted they be kept. She could almost smell the rumors floating in the air from the employees who were already at work.

Why not start the day with a bit of lighthearted fun? She approached the guard's desk. Pete had already noticed her.

"Mrs. Radley, seeing you here is a bit of a surprise. Please accept my condolences for your loss."

"Thank you, Pete." She could see the questions fighting to come out: What really happened? How could she be so calm just days after her husband's death? What's she doing here? Why wasn't she in mourning? Who was going to run the company?

"Is there something I can help you with?" Pete asked.

"Not really, but thank you for asking." She started to walk past him into the building.

He stood. "Forgive me, Mrs. Radley. I feel awkward saying this, but I have strict instructions to follow security protocol…with everyone. I'll call someone to escort you."

"That's not necessary, Pete." She returned to the desk and held out her ID badge.

His mouth opened and froze there for a moment. "Oh. I didn't realize— It's just that—"

"I know, a lot has happened. You perform your duties perfectly. I expect you to challenge *everyone*. Now, some government people will be here this morning to talk with me. I'll let the security office know to have badges ready for them, but make sure you check their credentials. I'll be in my office."

"Yes, ma'am… *Your* office?"

She leaned over the desk. "Ethan always hoped Drake would take over the company one day. He starts college this summer, and he can't take over until he's at least twenty-one. I'll be running it in the meantime."

Lightning Source Inc.
Breinigsville, PA USA
14 August 2009

222343BV00001B/5/P